With Her Fists

With Her Fists

Henry Roi

"Fights are not won in the ring; they are won in the gym, in preparation."
-Fred Williams

Part I

Chapter I

Biloxi, Mississippi
March 16, 2010

The gun smacked into the man's face with a sound only solid metal hitting flesh can make. An arch of pink sweat glistened in a ray of sunlight before sticking to a shadowed wall.

The man's head rolled around his shoulders, eyes showing whites, his mouth slack. A garden hose was pointed at the man, turned on, spraying him in the face. His eyes puckered, head thrashing side to side to move his mouth and nose clear of the water.

A second assailant stepped forward with a small taser in his hand. Stuck it to the man's neck. Jolted him with a low current, zapping him back to consciousness.

A loud slap resonated throughout the building. "Tell me where it is, Jose. Where did you hide it?"

The slap again. "I will beat you to a slow death. You know this. I will saw off your fucking balls. Where's the goddamn money?" demanded a man of enormous girth.

Tall and pale with a hair-trigger temper, his face was stained with a permanent flush, his breath an incessant wheeze. He slapped Jose with a hand swollen with hate.

"Where is it?" he shouted with spittle on his lips, veins in his neck and forehead bulging, turning his skin shades of red into purple.

"Jose, come on, *amigo*. You don't have to go through this. Just tell us, okay? *Dónde esta*?" the partner said, playing his role. He really believed he was a good guy. Doing what needed to be done so that he could take care of his family, watch his partner's back. Though the term 'good' was taken to a new level today, he thought. He fidgeted, his fireplug body and chubby Latin face filled with worry.

The place stank of mildew, rotten wood. Of blood and sweat. Of fear. Odors that imbue paranoia. Hector was constantly scanning the room, listening to the silence of the building and the lack of wind or natural noises from outside.

It was unsettling.

A train horn sounded from miles away, seeming to crescendo inside the death shrouded room, causing Hector to jump and curse a string of Spanish. He inhaled, slow, to steady his heartbeat. Tried to focus on the job at hand.

The sweat on Jose's throat shone as he coughed to clear it. He lifted his head and glared at his enemies. "*Cabrones,*" he spat. "La Familia has shown you loyalty. Has taken care of you. And you show your gratitude with betrayal? Goat fucking pigs! The worst kind of traitors." His chin sank to his chest, arms tense with ropey veins. Struggling to overcome it, he continued talking. "I was only mildly surprised by your treachery, *gordo,*" he said to the huge white man, then spat blood at him. His eyes moved to the other man. "But you, Hector. You are Mexicano, with roots in Juarez. The cartel is your blood. This betrayal will crush your family. They will be hunted. And exterminated. *Cucarachas.*" He spat blood seeping from his lips, his glare roving between them.

Jimmy wasn't impressed. He stepped forward, grunting with the effort as he threw a fist into Jose's stomach. The thud knocked the wind from him, expelled breath thickening the air with more blood and sweat. The ropes holding Jose to the chair strained as his body tried to double over from the pain.

"Where is it? Where the fuck did you put it?" Jimmy shouted in rage, shaking with something far beyond impatience. He screamed and started throwing punch after punch into Jose's face, stomach, and ribs, his gloved fists dishing out bruises and fractures with every blow. The abandoned apartment building echoed with the fury, but its filthy walls, trash-strewn floors and busted windows were unconcerned witnesses to the brutality.

Jimmy stooped with both hands on his knees. Bent over and wheezing like he was the one being assaulted. He looked over at his partner. "Hose...Him...Taser."

Hector grabbed the hose and twisted the nozzle. The cold stream of water revived Jose enough so that he didn't have to use the modified taser. "I don't think this was a good idea, Jimmy," he said, turning the hose off. "He's not going to talk. Jose didn't get to be a lieutenant by being weak."

"What, are you scared now? Getting a conscience all of a sudden? It's too late for that. We can't just quit and let him go." He paused and looked at his partner and only friend. "Look, these greasy motherfuckers owe us, Hector. Everybody owes us, this entire community. We have served the public on these ungrateful streets for ten years, saving lives and sending the trash to prison. And what do we have to show for it? An anorexic bank account and more time on the goddamn streets! They owe us, and so does this trash right here," he said, pushing a branch-like finger into Jose's forehead. "He owes us for not putting him away years ago." Dark red splotches appeared to rise from the sweat pouring off his brow, eyes enormous with lack of circulation.

He spun back to Jose, who was laughing.

"Hector is right, Jimmy," Jose croaked, still laughing. His slight frame shook in his yellow silk shirt, eyes alight with the antagonizing desire he felt towards the man he knew would kill him. "And you are wrong in your justification. There is no just due.

Nobody owes you. It is greed that controls your life now." His teeth showed in a bloody smile. "It's greed that has sentenced you to death."

With a ferocious grunt Jimmy reared back and slapped him again, putting his whole body into the swing, knocking the chair over. Jose's body slammed on the floor, thumping his head on the filthy tile. Jimmy leaned down and grabbed his shoulders, pulled up, setting the chair upright again.

He growled in Jose's face. "Now, you listen to me, big shot, big shit, mafia wannabe greaser." His whisper was ominous, "You are nothing now. *Nothing*," he breathed hotly. "You have been screwing me for three years. Now I want to get paid." He gave a pleasant look. "You know, we learned quite a bit about serial killers and torture methods at the academy. I would love to try out a few of my favorites on you. You will suffer in pain beyond comprehension. I'll give you blood transfusions and bring you back to life with a fucking defibrillator so I can kill you and revive you again and again. And again." His big nose wrinkled over bared teeth. "But it doesn't have to be that way. Tell me where you hid the money and I'll end it quick and clean, right now." He snapped his fingers.

Jose whispered, features going slack. He grunted with a swing of his head, motioning Jimmy to come closer. Jimmy leaned down with his ear to Jose's mouth. "*Chinga tu madre*," he said, then spat blood on the side of Jimmy's face.

"You're dead! You're fucking dead, greaser!" The folds in Jimmy's neck trembled, fists rose up on either side. He unleashed blows into Jose's face once more, wheezing and missing as he tired. He fell on one knee, sharp breaths stirring dust between his boots.

Jose managed to laugh through the final barrage, laughing even harder when he quit. "No *gordo*. It is you who are dead. Traitors... *las estupida putas*. Always make mistakes." He coughed, blood ran out of his mouth and down his clean shaven chin and neck. His diehard manner and righteous final words would honor his Aztec warrior ancestry. "If my *hermanos* don't avenge me, someone else will get you. Sooner, rather than later."

Face purple and bellowing between breaths, Jimmy drew his gun and shot Jose in the face from where he knelt. The .40 Black Talon entered at his chin and went through his mouth and out the back of his neck, severing the spinal cord and traveling through two sheetrock walls before lodging in a wooden stud. The explosion covered the wall and floor behind him in bits of bone, blood, gray matter, chunks of hair and skin. Pigeons cooed and flapped away from the open, busted windows, emptying their frightened bowels on the concrete and lawn below.

From the wall of gore an incisor fell free, hitting the floor tiles with a chink in the silent aftermath.

Hector's swallowed a powerful cry and stumbled forward. "Oh, Jimmy. No! Not the Sig. Why did you use the Sig?" He stood with his hands gripping his hair, staring at what was left of Jose's neck. He whined, "This is bad, amigo. Really bad. You were supposed to use the .38, the throw-away. Not your issue!"

"Shut up, shut up! I know that." Jimmy said, huffing from an inhaler. Asthma under control, he realized the consequences and made a serious effort to get his temper down, to compose a new plan. "Don't worry about it. It was only one bullet. We'll take his head and throw it in the bayou. They'll never find it. Our cartel guys will think it was an MS-13 hit."

"Take his head? You want to take his head?" He whined, "*Madre de Dios*," and crossed himself.

"Yes. Listen to me, goddamn it. We needed to do this. This piece of shit was in our way. We talked about this. He's the reason our cut was only five percent. The ungrateful prick is out of the way now, so we'll get more money. Your family will get more money now. Let's stay focused on why we had to do this, Hector."

"All right, Jimmy. Let's hurry, okay? We have been here for way too long already."

Jimmy unsnapped his knife sheath and slid out his six-inch serrated Gerber blade. Grabbing Jose's hair with one hand, he sawed through the esophagus, muscles and tendons, then dug around and found a spot between two vertebrae to complete the severing. Blood nearly as dark as his gloves ran to the floor in rivulets. He didn't get what he had come for, and the dead eyes and death's head grin seemed to mock him for his failure. His neck quivered below his gaping snarl.

"I found it, Jimmy," Hector called, relief evident in his voice as he walked from the hallway holding a deformed slug between two fingers. He stuck it in his pocket with a grimace. "It was stuck in a stud, in the back room. Got lucky, *ese.*"

"Right. Good. The crime scene unit won't have a bullet or a head to find out what kind of gun was used. But they could find our hair, prints, or something. We'll have to burn the place. That'll clean it up. Do you have a lighter?" he asked, knowing his partner sometimes smoked.

"Yeah, Jimmy. I'll make a fire. Let's just go, okay? I'm getting spooked."

"All right, all right! We're going. Don't start that Mexican spirits of the dead crap again. This is one greaser that won't be haunting us, I promise you. He'll be haunting some stinking bayou in about fifteen minutes."

"Whatever you say, Jimmy."

Hector shook his head and walked back down the hallway, stepping over an Arby's bag with holes chewed in it, stopping where he had earlier found a jug of paint thinner. He picked up the container, wondering if someone had abandoned it along with their plans to restore the apartment. The entire neighborhood had deserted the area, unable to afford to rebuild after Hurricane Katrina had caused the building codes to change. The police kept out squatters and junkies very effectively.

And the officers that made that extra effort are the same ones that used this neighborhood for their personal affairs, he just realized. He shook his head again.

"Well, no one will use this place again. Sheesh. What have you gotten yourself into, Hector?" he muttered to himself, unscrewing the cap. He poured the mineral spirits all over the floor and walls. Walked the liquid trail down the hall and into the front room with Jose. He splashed it around the body but couldn't quite bring himself to throw it on the cartel lieutenant. Squatting down, he struck his lighter and the room slowly bloomed with firelight.

Walking outside, Hector saw Jimmy rummaging through Jose's car, a new champagne colored BMW M3. The glass had been recently cleaned and reflected a morning sky that seemed supernaturally clear and pure in contrast to the street below. The yard was a trashed clone of the other lots on the abandoned street, overgrown with weeds and littered with fast food packages, old, rusted kitchen appliances, and diapers. It was diseased. Clusters of pox on hairy, filthy skin. The apartment buildings were mere skeletons of their pre-Katrina glory, gutted and ugly with stripped paint and rotten wood that could be sensed every time a breeze drifted through.

The scene matched Hector's mood, compounding it.

Maybe a fire is what this place really needs, he reasoned, looking around and envisioning an inferno consuming the filth and corruption. "We are going to burn for our corruption one day, too," he prophesied to the neighborhood.

"What?" Jimmy yelled, still digging around in the car.

"I lit the fire."

"Good. Set this car on fire, too. There's nothing in it worth anything. Dammit!" He threw down some papers and slammed the center console shut. Got out, looked Hector in the eye. "I wish I could bring the bastard back to life so I could kill him again. They owe us, Hector. They fucking owe us!"

Kill him again? Hopefully you'll use the .38 next time, Hector thought to himself. He didn't say anything, knowing that continuing to talk about the money they didn't get would only make the situation worse. And, he discovered, he was scared to say anything. Scared of the person his partner had become.

He popped the hood on the BMW and used his knife to cut a fuel line. Then he walked back to the driver's side and turned the key on. The fuel pump cycled on and off to prime the engine, spraying gasoline all over the engine compartment and ground. He turned the key off, then on again to spray more fuel. Then, he squatted down and struck his lighter.

The car burst into flames.

"Let's go, Hector. We have to dispose of this son of a bitch's head and get back to work." Jimmy got into their car, closed the door.

"Yeah. Let's get back to work," he replied, adjusting his uniform back into regulatory position. For a moment he stood there, studying the side of their patrol car, noticing how the name of the place he once swore to protect and serve mocked him in return.

City of Biloxi Police, its bold, black presence stood out in sharp contrast against the pristine white of the front and rear door panels. The dark letters seeping in and scarring the rest of the sanctified body, abusing their place of honor much like the two men who rode inside.

He fell into the passenger seat with a defeated slump, closed the door behind him, and sighed. Flames from the BMW's carcass danced like victorious, evil spirits across the cruiser's mirrored surface, echoing their laughter along the side of Hector's sullen face as they drove away from the scene.

He dug a pack of Winston's from his uniform pocket and placed a crooked cigarette between two nervous fingers. Turning slightly so as not to arouse Jimmy's suspicion, he crossed himself, resigned to the chaos ahead.

Chapter II

Philadelphia, Pennsylvania
March 19, 2010

Twelve miles from the Philadelphia Airport her destiny awaited. The cornerstone that will cap the legacy of Shocker the Fighter and initiate a new era for Clarice the Woman. The Wife and Mother.

North Broad Street was filled with old buildings, but none was more distinguished than the four-story beauty that was the Blue Horizon. The legendary boxing venue was over a hundred and forty years old. It pulsed with an ancient force beyond its years, a residual energy that permeated the structure's core from the hundreds of thousands of fans that had screamed within these walls. She could feel that energy now, revitalized from the crowd of fifteen-hundred that surrounded the ring and voiced their joy from the previous fight, a ten-rounder between welterweight contenders. If she read the commotion correctly, *someone got knocked the fuck out.*

The exterior and design of the Blue Horizon were exquisite, but the interior showed the aged and worn characteristics of an establishment with a maintenance budget deficit. Well loved, well used. Reminded her of the patina on her El Camino's 1959 paint and body. It had needed to be restored but broke her heart to do so because she was reluctant to change his O.G. personality, rough and gruff. This joint had that O.G. effect. Rough, dirty, powerful, like it was the Grandpa of Philly. A mean old son of a bitch of a grandpa that would outlive God, kick His ass every time it thundered, and turn His angels into his own personal harem with a schlong as big as a mountain.

Old School, architectural pimp.

The locker room floor tiles were white, chipped and pitted with black mold stains, and sprouted benches along the walls and down the center of the small, rectangular room. The walls were thick concrete with peeling white paint and brown stains from strong disinfectant that didn't like to wipe off. Fluorescent lights with dirty globes shined dimly over their heads. It smelled like it looked, old and dank, with detergents that couldn't quite mask the odor of degeneration.

Like my grandpa, she thought.

The walls vibrated with the crowd's energy, towering resonators that shook her little bones with immeasurable power and buzzed her head with sensations that mirrored her thoughts and intentions for the upcoming battle.

Hyper thoughts. Violent intentions.

Her mouth was suddenly dry, her bladder full. Symptoms a soldier experiences before going into a deadly war she knows she may not make it out of in one piece. That feeling of High Risk that takes the mind into an alternate reality where instincts do all the driving and leave all the drama and whiny emotions in the dust. A nervous want. A fear of blood loss and a desire for blood lust.

A Sweet Science.

The strategy of Hurt and Not Get Hurt. The strategy of You Better Fucking Win Because There Is No Second Place.

She wanted it.

Her monster wanted it, the fight junkie dwelling in her head.

"I want it," she told Eddy. He straddled the bench in front of her, wrapping her hands, ignoring the Philadelphia Boxing Commission representative and the Latino dude from Team Torres that looked over his shoulder to monitor his work.

"Believe it, girl. You'll get it. She's all yours," he said, adjusting the sleeve of his black and pink Team Ares jacket, unrolled another length of tape. The white athletic tape he layered on her fists tightened, hardened her hands into lethal weapons. Grenades she planned to decimate Torres' head and body with. She tensed, foot started bouncing. Eddy started taping faster, his mind on the same alternate realm as hers.

She wanted it. He wanted it.

Now.

"Tell them to just play the song. I can't sing it. Don't know what the hell I was thinking," she told him.

Eddy looked over at her promoter, Silvio, who sat on a bench to their left, brushing imaginary dust off his black Hugo Boss suit. Smiled at him. Looked back at her, underbite sticking out with a grin. "I already took care of it," he said.

Her mouth turned down, brows rolled into one. "Really," she said.

"Don't worry, darlin'. No one doubts your singing ability. Your ability to overcome the killer instinct you feel now, and perform a song you've only practiced in your car. That was in doubt."

"Really."

"And like you just said, what were you thinking? This isn't a singing contest. Forget about it."

"Yeah, Shock. Forget about it," Silvio said, adding his two cents and earning a glare-scowl from her. The Commission rep snickered and she aimed her mean mug at him. His expression became focused once more.

"Let's get these gloves on. Then you get your butt in that contraption. It's show time," Eddy said.

"Yes, Coach," she snapped at him. He just continued his stupid grin and unwound the final length of tape. Cut it, stuffed the roll in a jacket pocket. Taped her hand.

Silvio had several event assistants running around double-checking his commands. The referee walked in, a late-fifties white dude with smooth movements and a tan, cosmetically enhanced face and Just For Men gelled brown hair. A herd of people and cameras followed, HBO Pay-Per-View staff. The commission rep signed his mark on her hand wraps and she stuffed them into the gloves Eddy held. Eight-ounce Cleto Reyes, black. He taped the wrists of the gloves quickly, securing the laces. The commission guy scribbled his mark over the tape, a seal that proved the gloves weren't loaded and prevented tampering between here and the ring. The ref stepped forward and did his thing, instructing her to avoid illegal punches and obey his commands at all times. The cameras zoomed in on them. She agreed to obey. He turned and walked through the HBO staff, who directed cameras after her as she walked into the hallway.

The 'contraption' sat outside the locker room door, in the hall that led into the Carmichael Auditorium where the crowd and ring awaited. Event assistants swarmed her. The huge mutant rat costume was thrown over her shoulders, around her pink and black trunks and legs. Zipped up. The head was placed over hers so that her eyes, nose, and mouth popped out under the rat's snout. The clear plastic spikes that ran over the rat's crown and down the spine were turned on, LEDs flickering white and purple. The feminine mask and wild, mutated dark brown furry body made her feel like Godzilla's bitch.

She noticed the microphone had been removed from the snout and figured Eddy had done it before she even arrived.

Old bastard, doubting my singing skills. I ought to take him to the fried seafood buffet and order us salads. Watch him sweat like a druggie in a crack house that's only allowed to smoke cigarettes. Teach the ol' geezer...

Music started, interrupting her thoughts of revenge. *She Wolf* by Shakira blasted from the auditorium, pummeling the walls and pillars with the Latina superstar's lilting voice and dance beats. The crowd roared its delight and she could picture women of all ages shaking their hips and waving arms over their heads.

Silvio appeared beside her, waving the cameras back. "Shocker, baby. You look fierce! Phenomenal!" he yelled over the resonations. The hallway was like a huge bass port, the air moving with the sound waves and fluttering all around them. Silvio's cologne wafted in her face. Polo Black with a dash of Cuba's finest tobacco.

"You're wearing too much cologne," she told him.

"What?"

"I'll miss this when I get home!"

"I will, too. You're the best, doll!" he yelled back.

She hugged him, decided against informing him that no amount of Polo could hide a Havana Sweet; he'd never fool his nagging wife. Stepped into her cage. Assistants stepped forward and secured the

Plexiglas door. A toggle switch was positioned next to the door frame. She flipped it. The clear liquid crystal displays on the outside of the Plexiglas walls, roof, and floor burst with bright blue, white, and purple streaks of lightning. It was so realistic looking it made her believe she could hear it sizzle and pop, anticipating thunderclaps. She smiled, thinking of her husband, Ace, and the mad scientist laugh he must have guffawed after creating this thing.

Shakira quit shaking the fans' rumps, returning to dormant 0s and 1s in a digital hard drive somewhere in a tiny control room out of sight. The crowd calmed to a simmer. The ring announcer boomed his intro for Consuela Torres, giving her kudos for being the WIBF champ with a record of twenty-six wins, zero losses, and eight knockouts. A nice account with ample embellishment.

The sound system started wailing again, this time with the heavy guitar chords of Smashing Pumpkins. Billy Corgan, *Bullet with Butterfly Wings.* Her gloves and boots started moving of their own volition, anticipating the show they had trained so hard for, bouncing on her toes, shuffling fists. Four huge bodybuilders in white lab coats walked into the hall, scientists to carry their experimental rat beast in a cage. They took up positions at the four corners, grabbed the handles and lifted the eight-by-six box of lightning above their shoulders, started walking slowly towards the auditorium.

I am the Shocker.

Thirty-one fights and twenty-nine knockouts. A feat that hasn't been matched in her weight class, or in any of the classes below a hundred-and-sixty-eight pounds. She looked at her right arm. All of the KOs owed credit to it. It's a lot bigger than her left. Not as fast, but a hell of a lot more powerful. A sixteen-year mechanic's arm, formed since she began turning wrenches at ten, that made her pound-for-pound the hardest hitting gal in boxing history. She wanted to use The Mechanic as her fight name, but inadvertently let Silvio see her shock herself one morning when he came into her shop.

Hey, she was out of coffee. Had a shitload of work to do.

He wouldn't let it go. Insanely original, and would pique the interest of the world, he said. The slick hustler was right. That stunt had landed them some pretty big pay days, for women's boxing, and landed her the name Shocker. A huge portion of the crowd was chanting it right then.

Goosebumps tingled up and down her arms, little icicles sprouting up under the beads of sweat.

Hyper thoughts. Violent intentions.

"Despite of my rage/ I am still just a rat in a cage!" Billy Corgan sang as they entered the auditorium proper, verse timed perfectly. She started shadow-boxing, dancing, dipping, pivoting, boots squeaking on plastic, throwing combos with easy speed, a freak in an electrical storm. The crowd loved it. The scientists and their insane creation, a monster they intended to turn loose inside the ring.

She rocked her monster, feeling the crowd's pleasure fuel her drive and really get her motor running. She lived for this moment. Nothing else was ever important or ever would be. This was, is, and will be her life, her destiny, her legacy. Her life was on the line, and she planned to shine.

The music ended, the cage was lowered, the door was opened. She bounded out in a crouch, still shadowboxing. The crowd stood to see her costume and bellowed their approval. The monster was loose. Huge TV monitors above the ring showed Godzilla's bitch bounding toward the ring's steps in a frenzy of pumping gloves, snarls, whipping tail and lightning Mohawk, clowning and working her Monster Mash.

She didn't remember climbing the steps or ducking under the ropes. Suddenly, she was in the ring, in a frenzy, in character and mashing her role to the fullest. She stopped on cue, as the music stopped, and Eddy lifted the mask off her head. Assistants unzipped the costume and it disappeared under the ropes. The TV monitors showed Eddy standing behind her, rubbing her right shoulder. She looked up at herself looking at herself. Face a thunderhead, brows furrowed, eyes dark and ominous, mouth in a snarl, boobs strapped down under a black tank. She raised a glove to salute the fans. They cheered and raised their arms in reply.

The ring announcer grabbed the microphone that was lowered from the overhead scaffolding. "Ladies and gentlemen! Introducing the reigning WBC world bantamweight champion!" His smooth voice boomed with super-sized garnishment to make it all sound pretty and important. She loved his voice. A brief pause to let the audience applaud, then he continued. "With a record of thirty-one wins, zero losses, and twenty-nine knockouts! The UNIQUE and PETITE! Clarice–'Shockerrr'–Arreees!"

The cheers lit up her pleasure centers like they never had before, pumping her full of her favorite drug: Invincibility. The rooty-poot term 'confident' didn't begin to describe her current mental state. The wonder drug the fans had immersed her in had inflated her ego to universal proportions, expanding like the Big Bang, flowing through her entire body and bonding to every molecule like armor.

I'm bulletproof, baby. An invincible predator. And tonight I'm going to jail for murder.

Torres is going in the ground.

The referee called his combatants to the center of the ring. Put his latex-gloved hands on a shoulder of each of them and spoke into the microphone, reminding them of the instructions he gave earlier in their locker rooms. She glared at her enemy. Looked her up and down. Growled because her light blue trunks with gray fur looked way cuter than hers. Torres' gray tank, no boobs, and manly shoulders didn't match her very feminine heart-shaped face and button nose. Big eyes and thick lips, dark hair in microbraids, tied in a ponytail. Prominent Latin features. She looked down at the mat, a psychological tactic that worked as a confidence tool for most fighters. Clarice had Invincible overconfidence shooting out of her like lunch from a supermodel, so glaring was the only function she had at that point.

The ref wrapped it up, the microphone was reeled up. The trainers and Teams ducked out of the ring. The fighters went to their corners.

Ding! Round One.

The blue mat didn't sound a peep as their bantam-weighted boots circled the Tecate beer logo in the center of the twenty-foot square ring. Circling left, two right-handed boxers dipping knees, weaving heads. Feigning jabs. Torres lunged forward with a double-jab and Clarice pivoted right while countering with a quick right-hand punch. Missed. Torres avoided it with ease, obviously having trained for that move. They circled some more. Clarice stopped, flat-footed for a ruse. Torres lunged again, a viper striking with liquid grace. Shifting her weight to her right foot, Clarice threw a jab that slid right down Torres' arm and, *bam!* Solidly thumped her button nose.

Damn that felt good.

First landed punch is always the best. Like an alcoholic taking her first sip of the day.

Give me more.

It is on, you little bull. Toro, bitch! TORO!

Torres' corner started yelling to her in Spanish. She attacked, jabbing, trying to sneak in an uppercut to the body. Clarice jabbed to fend her off, pivoted left, back to the right, catching Torres' punches on her gloves, waiting on her to fire another right-hand. There it comes! Focus so acute everything slowed

23

down like a scene in The Matrix, surreal, *megamo*. Torres' punch reached the end of its range, Clarice ducked under it, weaved out over her left foot, shot a left-hook towards Torres' ear like a Tomahawk missile, really thrusting up from legs and transferring that weight and momentum into twisting shoulders and through the punch.

Through her head.

Sweat exploded off Torres' head, spraying the panel of judges that sat ringside behind a table. One of the judges, an elderly lady with snow white hair, wiped her face and grinned.

Torres wobbled into the ropes and Clarice attacked with four and five punch combinations that had the crowd on their feet, screaming with glee. The Invincible dope and bloodlust overcame her and she stupidly wasted more energy than she should have.

Torres was hurt but still firing back, still defending. As it turned into a slugfest, the cheers became deafening, teasing, taunting and enticing Clarice with more of the Good Stuff, urging her to keep throwing. Keep chasing that first-hit reward. Torres felt it, too, and was beginning to land more punches as Clarice's shoulders tired.

Eddy yelled and Clarice's senses returned, telling her to get out of there, let go of the bloodlust, put a leash on the fight junkie. "Box! Box!" Eddy shouted. "Move your butt, girl!"

She needed to get Torres back on her terms, control the fight with boxing instead of punching. Slugging is what Torres did best. Clarice needed to pick her apart like a surgeon. She jabbed out, away from Torres, moving back to the center of the ring for more movement options. Torres followed, gliding smoothly and showing no signs that she had been hurt.

Did I hurt her? Or did that bitch trick me into punching it out with her?

"Ugh!" she grunted in frustration.

Torres jabbed, threw a right that Clarice blocked. She did it again, but feigned the right. Too late, Clarice fell for it, threw a counter-right that missed and gave Torres the opening she had set up. Torres snapped her hips and whopped Clarice in the chin with an uppercut.

Backwards Clarice went, arms pin-wheeling in an effort to keep the balance her brain had temporarily forfeited. Her butt hit the mat. She squawked in anger.

Mother... fucker.

Torres' fans roared. The ref counted. Eddy started cursing. All really bad signs. Clarice took a few deep breaths and concentrated on the ref. He focused clearly in her vision so she got up, shrugged shoulders and rolled her neck, bounced on her toes. She took the standing eight-count to recover, then nodded to the ref that she was ready to continue. Nodded that she was ready to murder.

Oh, baby. She will pay for that one.

The ref told Clarice to walk to him, rubbed her gloves on his shirt, got out of the way. "Box!" he said.

She launched a series of jabs that backed Torres into the ropes. Torres tried to pivot and counter, but

Clarice anticipated the angle and dropped down below it, throwing a steaming right-hand into Torres' stomach, immediately stepping with her left foot to throw a hook. Torres clinched to catch her breath, grabbing Clarice's arms, then tried to sneak in another uppercut. Clarice blocked it with her right glove, reached up and grabbed the back of her head with her left and pulled down. Instinctively, Torres raised her head to pull away, wasting precious energy and prolonging her recovery. Clarice held her.

"You can call me Herpes, bitch," Clarice spat at her. "Because I always come back."

Growling in pain and anger, Torres struggled loose and sprang off her back foot with a wild four-punch combination that Clarice danced away from, landing jabs on Torres' forehead. Snapped a wicked right-cross that landed with a satisfying smack on Torres' cheek, the crowd echoing it with a collective "Oooh…"

How you like me now?

Ding! The ref jumped between them and pointed to their corners. The crowd was on their feet cheering and clapping raucously. They raised their gloves to acknowledge the fans' support as they walked to their respective corners.

Eddy propped the stool on the mat and tore Clarice a new one as soon as she sat down. "What the hell were you doing? You abandoned the fight plan! I know you're smarter than that. When a jackass brays at you, you don't bray back! You trick him into carrying your load! Stop being stupid and listen!" he bellowed right in her face. His breath smelled like peanuts, but it felt like fire. The angry passion he emanated was super scary. Realizing how bad she had fucked up, all she could do was nod vigorously and agree to get back on the game plan.

"Yes, Coach!"

"I told you. When she wants to punch, you box! Get it through your thick head, girl! Box!"

"Yes, Coach!"

"Remember: weave, hook, weave, hook! Trick her with the right, then hook!"

"Yes, Coach!"

"You got knocked down, so you lost that round. You better not lose another to this girl."

"Yes, Coach!"

He ducked under the ropes, the cut man smeared Vaseline over her eyes and cheekbones, put her mouthpiece in. She stood. The bell rang.

Ding! Round two.

Clarice's ponytail, tank top, and trunks were soaked, sweat pouring off as if she were standing in a steam room. A towel flashed between her legs, wiping up the puddle she had left from the sixty-second break. Her cheeks were beginning to throb, the jaw muscles inflamed from absorbing that bomb Torres had nailed on her chin. Motherfucker would be sore as hell later.

Super-duper.

Clarice made a conscious effort to clear her head and focus on nothing, an illusion of elsewhere that erased all emotion from her body and allowed her muscles to connect directly with her instincts, the muscle-memory that was programmed with Eddy's custom pugilistic software. Thinking slows a fighter down, inhibiting the mind-muscle connection with unnecessary pulses of information. Like spam, all in the damn way. Acting without thought or emotion is the recipe for speed.

And you know what they say about speed… It kills.

Torres darted in like a jackhammer, jab pumping as her feet pumped across the Tecate logo towards Clarice. Right-hand cocked. Clarice slipped the jabs, staying right in Torres' face, watching for her right as she watched for Clarice's. Let Torres chase her around the ring for a minute while she got into position for a counter punch. Torres kept coming straight at her, relentless, homing in, being the aggressor as part of a strategy to impress the judges and gain favor in the event that the fight went the distance. Aggressor is the only role Torres knew, a Mexican style of fighting she was taught, and taught well. Problem is, it's one-dimensional, all attack with little defense or counter punching involved. She would be in serious trouble if the roles suddenly reversed. That's why she's good at standing her ground and slugging. To prevent role-reversal, survival, protection of her style. Clarice needed to hurt her to reverse it, get her out of her rhythm and off her game.

Hurt her bad… Speed speed speed…

Clarice pivoted the wrong way, seemingly by accident, as a result of frustration, let Torres chase her into a corner, raised her gloves to cover her head, elbows close together to cover her body. Pop-pop *bam!* Torres wailed on her gloves and arms with a beautiful three-punch line drive. A half-second later, she reset and wailed again. This time Clarice turned to the right and caught the third punch, a heavy right, on her left shoulder.

"Gaah!" she cried, grabbing Torres' forearms and clinching. Having sensed the injury, Torres yanked up hard on her left arm, grunting sadistically, spraying spit and hot breath on her arms. Clarice cried out again, grabbed Torres' elbow and pushed her left while pivoting right, spinning her into the corner, trading places. Clarice backpedaled to the center of the ring, shaking out her arm and grimacing like her shoulder was torn or out of socket.

Torres paused in the corner and smiled at Clarice. A green, white, and red flag of Mexico appeared behind her lips, a fierce grin representing the country she was kicking ass for. "*Muerta, puta,*" she said, bringing her gloves together in front of her face. She raised her Cleto Reyes and jabbed after Clarice, explosive and feline, a lioness pouncing on her hamstringed prey.

Standing with her left arm hanging, Clarice stepped and weaved her head as if she actually believed she could slip punches and fight with just her right arm. Torres went right at her with a one-two. Clarice shifted onto her back foot to avoid the punches, right glove brushing her nose. Clarice stepped toward her hard and quick, throwing her 'useless' left arm up horizontally into a hook that had all of her legs, hips, and shoulders behind it, leverage and weight distribution in perfect textbook form.

Her glove hit Torres' chin and she tightened her fist, forearm and shoulder as it connected, solidifying it, driving it through the girl's face. Torres' head twisted, her eyes rolled, she flailed her arms reflexively, punches her brain triggered while forgetting to tell the rest of her that she was going down for a crash landing.

Clarice stood over her, glaring, snarling, ignoring the referee who urgently motioned her to a neutral corner so he could count out her victim. But Clarice didn't want him to count her out. She wanted Torres to get up so she could ride that roller coaster again. Feel that satisfying crunch of her jaw that made her eyes flash like flags of surrender.

The crowd was going mad from the action, feeling the blood-lust and cheering the violent skill they had paid good money to witness, voicing their appreciation for not being disappointed.

Well, how about an encore?

"Get up, Torres!" Clarice shouted. "You're not done yet. Get up!" Spit flew out of her mouth, drooling down a sweaty chin from lips that wouldn't seal properly around the mouthpiece, pink with tiny white bolts of lightning for teeth. The huge TV monitors showed Clarice screaming at her inert opponent, shaking the glove that had knocked Torres down, spit and drool flowing from her snarl, rabid.

Eddy's voice broke through the noise and her zone of rage. "Get your ass in that corner! Now! Shocker! Get your goddamn ass in that corner, girl!" he roared, spitting, snarling with even more rabid nature.

Clarice glanced around, expecting a mob of people to be running away from her coach's vicinity, listening for a siren to start blaring a warning. Remembering why she was suddenly scared, she trotted to a neutral corner, turned and watched the ref count, refusing to look at Eddy and his heated glare directed at her.

Torres was on one knee, slowly recovering from the extra seconds given to her, staring at her gloves on the mat in front of her as her corner and her fans yelled and cheered encouragement to get up and fight. She stood, eyes wide and not completely focused, nodded to the ref. The ref told her to lift her gloves and step towards him. She did so without stumbling. He wiped her gloves on his shirt, asking if she was okay to continue. She nodded, stoic, a true warrior's reaction, showing her people she wasn't a quitter and would fight on regardless of consequences to her health.

Gotta give it to the broad. She's a soldier. But she's still gonna be Shocker Victim #32.

The ref signaled them to continue. They raised their gloves.

Eddy yelled again, "Thirty-seconds! *Get in her ass!*"

Torres was game and tried to work a few power punches behind her jab. But Clarice just bowled right over her, hammering her into the ropes with hard, driving, blistering quick right-hands that busted her nose and lips, spraying pink sweat all over the mat and outside the ropes onto the Beautiful People that sat nearest the ring. Torres bounded off the ropes with a wild hook. Clarice ducked it, banged a right-hand, left-hook to Torres' stomach and ribs, springing up to make it a double-hook to her head, landing it hard.

Sideways Torres went, grabbing the ropes for support. At that point, the referee should have stopped the fight, but he didn't.

And Clarice wasn't mad about it.

Torres hit the corner post and covered up. Clarice jumped in and out at her, throwing a right-hand bomb every time her weight came forward, rocking her monster, rocking Torres' head even though Torres caught the punches on her gloves. Threw a ridiculously flashy over/under combination of about ten blows, mostly ineffective, showboating her speed demon to please the crowd. Torres fired back before the ref TKO'd her for not defending herself. Clarice paused and laughed, relaxed her shoulders for a fraction of a second, launched what she knew would be the *coup de grace*.

Right-hand, left-hook, right-hand, left-hook, over and over, harder and faster, flowing, rocking Torres like a bobble head dashboard toy. Switched, right-uppercut, left-hook, over and under, upper-cutting between her elbows to split her guard, tagging her chin, popping her head up behind her gloves to meet a perfectly thrown hook.

Clarice's left glove compressed against Torres' jaw, twisting her neck sharply, disrupting the flow of nerve impulses between her brain stem and spinal cord.

Incommunicado. Lights out.

Torres' eyes flashed surrender, her body dropped like a sniper had picked her off. The ref jumped in front of her, his back to Clarice, waving his arms like he was doing jumping jacks. The fans were literally off their feet, jumping up and down screaming, spirit and spittle flying in joyful chaos. Someone grabbed Clarice's legs from behind and hoisted her above the people that flooded the ring with towels, cameras, and pumping celebratory fists. Eddy held her up on one shoulder like a trophy, his prize, a winner that made him a winner. She leaned sideways and kissed the top of his curly head.

Several officials in suits of grays and blues appeared in the twenty-foot squared circle, a sea of boxing's privileged locals, shuffling, pushing, turning through the throng to stand next to Eddy. He lowered her. Clarice's boots hit the mat and she looked up at huge men that lowered championship belts over her. One over her head, one around her waist. Eddy stood behind her and held the belts in place. The towering suits flanked them and a dozen cameras flashed, zoomed in. The TV monitors showed the WBC and WIBF world championship belts wrapped around an emotional girl who was visibly relinquishing the killer instinct in the form of tears. The giants surrounding her were blocking the view for most of the fans so Eddy lifted her again, slowly rotated her, his trophy holding her trophies. Clarice basked in their adoration for what she knew would be the final time, tears pouring like sweat, smiling and sobbing, trying to breathe through an emotionally constricted throat.

She kissed Eddy's head again and choked out, "We did it, Coach."

He patted her leg. "You better believe it."

He lowered her, hugged her. Grabbed the belts she shrugged out of and looped them over a huge arm like bracelets. Flicked out a knife and cut off her gloves. She waded through the suits and media, ignoring the microphones shoved in her face, until she saw Team Torres jackets. Her opponent's people saw Clarice and made way so she could hug her no-longer enemy. She raised Torres' hand. Cameras zoomed in. The TV monitors showed two serious combat women acknowledging respect for each other's lethal skills in battle. Clarice hugged her again. Hugged her trainer. Waded back to Eddy.

And started sobbing harder. It was all over.

Forever.

"Let's get out of here, darling," Eddy said, wrapping a protective arm around her. He marched them through the suits and pursuing media like a cruise ship plowing through small waves.

Chapter III

Biloxi, Mississippi
March 20, 2010

The flight from Philadelphia to Atlanta was uneventful, other than the event that began inside of her. An anti-climax that happens immediately after every fight. She's never experimented with drugs, but knew what it felt like to be seriously high, to soar above everything and everybody and never want to come down.

She knew what it felt like to come down, hard, a vertical drop without declining in gradients. No levels of descent to get the body sensitized to running on less Go-Go Juice. Just an abrupt loss, a *snatching*, a dream life lost and never to be lived again.

And she knew what it felt like to want more. To go mad for another hit.

Clarice was in agonizing withdrawal when she and Eddy changed planes and landed at Gulfport International an hour later. Her home was close by, in Biloxi, about a fifteen-minute drive. Ace picked her up in his Dodge Ram. They said their goodbyes to Eddy and he drove them home in silence. Her man understood that she needed this time to think and readjust to being human again after playing the super hero role in the ring. Emotional decompression. Ace was lucky this process worked. Otherwise she'd have him on a steady diet of Ms. Bad Bitch, with liberal servings of Wicked Narcissism on the side, and, perhaps, served up on a lovely platter of I Run This Shit.

And feed it to him for breakfast, lunch, and dinner...

So she fought for decompression. He stayed quiet. And lucky.

They exited Interstate-10 in Woolmarket, in north Biloxi, and turned onto Woolmarket Road. Headed east for about a quarter mile before turning into a driveway. A two-hundred foot steel building sat on five acres of grass surrounded by pine trees and residential streets behind it. The building had a granite stone front, dark blue steel sides, and a white roof with half a dozen skylights showing on the front, with more on the other half of the building.

Huge windows with awnings on the front entrance were dark, reflecting the street lights. A large blue and gray sign stood guard at the left of the gravel drive, ten feet of fiberglass and wood, a tattooed chick bending over and reading the side of a door on a hot rod. The door advertised that this was a united business: Tattoology, her high-tech tattoo studio. And Custom Ace, the all-purpose mechanic shop that she renamed after marrying Alan "Ace" Carter.

They got out of the truck and were greeted by crickets that one by one started up their violin wings again once the Viper engine stopped growling at them. A dry breeze brought the fragrances of dozens of flowers and weeds that were blooming all over the yard. The smell of home, the ultimate aromatherapy. Clarice walked inside, passing through the tattoo studio area and into a hallway that led to the auto shop in the back. The studio's lobby, office, and partitioned parlor were spotless, furnished with state-of-the-art equipment, and smelled similar to a hospital. Ace took her hand and we walked up the wooden stairs in the center of the hallway, into our home over the top of the studio.

She was struggling in a strange daze. An empty, numb, and wanting sensation that had nothing to do with jet lag. She was too spaced out to seriously analyze herself, but was sure the feeling is what others experience from traumatic loss. Like when a family member dies. A brother or sister, a twin, and you feel like you've lost a part of yourself.

A part of myself.

She could still hear the crowd cheering as she left the ring. Could still hear the roaring, vibrating echo that was the hypodermic for her Invincible dope, as she sat in the locker room, sobbing, as Eddy cut off her hand wraps and her promoter hustled the media that crowded in after them. She could still feel it happening…

But it wasn't happening. And never would again. She just didn't want to let it go. It didn't want to let her go, either.

Let her go.

Shocker Ares. She's gone.

I'm gone. I'm there. Now I'm here. Without her.

A part of myself.

"Are you okay, Clarice?" Ace asked, stroking her hair. He knew how much she loved that. And it helped, was soothing on so many levels. They sat in their comfy living room, in a huge leather chair that was their favorite spot because they could view the room and the artwork on the walls, the Turkish rugs that checkered the hardwood floor.

Mostly earth tones, the ambience was tranquilizing until your eyes wandered onto the mythological paintings dwelling like three-dimensional beings on the walls. Dragons, gods, and goddesses. Eight life-sized paintings with layered backgrounds in striking realism, seemed to lift off of the canvases and reach into your imagination. Monsters from the sea and the land, myths and legends that were created and accepted as real in everyday life thousands of years ago. Clarice painted them once she knew she was going to be building a home. Kind of like a home warming gift to herself, a series her Greek ancestors would surely appreciate.

A low moon white ceiling with small fluorescent spotlights lit up parts of the room and the paintings behind the sofas and the chair. The skylights were trimmed in dark blue, even darker now because of the night sky's lack of illumination. The forty-foot square floor was dark shiny wood with rugs in geometric patterns, though there were settings of furniture as well. A circular white leather sofa cornered a large flat screen TV and stereo entertainment center to their right. Tall corner windows with beige and white curtains were behind it and six-foot Apollo and Aphrodite renderings were on the far side of the windows. A small glass coffee table held remotes and coasters in front of the sofa. Behind that and almost directly across from them on one reddish-brown wall was another sofa. Long and white brushed leather with dark red throw pillows. A behemoth dragon on the wall above it floated in the air the entire length of the sofa, blowing flames on a tiny village far below its muscular wings, furious. Twin glass tables flanked it with red lamps and more coasters.

Behind them was another six-foot painting, this one with the goddess of the moon, Artemis. She was hunting for something, though Clarice left that up for the observers' interpretation. Honestly, she didn't know what the hell the ancient broad was hunting for. So she didn't put it in the painting. But it looked kickass over their chair.

The chair had the appearance and feeling of a king's throne, with an aura of cunning emitting from the scenes of sprites and fairies carved into the thick oak legs and arms, the little creatures twisted around each other erotically, expressions of carnal magic that seemed to honor a superior being. Like it was crafted so Conan and his concubines could have an orgy on it.

Maybe I should paint that and hang it over the chair...

She leaned back against her man and sighed, eyes closed. Then remembered he had asked her a question. "I know I'm being a drama queen. I'm having issues here," she said by way of apology.

"Just relax and tell me when you feel like it," he murmured, wanting no part of Ms. Bad Bitch. Wanting to stay lucky.

That made her smile. "Relax? What is that?"

"Shh. Don't do that. You know you'll feel better if you just talk it out," he murmured again, brushing his vibrating lips on the side of her neck, kissing it. He moved her hair and kissed her nape.

Oh, *god*. The man knew how to get her mind out of the gutter, and off to frolic in a different kind of gutter. Clarice started squirming, thinking of the Orgy Throne painting again. Giving it a title made it real in her mind, a fantasy, one she wanted to bring to life, lose herself in at that very moment.

"You're absolutely right," she whispered in a tight, I Have An Idea Voice. Her tone rose louder, husky. "Let's talk this out. Come on. Get up. I need your help with something in our bedroom. Let's scream that motherfucker out." She stood and grabbed his wrists, snatched him out of the chair.

I need this, as a cleansing of sorts. Yeah, this feels right...

Yeah. And Nolan won't be here until 6 a.m., when Mom drops him off. Plenty of time to deal with this...

She gripped his arms tighter.

"Are you going to hurt me again?" he said with a little worry laced in it. But excitement, too. Like he was about to get back on a theme park ride that scared him stupid, but he kept getting back in line anyway.

"Probably so."

"That's cool."

He laughed nervously as she led him down the hallway to their bedroom.

Chapter IV

Biloxi, Mississippi
March 21, 2010

Main Street in Biloxi was a curious mix of life. The buildings of the numerous businesses were in as many variations of shapes, colors and sizes as the people that populated the area. A real potpourri of humanity. But there were clear distinctions between two elements, unmistakable patterns that contrasted one class from the other.

There were the legit folks, mostly overweight whites with some older blacks, Asians, and a few Latinos. They drove nice cars and wore nice clothes, walked and talked in a manner that proclaimed them as law-abiding citizens. The suspect crowd, mostly blacks, with groups of young Asians, Latinos and whites disseminated throughout the area, drove old hoopties that branded them as probable drug users, or rode in customized bling rides that screamed illicit gain. Their fashion tastes favored sports jerseys or tank tops to show off tattoos, sagging, baggy pants and huge boots with loose shoe strings, or basketball shoes in loud colors.

The legits waved, nodded, or were oblivious to the police cars that drove by, confident in their citizenship and showing no concern at being observed by law enforcement. The suspects pretended to be oblivious, mostly unsuccessfully, by suddenly finding something to make them look busy or show they had a completely legal purpose for their present actions. Behavior that suggested the potential to break rules and a lot of guilt on their collective conscience.

"Look at that guy over there," Jimmy said, pointing at a young black man that had obviously been up all night. The teenager's pants were dropped below his butt, showing red boxers and a Tommy Hilfiger logo. The hustler saw the cop car and automatically pulled up his pants, an unconscious response that was nearly instinctual among street thugs because it made them a target for the boys in blue. "Jerkoff could at least wear clean drawers, you know? I mean, look at his ass. It looks like a fucking bruised apple. Who wants to see that?"

"I don't get it either," Hector replied, chuckling. "Personally, I don't mind the saggy thing. Makes them easier to catch." They shared a laugh. "One time, I chased an Asian kid through his house and into his backyard. He made it about fifty feet before his pants fell around his ankles and tripped him. Dummy busted himself."

"Oh, yeah! I remember that." The car swelled with loud belly laughter. They pointed out more suspects with bloopers potential as they prowled the dawning neighborhood. Some of the people were so obviously up to no good that they panicked and fled at first glimpse of the patrol. The guffaws continued, with wheezing, coughs and tear-welled eyes.

"Hey, Jimmy. They are like little raccoons with their robbers' masks, right?" Hector choked out between laughs.

"We caught them with their paws in the trash and they ran back into the woods! Yeah!" Jimmy exclaimed, wheezing and executing a few unplanned swerves.

The street light timers sensed the presence of the sun, blinking off the lights and erasing that eerie yellow-orange color that dominate the night in cities. A glare in the eyes that made the sky and buildings less distinguishable, and hid most of the ugliness of concrete and people alike. It was morning. The illuminating glow of the rising sun chased away the cloaking shadows to reveal the true nature of the area in all its glory: Filthy. Ugly. With random symmetry and appeal. Wrinkles, cracks, and dirt became more visible on the faces of stores and the people that walked into them.

"He should have called by now," Jimmy said, switching into the left lane without the courtesy of a blinker.

"Who, El Maestro?" Hector asked.

"Yeah, who else? I thought you said he would call by now."

"He said he would text. And to be on Main Street at sunup. We're here. I don't know what to tell you, Jimmy."

"Great. Just fucking great. What kind of an organized crime boss is he, huh? Can't keep a fucking appointment with his security team. I swear, these greaser —"

"Wait a minute, Jimmy. Just got a text." Hector's phone finished its chime as he took it from a compartment on his gun belt. He flipped open the purple Samsung, read the message. "It's him. He says to pull over the green Chevy Cruze in front of us."

"What the hell?" Jimmy leaned forward with his head over the steering wheel, squinting ahead into the shadowed traffic, searching through the people hurrying to work or school. He spotted the car and maneuvered to get behind it. Hit the lights for a routine traffic stop. "Is this him?"

"I think so."

"Be ready for anything."

"I know." Hector unsnapped his gun.

The Cruze pulled over to the right side of the road, stopping in front of a dress shop with mannequins in the windows displaying wedding gowns. The driver parked and waited without movement, both hands on top of the wheel.

Jimmy got out, blasts of wind from passing cars tugged at the door, assaulting his nose and lungs with smog particulates. He coughed and wheezed. Unsnapped and drew his gun. Held it against his leg as he approached the back of the green Cruze. Horns honked at an intersection nearby. Tiny rocks tinkled against the police cruiser from churning tires as a duo of dump trucks rumbled by. Hector approached the car from the passenger side.

The driver rolled down both windows simultaneously. "Hector. Jimmy. I think I would feel more pleasure from seeing you if you weren't holding drawn guns," greeted El Maestro. Clean and trim in a blue Nautica button-up with gold sailboats all over it, his light brown skin and black chin beard looked deceptively young on a man in his late sixties. The short dark hair on top with specks of gray, bald spot showing through, were the only indications of his age. He smiled, showing teeth as bright as his watch and rings.

"Good to see you, El Maestro," Hector said, holstering his gun.

"Yeah, as always," Jimmy agreed, still holding his gun and glancing in all directions.

El Maestro looked down at the weapon, back to Jimmy's nervous face. He said, "You seem overly anxious. Do you not trust me anymore? Or have you a guilty conscience about something?"

"It's not that." Jimmy allowed his anger to show, masking the paranoia. "We're a security team. I'd prefer to stay ready for anything."

"So you've heard, then."

"Yeah. We heard about Jose," Hector said. "Big news at the station yesterday."

El Maestro turned to Hector. "A victory for law enforcement, certainly. Jose was a warrior with status, and has been wanted for over a decade now. He will be remembered for his loyalty to La Familia and his sacrifices for his countrymen," he said, voice beginning to break with emotion. He cleared his throat. "I want you to investigate his death. Find out who did this and you will be rewarded."

"Any idea who did it?" Jimmy inquired, staring El Maestro in the face without blinking.

He didn't respond right away. Looked down to gather himself. Turned to the right, locking eyes with Hector. "Traitors," El Maestro growled. Hector flinched. Jimmy brought his gun up and pointed it at the back of El Maestro's head. "It was traitors," he continued, unaware of the instrument of death aimed at his cranium. "Somebody from inside the organization. Either La Familia or one of the associates or security teams," he told Hector, his stare watery and smoldering at once.

Jimmy lowered the gun. Glanced around to see if anyone was gawking. There wasn't. A wheeze slithered through his gritted teeth.

"Traitors?" Hector tilted his head. "Who? Who do we investigate?"

"If I knew, you wouldn't be investigating. It happened in your district. There are only so many people linked to us that could have arranged a meeting with Jose. Find out the 'who' and eliminate them. If you

47

need reinforcements, you know where to find me," he said, looking back to Jimmy.

"We'll take care of it. As soon as we know anything Hector will text you," Jimmy assured him.

"Excellent. We must show our enemies we don't let transgressions go unpunished." He looked over at Hector. "And we must show our family that vengeance will be pursued. *Pronto.*"

Hector just stood there, dark hair cut clean over haggard features.

"El Maestro," Jimmy said, calling his attention away from the look of guilt controlling his partner's face. "You said we would have a detail today. Where are the mules? Let's take care of business."

"You are right, of course," he replied, taking a phone from his pocket. He texted a quick note, pressed Send. "Let us not waste time chatting of unimportant matters."

"El Maestro, I don't think he meant –" Hector began, but was silenced by an upraised hand.

"I know what he meant. And we are wasting time. That car," he said, pointing at a late-model white Pontiac GTO that had pulled over to the opposite side of the road fifty yards ahead of them, "is your security assignment. Instead of the usual switch-off in Gulfport, I had the Hancock County team escort them here. All switch points will be changed randomly from now on. Follow them north and you will receive a text with the next switch point." He opened the center console, removed a gray Nokia cell phone and handed it to Hector. "Your new phone. I now have a GPS app that shows me where all my security teams are, so coordination will be more efficient."

"Okay, still business as usual. We'll take care of it," Jimmy said.

Dammit, he thought. *I'll have to figure out a way around this tracking and random switch point shit now.*

He holstered his gun, grimacing, walked back to the patrol car.

El Maestro turned to Hector. "Find the person who is behind this betrayal, Hector. Kill them. I will personally make sure your family in Juarez benefits from your dedication to La Familia. Good deeds earn great honor, *hermano.*"

Hector didn't reply, just stared after the green sedan as it pulled into traffic and turned its lights off, the morning air brightening.

Seagulls cawed overhead, grabbing Hector's attention, the sound like an omen of consequence. He stared up at the scavengers, eyes glazing, mystified.

His heart quickened.

A premonition sneaked its way into his thoughts, like a diseased mouse squeezing through a tight crack and entering a room that had never before been invaded by an infectious entity. The realization that he was a traitor as well as a dirty cop did not sit well in his mind. Uncoordinated from looking up, he stumbled to the side. Looked down at the concrete and his boots. To the left at the patrol car.

Jimmy stuck his head out of the driver's side window. "What the fuck are you doing? Let's go, let's go!" he yelled, pointing at the Pontiac up the street like Hector was a deaf dummy that needed blunt, elementary gestures to comprehend his meaning.

Hector hurried to the car, got in, and they pulled into traffic. Made a U-turn to get behind the GTO and followed them to the interstate.

"What the hell was that all about? What did El Maestro say?" Jimmy wanted to know. He divided his attention between driving and trying to analyze his friend.

"He just said he would take care of my family if we found the traitor." He shrugged.

"And what did you say?"

"Nothing."

"You didn't say anything?"

"I just said I didn't. What's your problem?" Hector folded his arms.

"Nothing, nothing. I'm sorry. I'm just a little stressed. I almost shot El Maestro a few minutes ago. Look, forget it, okay? Let's focus on the job. You know those guys?" he asked, indicating the two men in the GTO.

"No. Don't think so."

"Wonder how much product is stashed in that car. Probably a million worth, at least." They drove in silence until they reached the on-ramp to Interstate-10 West, which would take them to Highway 49 North. Jimmy tapped his meaty hands on the steering wheel. "Hey, how'd he get the name the Teacher, anyway."

"He really is a teacher." Hector watched the woods that lined the side of the interstate. He didn't look at his partner, hoping Jimmy would take the hint that he didn't feel like talking.

He didn't catch on. "No shit? From where?"

"University in Juarez. Economics and commerce professor."

"Commerce, huh? Yeah, that makes sense. No wonder that guy's like a fucking secret agent or something. Controlling a drug commerce relay race by using our government's own security structure to facilitate it. That GTO is the baton, and we are the runners that have to pass it off to the next runner."

"It's brilliant, *ese.*" Barely audible, his words sounded like they were dragged out of him. "No cop would think to pull over a car another cop is already following. And buying a cop or two in every county on the route is cheaper than losing shipments and drivers to law enforcement. It's nearly foolproof."

"Nearly," Jimmy agreed. "But I don't plan on passing these fucking batons much longer, brilliant or otherwise. I've done my tour of duty, Hector." He patted the badge on his chest. "For both sides of the fence."

They fell silent again. Another mile passed and the GTO pulled over to the side in the emergency lane, hazard lights flashing.

"What the fuck?" Jimmy roared, slowing and pulling in behind them. "Be ready." He unsnapped his gun. Shifted into Park and opened his door.

A slim Latino of medium height in his early forties stepped out of the Pontiac, loose fitting white pants and peach pastel shirt fluttering like flags as cars sped by. He shouted back at the patrol car. "Something's wrong with the *coche!*" he hollered over the din.

"What's the matter?" Jimmy yelled back. Stuck a fist to his mouth, coughed several times.

"The dash lights are going *loco!* And the car is losing power! *No se*," he said.

Jimmy stuck his head back in the car. "Hector you know more about cars than me. Check it out while I cover you."

"I'll take a look," he said, sighing. He opened the door, got out and walked to the white sports car. Asked the driver to step aside, sat in the seat and turned the key on.

Jimmy stood behind his door, hand on gun, watching the trees lining the side of the interstate and the cars approaching that may suddenly stop and sprout enemy targets. His energy abruptly failed him, dipping so low his knees nearly buckled and dropped him where he stood. Tiny dark spots appeared in his vision, little black holes that sucked in the light and matter in their vicinity. He leaned on the door, scowling viciously as he recovered.

All this damn greaser stress, he thought. *Motherfuckers are determined to put me in the ground before I get a chance to get out. I'll have to get stronger blood pressure meds this week.*

Fuck!

Hector trotted back to the cruiser. He and his partner ducked into their sides, closed the doors. "I don't know what the problem is, maybe something electrical. It will still drive, though. I gave them directions to a shop in Woolmarket. Only one exit away."

"You're talking about Custom Ace, right? Good idea. They're fast."

"Hopefully, it's only a minor problem and we'll be back on the road before lunch."

"Has anybody replaced Jose?"

"Don't think so. El Maestro mentioned that new GPS app, so I think he's running the show until someone gets promoted to lieutenant."

"So we report this directly to El Maestro. Text him a report. We'll park down the road from Custom Ace and stay on point."

"Sounds good, Jimmy." Hector took the Nokia out of his belt.

Chapter V

Biloxi, Mississippi
March 21, 2010

The alarm clock went off and they awoke to the Kings of Leon belting out *Sex on Fire*. Last night's experience ran through Clarice's head in vivid emotion and she started laughing. Ace obviously had the same thoughts because he was laughing and singing along as he got out of bed.

"*Your sex is on fire!*" he sang, playing air guitar and stepping around the room like he was performing for a crowd. Except a guitar wasn't what he was slinging around. He had absolutely no butt, and his narrow hips made his penis seem comically out of proportion. Like it could eat peanuts out of her hand.

She laughed harder.

He turned. "What?"

"Nothing. It's just that, well, did you eat Corn Flakes as a kid?" she asked with a big-eyed innocent look, already knowing the answer. She sat up. The blanket fell down, bunched under her bare breasts.

Ace looked at them and waggled his eyebrows. "Corn Flakes? Nope."

"Oh, that's right. You ate Noassatall Flakes." She looked at his hips. "Gigantic bowls of it."

"Hey, who needs a butt when you have this?" he responded, holding his 'this' in both hands and playing a solo on it. "Your sex is on fire!" he jammed, dancing around again. He was really getting into it, whipping it up and down like Hendrix at Woodstock.

Clarice laughed so hard her eyes had rivers pouring out at all corners. She wanted to spend the rest of her life right there, feeling that exquisite joy. "Oh man, that's good stuff." She wiped her eyes. "You won't win any mainstream talent shows, but I think you have a bright future in adult comedy. Let's set up a stage with tiki torches. We'll put on grass skirts and I'll drum on your coconut knees while you play your instrument."

He stopped and his eyes closed and opened slowly, head shaking. His fingers gestured at her. "It won't work."

"And why is that?"

"We would need a bass player. A bass guitar is bigger than a regular guitar. Where are we going to find a bigger guitar than mine?" he said, face serious again, gesturing at his crotch like it was the tallest skyscraper in the world.

"And the ego has landed." A fit of giggles grasped her and she lay back on the bed. *Oh man, that's good stuff.* She sat up again. "I could get a strap-on, but the competition might —"

"And we would need a singer," he interrupted, pretending he hadn't heard the solution to finding something bigger. He turned and walked to the bathroom, the sight of his no-butt dropping her back on the bed giggling once more. He gave it a smack, then yelled, "And you can't sing!" The shower turned on.

Clarice jumped up, laughter cutting off. "I can too sing!" she yelled back, a little girl in a My Daddy Can Beat Up Your Daddy argument. She stormed into the bathroom, slammed the door, tagged Ace with a quick combo to the body that knocked him off his feet in the tub. He fell, flailing his arms and ripping the shower curtain off the rod, thumped down on his no-butt. Water cascaded from the shower head, bouncing off his legs, sprinkling on the floor. The Giggle God struck her down again and she tumbled into the tub with the cute jerk.

* * *

Their bedroom was quiet, dark, with the comforting aromas of hygiene products and natural scents that accumulated from a couple's active life. It was their sanctuary, a chamber with no technology to distract from sleeping. As a fighter, she'd studied the science of the body, so she knew how important quality sleep was for recouping sharpness in the nervous system, for mental and physical keenness. Deep sleep is important for so many bodily functions. So that's all they did in there.

Well, and play air guitar…

The bed was large, low to the floor with white pillows against a black wooden headboard, huge white comforter, rumpled, hanging half off the mattress onto the gray carpeted floor. The thirty-foot square room had dark blue and white walls, two dressers with mirrors, black wood, and a small walk-in closet. Relatively bare bones.

Wide awake from the energizing shower, they dressed in work clothes. Clarice really didn't care for traditional mechanic's uniforms of dark blue. That's all good for shops that service factory cars, or whatever. But a custom shop like they ran was highly artistic, and she believed their uniforms should show more style than the usual, boring attire.

So…

She got with a friend that sewed for a living and designed Custom Ace and Tattoology uniforms with a blue camouflage base. Blue, gray, and white deals. The mechanics had combat-type pants with Custom Ace logos on the side cargo pockets, and zip-up tops with logos on the back. There were plenty of random sized pockets and matching mechanic's gloves. Her top had a MIG welding machine for a name badge backdrop with CLARICE in wicket tribal letters. Ace had a diagnostic machine name badge, their painter had a spray gun, and so on, each employee labeled with their specialty.

Clarice's tattoo artists, who would open the studio after noon, had blue camo shorts for the guys, a skirt for the manager, and tank tops to show off their tatts while advertising Tattoology on the front.

You know the famous statue of soldiers raising the American flag on Iwo Jima? The Custom Ace logo was soldiers raising a wrench. The Tattoology logo was a soldiers raising a tattoo machine. The colors matched the building and went with a theme that they are soldiers of creation.

Bring in any tatt idea or car idea you can imagine. Their soldiers will create it.

Down the stairs they went. The thick cedar wood lacked the creaks and squeaks that plagued older steps. The sheetrock walls were dark blue and bare except for a huge Avatar movie poster halfway down on the right. The only light was a black light over-head that made the Avatar's eyes and skin glow with unnatural blues and greens. Shampoo drifted up from her man's freshly scrubbed hair. He paused at the poster, turned his face up to her and did an uncanny impression of the Avatar. Mouth wide, eyes large and glowing. He grinned. His teeth glowed green.

Stepping off the stairs into the hallway, turning right, they walked through a heavy steel door that insulated the tatt parlor from most of the incredible racket they made banging on cars. Ace held the door, a perfect gentleman, closed it with a click of the latch and snip of pressurized air, sealing the quieter half of the building.

He inhaled and his look went all dreamy. "I love the smell of diagnostic machines in the morning."

"I hate to tell you, Bread Stick, but that's the smell of burnt diagnostics this morning," rumbled a black man in a blue camo suit, walking up to them, cleaning his hands on a rag. BOBBY stood out from a paint spray gun on his name badge. Taller than Ace and a hundred pounds heavier, he looked and sounded like Vingo Rhames, if Ving looked like he just stepped off the Mr. Olympia stage. All Bobby needed was posing trunks and oil.

"Uh. Okay. When you say 'burnt'…" Ace said, looking at Bobby like a kid who was just told his favorite pet had been murdered.

"Burnt means just that. When I opened the shop and turned the equipment on, your girlfriend growled and spit sparks at me. The transformer circuit is blacker than I am." Bobby smiled at the look of pain that took hold of Ace's face.

The poor guy ran off towards his machine yelling, "Daddy's coming!"

"No running in the shop, you idiot!" Clarice yelled after him, grinning.

"Now that was some funny shit," Bobby told her. He stood with hands on waist, staring at his running friend with a big silly smile.

She looked at his arms. They were as big as her legs. "What?"

"His face. That geek really thinks those machines are his babies."

"They are," she defended her guy. "He created them, gave them life." She patted the soldiers and wrench logo on Bobby's side pocket.

"If you say so, Boss," he rumbled, smiling and walking back to his work station, a paint booth surrounded by tables full of paint and body tools. His chuckle sounded like a 500hp CAT engine.

She did her morning inspection. Walked from station to station to make sure the apprentices had cleaned and organized the tools, and also to check on the progress of various projects. Everything looked spectacular.

The shop was a hundred and fifty feet long and one-hundred feet wide, with six bays and five car lifts. Huge red and black Craftsman tool boxes towered next to the lifts, with black air hoses snaking down from the ceiling and around the boxes to rest on metal work tables. Pneumatic tools and bench vises on one table drew her eye. Certain tools had the ability to ensnare her on sight. To attract interest with their scents of petroleum, amazing geometry and unique capabilities. Each station had a mélange of oils and degreasers that glistened from forged steel, twinkling with the promise of lighting up the innovative half of her brain, if only she'd stop and pick something up. She swore she could feel it tingling right then.

Or maybe that was just the fumes.

The twenty foot ceiling with I-beams overhead held rolling electric wenches that were used for everything from lifting car engines to holding an employee upside down for a birthday spanking. They even had Bobby's big ass up there one day.

A grinder suddenly clicked on with an air whine, buzzing a wire wheel on metal. The 20hp air-compressor added to the racket, cranking up its thump-pump to replenish pressure in the reservoir. Bobby, standing in front of an old Chevy with a clear face shield strapped around his muscular head, ground rust from a bumper, sparks fanning.

A white Pontiac GTO drove up to the side of the shop. Clarice guessed it to be a 2005 model, factory spec, but still kickass. She motioned for them to pull into an empty garage bay. The two men in the car waved and nodded, backed up and drove the Goat into the shop, rattles and clangs from one seriously disgruntled drivetrain reverberating loudly. She winced, looking at the poor car with a feeling that put a heavy frown on her face. God, like seeing a sick animal that would be a wondrous beauty if someone would just mother it. She wanted to give this car some TLC, a quirk she indulged every time high-end wheels rolled in there.

She walked over to Bobby, who had put aside his work to attend to the customers. He was explaining a delay and technical problem to the two men who stood in front of their car looking like characters from Miami Vice, white dress pants, pastel shirts, and all.

"...but the diagnostic specialist is here now," Bobby said, nodding toward Ace, the muttering nerd with dozens of colored wires strewn over his lap, shoulders, head inside a huge machine. "He'll fix the machine in no time and we'll scan your car for the problem."

"We need the car working by lunch, *Señor*," the guy in the peach pastel said to Bobby, looking nervous about something. Possibly intimidated by Bobby's presence. Lots of customers were. "We have an important meeting we cannot miss. I will pay you double if you will hurry, *por favor*."

Bobby's eyes widened just a tad at the mention of a double payment. He blinked and Clarice heard, cha-ching! Bobby said, "I understand, sir, and we will do that for you. But we have to wait –"

"Bobby, don't sweat it," Clarice said. "I'll take care of these guys. Have to do it the old fashioned way, but hey, these gentlemen are offering incentive for the effort." She smiled at them. "First-class service for two first-class gentlemen." *Pay us double? Go to the front of the shop, sirs.* They smiled back, relieved, stroked by her charm, happy that they would make their meeting on time. She could sense they were seriously scared of missing it, and were willing to go to great expense to avoid that fate.

Hmm… Two Mexican dudes with deep pockets of cash, a boss car, going to a meeting of consequence.

Doesn't take a genius to figure this one out.

"*Gracias, Señora.* We cannot thank you enough," Peach Pastel said, speaking formal, audio taped-learned English without contractions.

She looked at Turquoise Pastel, wondering if he could speak any English at all. Looked back at Peach, smiling. "Hey, we believe in customer service. You guys be sure to bring this baby back for an upgrade. With a supercharger and a little electronics package, this Goat could have the power of five-hundred horses."

"We will consider it, *Señora. Gracias,*" he said, beaming.

Clarice knew they wouldn't return for her suggestion, but she beamed back anyway, thinking it was a good idea to be courteous to men who could potentially turn into villains from a Don Johnson show. "Looking forward to it. You can wait in the lounge if you like." She pointed to the hall entrance. "Walk through that door there and go into the parlor to the right. There are computers with Internet, video games and free coffee. Help yourself, guys."

"*Gracias,*" they both said, smiling and heading to the lounge. The heavy snip of the door closing was masked by the running grinder once again wielded by Bobby, the biggest rust racist on the planet.

She opened the driver's side on the GTO and sat in the leather seat. Gave it a squirm. Weird, hard, didn't agree with her. Turned the key to start the engine. It turned over, idling roughly and shaking the whole car, the view behind her blurred in the mirrors. It had oil pressure and wasn't overheating so she left it running, stepped out, grabbing a multi-meter from a tool box. Got back in and ducked under the dashboard to find the fuse box. Used the meter to make sure the fuel pump and ignition were getting the juice they needed.

Everything was in spec so she crawled out from under the steering wheel and turned the key off. Pulled the hood release. As she pushed off the seat to stand up, she noticed the carpet around the base of the seat wasn't aligned properly. Looked closer and discovered that someone had removed the seat before, possibly to access the ECU, the main computer that was bolted under the seat.

Hmm. Maybe something on the wiring harness vibrated loose or wasn't installed properly.

She jumped out, grabbed an air ratchet and speed-rack of sockets. Ducked back in and unbolted the seat like she was on an Indy car pit crew, pneumatic ratchet buzzing. The fantasy pit crew radio chatter she voiced should have made her feel silly. But it didn't. Foolishness is normal for a woman that is getting acquainted with a manly beast such as this Pontiac. The seat base lifted off of the carpet and exposed the wiring harness, part of it smashed beneath it. The wires were grounding out on the metal rail.

Hi there Problem. Let's get you outta here...

She pushed the seat over backwards to get some elbow room and noticed some seriously bad repair work on the base of the seat where the leather attached. "What upholstery hell is this?" she muttered at the terrible work. *Who repaired this thing, Hillary Clinton?* It was that bad. Like some hag with kindergartner skills crawled her mammoth behind in there, butchered the seat and scammed the owners.

Shit. Drug guys... This seat is probably loaded with dope for their VIP meeting.

Oh-my-just-fucking-lovely-god.

"It's a beautiful morning." Lips pursed, she tapped the ratchet on her palm.

What do I do? Report them? Pretend I never noticed? The How To Start A Small Business book I studied before opening this joint neglected to offer a solution for this particular situation. I can't just let these assholes go and have this shit land on the streets for kids like mine to snort and smoke and fuck up their lives...

A sickly chill pulsed in her stomach.

First things first, she calmed down. And checked it. It's entirely possible her intuition was wrong and the seat was victimized by someone who couldn't tell the difference between foam and sand when they repaired it.

She grabbed a serrated knife, made an incision where the plastic and foam joined. Cut a six-inch gap and stuck a finger in. Felt something that wasn't supposed to be there.

"No," she moaned. Her stomached cranked up the sick feeling, jumped into another dimension with zero gravity and pterodactyls crashing around. Much worse than a case of nervous butterflies. "Oh shit," she breathed, seriously not liking this unknown territory. She opened the gap a little more, took off her gloves, reached in and pulled out a duct taped brick of dope. No wonder her squirm had been rejected. There must be six bricks of crap in the seat base.

She looked at the other seats, suddenly able to see with x-ray vision, bricks of dope crammed throughout every cushion in the car. "Oh *shit*." Her heart started thumping harder, filling her ears, veins aching, as she thought about the risks involved in what she could or should do. These guys could have guns. Nolan would be down here any time. He usually explores the shop before going out front to the bus stop.

I have to tell Ace and Bobby.

No.

They may act suspicious or get all protective if the drug dudes come back to check on their car.

Okay, lady. You can do this. Get it together here. Your family and employees are in danger, but you can still think straight. So stop being an idiot and just call the freaking cops.

Yeah. Then I'll act like I'm working on the car until they get here.

She unzipped a side pocket, took out her phone and dialed 9-1-1. Waited a hundred-thousand years for someone to answer. It rang once. "Nine-one-one emergency," chirped a professional female voice.

"There are drug runners at my mechanic shop. I'm working on their car right now and the seats are loaded with dope," she said in a low, rapid voice. Her top pocket and collar vibrated, palm sweaty on the phone.

"What's the address?

"Custom Ace on Woolmarket Road." Clarice gave her the street number and hung up before she was asked to stay on the line or some nonsense. She needed to look busy there. Squatting down, she put her phone away, then froze at a sound that was ridiculously unexpected in her present mental state.

A disturbing, haunted house laugh began in the back of the shop, over in Ace's corner of gadgets and contraptions. Starting low and throaty, Ace laughed higher and faster. His incredibly retarded but adorable mad scientist laugh. Damn thing caught her off guard every time he did it. He must have fixed the diagnostic machine.

"It's alive! IT'S ALIVE! Hoo-hoo-hoo Ha-ha-ha," the crazy bastard trumpeted.

Well. There it is. Let's hope that madcap exhibition didn't attract -

"Dad! Dad, did you fix it?" Nolan said, running into the shop. The hall door clunked closed behind him. He saw Clarice, frowned, stopped running and walked like a good boy over to his father. The Khaki school uniform made him look mature only until the grease stains appeared. And they would. And she would have to clean them.

"Fuck," she grumbled, cursing grease stains and the entire situation in general. The day had started off great. *What happened?* She stared at the overturned car seat, distraught, indecisive. Scared and pissed off. She looked back at Nolan, mind racing.

"I heard your Fixed It laugh," Nolan told Ace.

"Yeah, my guy. I fixed it," Ace replied, bumping fists with him. They both wore identical Kool Aid smiles. She felt left out so she tried one on, but it literally shook off when she glanced at the brick of dope. Ace held something up. "See this wire?"

"Yep," Nolan confirmed.

"It's broken. It got too hot and melted. Grab a flat-head screwdriver and unscrew this clamp. I'll show you how to replace a melted wire."

"I thought it was a 'faulty' wire," he said, smiling.

Ace bumped fists with him again. "You're too smart for me, son."

"Yeah, right!" He laughed. Opened the top drawer on a tool box, rummaging around with pure glee.

Damn. Here come the stains.

Realizing her indecision was getting out of hand, she considered if other people had weird thoughts in times of crisis. Like a shock buffer. Whatever it was, sitting there like an ignoramus was out of character for her. She's never been this passive under pressure. She needed to get that kid out of there, and do it without causing a panic or triggering a dramatic hissy fit.

Ugh. This could be harder than just going head-to-head with the Miami Vice villains.

With that prioritized thought, Clarice stood to walk the Gauntlet of Nolan, but spun back the other way when the hall door opened.

"*Señora*, how bad is it?" Peach Pastel said, walking toward the Pontiac.

She took a calming breath and smiled at him. "Shouldn't be much longer now. I think I found the problem." She sized him up with a glance, reminding herself this wasn't boxing with illegal punches, anything goes, zeroing in on possible targets of chin, throat, abdomen, groin, knees, marking him as an Enemy. Stepped over to him quickly, hoping to distract him from seeing –

"The seat, *Señora*. Is there a problem with it?" he said, leaning into the open door, inspecting the cut she had made.

Ugh... dumb. Why didn't I reposition the seat? That's one could'a-should'a-would'a that will haunt me for the rest of my life.

He saw the duct taped brick on the floor board. Then drew an enormous silver revolver from under his shirt, eyes narrowing as he brought it up to point at her.

Without thinking, she lunged forward and drilled him with a lead-right.

* * *

"All available units, respond to distress call at Custom Ace on Woolmarket Road..."

"*Hijo de puta!*" Hector stared at the radio. "What happened, Jimmy?"

"Fuck, fuck! I don't know. But we'll be the first to find out," Jimmy said, shifting the patrol car into Drive. "We'll be there in two seconds. Maybe we can clean this mess up before any other units arrive. Our priority is to protect the cartel guys."

"All right. But no killing, okay? I can't take any more of that."

"What? Who the fuck said anything about killing?" he yelled, face reddening. He coughed several times. "Just calm down. We don't know what's going on over there." He floored the gas pedal, darting the car out onto the road, rear tires spinning, squealing. The Custom Ace sign was visible a quarter-mile up the road.

* * *

The air ratchet in her hand made her fist heavy and solid. Lethal. She didn't just strike the guy, she hit his chin so hard his head looked like it would twist off his neck. His owl impression lasted one second, his head twisted back straight, his knees buckled, crumpling him over the door. The gun dropped, clattering as he slid off the door and sprawled on the concrete. His eyes danced epileptically before closing completely.

Clarice stood over him, panting, excited. She'd never hit anybody that hard before. A horseshoe-loaded boxing glove couldn't have executed a better knockout. Under different circumstances, this would have been a toe-curling aphrodisiac.

She took a deep breath, ignoring her curling toes that defied that last thought, reached down to grab the pistol.

And saw it kicked away by a very nice Perry Ellis dress shoe.

She followed the shoe up the leg of white pants to find the other Mexican dude, Turquoise Pastel, pointing a matching revolver in her face. "Oh shit," she said, her highly intelligent response of the day.

"*Señora*, please be calm. No one has to get hurt here. *Comprende*?" he said, squatting down and grabbing the gun off the floor. He stuck it in his waistband, caution in his darting look.

He looks... scared of me?

The flock of pterodactyls in her guts didn't agree with that assessment. She held up her hands, peripherally noticing the air hose had somehow disconnected from the ratchet still gripped in her fist. "Okay, sir. I'm calm. We're all calm. We just have a misunderstanding here. I'm sure we can figure this out."

He looked at his friend, muttering in Spanish, something about being shamed by a *gringa*. Looked in the car and spotted the brick of dope, eyes threatening to pop out of their sockets. He looked back at Clarice and she could see his Scared circuit switch over to Panic. He had no clue how to handle this situation. Not that she had much room to talk, but this guy did things like this for a living. His How To Be A Miami Vice Villian book should have explained this scenario to him.

Stupid How-To books.

The shot-caller must be the peach pasteled turd sleeping on her shop floor. The day just keeps getting better.

"Whoever installed that, uh, stuff there damaged some wires to the ECU. I was only doing my job."

Wasn't my damn fault. You jackasses should hire better mechanics.

Mexicans are legendary upholstery experts. How could an entire cartel of them allow Hillary to fabricate this seat? She kept that to herself and looked around the shop real quick. Not really surprised that no one had noticed the situation. Bobby was sanding an old primer gray Chevelle, bobbing his head and humming along to a Temptations song jamming from the car's radio. Ace and Nolan were chatting about the machine they tinkered on. Getting grease on his damn clothes. No one else had made it to work yet, thankfully.

Perfect time to stop being stupid and make a plan. "So what's the plan?" she asked Turquoise Pastel, hoping he could think of a less violent idea than the one she held in her fist. He looked as stupid and inconclusive as she did, so she stepped closer to him.

If I can get him in punching range...

"Is the car fixed?" he said, waving the gun at the GTO.

"I-I don't know. I just found the problem. The seat was smashing the wires. It might work now."

"Put the seat back. We are leaving."

Sounded great to her. She moved to do as he said, then hesitated when she heard the footsteps. A child's footsteps.

Her shoulders sank and she stilled.

"Clarice!" Nolan shouted, running over. He saw her look and must have thought she meant to scold him. He slowed and walked. "Dad showed me how to replace a faulty wire. See?" He held up a deformed wire like a trophy.

She smiled, inwardly cringing because her worst fear was happening. Her son was merely feet away from a dangerous man with a gun. *With a big grease stain on his uniform... Dammit!* She inched closer to her target, chin, throat, abdomen, groin, knees. Her heart started beating again. Her breathing resumed. "Nolan, honey. I'll look at that later. Right now I have to take care of this customer."

"Why does that man have a gun?" he asked, pointing at the weapon with perfect innocence. "Can I hold it? I had one just like it on *Metal Gear*."

"Nolan —"

"All right, *niño*. Get close to the *Señora* there," Turquoise said, starting to panic again. Nolan just looked at him, completely unaware of what was happening. *"I said get over next to her!"* He waved the gun at her son and took twenty years off her life span. When Nolan still didn't move, only stared, confused, Turquoise took a step towards him and pointed the gun at his head.

The weight of the tool in Clarice's hand should have been a cold weight. But it burned. Like an iron. Like an explosive that was a millisecond from going *boom*.

As soon as the Enemy moved in Nolan's direction, she sprang off her back foot with all her weight thrown behind a right-hand, extending it to a spot on the other side of his head. It hit the side of his neck with tremendous force, a gruesome crunch. She followed with a left-hook that smacked into his cheek, feeling like a slap after that crunching lead punch. The target crashed over the hood of the GTO, denting the metal panels with loud impacts, flailing his arms and the gun with no equilibrium.

Bobby appeared out of nowhere and swung a telephone pole arm down on Turquoise's gun hand, smashing his wrist against a fender, knocking the pistol to the floor. It clattered on the concrete like a heavy tool. Bobby grabbed him in a bear hug, roaring angrily with the squeezing effort as the man groaned out a painful breath. Stepping up to the giant and his catch, Clarice snatched the pistol from Turquoise's belt. Bobby roared and squeezed again. The guy barked out another painful breath and lost consciousness.

Without meaning to, she mimicked his tortured noise. It was painful to watch.

"Nolan, go into the parlor!" Ace yelled, running up and grabbing the other revolver off the floor. Heavy footsteps pounded in the shop and he whipped the gun towards the open bays.

"Get the fuck on the ground!"

"On the floor, now! All of you!"

"Get down now, motherfucker!"

"Drop the guns, now! Put the guns down!"

Two cops came rushing in, guns drawn, screaming at the top of their lungs. Clarice dropped the gun. So did Ace. They put their hands up but didn't get on the ground. They weren't the bad guys.

"I said on the fucking ground! *Now!*" Some huge red-faced dude grabbed Ace and threw him on the concrete. Then he grabbed Bobby and, well, that was as far as he got. He tried his best to shove Bobby down, but the Custom Ace painting specialist just scowled at him. Clarice almost laughed. The other cop, a Mexican guy with a look as nervous as the Pastel Brothers had, pointed his gun at her and motioned to the floor. She got down. She watched *20/20*. Scared people with guns will kill you.

"Bobby, just get down, man. They'll figure it out," she told the big lug, almost laughing again. He took his time kneeing on the floor, glaring at the policemen and their misdirected authority.

"Hands behind your motherfucking back. I said now!" the big cop yelled, pinning Bobby's arms, cuffing his wrists.

"Hey, asshole. You need to be handcuffing those guys, not us," Clarice said.

"Shut up. Shut up! Just shut the fuck up, lady! I know how to do my job," the bastard shouted. He coughed several times, looking around, deciding what to do next. She was tempted to get up and crack him with the air ratchet. She looked at it. Couldn't believe it was still in her hand after that last blow. Her knuckle bled freely, cut deeply, making the palm of her hand wet and sticky. She looked at her knockout victims. Both were sprawled in odd positions, looking like crash test dummies that had been thrown through windshields. The bruises on their jaws were already dark purple and swollen, split, leaking blood.

An intense feeling of pride welled up in her, making her eyes water, stretching a tight smile, throbbing to the beat of her split knuckle. She had protected her tribe. And it throbbed so good.

But her proud disposition was short-lived. She began to get a bad vibe from the police continuing to treat them as the criminals and the Pastel Brothers as the victims. Pride devolved to fear, consolidating with words from the asshole cop with the ugly asthma face.

"You're under arrest. Give me your arms. Hold still!" he shouted at Ace, pinning him down with a knee between his shoulders, pressing his cheek into the concrete floor, distorting his face. Ace huffed with indignation, with pain at the four-hundred pound knee-log pushed into his vertebrae, popping them with dangerous flexing.

His hands were cuffed. He was jerked up. Clarice found herself jerked up simultaneously. By instinct. Reaction to outrage. Her man would not be treated this way. *How dare he think he can come in my house and touch one of mine like that?*

How dare he?

She bounded towards the huge sonofabitch with rage thrashing in the depths of every muscle. Powering hard off the balls of her feet, she zipped at her new target with unnatural speed, fueled by anger so intense her vision flamed red, and her hearing could only sense a high-pitched fizzling. The lit fuse on the Vendetta Cannon that boomed from her shoulders with a bestial snarl, thrown with all the explosive anger she could muster.

The cop turned his eyes to her as soon as she sprang, flinching, reflex from the startling movement in his peripheral. Clarice was too far away and he had time to snap his head to the side right as her punch hit, neutralizing half its power as it plowed into his ear, ratchet scraping up his scalp, hair. Forward momentum rammed her chest into his side, an immovable wall that promptly knocked the wind from her on impact.

"Oof!" she sputtered. This was probably a little out of her weight class. She went for it anyway, vision deepening with red fuel, high-pitched fizzle threatening to blow her ear drums, the fight junkie out of her cage and swinging as hard and as fast as she could, arms blurring with knockout power in either fist. The target swung his gun towards her, caught a few punches on his face, arms, stumbled, dropped his gun arm to crank it through the air a few rotations to gain balance. She dropped the ratchet so she could throw faster and pounced on him again, five-punch combination that only brushed his face as he fell backwards, not quite fast enough to beat the pull of gravity on a huge falling body.

Dammit!

He hit the floor with a wallop, keys clanging on concrete, gun belt and vest creaking, elbows and boots thumping. "You stupid cunt!" he coughed out, wheezing, face scarlet. "I got something for you."

Clarice had a moment to realize she should have jumped on top of him. She wasn't in a ring with boxing rules. He unsnapped a large cylindrical compartment on his belt and removed a can of pepper spray. He drew it with a well-practiced fluidity and sprayed the motherfucker right in her eyes, covering her entire head and upper body with incapacitating chemicals.

"Gaah! You prick," she spat. Then sneezed. Sneezed again. Her eye muscles locked up, squinting hard enough to give her face thirty years of wear. Eyebrows pushing down. Forehead flexing. Mouth puckered, throat sucked in, a vacuum attempting to pump some air through an esophagus she knew was uncontrollably inflamed and constricted. Every little breath sucked in more pepper particles, circulating them deep into her lungs and further arresting her respiratory system. No air, no muscle power. The Mexican cop finally decided to assist his partner and had her face down within seconds, hands cuffed painfully behind her back. Her oxygen-deprived brain could only wonder at the trained ease the officer had shown in trussing her like a rodeo animal.

"Clarice!" Ace yelled. Dust and Oil Dry stuck to his lips that were pressed to the concrete once again.

"What?" she croaked. Gasp air, resist the choke, gasp air, resist the choke. *Sneeze!*

Shit. This stuff handed my butt to me. My first TKO. But a TKO is not a KO…

"You okay?"

"Great…Never…Better," she wheezed, snot running out of her nose like water. Gasp air, resist the choke…

"Shut up, shut up!" the Nazi cop shouted. It took him a year and a half to get up. He coughed several times, looking back and forth between Clarice and Ace, angry, confused. He coughed again. "You!" He pointed at her. "Are under arrest for assault on a police officer." He looked over at Ace, at her again, determining that they were securely detained for the time being. He walked over to Bobby, moving stiffly

78

on legs that weren't used to so much excitement, squatted down and stared at his face. Holstered his gun, but kept the pepper spray handy. He frowned at Bobby, trying to get an impression of how he would fit into the situation. The cop shook his head, coming to some kind of decision, stood and walked over to the Pontiac. Stuck his head in the open driver's side. Glanced around and spotted the drugs and cut open the seat. He nodded and grunted, limped over to stand between Clarice and her husband. He said, "You are under arrest for possession of narcotics."

"You got me fucked up, fat boy!" Bobby exploded.

"You're making a huge mistake," Ace sputtered from dusty lips.

"Gonna… kick… your… big ass." Gasp air, resist choke…

"Shut up, shut up! *The law is what I say it is!*" he continued, yelling over their protests. "And, you're under arrest for conspiracy to traffic narcotics."

"You got me fucked up!" Bobby cursed, rolling over to try and stand. The pepper spray was aimed at him and he quit.

"Not you, nigger! These two! *These two!* Shut your stupid black hole before I charge you, too. Shut up!"

"Soon as… I get… my breath," Clarice gasped, squinting through one barely opened eye to focus on her target, chin, throat, abdomen, groin, knees, completely ignoring his fraudulent arrest in her mission to stop him. She gained her feet, he noticed her intent and ruthlessly dosed her with another burst of chemicals, dropping her to the floor.

Her face locked up again, squinting so hard her eyes felt like hot irons being driven into her head. Diaphragm frozen as if she had been nailed with a solid body punch, inflamed nerves cut off from communication pulses that told her lungs to breathe, *breathe, Clarice.*

The tiny gasp she finally sucked in turned into a sneeze, ejecting the precious air before her lungs had a chance to utilize it. This was undoubtedly the most inconvenient feeling she'd ever experienced. The motherfucking cop had TKO in a can. She was immobilized and completely helpless. And humiliated, to boot.

And suddenly very frightened.

This isn't happening. I saved my people, took out the bad guys. The cops were supposed to be on our side, dragging these criminals off my shop floor and congratulating us for calling the police and overcoming the perps.

Her fear grew, fumed in her near-unconscious daze, blooming with cold fire that spread down her arms and legs, up her spine and neck, steamed from her ears in a renewed fizzle, lighting another fuse. Her eyes cracked open, blurry, red, pried open by a will that didn't know the meaning of surrender, having every intention of slaughtering the pig that had so quickly turned their big win into a nightmarish setback.

She wanted a taste of those pork chops big boy was holding.

Her fists flexed and trembled, willing to work without oxygen, engines that continued to run hard even when starved of fuel. But they were cuffed, rendered obsolete. Her legs were not much better. Free, but practically useless, flaccid of all but slight tremors. Willing to kick, but unable to. No matter. She only needed them to hold her up for a few seconds.

The Enemy pointed the pepper spray at Bobby, at Ace, daring them to give him an excuse. "Anybody else? Keep your mouths shut or I'll shut 'em for you. Like I said." He coughed, looked at his partner. "Hector, call it in. And check the ETA of our assistance."

"Okay, Jimmy," Hector said, nodding. He turned his back to them and spoke codes into his walkie-talkie. The air-compressor turned off, its rapid thump-pump petering out, stopping completely, hissing a release of pressure that was built up in the hoses. The shop became silent except for Clarice's soft wheezing and Pork Chop cop's coughing fits.

Engines raced outside the shop. With surreal detachment, Clarice amazed herself by taking a second to admire the exhaust notes of what she knew were 4.6 liter Interceptor engines. Crown Victoria police cars. Hopefully carrying cops with common sense.

Footsteps and voices sounded from the front of the building, talking, questioning loudly, moving through her parlor with rude disregard. Two men in uniforms rushed in through the hallway door, slowing and relaxing as they took in the scene and deemed it secure. Three more officers popped in through an open garage bay, ducking around a car lift to walk toward them quickly while searching the rest of the shop for activity. They crouch-walked, guns and heads whipping around with no wasted movement. A single policeman ducked in through the rear bay door, completing their grid of the building.

"What's the status?" asked one of the new arrivals, a muscle-bound ego on legs, with a buzz cut and sunglasses that came from the same cookie cutter as the rest of his pals.

Pork Chop answered, "We came in and found the perps holding the victims at gunpoint. We disarmed them, determined they were conspiring to traffic drugs with this white car here," he said, pointing at the GTO.

Clarice's legs straightened like hydraulic cylinders, standing her up, speechless. Ace and Bobby found their voices, however.

"You're the perps!" Bobby bellowed, voice booming off the steel walls with startling effect. Everyone cringed and looked at him. Ace flopped around trying to get his feet under him, outraged, fuming protest from dusty lips.

"Possession of narcotics, assault on a police officer, aggravated assault on both of the victims here," Pork Chop said, counting off on his sausage fingers. The officers nodded, one of them patting Pork Chop on the back. Several thumbs-up directed at Hector.

Clarice started in the Enemy's direction, just sort of stumbled on numb legs with the same detached, oxygen-deprived thoughts that had noted the engine exhaust tones, staring at a big red face that she wanted to hurt, to make it stop talking, stop lying, stop hurting her family's future with every jounce and jiggle of its jowls. She noted an angle, a bull's eye on the target that would accomplish her goal, stop the bastard that had instigated a stunning catastrophe.

Ooh, come and give momma a taste of those pork chops.

She stumbled, unnoticed by the collaborating police, over to ol' Jiggle Jowls, devoid of emotion, focused only on the *intent,* angling toward the bull's eye that would surely make this nightmare cease once she hit it.

She stopped in front of the target. Looked up at her bull's eye with lust. She noted, like a hawk dispassionately eyeing a lesser bird, that her bull's eye was still flapping away, huffing emphysemic fabrications about what had taken place here.

Clarice looked at Hector, the only officer there that didn't look like he was enjoying a hard-on from arresting innocent people. "I was the one that called you guys," she wheezed at him, then she gripped her handcuff chain and lunged forward with a head butt aimed at his partner. The crown of her head rammed into Pork Chop's chin, arcing up to smash his lips against his teeth and bust his nose, warm blood spraying down her face, into her eyes. He gave a monstrous grunt as the pain and shock from the blow set in, setting off a chain of coughs that made her think she had hit his pepper spray somehow, spraying him with a nice dose. His pals rushed her. Pork Chop fumbled at his belt, roaring with fury, up came the spray again, hosing her and the three that had grabbed her legs and shoulders and tackled her to the ground in a cloud of no-breath. She had a moment to realize the chemicals in her hair are what had caused Pork Chop's coughing attack, and would probably cause him to die a slow, painful asthmatic death.

The shop floor rudely contorted her face, smelling strongly of oil. Ten feet away Ace was still flopping around. Bobby was cheering for her to hit him again. The officers yelled over each other trying to establish procedure, coughing, squinting angry eyes.

The last thing Clarice heard before the no-breathe KOed her was her own impartial thoughts wondering who would get the grease stains out of Nolan's uniform.

Chapter VI

Central Mississippi Correctional Facility
October 10, 2011

"Carter! Clarice Carter! Visitation," the officer announced. She stood in front of a stainless steel picnic table flipping through a count roster, a list of inmate's names, numbers, and bed assignments attached to a clipboard. Her blue uniform top labeled her as a CO 1, her thin ponytail and short fingernails labeled her as a black woman on a budget.

The CO smiled as Clarice approached, and Clarice reminded herself that the officer was usually a *nice* black woman on a budget, a person she should at least attempt to be cordial to. One of the few officers she'd met that wasn't a power-tripping retard. Unfortunately for the friendly COs like her, the situation that landed Clarice in that dump had made her, let's call it, 'sensitive' to police authority in any form.

Several of the power abusers were on the receiving end of some very eloquent threats, and a few thrashing haymakers, from a former pro fighter now known as offender J1332. One extremely unfortunate lady caught a left-hook to her muffin top after pepper spraying Clarice, twice, and another large and lovely lady ran head first into a wall after Clarice fought loose from a group of COs attempting to hold her and turned her fury in the lady's direction. Wanting to press charges, the victim abruptly ended her hissy fit after Clarice pointed out that a jury wouldn't convict a cinder block wall.

Clarice had been sprayed and locked down five times already. She simply couldn't stand people telling her what she could and couldn't do. An almost exact repeat of what happened when they first locked her up in the county jail. She'd had twenty bosses, and the higher they ranked, the higher they rated on the Idiot Scale.

And I just got here. For Christ's sake, people.

Grumbling, she walked away from another source of strife, a group of women she had no wish to be around, but was forced to live with. They watched soap operas on a small TV mounted high up on a wall. Around thirty black women, a few whites, and one Latina, lounged around picnic tables, plopped in plastic chairs or sat on the floor bundled up in blankets or thermals, oblivious to anything outside of that little world. Truly products of their environment, they were broken long ago to submit and accept those conditions as their home and life. Some were serving life. And instead of hitting up the law library every week looking for a loophole in the system, they were yucking it up at the card tables or staring at eye candy on the idiot box.

Incarceration, Clarice found, is a serious education in human behavior. It is simply amazing what a person can adapt to. And confounding. And scary.

And it pissed her off.

She shook her head in renewed anger, struggling to refocus it so she wouldn't start bitching about all there was to be mad about around there. Stopping in front of the CO she planned on being nice to, she planted a big fake smile on her face to challenge her will. It was a wretched mug, like you'd see on Mrs. Potato Head.

"Hello, Officer Pruet," Mrs. Potato Head said.

"Hello, Offender J1332."

"Any idea who is here to see me?"

"Your attorney."

"Great. I've been working on a new lawyer joke to tell his sorry ass," Clarice said, losing the smile. The women behind her ah-ed together at something on the television. Damn whiny soaps.

"Oh, come on now. He might have some good news for you this time."

"Uh-huh. Like the truth? As in, I'm innocent and get to go home?"

She smiled, raised her eyebrows. "They're all innocent," she sighed, rolling her eyes. Made Clarice want to slug her. "Let's go, now. You ready?"

"Sure," she said, thinking about doing ninety days in lock down for assault. Deciding against it, barely, she refreshed her cordial Mrs. Potato Head and grinned and bore it. Attempting to regain their positive rapport, she said, "Got my mani-pedi, boss tan, Karen Millen dress and Gucci heels. How's my hundred dollar hairdo look?" She posed and patted her hair like it was styled and shining like diamonds. It was in a short, ugly ponytail just like Officer Pruet's.

She laughed. "Looks fine to me. Have ya taken your medication today?" She pointed at Clarice's prisoner's uniform of black and white striped pants and white pullover with MDOC CONVICT heat-stamped on the back. "Looks more like Barker than Millen, honey. Even Halle Berry would look rough in that."

That brought a small smile. Bob Barker made everything from toothbrushes to mattresses for prisons world-wide. Mistaking the Price Is Right geezer for a fashion designer would certainly make Clarice eligible for anti-psychotic meds. Her smile widened. "No biggie. I'll rock my Barker getup. And anyways, if I go too feminine I start to look like a transsexual."

Officer Pruet snickered, pinching her wide nose. Eyes glittering with humor, she shook her head at Clarice and turned to walk toward the zone's main entrance. Clarice followed, glancing left, right, at the empty beds, wondering what time it was. Most of the women there could tell you the time according to what soap opera was on. Clarice was determined to never become so institutionalized or media pro-grammed, so she asked the CO.

Pruet looked behind them at the TV, then gave Clarice a look like she couldn't have asked a more stupid question. "It's one o'clock. General Hospital just came on."

Clarice's lips thinned. *It's like she's doing hard time like us.*

"You late for an appointment?"

"Nah, nothing special," Clarice said, gritting teeth.

Just late for the Big Show, lady. That's all. The mega event of knocking the crusty grills out of all the smart mouth COs like you. Real late for that. Perhaps we'll reschedule.

She kept glancing at Clarice, an uneasy expression forming as she noticed the feral grin suddenly bloom and hint that Clarice just might have a special ap-pointment after all.

The grin had to be ugly, scary, Mrs. Evil Potato Head. But she kept it there.

It felt good.

The concrete building was L-shaped and divided in two sections, A-zone and B-zone, with fifteen foot tall circular guard towers in the center of each zone. The tower windows were square, covered in steel grates, and gave the tower officer a panoramic view of the zone, cubicles, and showers. The concrete floor was painted a soft psych ward blue, chipped, scraped, faded and stained with everything from or-ange pepper spray, blood, to homemade black and yellow hair dye. A low cinder block wall, maybe four feet high, sectioned off cubicles not unlike an office building. Instead of desks and computers, the cubicles encompassed two steel bunk beds, black, with green foam mattresses, white sheets and pillow cases, locker boxes, and four female convicts with all their collective drama.

The concrete walls were odd white tones of the lowest quality pigments. Like someone put a spoonful of mustard in a jar of mayonnaise and slathered it all over everything, uneven, thick and thin, with too much mustard in the mix here and there. The lack of quality control made Clarice's obsessive-compulsive axe really grind. Like fingernails digging into a chalkboard so hard it flashed sparks and little wisps of foul smoke. The few prisoners that were intelligently aware of their surroundings, and understood what it all meant relative to the rest of the world, lived in a perpetual state of cringing pooh-pooh face.

A Thorazine patient stumbled by. Uncoordinated, pants so dirty the white stripes looked black. Natty, filthy hair and unhealthy skin. She was white, though had evidently tallied up enough days away from the shower to make her look Hispanic. But she was so content, so damn gleeful, dancing around in her own little world. Planet Happiness, with bright sunshine and friendly, cuddly moons of Everything is Funny and I Love Laughing-Drooling-Snotty Expressions orbiting around her silly smile. If Clarice stayed there much longer, she would start to envy the woman. Though she was sure she would never take the ultimate step like the woman did, give up hope for a super tranquilized life of unawareness.

"Ignorance is bliss," she murmured.

Pruet followed her eyes over to the woman joyously doing the Thorazine Shuffle, giggling, clapping, twirling. "I guess it really can be," Pruet agreed.

The zone's main entrance was next to the tower. They stopped in front of it and Pruet keyed her walkie-talkie. "B-zone tower, open thirty-five," she said, releasing the button and looking up at the tower window. The tower CO stepped to the window, waved, turned a knob on the control board. The heavy steel lock buzzed, clicked, the white door whined open on its dry scraping track. They walked through into a long hallway with more psych ward blues and mustard whites. The chemical scent of industrial floor wax burned Clarice's nose. A slim black lady in prison stripes was wrestling with a floor buffing machine behind them as they walked toward the administration section of the unit. Officer Pruet followed behind Clarice as security protocol mandated, watching to see if she picked up or passed any contraband. She was a good girl and managed not to pass any shanks or pick up any drugs.

They arrived at the A-zone tower and turned to go through the main exit. Pruet did her thing on the radio again, advising the tower to open the twin gates in front of the door. They walked outside.

The October afternoon sky was gorgeous. Deep blue with fluffs and puffs of the smoothest clouds, mostly high-altitude cirrus with random jet vapor trails shot through. Reminded Clarice of one of Nolan's first paintings, making her smile.

The grandiose sky scene was ruined by the rotten tooth below it. Concrete buildings of the most despicable design sprawled desecration across the acres, each sectioned off with twin razor wire-topped fences, their variety of energies mixing and clashing to form an unpredictable economy.

Most of the quiet, frightened women had been shipped to the ape warehouse just because the capricious government figured out a way to make a buck on it.

Women afraid of everything in there and deteriorating on a sharp curve, confined to the lower rungs of the ladder where the hustled and the punked clung to existence.

The core members of the mix were more emotionally complex, more active in the range between inferior and superior and not likely to stay status quo for very long.

And then there were the very strong women. The Alphas. Some were respected for not using their abilities to take advantage of others. Most instigated cruelty and physical abuse to anyone they perceived as marks, inmates and officers alike.

Trapped. Scared. Feared. Animals vying for status.

Clarice turned left onto a concrete walkway with a corrugated steel roof that blocked the sun, cooling the air and casting a rectangular shadow on the freshly cut grass. Grasshoppers and gnats swarmed over the green clippings. The administration building was the same ugly formed-concrete structure as the other buildings, but with more dimensions, more doors for a cafeteria, barber shop, watch commander's office, and other penitentiary facilities.

As they approached the visitation section, a strong breeze blew through the walkway, scattering stray grass blades over Clarice's cheap white shoes, dislodging strands from her hair tie. A huge cumulus cloud moved overhead, hiding the sun, making the gushing wind chilly. As she finger combed her hair, she heard echoes of barking and smelled the stink of wet dogs, bloodhounds that were kept in kennels close by, at the Emergency Response Team headquarters. Those jerks were the worst power trippers. ERT loved to intimidate and assault prisoners, even more than the inmate bullies. Stripping a girl naked and tearing up her property in front of eighty of her peers was just a warm-up for them. Open your mouth to protest the degrading of your fellow convict and they'll strip you naked and tear up your property for your compassion. *Ask me how I know...* By then they'll be high on power lust and want another hit. The zone or the entire building could potentially get shook down, and ERT will rock their jollies from finding miscellaneous drugs and weapons and roughing up disgruntled women that fight like men.

They were freaking terrorists. Full of threats like the one that gave her chill bumps right then, barking dogs illustrating a scene with an escaped convict being torn apart by the pack.

Clarice scowled and tried to shake it out of her mind. But the image continued, premonitory, expanding on the idea of escape with her as the star of the stunt. It felt possible, all of a sudden. It felt like it was *meant to be.* She gasped as a jolt of anxious adrenaline flooded her arms and legs, priming her body to hold up for the mad adventure circulating in her mind.

Clarice paused and glanced at Officer Pruet, with what she knew was an odd, guilty look.

Stupid. As if she could hear me thinking about escape.

She couldn't, and kept walking.

Deciding those thoughts were too high-risk while in the presence of the blue shirts, Clarice made a mental note to consider the subject again later. Then focused on the door to the front and the hypocritical lawyer waiting to stick a fork in her.

The door, labeled "Visitation," buzzed and they walked through into a small room with white tiles and mustard walls, stopped in front of a small metal desk. A CO sat behind it, an obese black lady of middle age squeezed into a padded chair that was visibly flexing under her bulk. A beehive-shaped weave on her head reflected the light, a shiny cone with a chubby face at its base that held an oily sheen of its own. Her name badge said her name was Loquesha Howard, but that sounded too long and complex for this lady. She looked at Clarice and Clarice thought her name badge should say Thud or Oof. A box of Popeye's fried chicken perched on the edge of the desk and filled the room with its secret spicy grease. A door with a Plexiglas window was to the left. Clarice looked through it, into the visitation room, where she spotted her lawyer sitting at a table with a briefcase on it.

"I'll be back in an hour," Officer Pruet told her, signing a log on the desk.

"I thought attorney visits were longer." Clarice crossed her arms.

"They are. But they rarely last longer than it takes to deliver the bad news."

Clarice's arms dropped to her sides, stiff, as she reevaluated her opinion of the silly screw. *She may not abuse her authority, but that didn't necessarily mean she was nice or smart. In fact, Pruet had to be one* stupid *fucking broad to think she could keep talking to me like that.* She made a serious effort to unclench her fists, which couldn't wait for the next stupid thing to come out of Pruet's mouth. Turned and walked to the visitation room door. The CO struggled up from her chair, which gave a squeak and groan Clarice swore sounded like relief, and waddled over, fumbling with a large ring of keys attached to her belt. She selected a key, unlocked the door, tumblers clicking loudly. She apparently wasn't aware of her girth because Clarice had to suck in a breath to shimmy past her, cringing as she breathed her laborious chicken breath in Clarice's face. She locked the door.

Clarice's attorney stood up from a green plastic chair behind a long wooden table, a white dude in his late fifties, grayish hair, smooth shaved face with a bulbous, red alcoholic's nose and flushed cheeks. His gray eyes would probably look a really clear blue after a trip to the Betty Ford Clinic and several shots of vitamin B12. His brown suit was expensive but very unclean, rumpled, like he had just pulled it from the trunk of his car and hurriedly dressed in the parking lot before going inside.

"You look like a stool sample," she greeted the man, sitting down in a chair opposite from him. Rested her arms on the table.

"Ah-ha," he chortled. "No lawyer jokes this time?" He sat down.

"That was my lawyer joke. You officers of the court are a bunch of damn sewer surfers. Like evil Ninja Turtles in dookie colored suits."

"Ah, good to see you still have your sense of humor, Clarice." He opened the small black briefcase on the table in front of him. The latch snapped, echoing in the quiet room. She glanced up at the drop ceiling, around at the other tables and chairs, while he rifled through some papers, jerky movements that showed he had no specific item he was searching for. A make-work tic that all lawyers seemed to do. Hey, they have to at least look like they are earning your money, right?

"So. What's the good news? You work up any connections in the Court of Appeals?" Clarice inquired.

"Ah, no. I don't think a judge of that caliber would take a chance on overturning your case."

"Meaning what?"

"Meaning, ah, that there are numerous cases in the system that an appeals judge would reverse before yours. Cases with far less incriminating evidence. A judge would take serious political and professional criticism for favoring your case without significant new evidence that would warrant a new trial."

"What incriminating evidence? My trial judge was an idiot. Surely the higher judges can see through all that bullshit, see that it was made up," she said, leaning forward with a stormy look.

He dropped his gaze first. "Ah, we've been over this before, Clarice. The, ah, trial was horrendous, a slam dunk for the prosecution. Two arresting officers testified that you and your husband were found assaulting the victims. The testimony from a police officer holds serious weight in court."

"Wait a minute. Victims? *Victims?* Do you think I'm guilty, too?" Her voice rose to a shout.

The CO at the visitation desk stood up. The lawyer waved at her, signaling everything was okay. "Ah, sorry. I've been reading the Attorney General's response brief. The, ah, cartel men claimed they came to your shop to use the phone. They said you unfairly stereotyped them, assumed they were drug guys just because of the way they looked, and tried to employ them to drive the shipment of drugs to an unknown destination. When they refused, you allegedly tried physical persuasion, with your fighting expertise, that got out of hand."

"But I'm the one that called the motherfreaking cops!" she said for probably the thousandth time in the last year and a half. She closed her eyes.

"I know," he said, making soothing gestures with his hands. "Prosecution said you called in an attempt to clean up your mess." He touched his fingers on the open top of the briefcase. "Your fingerprints were on one of the bricks of cocaine. Theirs weren't. And both you and your husband's prints were on the guns. The car had untraceable license and VIN plates that prosecution claimed could have been easily attained through your automotive connections. And to put the icing on the cake, those cartel guys had spotless records." He grunted. "The evidence, however false, was overwhelmingly against you. My firm has studied your case from top to bottom for eighteen months now, and we can't see any new evidence that can be presented to the Court of Appeals or the Mississippi Supreme Court." He paused again, a dejected frown appearing to show her how sorry he was for taking her money for such a stick-in-the-ass result. His eyes watered a little, lawyerly showmanship kicking in to sell it, like a good final argument to a jury that's been unimpressed with his performance thus far.

"Shit."

"I'm truly sorry, Clarice. I, ah, have to recommend that you and your husband hire another firm, though for the life of me, I don't know what they could do to get you out of this. I'm sorry," he said again, dropping the papers back in the briefcase, ending the ruse.

"It's over, then," she breathed to herself, exhaling long and slow as a numbness enveloped her. Eyes wide, staring at nothing, she sensed but didn't see the attorney stand up and leave, a warm shadow tinged with high-quality vodka retreating silently to the far left of the room. A buzz of the lock. Heavy click of a security door.

And all hope of freedom walking out with him.

After months of hassle with the feds, Clarice had convinced them her home and businesses were bought legally, but failed to convince them about the property in the buildings, which they confiscated. She sold everything they had left to pay the firm to represent her and Ace. They took all their money. She couldn't afford to hire more attorneys if she wanted to. She was sitting on absolute rock bottom.

Her scalp suddenly hurt. She became aware of her hands gripping the sides of her hair, white knuckled fists squeezing, grasping it. She didn't know why. Maybe just to make sure she could still feel something.

Feel something.

She gripped harder, pulling her hair tie loose and bunching big clumps of hair above her ears. Cheap shampoo offended her nose, Bob Barker crap that had the odor of dog shampoo and made her feel like a flea scratching degenerate for using it. Her hands caught another gear and red hot swords pierced her skull, yet she couldn't quite feel it. She was far beyond awareness of pain, fully desensitized to the scalpel of stress that carved her guts into ribbons and made the tears streaming down her face burn like acid, an auto-reply her body produced to show her it still knew how to do its job even though she had vacated the driver's seat.

Her body was crying. Her mind was down the rabbit hole.

Her nose dripped onto the table, thick cloudy drops that splattered and darkened the wood. She stared at the puddle, feeling her diaphragm trying to expand to sniffle the mess from her nostrils and cease the indecent display. An involuntary snort filled her throat with warm, salty fluid that nearly choked her, forcing her to wake the hell up and swallow.

Clarice searched for sensation other than the hot and wet no-crying and found none. There was nothing to sense, a desolate embodiment that was once mighty and bountiful, but was now torn and stripped from heart-wrenching losses, one right after another.

She recognized the despair threatening to consume her as being deeper and more profound than anything she's ever experienced, far worse than the loss she felt after retiring from fighting. Her family, her husband and son, her home and businesses, friends, employees. People that depended on her to provide for their homes and families and friends. Lost. Gone.

Taken.

Everything was taken from me.

Somewhere deep inside of her a switch was suddenly flipped. A switch so heavy with life-changing consequences weighing it down that it required fight-or-flight instincts and immense psyche power to even budge it. It clicked so hard and so fast it felt like a giant had snapped a twig. Sensation approached, far in the distance, she could feel its heavy chugging towards her, a freight train a thousand miles long, heavy tonnage speeding on a track that just barely guided a massive, violent beast.

Her hands gripped even harder, anticipating, spreading the pain from her scalp down her face like a red blanket, tinting her vision. Her arms flushed, tingling with heat. Her throat constricted with emotion, boiling rage that came to a head as the violent freight pulled in to station. Her arms flexed, vascular and alien, the arms of a being ruled by instincts of dominant, physical action. A new driver was behind the wheel. One that knew violence like an old lover, knew how to mold it into many shapes and forms of hurt without regard to morals or mercy.

A driver that understood Clarice the Wife and Mother could never break the laws and soil her pretty pink fingernails with what must be done.

A driver that knew how to *take*.

Clarice felt like people should be watching her do something, do something to some *body*. Cheering for pain infliction and blood and bodies slapping down on the mat.

Mat. Ring. Where's the ring?

She glanced around, expecting to see a roped off square with a beer logo and referee dancing and dodging while a spirited crowd shouted her name all around us.

My name...

Her flushed arms lightened, her veins receded, and with it all feeling of doubt. A transformation had taken place, leaving her with many certitudes. The first and most obvious was she no longer felt alien. She *was* the alien. And confidence of the most supreme form had replaced the plague of fears. She felt the dried tears on her face and wondered how she could ever cry, how she could ever submit to such a superfluous, counterproductive emotion. She was the Shocker.

I am the Shocker!

Having never experienced this persona outside of boxing relations, it took her a moment to accept what had become of her. But only a moment. She smiled.

Oh, yeah. This is just what I needed. Welcome back, baby.

She hugged herself.

The homecoming was rudely interrupted by the door on the far side of the room buzzing and clicking again. It opened, a Latino gentleman entered like he owned the place. Middle-aged and of medium height and small build, he was well-groomed with salt and pepper hair combed to the side, smooth face with a black mustache and chin beard cropped short. Tasteful cream suit with darker toned patches on the elbows. Bow tie. He looked like a college professor. Clarice stared at him. He stared back, dark eyes squinting and flickering to analyze her tear-stained face, bloodshot eyes and disarrayed hair, puddle on the table. Back to her face. Her stressed appearance was in stark contrast with her relaxed, focused, and smiling expression.

The professor walked toward her exhibiting a swagger that told her he either wielded great power or had really big balls. He stopped on the other side of the table from her. Unbuttoned his jacket. Sat down in the chair the attorney had used. He continued to stare into her eyes. *Through* her eyes. Like a damn soul gaze.

"You are not Clarice Carter," he said in a pleasant, lecturing tone without accent. She remained silent, smiling, relaxed. Confident. Patient and unconcerned. He looked at the puddle of tears and snot again, pursed his lips. "You are Clarice Ares. The Shocker. Now. Again."

Whoa. This dude really did gaze into my soul. Her expression didn't change, however.

"That is correct. Recently reconciled." She hugged herself, then waved a hand in his direction. "I admire your insight."

"It is what I do."

"And what is that?"

He didn't answer, just squinted and analyzed. She guessed she should've wondered who he was and how he got in here to see her without being on the approved visitation list. Clarice would have fretted about that, she supposed, but not her. Maybe later.

Who gives a shit? She laughed.

He stared for a moment more, then said, "My name is Ignacio. Your predicament regarding the appeal recently came to my attention and I wish to help you."

"Really."

"Sincerely, yes."

"How is it that you know the Shocker? You a boxing fan?"

"Indirectly, yes. I run a corporation that owns many smaller businesses, some with charities that fund even smaller establishments. One in particular is a quaint little boxing gym in Juarez that had the pleasure of producing two world champions. You destroyed one of them in your final fight at the Blue Horizon." He paused and gave an amused smile. "I lost a considerable sum of money."

"You bet on the wrong horse."

"Admittedly, I knew that before placing the wager."

"You knowingly bet on a loser?"

"She was no loser, and I am nothing if not loyal to my people," he said, deadpan serious.

She smiled. "Consuela Torres. How is she?"

"Not good. She was never the same after you knocked her out. She fought three more times, lost twice, then retired. Señora Torres now works at one of my garment factories. A manager, I believe."

"Damn. You rarely hear a happy ending to a boxer's life."

"Es verdad."

"I mean, they usually end up broke, OD'ed on drugs, or in prison. Like me." A menacing look flashed over her face. *From* her face, a solar flare erupting from a riled sun. Teeth gnashing, she said in a clipped voice, "Even though I'm innocent."

"I know you are innocent," he said quietly, without hesitation, looking her in the eye.

She sat up. "Really."

"Sincerely, yes."

They engaged in another stare down. "Great power and big balls, both," she murmured.

"Pardon me?" He raised his eyebrows.

"What do you want?"

He laid his hands flat on the table, thick gold rings over perfectly manicured nails. They gleamed with clear polish.

"Truthfully, I wish to ease my conscience. To aid you in some way, perhaps influence the locals so you can live comfortably in here."

"And you have that kind of influence?"

"I do."

"Know anybody in the Court of Appeals?"

"Regretfully, no."

"Then you can't help me."

Silence again. The fluorescent lights overhead hummed. A door buzzed-clicked behind her. She turned to look and through the Plexiglas saw an older lady in green and white stripes, a trustee, that she recognized as a high-ranking Latin Queen. The trustee had a mop in her hand, the head of it in a bucket of soapy water that rolled as she pushed it into an adjoining room with snack and soda machines. The lady glanced at Clarice, did a double-take and stared at Ignacio. She put a latex gloved hand to her mouth. In the silence we heard her say, "El Maestro."

The Teacher. Hmm. Clarice looked back at her visitor, menace flashing again. She had read about this guy. "I don't mean to be presumptuous, but a Mexican business owner, one that runs a 'corporation', usually translates into laymen's English as a cartel kingpin."

"I cannot refute that," he said amiably. "However —"

"Scum of the earth," she growled.

His jaw flexed. His look became dark and ominous, displeasure at having been goosed into showing emotion.

"And you want to ease your conscience, as you say, because those drugs and those two Nash Bridges thugs that came into my shop were yours."

"Again, regretfully this time, I cannot refute that."

"And those asshole pigs that ruined my fucking *family's life* were on your payroll, as well." Her solar glare looked like it was burning his face. She whispered to him, lips quivering, "I was just collateral damage to you, right?"

He flinched, slowly regained his composure, but remained silent.

"I'll take your silence as assent. Tell you what. I would like to make it through the rest of today without murdering a sonofabitch with my bare hands." Her fists flexed hard, started shaking in anticipation. The Teacher put a hand to his waist. "If you don't leave right now. I. Will. Kill. You." She enunciated each word with her lip angling off her teeth.

The Teacher held up a hand. With the other hand, he pulled aside his jacket and showed her a giant gun in a shoulder holster. She couldn't believe her eyes. In prison.

Great power and big balls!

He said, "I wasn't worried about Mrs. Carter. But I expected nothing less from the Shocker." Closing his jacket, he stood. "My people and I respect you greatly. We will continue pursuing avenues to aid your release. And, for what it is worth, I am deeply sorry, Señora Shocker."

Sorry?

Clarice sprang up, knocking her chair several feet behind her in a loud clatter of plastic on tiles. The Teacher was slower, jumping backwards, almost tripping over his chair, hopping around to get balanced. He stepped around the chair, eyes on her, backed away quickly, unholstering the gun. The Latin Queen in the snack room burst into a stream of desperate sounding Spanish.

"That gun doesn't scare me, El Maestro. Leave before my fists taste your blood." She was panting, nearly foaming at the mouth in her desire to attack the man.

He nodded, gave a look of sadness and regret before bravely turning his back and holstering the weapon. Swaggered over to the door. It buzzed, clicked, closed behind him with a heavy finality.

Clarice turned around to see the Latin Queen looking at her like she was Satan incarnate, still muttering rapid-fire Spanish in what sounded like prayer.

The CO at the visitation desk was standing, bent over the box of Popeye's, wide butt jacked up and looking like the rear tires on a dune buggy. Clarice walked to the door and motioned for her to open it. She looked at Clarice's Power Puff Girl hair, feral grin, blood red eyes and veins standing up from fists. Back to Clarice's grin. Her eyes widened, mouth opened.

She shook her head no.

Chapter VII

Juarez, Chihuahua
Mexico
October 11, 2011

The dark blue Gulfstream IV shot out of the bank of clouds above the Rio Grande at over 300mph, streamlined aerodynamics and precise navigation performing a turbulence-free flight. Small red lights on the wings blinked at intervals. The down-flaps shifted slightly, angling the aircraft on a descent that broke up more ranks of clouds, most bright and fluffy white, some dark and thickening with ice, dust, and precipitation. Tempests in infancy.

The ground appeared a few blinks later, *terra firma* that looked especially sharp after hours of immersion in the fluffy canopy of potential thunderheads. Beams of sunlight filtered down in rays that faded but still brightened the greens and browns of small dry climate shrubs and cacti peppering the desert as far as the eye could see. The sun hid behind a mass of blinding whiteout to the left of the southbound jet, nearing its peak and alerting the agenda, conscious that it was time to prepare for the noontime siesta.

El Maestro sat in a roomy recliner next to the first window facing the sun, the only passenger on board. An irritable expression seemed permanently stained on his face. But the mood didn't keep him from gazing out the window and appreciating the aesthetics of the sky and land surrounding his desert home.

The jet banked slightly to the west. What appeared to be a small airport came into view. As the pilot maneuvered closer, the vague airport became a large estate with a private airstrip. A huge villa with a brown tiled roof commanded the center stage, with a smaller structure of similar build off to one side. Several acres around the buildings and runway were fenced in, thick red brick columns with steel poles in a pleasing octagon, with smaller fences inside corralling horses, chickens, pigs, and *burros*. Large steel roofed sheds stood next to the corrals.

Men, and a few robust women, were on horseback or riding ATVs, going about their tasks like busy ants, herding the animals and hauling loads of various ranching by-products.

The pilot circled the area and lined up with the runway, descending smoothly. Seconds later, a muffled chirp of tires and compression of struts could be heard in the cabin where El Maestro was calmly unbuckling his seat harness. The plane taxied toward a large hangar where a yellow truck with adjustable stairs mounted on its side was driving out, turning in the direction of the new arrival.

The jet stopped, turbines winding down. The co-pilot, a small-framed black Cuban gentleman with a puff of gray for hair, exited the cockpit and opened the main door. The cabin depressurized with a subtle, hollow sensation, an impossibly huge breath being exhaled. The truck parked with its stairs aimed with practiced precision, raised them to the jet's door. The hydraulic pump under the stairs cycled loudly, an oily whine that resonated over the distant boking of startled chickens and oinking of hungry pigs. El Maestro stepped out and down the steps with his customary patience and collective, analyzing glances in all directions.

"*Hola*, Marcela," El Maestro greeted the stair truck driver, a sixtyish Mexicana with slicked back hair and a charming, toothless smile that pushed her cheeks out wide. He walked past the vehicle and turned to face the two men who were jogging from the hangar to meet their employer. Tall with dark buzz cuts and thick mustaches, both muscle heads wore blue mechanic's coveralls with patches on the top pockets that named them as Erik and Felix.

They stopped in front of El Maestro. "*Hola*, El Maestro," Felix said, smiling briefly. "*Como esta?*"

El Maestro didn't respond right away. He stared into the distance, searching the dazzling horizon as if it held solutions to the troubles plaguing his current operations. Looking at his men, he acknowledged them with a curt nod, motioned for them to follow and walked toward the red brick building that squatted on the north side of its larger sibling, the main house, a brick villa well over two hundred feet wide. Spanish style doors and windows on both buildings were footed with small flower gardens that struggled to absorb moisture in the arid environment. El Maestro noticed movement in the garden mulch, a tiny scorpion that chased a spider twice its size into a patch of barrel cactus.

"Has the security team in Biloxi reported in today?" El Maestro asked, knowing everyone on the ranch awaited news on the murder investigation and gossiped about any updates, even after all this time. His loafers whispered over the stone walkway, silent steps that seemed to compound the heavy boots thudding behind him. A hot alkaline wind pulsed across the estate, dislodging sand from the dry, cracked dirt yard. The scent of manure stirred within the currents, at times so strong one had to hold one's breath.

Erik glanced at Felix, then answered, "*Si, El Maestro. Esos policios —*"

"Practice your English, Erik."

"*Si*, El Maestro. Those policemen say they no hear anything yet. Everyone has lost hope, and no more believe the policemen will find the traitor."

El Maestro nodded, muttered several brusque words. The mechanics shared a worried look, concerned about the irresolution not normally shown by their leader. Felix shrugged at Erik, said, "I can no be-lieve El Maestro risk himself on the street."

"He wants to avenge Jose," Erik said, pride in his voice.

"*Si.* But now he wants to save the *gringa.* She de-served the honor, but this no good for him."

"*Ay, iy, iy,*" Erik breathed, shaking his head. "It is good to worry about El Maestro, but no good to ques-tion him."

"Enough from you two," El Maestro said, stopping in front of the ranch office. He opened the stained oak door. It opened quietly, weather seals brushing over the floor, allowing hot air to flow into the cold room. They walked inside. The mechanics sighed as the air conditioned coolness enveloped their over-heated muscles, even cooler in places where sweat had accumulated.

The modern furniture was tasteful, businesslike, not overly expensive, as were the electronics that were visible. Consumer products that law enforce-ment raids would quickly dismiss as affordable on a rancher's income. Tall floor lamps stood behind a desk, a small sofa, and next to a chest-high bookcase, illuminating the room from the neck down, showing clean blue carpet and cream colored walls that looked new but smelled pleasantly well-lived in. El Maestro sat behind a large birch desk with a dull natural fin-ish, leaned back in the padded swivel chair and inter-laced his fingers over his belt. Eyeing his men with renewed irritation, he said, "Report."

Felix glanced at Erik, who nodded. Felix said, "The Gulfstream has another three hundred hours before the turbines need overhaul."

"Overhauling," El Maestro said.

"Overhauling. It will take one week."

"When?"

"We reviewed your traveling habits and estimated four months from now. Your secretary was informed for scheduling."

"Your English is improving, Felix," he praised, looked over at Erik. "And what of the ranch vehicles? Any repairs that exceed the usual maintenance costs?"

"No, El Maestro."

"Very well." El Maestro spun in his chair, grabbed a walkie-talkie out of its charger on top of the bookcase. He keyed it, spoke a request rapidly in Spanish, replaced it in the charger, chair creaking. A framed portrait hanging above the books caught his eye, riveting his feet and erecting his spine as he inhaled sharply from the grieving pain that attacked him once again. It was an artist's rendering of his longtime friend and business partner, Jose. A memorial drawn in pencil by a child in a poor village that was alive today because of Jose's compassion for his people.

Tears welled in El Maestro's eyes.

I am sorry I have not avenged you, mi compadre, he thought, looking into the drawing's eyes and experiencing a sort of metaphysical connection. *I will never stop searching for the* cabrone *that took your life and*

betrayed La Familia. And I will continue your charities,
helping those that were unfairly wronged or simply de-
serving of a chance.

Like the girl.

I will help her, because that is what you would have
advised me to do.

A tear trailed down his cheek. He pulled a handkerchief from his top pocket, yellow silk, perfectly
folded. Wiped the tear, sniffing and turning back to
his men. He said, "*Con permiso.*" Cleared his throat.
"Now. Report, off the books." He interlaced his fingers again.

Felix went first, speaking with the excitement of a
true gearhead. "The new go-fast boats are *mucho* better than the old models we had. Five-seventy-two big
block Chevy engines, twelve hundred horsepower in
each boat." He smiled, eyes widening, hands gesturing energetically with his words. "They are longer,
with *mucho* payload capacity and upgraded navigation equipment that will temporarily jam the Coast
Guard's radar."

El Maestro pursed his lips thoughtfully, nodded.
He waved a hand at Erik.

Erik took a deep breath, concentrating on his second language. "The ATVs were equip with—"

"Equipped."

"*Gracias.* Equipped with infrared lamps for night
vision driving in the desert. They now have ten gallon reserve tanks, and we experimented with small
trailers to pull behind them, but they were no good.
Too clumsy over the terrain. Instead, we fabricated

larger luggage racks and cut the seats to accom, ac-como—"

"Accommodate."

"*Gracias.* Accommodate the racks. They now carry one-third more product, and they get two-thirds more range."

"Very well. Good work. On the English, too."

A double tap sounded at the door. El Maestro nodded and Erik got up to open it. A thirty-something Mexicana in a maid's uniform of soft pink walked in, pushing a vacuum cleaner in front of her. She gave a brief bow for her boss, avoiding eye contact and ignoring the mechanics, who were shooting appreciative looks at her legs. She found a receptacle on a wall, plugged in her machine.

Before she could turn it on, El Maestro held up a hand to give her pause, waved for her to come to him, a specific motion that conveyed a specific meaning. She rolled the vacuum up to his desk, around it, stood it next to his chair. He turned to face it and unlatched a plastic panel on the front. The cover popped off and revealed an iPad integrated inside, a factory-quality installation. Turning it on, he used the touchscreen to scroll through coded files only he and the maids were versed in. After several minutes of browsing, he grunted ambiguously, gestured at the screen inviting elaboration.

The maid bowed again, moved around the machine and squatted down to read the encrypted language. "*Inglés?*" she asked. English?

"Yes, please."

"Profits on the books will cover the maids', mechanics', and *rancheros'* salaries. Maintenance costs for the jet and airstrip have not yet been calculated, but projections show those expenses will make your personal salary miniscule." El Maestro waved a hand, unconcerned. She continued, scrolling through the files. "Livestock markets are unchanged. Off the books profits for this quarter were as expected, though I'm predicting the next quarter will be slightly below our target due to inefficient logistics." She cleared her throat. "*Señor* Jose's replacement is not as effective as we are used to." She bowed her head. Crossing herself, she murmured a quick prayer in Spanish for her late underboss, kept her head down, awaiting further instructions.

El Maestro's face flushed with sudden anger, a fleeting change that danced over him, head to toe, before vanishing from ruthless suppression. Equilibrium regained, he took a calming breath and looked at her. "Thank you, Elena. Notify the maid's team leader that I want encryption software upgraded every ninety days from now on. Every iPad and laptop in every company with off-the-books income. Several of the cartels have employed hackers, and I fear our current truces hold no sway in the virtual world."

"*Si*, El Maestro."

"That is all. Thank you, Elena."

The maid/accountant turned off the iPad, replaced the plastic panel and began vacuuming the already spotless floor.

Chapter VIII

Central Mississippi Correctional Facility
Pearl, Mississippi
December 24, 2011

"Is that weed you're smoking? I haven't smelled that stuff in years," Clarice asked her cubicle mate, Patty, who sat on the bottom bunk amid a cloud of reefer smoke.

"Yep," she replied, a puff wheezing out from the huge hit she held in.

"I thought you were going to church. For the big Christmas deal."

"I am," she shrugged. "I like to catch a good buzz before I pray. Gets me closer to Jesus."

Clarice laughed, watching Patty's face change colors from no oxygen. Unable to hold it in any longer, she gave a loud expulsion that curiously emitted little smoke, most of it apparently absorbed in her bloodstream by cavernous lungs. She stood up, smiling, eyes squinted nearly closed in pleasure, steel bed popping its released tension, swayed a little. Over six feet with a large waist and brawny arms, very white skin with freckles and shining blonde hair that fell in waves just below her shoulders, Patty was a formidable woman. Smart, funny, and capable. Clarice had liked her from the moment they met.

Clarice's other cube mate was a different story, however. Yolanda sat up on the top bunk above Patty. Slim with protruding cheekbones, long dark hair and acne scars on her brown skin, the young Ecuadorian cocked her neck a few times with attitude, said "You've changed."

"They say prison will do that to a girl," Clarice responded with attitude of her own.

"You used to be nice and understanding. Ever since you got a reputation, you've been judgmental."

"Reputation? Judgmental? No, Yolanda. I just call it like I see it. You're a fucking leech. If you can't pay me back, just say so. Don't connive over a few dollars in canteen. Good way to get your head busted."

"Wow," Patty said. "You have changed."

"You're just high," Clarice said.

"True," Patty agreed, then started pinching the muffin top that hung over the waistband of her black and white pants. She sucked in her stomach. "Am I like really fat, or can I make the pathetic claim that I'm 'big boned'?" she asked, turning like she was trying to find a skinny angle.

"Oh, Patty. Your body has to be big, to be able to hold such a big heart," Clarice assured her, smiling. "Large and lovely."

She returned the smile, eyes glittering with merriment. And quality weed. "That's the nicest way I've ever been called fat. Thank you."

"You're welcome."

She sat down again, opened her locker box and took out a giant Honey Bun. Closed the box, unwrapped the pastry. Noticing Clarice's smirk, she told her, "Hey. Fat people have to eat, too."

"What about the church service? Don't they have food?"

"Damn. I forgot. I need to get going," she said, stuffing the Honey Bun in her mouth and standing up. "I'll eat there, too," she mumbled around the bun.

"What are you having?"

"Traditional hooker meal."

"Traditional?"

Walking away, she turned her head, swallowed, and said, "Two missionaries in a sandwich."

Clarice laughed, then yelled after her. "Don't molest those holy men. They'll stick your crazy ass under the prison!"

Yolanda and Clarice giggled for a moment, then remembered they were beefing and resumed their antagonizing mugs. Yolanda sniffed, stuck her nose up and looked away.

Clarice sighed. "We'll talk later. I'm off to clean toilets. I think."

"I thought you were sweeping and mopping."

"I'm not sure. The Latin Queens got me a job in the lockdown unit. Sounds thrilling, whatever it is."

"Well, there aren't that many jobs. And there are too many hoes trying to work. You should feel fortunate."

"Yeah, fortunate. That's what I feel."

Closing her locker box, Clarice secured the lock, stood and walked past a pouting Yolanda to tell the tower officer she had to go to work. After leaving her ID with the CO, she walked out of the building and down several walkways before the unit she was looking for came into view. Heavy rain clouds seemed poised over its roof. A promise of ruining the rest of the day by canceling yard-call and other outside activities, potentially causing an institutional lockdown if the storm proved furious enough.

Cold wind blasted from the gray morning sky. Goose bumps prickled her arms, making Clarice regret the decision to leave her jacket. She had planned to work hard to stay warm, but that wouldn't work out very well if she froze before getting there. She walked faster.

The lockdown unit was legendary on the compound, having a long history of horror stories. Beatings, stabbings, self-mutilating psych patients. As the main entrance buzzed and she walked inside, she sensed anxiety that was not quite hidden in the body language of the COs that meandered the halls and loitered by the tower doors. They bantered with each other, loudly, laughing and appearing at ease, but their quick glances at unlatching door locks and nervous eating of too much snack machine food showed the constant fears they dreaded. Of being fired for opening the wrong cell door, getting stabbed or scalded, or having feces thrown on them by a disturbed woman who has no qualms about engaging in biological warfare.

Real fears, from real experiences.

Clarice had actually seen a CO scalded with sugar water. It wasn't pretty. Her normally dark skin was blistered white, pink in places where the skin had completely melted off. And she's seen COs walk out of there with their heads down, dejected, after being fired for opening cell #23 when it should have been #22, causing a brutal stabbing and ending any future career in corrections. Those sorts of incidents and the people involved in them were talked about for a week or so, then forgotten. A common occurrence not worth dwelling on. A terrible one, sure. But no one wanted to remember it.

For some reason, Clarice didn't feel sorry for the officers. None of the COs took an interest in her, as usual. She wasn't feeling any urge to gain recognition or ask one of the idiots for instructions, so she went down the hallway between the zones looking for the door marked STORAGE, knowing all those buildings were of the same basic design. She found it quickly. Pushed it open. Mops and brooms stood haphazardly behind boxes of paper towels and detergents, bottles of industrial strength cleaner. Stepping inside the small room, she held her breath. There were dozens of chemicals and no telling how many molds and fungi vying for a chance to lay spore in her lungs. She pulled the collar of her shirt up over her nose and mouth, grabbed a yellow mop bucket and hurriedly filled it with hot water from the filthy porcelain sink that clung to the back wall like a drunken bum, slouched, crooked and beat up. Grabbed a packet of liquid detergent and squeezed it into the steaming water. Suds and bubbles popped, adding fresh fumes to the tiny room, making her sneeze several times. She grabbed a mop and broom at random, backpedaled the hell out of there, gasping deeply at the much cleaner air in the hallway. Rolled the bucket to the A zone door, waved at the tower. It buzzed, clicked, and slid open with mechanical complaint. She walked through.

The zone had sixty cells, thirty in a horseshoe shape downstairs, thirty upstairs. Clarice's job was to clean the dayroom floor and tables, the upstairs tier floor, and stay away from the cells. No problem.

As she went about the mindless work, she thought about the months since she met Ignacio. Or El Maestro. Whatever the hell he called himself. His influence had certainly made her life in prison more interesting. That dude was a legend among the street savvy, which was the entire population of this joint, including the officers. Word of their visitation showdown got around fast. It was like a mass text message hit the hundreds of contraband cell phones in every unit with the details, elevating her status to instant criminal celebrity. The weird thing was, she kind of liked it. She missed fame, She wasn't ashamed to admit it . This deal was deep in the infamous spectrum of fame, but all the same, she was rocking it.

She remembered walking back from visitation that day and passing other inmates who stepped away from her, making sure to maintain a respectful distance. And walking by officers that looked at her nervously but neglected to question her intended destination. Pretended she wasn't there.

Of course, by that point she looked like a stunt double for *The Poltergeist,* and would probably frighten Charles Manson with a glance. So maybe she was assuming too much. Maybe they hadn't known so fast.

But they sure knew now...

Finished with the broom, she dipped the mop in the bucket, in the soapy water that instantly turned brown from the repulsive mop head.

"That's just wrong," she grumbled, thinking about how unorganized the place was, that they couldn't even clean up a mop before storing it. *I'll be here all day working on that damn floor. Well, it's either that or getting stuck on the zone listening to all the incredibly loud stupidity between groups of women. One Life to Live discussions. Screaming, card slamming games. My Baby Daddy A Loser drama.*

Excedrin Headache #976,860,000.

Deciding this was a comparable heaven, she placed the mop in the wringer, leaned all of her one-hundred-and-thirty-five pounds on the lever and squeezed the Mississippi mud out of the old, thin cotton strings. The plastic and springs groaned loudly, echoing off the brick walls and steel doors.

The zone was full of women, every cell occupied. Clarice caught several of them staring at her, or ducking out of their windows when she looked up. A few waved, most just gave her blank or nasty looks. She gave the same response to all of them. A simple nod, civil, not friendly, just a girl doing a slave job for a day off her sentence as payment.

Clarice had been in that same unit several times for fighting officers. *Which, on reflection, makes me incredibly lucky to even have this job, and eligibility for Good Time.* So she was familiar with disrupting the orderly running of the institution and doing dungeon time. The women there couldn't make it in general population for many reasons. Fighting, robbing, extorting the weak. Or just getting in touch with their inner dumbass because they were bored. Several were on protective custody to be sheltered from such predatory behavior.

Not an ideal place to do time. Or work.

The mop plopped wetly on the floor. As she swirled and swayed with the strokes of cleaning, she hummed an unknown number, a tune written by happy thoughts, and imagined what Yolanda would look like wearing a Ringside Products tee shirt. Her peanut head would make a fine double-end bag. Clarice could trick her into thinking they were going to work out together...

Then Clarice would start hitting her, and, too late, she would realize that she was the workout.

Ha-ha...

She stepped backwards and swung the mop as far as she could to either side, being careful not to get too close to the cells. The Yolanda workout plan almost got her doused with coffee and juice, thrown by two childish black girls in neighboring cells, laughing like they were teasing a smaller kid on a playground, giggling and slapping their thighs in the safety of their cells, unable to think of consequences. Freaking ignoramuses. Definitely in touch with their inner dumbass.

Clarice ground her teeth but ignored them, quietly thanking her quick reflexes and placing them at the top of her Proud Attributes list, which dropped her glutes to the #2 spot for the first time ever. *Sorry Perfect Booty... Survival trumps the self-esteem ya gave me.* Threats and crap like that happened to her during previous visits there. It seemed it would increase in frequency now that she was working the floor and had become a kind of sport for the arrested development windbags. For whatever reason, all those tough, hard black women couldn't stand to see a little ol' white chick trying to make that bacteria pit look and smell better. So much racism and tribalism was new to her. It was irrational, and really frustrating.

Stupid. She shook her head.

She grinned and hummed louder through clenched teeth, imagining Ringside tee shirts on all those crazy bitches, more of them joining in now that the first salvo had been thrown. She swayed and swirled, dancing with the feeling of the pleasant fantasy.

Added a few la-dee-da lyrics to the inane jam, shouting melodiously in response to the derogatory comments. Once they realized she wasn't fun anymore, they quit.

Hey, I can out-crazy-bitch any crazy bitch. Sometimes you have to fight fire with fire. Stupid with stupider.

Walking back to get the bucket, she passed a cell that had an enormous head filling the window. The light was on, barely peeking through gaps around the hippopotamus face in silhouette, whites of eyes the only thing distinguishable. Jeepers creepers, it was abnormal. Clarice couldn't help looking again. The hippo bared its teeth at her, then punched the crap out of the steel door. It thundered like a bass drum throughout the zone, startling some of the women, who jumped away from their windows. Shouts for quiet followed.

"You shut up!" the hippo hollered back.

"Who that is? That you Boogerilla?" someone a few cells down said, speaking through their tray slot.

"Yeah. That me," the hippo replied, thumping her door again. "This white bitch be looking me all in my face. Like she wanna fuck me, or some shit."

"Excuse me?" Clarice said, standing up straight, unconsciously gripping the mop like a weapon.

"Who that is?" the tray slot said again.

"This white-bread nothing in front of my cell," Boogerilla said.

"What you be, girl?" the tray slot said, demanding to know what gang Clarice represented.

"I'm just me," she responded.

"Oh. You nothing then."

Leaning the mop against a wall, Clarice walked down to the talking tray hole, squatted down and looked into the eyes of a very rough featured black woman that could have been twenty-five or fifty-five. Scars ran thickly down one side of her face and continued even thicker across the contours of a shoulder and down the arm. Battle wounds from knife fights. Clarice liked the scars, and the girl had some boss corn row braids. But Clarice held her compliments.

I can see she and I are to be unfriendlies.

Clarice let the girl get a good look at the beast lurking behind her eyes. "Oh, you can believe I'm something."

She narrowed her eyes. "I remember you now, small fry. You just left here. I know you supposed to be some big shot fighter in a ring with gloves. But I don't use gloves, small fry." Her hands out of sight, she grinded something heavy and metallic on the concrete floor. "I use iron," she breathed, then held up a length of metal longer than Clarice's hand, angle iron that she guessed came from the inside of a fluorescent light housing. The girl licked the blade, staring into Clarice's eyes.

Unimpressed, Clarice told her, "If you call me a nothing again, you may have to use that flimsy piece of tin."

Outrage rippled across the girl's features. Clarice walked away and the girl screamed at her back, "You dead, small fry! Nobody insults Chiquita like that. I make the best blades. The best!"

"I'll get her ass, Chuiquita," Boogerilla said, hippo eyes alight as Clarice walked past her cell again to grab the mop. "This door gonna swing one day while she be in the zone. Them tower officers always push the wrong buttons. That's how I got Mimi. I'll get this white-bread hoe, too. Only a matter of time."

Clarice stopped and looked over at Boogerilla, tilted her head. "What does Boogerilla mean, anyway? Booger gorilla? You drag your knuckles before you pick your nose? How the hell did you get such a fucked up name?"

"I'm going to kill you and fuck your dead body," she promised, punching the door hard enough that Clarice had to catch herself from flinching. Someone upstairs squeaked.

Clarice grinned at her. "I hope you have a big one so my spirit will fly away with a satisfied smile."

"You think this is a game, bitch. You see. You will see."

The hippo disappeared, allowing light to show through the window. As Clarice rolled the mop bucket to the stairs so she could go up and clean the top tier, she overheard Boogerilla talking to herself. Telling an imaginary friend what she would do to Clarice. And Clarice heard, actually felt, the hard grinding of a fresh piece of steel inside Chiquita's cell. A blade that would most certainly have her name on it.

Super-duper.

Not bad for my first day at work.

"Carter!" a CO yelled from the zone door.

Clarice turned to look. "Yeah?"

"Visitation. Let's go," she said, turning to speak to the tower officer.

Grabbing the broom and mop, Clarice pushed the bucket behind the officer to the storage room, tiny wheels squeaking as she mulled over comparisons with previous jobs she's had, finding none. She made more enemies there in an hour than she had in her entire professional boxing career.

At least I got to knock off work early.

Merry freaking Christmas to me.

* * *

The place had a way of deluding, forcing a person to think and behave, conform to the tribal conditions. *Lord of the Flies* with adults. Civilized people isolated, unable to use the higher evolved thought processes that are needed to survive in the social realms of the free-world. The processes Clarice once used daily had regressed, commandeered by the primeval fight-or-flight life she lived now, and shut out any distractions that might hinder its mechanism.

Like my family... The most distracting element that could lessen her chances for survival in prison.

She had been so immersed in the institution that she hadn't thought about what really matters in months. She hadn't been able to. And she hated herself for it.

My extraordinary, beautiful goddamn family. How could I forget about them? I'm a traitor.

She walked fast to the visitation room. Stood by impatiently as the CO that had escorted her signed the log on the desk. The visitation officer, the same jacked up dune buggy booty with Popeye's grease face that was always there, buzzed her into the room. Clarice's mother, father, and her trainer, Eddy, sat behind a table with huge inviting smiles. She stopped in her tracks, stunned by the beautiful sight, rushing with pleasure that made her glow a pure smile in return, chest tightening, making it a conscious effort to breathe, aggressive persona taking a hiatus, a sensation she felt physically, as if a part of her soul had gone into another room to give them some privacy.

Faces and memories flashed, seemingly in front of her eyes. A 3D movie where graphic scenes from her past jumped out at her through red and blue shades, filtering her vision. Dug up from a neuronal tomb where she stuffed all the information that made her feel like screaming, stifled and sad and head-banging-on-a-table pissed the fuck off.

She hated feeling like that.

So she chose not to, and could usually pull it off successfully. Or rather, Shocker could. But there's a penalty when it all came flooding back, like it was then.

It hurts.

Like a mother.

"Hi," she said, a loud whisper in the quiet room. Even the building was silent. None of the usual bumps, bangs and distant jibing from trustees pretending to work. Crashing silence. Their chairs scraped the floor as all three of them stood up, walked quickly around the table to give her a group hug.

Her mother took charge and backed the men out of the way. "Clarice! You look dreadful," she greeted with her usual criticism, touching Clarice's cheeks, hair, turning Clarice's head for inspection, fussing over her daughter as Clarice grinned and tingled at her touch.

Damn, that feels good... Clarice realized she had really missed this wonderful woman. The aromas of home permeated her mother, releasing a flood tide of even more memories. These more pleasant, thankfully.

An inch shorter than Clarice's five-eight, Jade Ares was the epitome of class. She was slim, handsome rather than pretty. Sported fashionable, short-styled blonde hair touched with the perfect mix of gray. Pro makeup highlighting her bright green eyes and high cheekbones, subtly diminishing the piggy nose that was the progenitor of Clarice's. Cosmetically enhanced lips that belied her fifty-nine years, glossed clear-of-pink. Thousand dollar green pantsuit, conservative black heels that knocked repeatedly on the floor as she walked around Clarice, scowling at her appearance, harrumphing.

How could anyone not love this woman? She was a hundred-and-twenty pounds of Make You Feel Good.

"Nice to see you, too, Mom," Clarice croaked. Turned to look at her father. He stood next to Eddy, watching his wife do her mother hen bit with pride emanating from every part of his body. Danny Ares was equal in height with Eddy, fifty pounds lighter, sixty with dark brown dyed hair. Ridiculous green bowling shirt he probably wore to please his wife in a color matching couple's scheme. It covered a small paunch that would earn him a lecture from his daughter if it got any bigger. Blue jeans and wing-tipped Doc Marten's. A lifetime coffee drinker, his unceasing smile shone like ivory rather than porcelain. Brown eyes squinted on his craggy face, distinguished with laughter lines and crow's feet. Clarice wanted to kick herself for not thinking about this loving, loyal man every second of every day.

Her chest tightened even further. Her boobs ached. But it felt awesome.

Jade completed her inspection, signaling the men that they were allowed to come forward again. Eddy stood back, anxiously awaiting his turn. He looked like a big bulldog told to stay away from his favorite toy, fidgeting with impatience.

"It's so good to see you, Clarice. Merry Christmas," Danny said, hugging her, twisting side-to-side. He smelled like a forest in the winter, clean and sharp. But he felt like the comfort of a day at the beach with a bottle of wine. His soft businessman's hands cupped her chin. "They treating you okay?"

Before she could answer Eddy's patience took that as a cue to vacate and he plowed her dad out of the way, grabbing her with arms that felt like they wrapped around her twice. Squeezed her in a crushing grizzly hug. Lifted her off the floor like a sack of feathers. Her smile was mostly a painful grimace.

"I think we should ask if she is treating them okay," Eddy rumbled in his basso voice, under-bite stuck out, grinning. Clarice's feet reacquainted with gravity. She grinned back at him, hugging his U.S.A. Team jacket, which felt looser on him.

Stepping back and indulging her own inner Mother Hen, Clarice grabbed his arm and turned him, like she was deciding whether to label him Accepted or Failed.

He didn't pass.

"You've lost weight," she told him, then sniffed. "Though I don't see how. Your breath smells like fried oysters."

"Yes. No. I haven't noticed," he said, dismissing her attention to his eating habits. "I've missed you, girl. Come on! Let's see that jab." He held up his meaty paws, big as punch mitts, and started moving around her in a circle with an intent expression.

She laughed, automatically stepping into a boxing stance and lunging at him with rapid jabs that popped like thunderclaps on his palms, causing Jade to tisk and shake her head. Clarice's muscles stretched and swelled with power. She felt like a race horse that had been left in the stables for too long, bursting with the need to go, the need for speed.

She doubled up, really clowning, feeling her monster start to rock, sticking his hand mitts with lightning stabs of her left fist, pivoting, weaving, lunging in and out. Shoes chirping on the floor. They laughed together, immersed in the movements that had been so intrinsic to their lives, responsible for so many joyful challenges and emotional moments of achievement. Cornerstones. Larger than life experiences.

A snarl gripped her lips. Killer instinct surfacing and taking control of her feet, stomping hard into a power jab, booming into his hand. Eddy roared with laughter, shaking the room like Pavarotti in a concert hall. She dropped below his hands and tagged his stomach with a five-punch combination that was almost too fast for ears to distinguish, sounding like a single blow. An ability she could use without the weight of hand wraps and gloves on her fists. She grabbed her trainer's waist and hugged him again. Nostalgic tears pooled in her eyes as the faint smell of boxing gyms crinkled off his jacket. Punching, jumping, grunting sounds seemed to accompany it.

Jade sobbed behind them. Grabbing her side for a purse that wasn't there, retained by an officer in the front where visitors come in. Tissues absent, Jade used the sleeve of her jacket to staunch her tears before her face became completely mussed. Clarice let go of Eddy and hugged her again.

"I missed you," Clarice told her, rubbing her back. Clarice buried her cheek in Jade's bosom. A nagging thought occurred to her. Like a smack in the face, she realized the person she wanted to see the most, needed to see, wasn't there. "Where's Nolan?" she said. Her son was staying with her parents while his own were incarcerated.

Danny stepped between them, answered, "He refused to come. We tried everything, believe me. But he wouldn't get in the car. Regina is watching him," he said, referring to their housekeeper. He cleared his throat. Sat down in a plastic chair.

"He said you aren't his mother and he never wants to see you again," Jade sobbed, sniffing, hiding her face behind her hands. "He said you broke your promise to never leave again."

"Now, Jade. That's not—" Danny began.

Jade dropped her hands and glared at him through tears and eyes of fire. An expression alien to her facial muscles, absurdly incongruous. "She deserves the truth, Danny. You always want to sugar coat!"

Eddy and Clarice looked back and forth between the couple they'd never witnessed in disagreement before, appalled at the outburst. It showed just how screwed up things had become because of the wrongful imprisonment. It showed how much Clarice had missed because of infrequent communication, how unaware she'd been of the deep impact of her imprisonment on everyone connected to her. Eddy noticed Clarice's horrified look and whisked her away. Grabbing her shoulders he marched her across the room to give her parents a chance to regain composure. And he wanted to speak to her in confidence. His baritone whisper felt like a ginormous bumble bee in her ear. "I was contacted by the Teacher," he said.

"What? Why?" she stuttered. A horrific feeling quickly took over the bliss she was enjoying.

"He explained his involvement in your case and wanted to help however he could."

"Okay. And?"

"And he sent me documents for you," he bumble bee-ed in her ear, glancing at her parents to see if they were listening. They were whispering in a furious argument, heads bowed together, pointing fingers all around. "Had a former colleague of mine deliver them. An old trainer I knew from Mexico. Two sets of driver's licenses, social security cards and birth certificates. Plus twenty large in cash."

Clarice looked back at Eddy and closed her stunned mouth. It fell open again. "No shit?" was the best she could come up with. *IDs? Cash?* Her head spun with the possibilities.

"Yeah. After I got over my urge to hurt that guy, I got to liking him - he's my kind of people - and agreed to help. Your folks know about this, but not about the documents and money. No one else needs to know the names on the IDs. And your poor folks can't handle too much involvement in underground activities, anyway. That's my forte." He chuffed and smirked, a quirk he used to do before brokering less-than-ethical deals during her boxing career. He had always shielded her from the shady side of the fight game, keeping her hands and image squeaky clean. Apparently, he was doing the same for her mom and dad now. He continued, "With the passports, you can get on a plane to anywhere in the world. The Teacher offered the same deal for Ace. But you have to get out first."

"All right. I'll do some homework and get back to you. What are the names on the IDs?" Curiosity was getting the better of her.

His cheeks sunk down. "Patricia on one. Connie on the other. I think. Cute, huh?" He waggled his heavy brows.

"I don't know. I don't trust the Teacher."

"I understand. Just let me know. In the meantime, we can plot the rest of it." He inclined his head at her parents. "Danny has something for you."

"What?" she said, turning to look at her dad.

"A cellphone." He grinned. "Untraceable. Also courtesy of the Teacher."

"My dad brought a phone in here?" she said. Her damn mouth was going to catch flies at this rate.

"Yep. Said he wanted to be the one to take the risk."

"That's insane!" she said too loudly. Jade and Danny stopped their fuming and looked over at them. Eddy clapped Clarice on the shoulder and they walked back over to the table, sat down. Her parents followed suit, both of them pressing elbows on the table, leaning towards Clarice.

Clarice looked at Danny. "You, um, need to tell me something?" Weird didn't begin to describe what she felt. The thought of her father, a Christian do-gooder, committing a felony was dumbfounding. She'd never heard of him breaking any rules, much less serious laws.

My dad? Heh. Right.

"Yes," he said, clearing his throat. He glanced at Jade, then at the CO through the window, who sat at the desk, flipping through a magazine. He continued, whispering, "The Teacher called us. We want to help."

"But you could go to jail if you get caught," Clarice whispered back in protest.

He held up a hand. "You were sentenced to forty years, Clarice. Forty. Years." He paused, tears glazing his steely eyes. "I won't stand by and let you waste your life in here if I can do something about it," he said, emotion flushing his face, love and passion for his only child. Jade patted his hand. "Well, I can do something about it. I was able to get past the metal detector because of the screws and pins in my leg. Your mother brought a medical report to prove it. Hang on a minute." His arms disappeared under the table. The room silent once more, his zipper peeling open was very loud. Clarice almost laughed.

A moment later, the tearing, ripping sound of strong tape pulling hair from skin grew loud in the room. His face turned a deep, painful scarlet as he held back an outcry. Clarice cringed at the sound and the excruciating look on her Dad's normally pleasant face. And the image of her father's pubic hair stuck all over a phone he was about to hand her. Eddy also cringed, hands ducking under the table, likely holding his junk in sympathy. Jade looked around, guilty, embarrassed, panicked. A range of reactions piqued by her morals from the blatant violation of the laws she had so loyally abided by up until that day.

Clarice nearly choked, holding back laughter. Yeah, weird couldn't possibly describe it.

Her dad's shoulders jerked a few more times and he bent over so his face almost touched the table. Rouge with hues of violet throbbing around veins in his temples, on his creased forehead. The poor man looked like he needed a stool softener in a bad way. A final jerk and his hands bumped hard into the underside of the table. He gave a grunt of surprise and something plastic clattered loudly on the floor. Four sets of eyes bugged out around the table. Jade squeaked, totally wigged out.

At that moment, the CO from the visitation desk walked in, ushering another inmate. The inmate, a white chick with greasy, stringy hair, maybe thirty years old with meth addiction written all over her abused body, spotted the phone and immediately pointed it out to the officer. Snitched on them. Clarice's stomach joined her jaw, bungee jumping to the floor. Her parents' responses mirrored hers, but Eddy was on a different level about the whole situation.

As the snitching slut pointed out the contraband on the floor, the CO maneuvered through the doorway and looked where the phone lay, eyes popping even more than theirs. Looked up at Eddy and jerked back from the murderous stare he directed at the snitch, at her, back to the snitch. Eddy sprang up a second later, chair flying out behind him as if he threw it. He snarled at the tattle-tale, then flipped the table over in her direction, roaring in anger, the booming rage vibrating Clarice's head, blurring her vision. The officer and inmate screamed in terror, piercing shrieks that would have more officers in there faster than any emergency code shouted into a walkie-talkie could accomplish. Their shaky legs propelled them against a wall, where they huddled together.

Everyone watched in stunned disbelief as Eddy swiftly grabbed the phone from between Danny's feet and sprinted to the restroom, his speed and agility for such a large man doubling the stun factor. The men's room door banged open. A toilet flushed.

A prison toilet. With enough flushing power to suck down a small dog.

Eddy had disposed of the evidence, his quick action saving her dad from five years in prison.

Whew, fuck, what???

A relieved vertigo overcame Clarice, allowing her to breathe again. As Eddy walked out of the restroom, still snarling, disgusted, glaring dangerously, footsteps and excited walkie-talkies approached from behind the hyperventilating CO and frightened snitch.

Jade sobbed. Danny held his hands over his face. Clarice banged her head softly on the table.

Chapter IX

South Mississippi Correctional Facility
Leaksville, Mississippi
January 5, 2012

The concrete floor was cold as the man laid his bare back down on it to stretch. Wearing white boxer shorts and prison issue shoes of poor quality, new but already creased and torn, Alan "Ace" Carter extended his long arms over his head, inhaling deeply. Stretching his diaphragm with a yoga method, holding for a count of eight, releasing and exhaling for another eight. Forcefully deflating his lungs for another few seconds, oxygenating his muscles in preparation for a workout.

Sitting up he reached for his toes, knees locked, continuing the deep breathing, grabbing his heels and burying his face between his knees. He exhaled and groaned with pleasure as his hamstrings loosened, burning with a gratifying sensation.

"If I could do that, I'd never leave my bed," lisped a man walking into the four-bed cubicle. Tall and as slim as Ace, Diamond paused to look at his friend, one hand on a hip encased in too-tight striped pants, the other bent at the wrist in a dainty, feminine posture. His yellow-brown skin glowed with moisturizers that weren't sold on the canteen, accentuating a wide nose and wider smile on a handsome, mid-twenties face. Shaved eyebrows replaced by pencil liner makeup. Red bandana styled like origami on his head, knotted in the front.

Ace laughed and flipped over to do some pushups. "Yeah, right. If you could do that, your freaky ass would get rich in the porn business," he said, grunting as he finished a set of twenty.

"As I said. I'd never leave my bed." Diamond giggled playfully before sitting on his bottom bunk, watching Ace's lanky, ripped physique with platonic admiration. He'd long since given up on the fantasy of them together as a romantic couple, happily resigned to having him as a friend and confidant.

Ace started another set, but faltered as the image his friend evoked settled in his mind like an uninvited guest, funny, though a little off-putting. Snickering, he forced his arms to pump again.

"What are you two dummies doing?" an officer said, stopping in front of Ace, High-Tech boots clumping, indicating a weight deceptive to his appearance. He looked at Diamond. "You're supposed to be at work, not pitching woo on white boys," Lieutenant Cole said, crossing arms over a barrel chest. His black, almost blue face broke into a wide smile, teeth extremely white in contrast. His bald head shone under light coming through barred and screened windows. Cole fixed his eyes on Diamond with something more than good-natured amusement, waiting on a response he seemed to know would be tart.

Ace continued pounding out pushups, ignoring the exchange between the men he suspected would be lovers before long.

If they weren't already, he thought, smirking.

"Your black ass be all up in my Kool Aid and don't even know cherry from grape," Diamond sassed, turning his nose up, looking to the side and rolling his eyes with dismissal.

Cole's eyes seemed to grow brighter. "My black ass will bust through your wall like the Kool Aid man himself. I'll make you any damn flavor I want," he said, still beaming his smile. He uncrossed his arms like he intended to make good on his threat.

Ace stood up, eyes wide and near to bursting with laughter. He choked it down, said to them, "Uh. You two need a moment? I'll hit the yard and get my run in." He grabbed a t-shirt and black and white pants off his top bunk.

Cole crossed his arms again, turned to look at Ace. "No, big guy. I'll deal with this cocoa butter urn later," he said, jerking a massive thumb at Diamond, who wore a pleased expression behind Cole's back. Ace kept a carefully neutral look. "Right now, I need to talk with you." He spun around to Ace's cube mate again. "So you need to skedaddle to the yard."

Diamond uncrossed his legs, unhurriedly, stood with a shrewish look at Cole. "Well, I'll let you get away with ordering me around, this time, but don't expect to be so lucky next time round," he said. Strutted out of the cubicle and down the center of the zone with a hand on his narrow hips, working his backside like a runway model. Cole watched with his big smile, appreciatively, eyes twinkling.

Diamond suddenly stopped, spun around with a smooth half-pirouette, knowing Cole would be looking, waved a hand in front of his face. "My-my-my-my poker face, nigga," he sang, cocking his neck side-to-side with his lyrics. He spun around again, resumed his strut to the end of the building and out an open door that exited onto the yard. Catcalls and loud greetings came through the doorway.

Ace's pent up laughter came rushing out.

"I think," he gasped, holding sore abs, "that he likes you." He wiped his eye before it teared.

Cole rumbled his own laughter, put his hands on his waist. "Yeah, that's my nigga." He looked around to see if anyone was near. The long rectangular steel building had cubicles lining both walls its entire length, all empty, the occupants at work or outside for recreation. The front of the zone had a small guard tower, security windows capped with a steel grate, caked with dust. A tiled area right in front of the tower had several shower heads on a wall. The clean tiles reflected the fluorescent lights, smelling strongly of bleach. The officer in the tower appeared to be sleeping, arms crossed on the control panel, head rested on top of them. Cole looked back at Ace. "I don't know what kind of business you were in on the street, but you have some powerful friends," he said.

Ace frowned at him. "I was a diagnostic specialist, at my wife's shop."

"Uh-huh. Look, big guy. I'm not the po-lice," he said, tapping the MDOC badge on his white lieutenant's shirt. "I'm a correctional officer. And I believe interacting with prisoners is the best way to make things run sweet around here. You feel me?"

"Sure."

"So you don't have to pretend to be innocent, or worry about me busting you for some petty bullshit. As long as niggas ain't robbing or jumping on the little guys, slinging shanks, I don't care what y'all do."

"Sounds good to me. But you should know that I am innocent. The arresting officers framed my wife and I. We got forty years, and we didn't do anything."

"Uh-huh," Cole repeated, bright smile showing once more. "Gee, I've never heard that before. And I've been here for eighteen years."

Ace looked down and shook his head, lifted his hands, dropping them in exasperation.

"That's cool, big guy. It's all good. Stick to your guns. We don't have to tell each other secrets to do business."

"Business?" Ace said, looking up quizzically.

146

"Here." Cole dug into a front pocket and pulled out a small bundle of brown paper towels, handed it to him. Ace looked around quickly, unwrapped the package to see what was inside. A Ziploc bag containing an iPod Touch, a credit card size Wi-Fi router and universal charger with USB wires. shocked All the moisture was shocked out of his mouth. He couldn't believe the sight in his lap. His dry lips opened and closed with a question that wouldn't quite come out, only making a clicking noise in the silent cubicle.

Cole chuckled at his reaction. "That shit looks tight, but I don't know how you're gonna use it. That new cellphone jammer they put outside won't let any calls go out. I have to drive about two miles away before my phone will work," he said, eyeing the electronics with an expression that showed he knew very little about technology.

Ace's shaking hands hurriedly rolled the paper towels around the bag again. Licking his lips, he said, "That jammer will block the Three-G network almost completely. This," he indicated the package, "is a Mi-Fi router that works on the Four-G network, and has enough bandwidth to get around that jammer. The Four-G Long-Term Evolution is the best network."

"Guess your people knew that, huh? Can you make calls on it?"

"Yeah. The iPod connects to the Mi-Fi. You can download an app called Text free with Voice and make Internet calls. Or do it with the Skype app."

"Skype. I've heard of that."

"Social network. Mostly video chat and phone calls."

"Damn, big guy. You're in there," Cole said, holding his fist out for a bump. Ace obliged him and they smiled at each other. Cole stood up. "Better find a good hiding place. If K-Nine or ERT finds that, your 'I am innocent' ass will go to lockdown for a good six months. Maybe catch a charge, too. That's a felony." He started to walk away, business finished. Another day at the office.

Ace stopped him. "Wait! Who gave you this?" He glanced around, lowered his voice. "I have to know."

Cole eyed him suspiciously for a few seconds. "You really don't know, do you?"

"Wish I did. I honestly don't know what the hell is going on. The last thing I expected was an officer to hand me an electronic felony."

Cole walked back to the cubicle and said, "You ever hear of El Maestro?"

"The Teacher? Heard of him, yeah."

"Big time cartel leader. Mexican guy. The Latin Kings around here idolize him. The real LKs, the Mexicans. Not those poor Mississippi white boys that got tricked into joining. Anyway. He pays well," he said, grinning and rubbing his index finger and thumb together.

"Latin Kings? Uh. I'm not Mexican. Or a tricked affiliate."

"I guess you are now, big guy. You just have to ask yourself if you're another poor Mississippi white boy that got tricked, or are you a business associate."

Cole smiled, winked, then walked to the tower. He slapped a hand on the steel door. The startled officer inside jumped awake and buzzed the door open for the lieutenant. He walked through and the door clunked shut behind him.

The low roar of the ventilation motor and distant laughter of convicts outside playing softball reassured Ace that he had privacy, at least for the moment. He ran a hand through his close cropped brown hair, blowing out a breath loudly. Glanced around for a place to stash the iPod and router, which seemed to burn with possibilities in his hands, heavy, full of promise. A hundred thoughts and emotions assaulted him all at once. His razor sharp mind prioritized each one.

I can call my son, he thought. Hell, we can video chat.

Smiling with anticipation of seeing Nolan's precious face on the touchscreen, several other scenarios rapidly overwhelmed his train of thought. His breathing and heart rate quickened, hands shaking, becoming vibrating instruments of multiple talents. Smile stretching to a grin, excitement from his dormant skills resurfacing to remind him of who he was and what he could do.

"I am the King of Hackers," he said.

Standing up, he clutched the package and began to pace back and forth between the bunk beds. Muttering, fingers twitching as if typing on a keyboard. There is plenty of lightweight hacking I could do with this baby, he pondered, recalling his old job as the top hacker at Wikileaks. Or 'researchers' as they liked to title the position.

All those iPhones I broke into or cloned that belonged to top military brass - I could recite the specifications in my sleep! This iPod Touch has the same interface and software capabilities as an iPhone...

"Ha!" he gloated as more ideas occurred, mind racing faster as his hacker's criminal mind took over, making a mental checklist of larger systems the iPod could access and control for even larger hack jobs. I could get transferred to CMCF and be closer to Clarice. Or send her 'legal mail' with any message I want, he considered, chest tightening at the thought of his wife.

I miss her so much!

An epiphany stopped him dead in his tracks, striking like a bullet, the train of thoughts colliding with an immovable wall of precedence. He now knew what must be done. What had to be done, and what was now possible because of the priceless fortune in his hands. Forget Skyping with Nolan. Or sending messages to Clarice.

I can be with them again, in person, he decided. *I can organize an escape. Mine and hers.*

A draft cooled the sweat that had appeared on his forehead. As he snapped out of his dazed contemplation, he started pacing again, muttering, "Son of a bitch. El Maestro, who the hell are you?"

Chapter X

Central Mississippi Correctional Facility
Pearl, Mississippi
March 1, 2012

Rude people suck, Clarice thought. Mosquitoes showed more courtesy than the ignoramuses in this joint. At least mosquitoes had a legitimate reason for their abusive behavior. The COs and administrators couldn't make that claim. Like the idiot pounding on her cell door at just that minute. Wham! Wham! Like a Neanderthal with a tusk club. *Ugh, me stupid cavewoman. Me no respect people. Ugh!* Couldn't be a polite knock, a light civilized tap of inquiry.

No. Just bludgeon the damn thing and show your true stupid blue colors.

Idiot.

She briefly considered playing opossum. Like the psych patients did sometimes. Then again, she thought, that sort of childishness would only perpetuate the rudeness, drive up the impatience level. That was the reason they did it; they threw a blanket treatment over all the prisoners, even the ones that didn't cause any trouble, because past experiences with immature prisoners had drained them of patience and courtesy. Or else, they were just mean.

Still, she didn't agree with that treatment, or any form of group punishment. Especially when it was directed at *her*. So she lay in her bed ignoring the loud, vaguely female voice demanding she come to the door. Spite was one of her few indulgences these days, and this psych patient opossum stuff was kinda fun.

Smiling, she rolled over, pulled the sheet over her head and said, "But I don't wanna go to school!"

"I'll write your ass up, convict! I'll make sure you get more lockdown time. Now bring your Lindsay Lohan-looking ass to this door!" the CO yelled.

The woman's fuming, spitting impatience gave Clarice the petty gratification she needed, so she dragged the sheet off herself, stepped into her shower shoes and padded to the door. Squatted down to peek out the tray slot at the officer who was already in the top five of Clarice's *Rude People That Suck* list.

"What's your name, convict?" demanded a tall black woman with captain's bars on the shoulders of her white shirt. Her forehead appeared to bulge from a tight ponytail, a weave of long hair pulled severely away from an almost masculine face. Strong cleft chin, long nose that extended in proportion to her forehead. Beady, creepy eyes. Her wide jaw muscles flexed as she smacked gum right in Clarice's face, bent over looking at her through the slot.

Smacking six inches from someone was rude and disgusting, Clarice thought. *Yeah? Wet, juicy, popping smacks. And the gum isn't doing anything to help her breath. Gross.*

The thought must have telegraphed on Clarice's face. The CO's gaze narrowed sharply.

"Clarice Carter, J-one-three-three-two," Clarice said, leaning back a little and holding her breath. She watched the CO's mouth cycle like a cow chewing a cud. She closed her eyes and suppressed a shiver.

"You got your job back, convict," the CO said. Then spat a stream of thick brown juice that hit the floor with such volume it sounded like a spilled drink.

She's chewing freaking tobacco! What the hell? Clarice couldn't recall ever seeing a woman with that nasty habit. It was beyond her comprehension as to how a woman could do that and still wear long hair, nails, and makeup.

Bizarre. Her throat burned as she tried not to vomit. *Eww.* "Um," she replied. "Great. I guess."

"Damn right it's great, convict. You can start by cleaning that shit up." She pointed at the tobacco spit.

Clarice's throat burned again, but with anger, heating her face and arms to the point she thought she would start emitting incandescent flares. "What's your name, Captain?" she growled, choking down several names that begged to form on her lips. She almost giggled, and the anger started to dissipate. Laughter really was the best medicine.

The CO's eyes flashed and narrowed again. "Correctional Commander Portsmouth," she growled back, managing to make it a snide remark, as if she wanted to offend Clarice with it.

What the hell was this broad's deal?

"What's the deal?" Clarice frowned, genuinely interested in the woman's motives. Besides being a nut job, something else was off here. Something that didn't equate with the take-everything-and-lock-'em-down mentality that was the norm for crazy, lazy officers like her.

"What are you bumping your gums about convict?"

"How did I get my job back while I'm in lockdown? And do I call you 'Correctional Commander' or 'Captain'?"

"You get your job back because I say so. Getting caught trying to get a cell phone in ain't no thing. You ain't no security risk. And maybe I like seeing your little cream tail shaking behind a broom. Maybe I don't. And you can call me 'Commander' or 'Captain' because that's what I be doing to you. Commanding and Captaining," she said, talking louder as she finished, standing up straight and putting hands on hips. Thick gold and platinum blinged from every finger. She spat again for emphasis. Even her chewing got louder.

Clarice failed to suppress the shiver this time. "Gosh, Captain. How can I refuse such a compelling personality?"

The woman shifted her weight to the other foot. Rolled her neck. "You ain't got no choice, Cream Tail. Nam! Now shut your sporty mouth and get dressed. You start now." She spat again, this time on Clarice's door, covering her tray hole with tobacco ick. Bubbles stewed in dark, stinking saliva. She walked away. A moment later her boots thumped heavily down the stairs. The zone door buzzed open, slammed shut behind her. Clarice let out a long sigh and grabbed a pair of yellow pants out of her locker box. Lockdown wear. She slipped them over men's boxer shorts that she wore like most of the other women did, white Bob Barker deals that hung to her knees and always embarrassed her by showing her panties through the penis access hole in the front.

Yep. This is what my life has become.

"Wrong. Just wrong," Clarice muttered, looking around her cell and hating it. She actually felt glad to be able to clean up Captain Yuckmouth's mess just to be able to get the hell out of the cell and move around some. The woman knew that, too. She had Clarice's number. She doubtless treated everyone else she had leverage on the same way. Probably did the same thing to her family.

Wow. I wonder if that thing has kids.

Nah. I doubt there's a man on this planet desperate or brave enough to hit that.

Feeling a little better with that façade of logic, Clarice murmured a quick prayer for children she didn't know and hoped didn't exist, just in case. Slipped on her shoes and tucked in her shirt, shivering as a blast of wind seeped through her window. She turned and looked up at the vents above the door and smirked. *My husband's farts blow warmer air than that heater. Piece of crap.*

She opted to leave the yellow uniform top off. Regulations be damned: she would rather freeze and risk a write-up than wear something that made her look like a sack of potatoes. (Tom boy, cute. Farm boy, *no.*)

Peeking out of her tray slot again, across the zone at the guard tower window, she searched for signs of movement that would indicate someone was awake and about their job. A silhouette moved. A big one, bigger than Clarice's upper body. Considering the diet and fashion in these parts, she determined it was just an obese woman's head with a cheap wig. She stuck her arm out and waved at it. "Hey! Officer in the tower! Let me out. I'm the floor walker!" she yelled, voice echoing as if she had shouted into a cave.

Several women came to their doors to investigate. The head in the tower bobbed up and down, looking in Clarice's direction. Or at least she thought so. Her door buzzed, clicked, opened. She walked out into air that felt like a cold spring morning, but smelled like feet and ass. They certainly needed someone to clean up around here. She was happy to do it.

I do not like the way this is going.

Her next step plopped into a puddle of spit, instantly staining the white canvas material her shoes were made of. "Yuckmouth bitch," she grumbled. "Lovely. Just fucking lovely."

Standing on one foot, she shook the other, slinging brown drool all over the floor. Giggles, then full-throated laughter pealed out of the cells on both sides of her. It was contagious. Really, the situation was so damn ridiculous Clarice just had to laugh. She looked at her neighbors and grinned, shaking her head in a *What Can I Do?* gesture.

Downstairs a door boomed from a massive blow. A powerful strike from a huge arm, a fist that had to be calloused like leather from such impacts all day and night. Tough girl posturing that could only come from one person.

"Boogerilla. You sexy hooker. You must have smelled me come out," Clarice said as the big woman struck the door again. She walked past several cells on her way to the stairs. Women watched her from their windows or tray slots, oddly quiet, like animals that sensed a storm was on the way. Clarice felt it, too. And wondered what would entice such distinctive intuition. Whatever it was, it didn't feel good.

It felt like trouble. Serious, mean biker granny panties trouble.

Boogerilla punched her door again, then yelled out of her slot at the tower. "Hey Officer Abrams! Captain Portsmouth gave me a job, too. Let me out so I can clean the showers!"

Uh-oh.

Clarice stepped to the handrail and looked down. A door buzzed open under her, the click of the heavy lock vibrating the metal under her hands, jolting her heart into a higher gear. Her lungs took the cue, inhaling deeply to pump her muscles full of oxygen for fuel, bellows feeding a fire until it roared with extreme energy. The cool air around her heated slightly from thermal radiation as her whole body primed for fight mode. An instinctual process that was a warm, pleasant rush, tingling with heightened senses and a promise of explosive, scary movement that could only end badly for the person on the receiving end of it.

Goddamn, what a great FEELING!

Her mouth clicked dry, her bladder felt full, and she knew she was ready. She knew what was coming. She'd thought about it for weeks, ever since this booger bear first threatened her. The booger and the other one, the knife maker. Chiquita. Clarice's fighter mentality had instantly analyzed them both and devised a game plan should they ever get a chance to make good on their threats.

Like right now.

A big girl like the Booger would run into a lot of problems going up against a trained pro that was slicker and faster than her. She was a schoolyard bully, a brute that would throw wide, looping punches, easy to block or counter. Though Clarice doubted she would have to do all that. If her plan worked, the Booger wouldn't get to throw a single punch.

Boogerilla walked right past Clarice's mop bucket and cleaning supplies. Grunted as her foot hit the first step and she started climbing, talking trash up the entire flight of stairs. Clarice guessed the woman was boosting her confidence more than trying to scare her. The Booger looked up at her and Clarice was sure of her plan the. It would work.

Let her believe I'm scared to death. She'll underestimate me. And I'll Shocker.

Hee-hee. This will be fun.

"I told you, white-bread ho!" the Booger bellowed up. "I told you I'd get your ass. It's on like Donkey Kong." She punctuated this prestigious statement with a crazy bark, a clipped explosion of her vocal cords that made someone squeak in a cell behind Clarice. Hatred twisted her face into a god-awful snarl, lifting her wide, plump cheeks back like hackles on a mastiff, baring teeth with driving energy and combat readiness. Her hair was shaped in a tall, thick Afro, clumped down on one side, making her head and neck look gargantuan, otherworldly, a beast from a low budget B movie. She wore a yellow uniform top, no t-shirt underneath, the dark skin of her upper breasts showing through the v-neck, more of a chest than a bosom. Huge shoulders and arms that made the 5XL sleeves look like Spandex. Barrel-shaped torso with rolls of flab a Sumo wrestler would envy.

Sheesh.

Her legs were short, but each as big as Clarice's waist, pulsing under yellow pants like columns of animated marble. Stomping down on shoes that bulged on the outsides from at least two-hundred-and-sixty pounds threatening to rip them open with every step. Clarice did a double-take, focusing on the woman's surprisingly small feet. They were wide, but short, abnormally out of proportion with her top-heavy body.

Yeah, she'll run into some problems. Literally.

"She'll come forward with no balance," Clarice muttered, then backed away to initiate her plan. Eyes wide, she held up her hands, a frightened posture, pleading. She shook her head as if she couldn't believe this was happening and was about to pee in her panties. "NO!" she cried in a high-pitched trill. "I'm sorry! I haven't done anything to you. Why are you doing this?"

Backing away along the tier, Clarice found it a chore to keep from laughing at herself. She could land an acting gig with this performance. Every cell door she passed had a head in the window. They stared, anxiously, excited about the drama unfolding and hoping it would become even more entertaining. A feeling Clarice could relate to. It was boring in here.

Well, let's not disappoint them, a voice whispered from the electrified part of her mind. *There's nothing else to do around here.*

"Oh, hell no," Boogerilla said, slowing her storming charge to a swaggering stalk. Confident she had her prey cornered and wanting to taunt and tease for the benefit of others. "I be boss bitch around here, you feel me? Real talk. You said all that tough shit while

I was behind that door and you felt safe. Now I'm gonna make you hold up for it." She stopped, looked around. "I be BOSS BITCH!" she roared. Clarice pictured her beating her chest while baring her teeth again. She gave several more battle cries, looking around at the other women to make sure she had their attention and were interested in watching the annihilation of this white-bread ho that had challenged her status.

Clarice freaked out, screamed with hands shaking on the sides of her face, pigeon toed, knees bent and saturated in terror. Then she turned and took off, running away from the scary giant that would certainly squash her like the pathetic gnat she was. "Nooo! Please don't!" she screamed, her little feet gliding lightly, in perfect balance over the floor.

Boogerilla charged instantly, and rather impressively for a big gal. Like a football linebacker spearing for a tackle she rushed after Clarice, whose pretend-scared legs must have lost their energy, *uh-oh*, allowing the Booger to gain a few seconds. As her heavy steps hammered behind, one-two-three, Clarice timed them, determined the woman was up to speed, spun around in a one-eighty pivot, hands up, weight centered, chin down and eyes beaming straight into the Booger's with boiling rage and unshakeable conviction that she would beat the woman senseless.

Time slowed, megamo, adrenaline hyping senses. The Booger saw Clarice spin around and crouch. Her fists, *Seek and Destroy*, rose in the Booger's direction with a look in her eyes that inexplicably zapped the energy that the woman had planned to demolish her with. The Booger faltered, her equilibrium wavered, her nervous system too sluggish to do anything about it. Confusion, then realization that she had been tricked, crossed her features a split second before she tried and failed to hit the brakes.

But it was way past too late.

"I was just kidding," Clarice said, shifting her weight forward and to her left, throwing an overhand right from the hip. Like a pitcher winding up to throw a fastball, her arm launched with slingshot action, forearm flexing, fist tightening right as it hit her in the face. The woman's forward momentum and weight compounded the punch with devastating results. Her knuckles crashed into her upper teeth and nose, crushing them. The bridge of bone and cartilage flattened between her eyes, tearing skin, instantly swelling both eyes shut with the trauma. Boogerilla wailed in startled pain as she plowed into Clarice's right shoulder and spun to the ground, huge body following an unperceiving head. Clarice pivoted to slip around her. Centered weight on her toes, hands raised for more action. Then stepped away from her opponent looking for a neutral corner while the referee did his thing.

"Christ," Clarice said, closing her eyes and shaking her head. "I'm not in a ring. I'm not even a boxer anymore." Looking up, she saw several women looking at her with open mouths. Laughing and clapping started from nearly every cell, muffled from behind the steel doors but still uproarious enough to make the joint sound like a real fight crowd. One of those things she hadn't known how much she missed, until she heard it.

I've missed that sound. So bad.

Boogerilla stirred on the floor, mewling the wet nasal sounds a person makes when knocked unconscious with a severely broken nose.

I've missed that sound, too. Ah, good times.

The Booger's hands flapped weakly around her head, which was pressed to the floor like a Muslim prostrating herself to Allah, butt in the air, stretched out with arms in the front. A position her body wasn't designed for. It looked painful.

So did the puddle of blood leaking from her nose. Clarice could smell it.

Ouch.

The thought of pain awakened Clarice's own. Her wrist, numb a second ago, throbbed and shouted at her every curse word in the book.

"Son of a mmm," she said, sucking in a breath and wincing. She grabbed her right wrist, squeezing like that would make it stop aching. It didn't. Opening her eyes, she looked at it. No protruding shards of bone or bulging deformations like her nerves told her were there. She tucked her arm under her boobs, gave Boogerilla another glance then walked back to her cell. This injury should get her some time off work. Hopefully. Or cost her the job. Likely.

Like I really gave a flying hoo-hah. One punch KO, biatch! That's what really matters, ladies and gentlemen.

Is there a better feeling than when a serious problem is solved, perfectly, according to plan? Clarice's wrist screamed bloody murder, but she couldn't think of a more satisfying emotion than the pure ecstasy coursing through her limbs at that moment. *Vivacious, baby.*

She walked into her cell and lay down on the bed. Smiling, unable to feel the crude discomfort of the mattress for the floating, drugged euphoria that levitated her into another reality. A sense of peace and sureness asserted itself in her mind. Comfortable thoughts familiar to her like a favorite cousin coming home after being away for years, welcomed with open arms by loved ones.

Why did I ever stop doing this? Fighting is in my blood, my first love, and will always and forever be my proudest talent.

The pulsating, rhythmic Feel-Good dope tingled in her hair and zinged in her loins. Her toes curled, and she stretched, groaning in a state of enjoyment that far surpassed the deepest levels of infatuation.

She was in love again. Completely, utterly in love. A fight junkie.

A loud clapping snapped her out of my reverie. She opened her eyes and looked at her cell door, which was closed but not locked. When she figured out that the clapping wasn't coming from another cell, she sat up, feet on the floor, and listened to the applauding hands approach.

"Bravo, Cream Tail," Captain Portsmouth said, opening my door, looking in at me. She clapped a few more times, then took a small camcorder from under her arm and waved for Clarice to come to her.

Frowning suspiciously, Clarice stood, walked the six feet to the door. "She started it," she said in an uncaring tone. She crossed her arms and looked at the video camera. Intuition kicked in hard, blaring a warning that a storm was brewing, and it wasn't going to be pretty. No rainbows. It dawned on Clarice that ERT or at least a herd of officers should have rushed in to stop the fight, and maybe even to kick the two women to sleep (or just Clarice, since Boogerilla was already snoozing...)

Clarice looked behind the Captain and said, "Um. This may sound odd. But why aren't I on the floor with a dozen boots upside my head, choking on pepper spray?"

For an answer, the woman simply smiled. A horrible, slow spreading thing that made horns extend from her already bulging forehead. A *cat ate the canary* smile. Thunder and lightning should have accompanied that look, ripping and booming above her head. Captain Stormmouth flipped open the camcorder's LCD screen. Powered it on. Pressed playback and waved an invitation for Clarice to view it with her. Clarice was too curious to tell her to *go sit on it*, so she stepped next to the woman and hoped she wouldn't catch any flesh eating diseases.

The video showed the zone from the guard tower's perspective. Thirty cells on bottom, thirty up top with a guard rail around the horseshoe-shaped tier. Four steel picnic tables bolted to the dayroom floor, spaced between the cells and the tower. Women looked out of their windows or tray holes.

A cell door on the top tier opened, the lock a faint snick across the cavernous zone. Clarice recognized her cell. She came out, glancing around. Took a step forward and froze. Lifted a foot and shook it as if trying to dislodge a dog turd. Looked at her neighbors, shoulders shaking with laughter.

Whoa. I look goofy!

Clarice had never seen a video of herself, other than fight tapes. Reality star material she was not.

The Goofy Clarice walked toward the stairs and paused as Boogerilla's bellowing voice megaphoned out of her tray slot, heard distinctly inside the tower, sounding just as crude and annoying on a video recording. Worse. A synthesizer probably couldn't have helped that guttural roar. Her titanic head blacked out the entire slot. She stood and the hole blinked with light. *Jeepers creepers.* The soft click of a lock and her door burst open as she charged straight for the stairs.

Wow. She looked twenty pounds heavier on video. Even managed to look more menacing as she trash-talked her way up the stairs. Our verbal exchange came through the camcorder's speakers in Stereo. Goofy Clarice morphed into Scared Clarice, did the freak-out, the backing away from an axe murderer bit... Clarice's opinion of reality show stardom changed.

She was pretty dang good at bringing the drama.

"Like you was really scared, Cream Tail," the captain said, chuckling. "That was mighty fine. I've never seen a fake-out like that before, and I've seen a lot of fights."

Clarice looked at the woman and almost started laughing with her. Praise was praise, and people respond to it even when coming from idiots. She looked back at the camera as Boogerilla started her war cries. Captain Portsmouth's chuckle turned into a full laugh, eyes squinting closed, making a face that was hard to look at or listen to. The LCD flopped as her arms shook.

"Her black ass be doing that every time," she said, wheezing and wiping her eyes with her free hand.

"Every time?" Clarice inquired.

She smiled her stormy promise again, thunder and lightning ripping, tumultuous. A tornado following a revelation that Clarice wasn't anxious to hear.

On the video, Clarice's whole body flipped its wig in terror, turned and ran from a charging beast. Boogerilla gained speed and ground on Scared Clarice, who suddenly stopped, pivoted, said her badass one-liner while drilling the woman with an overhand haymaker that smacked loudly into her head. The crunch-wail-shuffling-shoes mix strained the little speakers. Portsmouth and Clarice shared a collective "ooh" and cringed.

Clarice saw and felt the damage that punch did up close. It looked even more gruesome on video. *And way cooler, too.*

Scared Clarice was Shocker Clarice, pivoting away from the falling giant, hands raised, looking for the referee like a dummy.

Clarice shook her head, looked away from the camera. Her fist throbbed to remind her that the scene wasn't fifteen minutes old. Captain Portsmouth closed the LCD, stuck the camera back under an arm and smiled. Hands on hips. Stormy grin. Approaching hurricane status. Clarice steeled herself.

"I want you to fight for me," Portsmouth said.

Shit! I knew it. Clarice didn't say anything.

This was not happening. Un-freaking-believable.

"That video was streamed live on the Internet. We have almost a half-million viewers, and we get more with every fight."

"We?"

"We've never had a one-punch KO. Of course, we've never had a professional boxer either."

"Let me get this straight." Clarice unfolded her arms. "You set me up to fight Boogerilla, and made money for whoever 'we' is. And now you expect me to fight for you on a regular basis. Is that right?"

"That's right, Cream Tail. Pretty and smart. You the new star. You just knocked off the champ."

"I don't want it. I don't want any part of this. I've retired from that life," Clarice said, grimacing with reluctance as the words spilled from her lips. *What the fuck is your problem, lady?* screamed a familiar voice in her head. The fight junkie that only moments ago was lying on that bed basking in a multi-orgasmic sea. She tried to quell the wrenching urge, so she could maneuver out of this mess. To work for this broad would be a disaster in the making. Hell, she didn't even want to clean the floor on her shift! The woman kept smiling at Clarice with absolute surety that she would own her. Clarice got a sinking feeling in her gut.

The fight junkie was jumping up and down in her head, pumping her mental fist with a cheer. She wanted to fight! *Bring 'em on!*

Crap.

"Oh, I think you do want it, Cream Tail. Everyone has a price," the woman said, pulling out a wad of cash from her shirt pocket. Peeling off a hundred dollar bill, she handed it to Clarice. "My girls get a hundred bones a fight. And a fifty dollar bonus if you get a knockout." She peeled off a fifty, dangled it in front of her face.

With a mind of its own, Clarice's traitorous hand reached out and took it.

Holding the bills was empowering, a unique rush in its own right. She used to fiend for this stuff. Money. The texture, the smell brought out feelings of success and vivid, positive memories. Images of good times. She hadn't even seen money in two years.

But a hundred-and-fifty for a fight? For that much work she used to get a hundred times that. More . This pocket change wouldn't be worth the wear and

169

tear her body took in training. And her aching wrist certainly suffered more than a bill-fifty in damage.

Reason and plain common sense ganged up on the fight junkie, beating her down and winning a hotly contested battle. Just barely. "I don't want it," she told Portsmouth again. She folded the bills, held them out to her. Portsmouth just looked at her hand.

Tempestuous smile appearing again, eye of a Category 5, Portsmouth grabbed the camcorder, powered it on and pointed the lens at her. "Today is March first, two-thousand-and-twelve. Approximately ten-thirty hours. Captain Portsmouth conducting security check. Offender Clarice Carter, J-one-three-three-two, found with major contraband in her possession," she said in a surprisingly clear, professional voice, zooming in on the money in her hand.

Clarice jerked her hands behind her back, stupidly, looking even more guilty for the video. Goofy Clarice.

"Offender refuses to give up the contraband. A take down team will be notified, offender will receive a Rules Violation Report." She closed the camera, smiled at Clarice. The insane bitch even waggled her eyebrows. She didn't need to say anything else.

Clarice's wrist pounded harder as her heart switched gears in outrage, telling her it would hurt but she'd have no problem sacrificing more for the sake of drilling this yeast infection in her ports mouth. The fight junkie screamed and danced, not caring who she fought for as long as she got to feel the resistance of a human body as she hit it. She suppressed the conflicted opinions and tried to get herself together. She was in real trouble here. That video could get her at least another six months in lockdown, and a mark on her record that could affect her security level. Not conducive to her parole plans.

As her dear husband used to say, she was an inclined plane wrapped helically around an axis.

Screwed.

"Oh my, Captain. I wonder if you realize how persuasive your charm is. Of course I'll accept your most gracious offer," she said through gritted teeth, eyes narrowed.

Portsmouth chortled happily, clapping. "I'm glad you came around, Cream Tail. You just remember who be your captain and you'll do okay, hear?"

"Yeah. I hear you."

"Right, then." She turned and walked away.

The eye of the storm moving off, the powerful feeder bands had Clarice in their grasp.

Part II

Chapter XI

Juarez, Chihuahua
Mexico
March 1, 2012

"*Con permiso*, El Maestro," Felix said, stepping into the cool office and closing the door behind him. The density of the colder air clashed with the warm rush of outside, a hallow vacuum abruptly cut off as the thick oak door sealed shut. Mesquite particles stirred around the entrance and covered his dark brown hair, which poured sweat, staining his collar. A red grease rag twisted and strained in his hands in front of him. He stuck it in a pocket of his coveralls, kept his head bowed and eyes averted as he waited on his liege to take a break.

El Maestro finished sorting through a dossier on his desk, closed it and looked up. "*Hola*, Felix. Is there something I can do for you?"

After the long wait Felix needed a moment to reorganize his thoughts before answering. The air conditioner gave such a blissful relief from the hot desert afternoon that he nearly forgot the reason for leaving the mechanic shop to interrupt his boss's busy schedule. Phones from a desk in the backroom rang, reminding him of his quest. "You asked Erik and me to monitor the accounts and GPS on *los gringos'* phones," he said.

"Yes. And are they active?"

"Yes and no. The *gringo's* signal is working properly. La *gringa's* phone was on when it was given to her maestro. I follow the-"

"Followed."

"*Gracias.* I followed the signal to the prison, then it disappeared. Something had to have go, uh, gone wrong."

"Is the gentleman's account active?"

"*Si*, El Maestro. He uses the iPod and router in the mornings and late at night. But we can't track the sites he frequents. The cookies never appear in the servers. Should we assign the maids to investigate?" he queried.

El Maestro gave a secret smile. "No, thank you. That would be superfluous."

"Why do you say that?" Felix said, perplexed. "The maids can hack anything."

"The gentleman is in a class of his own when it comes to technology. They would be chasing a ghost."

"So, he is like the *chupacabra* of the Internet, eh?" he said. They shared a chuckle.

El Maestro pointed a finger at him, a mock scolding. "Don't joke about *la chupacabra*, Felix. He's real," he said. Felix burst into laughter, but quieted to a smile when his boss waved a hand. "Who gave the phone to the lady's father?" he said, leaning back in his chair. It creaked. The phones continued to ring.

"Señor Eddy," he replied, wondering how the man knew the father was the one to smuggle in the cell phone. Fascinating. He said, "I brought the E and E package to Antonio at the gym in the city. He drove to Mississippi to meet Eddy. He say, he said, they were old friends from boxing. Antonio also found an officer at the *gringo's* prison who does business with La Familia."

"A Chicano officer?"

"No, Señor. A negro lieutenant," Felix replied, embarrassed, as if it were his fault the Mexican race hadn't done a better job infiltrating the prison. "We had no one there, other than a few low-level Latin Kings. And they were prisoners."

El Maestro closed his eyes, shook his head. "Mississippi. Ay, iy, iy," he muttered. The phones finally stopped, ring tones echoing faintly. He leaned forward, looked into Felix's eyes. "Find out what happened to the phone we sent the lady. Make sure she gets another one. Use whatever resources you need. And tell Elena to give Antonio the usual bonus."

"*Si*, El Maestro," he said, bobbing his head enthusiastically.

El Maestro waved a dismissive hand as he picked up the phone, started dialing. Felix bobbed his head once more, turned around slowly, posturing subordination and respect. Walked to the door.

The scorching sun and dry wind welcomed him back to reality. Disillusioned, the hulking mechanic looked back at the chilled building with yearning and felt like a child about to throw a tantrum after seeing the ice cream wagon gallop away. Laughing at himself, he set out to find Erik so they could devise a plan to get a phone in to the *gringa* boxer.

How hard could that be?

Chapter XII

Central Mississippi Correctional Facility
Pearl, Mississippi
March 2, 2012

"Hey, look who's back," Patty called out as Clarice walked into the cubicle.

Clarice set a bulging pillowcase on her bed, a makeshift rucksack she had used since day one in the system. Various hygiene containers clacked together inside. She looked at Patty, tired, and struggled up a smile. "What are you doing up so early?" she asked.

Several women in nearby cubicles stirred, rolled over. One directed an angry sleepy eye at her and Clarice felt like a klutz, becoming aware of how much racket she was making. After the non-stop noise of the beasts in lockdown, she wasn't used to the quiet, soft rustling and snores of early morning sleep in a more civilized zone.

Patty smirked. "You know, they say only hookers and crack heads are up this early. So what does that tell you about me?" she said, eyes kindling with more than mischief.

"Um. You're hustling the male officers and smoking weed?"

"Like a motherfucker," Patty said, standing up. "*Got me feeling hella good - so I'm gonna keep on dancing,*" she sang, twirling an arm above her head, stepping in a circle. The angry sleepy eye beamed open at her, accompanied by a grunt that clearly meant *please shut the fuck up.*

Even acting like a clown, Patty looked like a fearless Viking princess. Big, strong, intense. And friendly. Clarice had missed her easy smile and constant humor, qualities that were rare in here. She held a hand pressed to her lips, trying to contain the high-pressured laugh that elated her stomach and throat. Attempted to unpack with the other. Opened her locker box and used toilet tissue to wipe out the dust. Neatly lined up hygiene products and folded clothes.

Patty sauntered over and looked in, whistled. "Damn, girl. You need some canteen. You're already cut up like Jesus. If your locker box stays anorexic like that you'll look like one of the Olson twins. Cute, but scrawny."

"You're right. We weren't allowed canteen in lockdown and I don't know how I'll get it now that my parents can't send me money."

"The po-lice banned your folks from sending canteen money?" she said incredulously, whistling again.

"Crazy, huh?"

"For sure. But don't worry your scrawny Olson self. I know how you can make some cheese."

"How?"

"Fighting," she said pointing at her wrist, which was wrapped up in a tube sock. She put on a sly smile, nodding with eyes half closed in an *I Know What You Did* look.

"You heard about that already? It was only yesterday," Clarice said, though she wasn't surprised. Gossip travels fast among women as a general rule. How fast do you think news spreads amongst two-thousand women stuck in one place with nothing better to do than talk about each other? Add cell phones and trustees passing notes and the entire compound could get word of your business in a matter of hours.

"Heard about it? Hell, I have the video." She looked around, stuck a hand down the front of her pants and said, "Crazy, huh?" in perfect imitation of Clarice, pulled out a kickass Motorola smartphone that attached to the inside of her pants by a clasp and string. Waving her over to her bed, they sat down and Clarice got to see Boogerilla eat her best punch again. It was no less impressive the third time.

"Ooh," they said together, cringing.

"Everyone in the fight clique is talking about you. Some say you were lucky. Most of us think you are the real McCoy," Patty said, sticking the phone back in her pants.

"We? You fight, too?"

"Sure. I make more playing the men's flutes and rattles, but I like a little smack down on occasion. Win some, lose some." She punched her palm. "Anyway, I'm with the group that thinks you're for real. I've seen about a dozen of your pro fights on YouTube, and there's no refuting that shit. You got some serious pizzazz, Olson. I'm a fan."

"Thanks."

"So, you one of Portsmouth's girls now?"

"I guess so. Didn't really have a choice. That crazy-ass broad set me up. Got me on video with cash in my hand."

"Yeah. That's her style. She caught me with three COs. I'm pretty sure she arranged it, though I haven't figured out how."

"Three?!" Clarice choked out, trying to keep her voice down. "What happened?"

"Well, it was two men, one Big Bertha looking hooker, and a small storage closet. There wasn't much room, and they were all nervous and shit. So I took the initiative, dropped my drawers and rang the dinner bell. Portsslut busted in with her camera, and you can imagine what happened after that. The COs became her lackeys, and she got a few fights out of me before I told her she could stick that video in her fat mammy's cellulite cratered ass."

"She let you off?"

"Yep. She knows I don't care about lockdown. Six months in the hole ain't shit. I have a life sentence to worry about. Fuck her." Her eyes widened as something occurred to her. She twisted to look at her. "You have forty calendars yourself, Olson. Why'd you let her sweat you like that?"

"Uh..." Clarice trailed off, thinking fast. She didn't want to lie to Patty, but she didn't know if she could trust her to keep quiet about her plans. Clarice looked at her long and hard, analyzing what she knew of Patty and considering her potential for gossip. She couldn't recall Patty talking about serious business and dropping names, telling exactly who was breaking the rules or laws. Her drug and prostitute stories were always told without names. Clarice decided a test would give her the information she needed. She had to be able to trust *somebody* in here.

Clarice hoped it would be her.

"Before I answer that, let me ask you something," she said.

"Say it."

"Who brought you that phone?"

She smiled, shook her head. "Olson we can talk about contraband all you want. But I don't discuss people that get it for me. Not gonna happen."

Clarice grinned at her and she narrowed her eyes, confused and suspicious. "Exactly the answer I needed to hear," she told her.

"Say again?"

"I need to trust you with something. I want to." Clarice took a deep breath, let it out. "I'm planning to escape soon. That's why I couldn't do six months in lockdown."

Patty's mouth dropped open. She stared at her, searching her face, hoping it was a joke. "Goddamn, Olson. I wish you hadn't told me that."

"You can call me Shocker."

"Okay, I'll go for that. I am shocked."

"You've been here for ten years, Patty. You know how other people have escaped in the past, or you know the people personally."

"I do. And I only know them because they were caught. If they'd gotten away, I would never have met them and only known their escape history from the papers. Trust me, you don't want to try what they did. Do you really want to attempt something that no one's ever been able to pull off?" She said it with compassion, a sad frown pulling at her normally cheerful face.

Clarice smiled and grabbed her shoulder. "I'm not like those other women," she said quietly.

Patty looked into Clarice's eyes and started leaning away, wary of the fierce intensity that was zinging from Clarice's irises. "Obviously," she said. She looked down, frown turning thoughtful as the revelation sank in.

Clarice was happy with her reaction. Patty didn't want to know about it. Women that were Nosy Nikis are the ones to worry about. She was sure she could trust Patty and confide in her whenever she needed advice or resources. Escaping from a maximum security prison was going to be one hell of a ride, and she'd need a few trustworthy mechanics to make sure her car got to the Finish line. All Patty needed now was a Custom Ace blue camo technician suit, with Viking horns as a name badge backdrop and PATTY spelled with letters that looked like flames. She was a Team member now. Clarice told her this.

"You designed your own mechanic and tattoo artist uniforms? That's so cool. The only thing I can sew is my fingers." She held up her large hands, raised her eyebrows.

"I didn't do the sewing. Just the art portion of it." Clarice paused. "On another note, I was thinking about building a tattoo machine and trying to get some supplies from the clinic. Do a few tatts to fatten up the parole fund. I'm sure I could make ten bucks an hour around here. I used to get two-hundred an hour for my work." Clarice stopped as an idea formed, then swatted Patty's leg. "Would you like to see what I can do?"

"Hell yeah. You can get down?"

"Go to Tattoology dotcom and click on my portfolio."

"Got it," Patty responded, looking around real quick before taking her phone out again. She logged on to the website in seconds, and was paging in awe through close-up photos of tattoos on Clarice's former customers.

Clarice leaned over to look at the screen. The sight of her shop in the background brought a lump to her throat. All of a sudden, she could feel the soft stool she had sat on while working on people of all ethnicities and personalities. She could hear the music and smell the disinfectants. She could feel the ambiance of the world-class studio.

Dammit.

The lump turned into a boulder. "Turn that off," Clarice said.

Patty looked at her, inquisitive, then said, "You're really passionate about it, huh?" She winked. "Being passionate about something you're great at is something I understand, Shocker. Me love you long time," she said in an Asian accent, hump dancing for emphasis. Clarice burst out laughing and had to wipe tears out of her eyes.

Patty nodded at her response, pleased to have turned her mood, then put her phone away. "You can build a tattoo gun?" she inquired.

"It's a machine. I was a metal fabrication specialist on the street. I can build anything," Clarice said with more than a hint of pride. Hey, it's not bragging if it's true. No false modesty here.

Patty's eyebrows came up again. "I believe it. Well, I can get you the dirt from the clinic. And maybe you can get with our scrub cube mate on the machine. She has one already."

"Yolanda does tattoos?" Clarice sputtered skeptically. "I bet everyone she worked on got infections!"

"I know. She's not exactly the cleanest person. And that machine sounded like something you'd buy in the lawn and garden section."

"That's horrible," Clarice complained. She took the tattoo business very seriously, following the professional ethics fanatically. Like a doctor takes an oath to always do what's right for their patients, her customers got one-hundred percent of her attention when considering biological safety. Whenever she saw or heard of slacker artists that neglected to create sterile fields around their machine and clean fields around their work area, she wanted to step in and stop the madness. Go to their studio or home and shut them down. Drill them with the procedures and discipline so they could honor the profession as they should.

You amateur ink slingers better not slip...

She looked around for Yolanda, a scalding rebuke prepared. No sign of her. "Where is she?" she grumbled.

Patty's sly smile resurfaced. "She went on court order. Had her drawers jerked up her cakes about something. Might've been the comment I made about her mustache looking better than Burt Reynolds'."

"Yeah, that's probably it."

"Come on, forget about her for now. Let's go outside," she suggested, leaning over to open her locker box.

"Sure."

Clarice stood, stretched. Cake wrappers crinkled loudly and Patty stood up with a Honey Bun jutting out of her mouth, smiling around it. Clarice giggled. Patty leaned down again to dig out a spare snack, stuck it in her back pocket, and must have become overly excited about the sugar rush. She tooted a quick, ripping fart that snapped her back upright with embarrassment reddening her face. The angry sleepy eye glared at her, grunting demands for silence for the second time. Patty pointed at her, finger jabbing and head nodding in her direction. The angry sleepy eye turned to her and Patty walked away quickly, fanning a hand under her nose while looking over her shoulder at her as if to ask what the hell her problem was.

It was nicely set up, and all Clarice could do was fall back on her bed and let out the pent up guffaw that couldn't possibly be held in now.

Ahhh, yeah. Clarice needed that.

A few women were awake now, shuffling around looking for their shower shoes so they could walk to the toilets. Patty and Clarice locked their boxes, left the cubicle, walking toward the tower and yard exit. They passed a slim black girl of about nineteen, sleep mussed and very beautiful. Patty turned her head and looked at the girl's backside as she passed them.

Clarice looked at Patty, mouth open in astonishment. "You just looked at that girl's butt!"

"You think she noticed?" she asked in a hopeful voice, grinning.

The laugh that came out of Clarice sounded like she was trying to hack a loogie. She didn't know how much longer she could hang out with the Viking princess before starting to hee-haw like a jackass with strep throat. Her abs were certainly getting plenty of work. They were pumped up, hard as granite. Patty could do her own ab workout video just standing around being herself while a crew filmed her. Poking around her stomach and feeling the individual muscles, Clarice decided she had buy the video. Clarice told her the idea.

"I already have some workout vids on the market," Patty replied, sticking her tongue out the side of her mouth and moving into a pumping motion with her arms and hips. Her abs did another set, burning like crazy.

Hee-haw!

Ahhh… Good stuff.

Bright morning sunlight spilled through the doorway as the yard exit buzz-clicked open. Patty danced to a song only she could hear, waving a goofy, flapping arm at the tower CO, skipping out onto the yard, high as a kite. Fresh cut grass and patches of red dirt made up the yard like a jigsaw pattern, glowing a mixture of bright yellow, greens and burnt orange from the horizontal rays of a sun still low in the sky. The air was incredibly fresh, thick and cool. A single woman jogged around the one-hundred-and-fifty yard square perimeter. Behind her, the twin fences topped with razor wire flickered with her trailing shadow. Clarice's legs became restless at the sight and started prancing of their own volition. It seemed to Clarice they were trying to tell her something.

"I need to run," she thought out loud.

"Oh, I thought you were getting hot in the ass from a contact buzz," Patty said, blowing out a cloud of reefer smoke and tapping the ash off a joint. She put her lighter down the front of her pants as natural as a person placing an item in a glove compartment, making Clarice curious about what else she might have down there. Sheesh. How big was her secret pocket?

Clarice considered the possibility that she was reacting to second-hand smoke. Then dismissed it. It seemed more likely the ants in her pants were from the workout she was about to get high on. She could get higher on running and boxing than I ever could on weed. She said as much to Patty.

"If you say so."

"I do."

We began waking a circuit, enjoying the air and the peaceful moment. Birds were going berserk in the under hanging of the roof behind them, and in the grass and dirt patches. Spring time friskiness. Female sparrows coyly fussing with multiple males. Happy pairs building nests from long strands of grass, trash debris, and one even flew by with what Clarice recognized as antenna wire stolen from a convict's window. It landed, dropped the wire, and chased its mate through tufts of clover, hopping on feet that couldn't walk because its hips were fused together.

Clarice looked back at the perimeter and her wrist throbbed, heart accelerating. She visualized herself flying around the yard in a blur, blasting by fence, buildings and convicts. The image gave her the second wind she needed. The flood of energy vaporized the effects of yesterday's ordeal, recouping stores of strength she usually only manage to recharge by quality sleep. It was a well-known but long-absent sensation that she hadn't experienced for some time, not since she last drove her El Camino and was anticipating the electric euphoria from a certain Blaster II ignition coil she had become addicted to. Clarice's body was planning to get a jumpstart, amped in anticipation, as if she were training for a pro bout. The urge felt so natural it frightened her. And it thrilled her.

The fight junkie has made me her bitch.

Hmm...

Clarice stopped and turned a slow half circle, searching the side of the building for a source of power. The dealer of her drug of choice.

Patty stopped, too, studying her through glazed eyes. "Shocker, you sure you're not high? You're acting like a snort junkie that just spotted a beach of cocaine," she observed, then touched the joint to a wallop of spit on the tip of her tongue. It fizzled out. Clarice looked at her with a grin that she knew was maniacal, stretching the cheeks of an alternate persona that gets off on challenging her physical abilities, a condition of such driving energy that medical professionals would recommend psychiatric treatment because they feared for their safety in her presence. Patty leaned away from her, blinking.

"Wanna know how I got my nickname?" Clarice said in a voice that didn't sound like her own.

"I assumed it was because of the spark plug tattooed on your shoulder. The mechanic job." She squinted. "That's not it?"

For an answer, Clarice turned and walked over to the side of the building. A metal conduit ran down the wall from the roof and ended with an electrical outlet at about knee height. Removing the two bobby pins from her bangs, Clarice squatted down and slid one pin in each slot of the socket. Touching her fingers on dew-soaked grass between her shoes, Clarice took several slow, deep breaths and tried to consult her rational self once more before she reached the point of no return.

Who was she kidding? They both knew how this would end.

Clarice grabbed the bobby pins with both wet hands and current entered her arms and felt like it shot right through her, jack-knifing her curled legs to launch her straight away from the wall and onto her back. She rolled easily with the impact, light and smooth, feet touching, jumped several feet off the ground, roaring and flexing her arms as if she were Ms. Olympia. Patty hooted out one boisterous laugh after another, holding her stomach, squinting her eyes as she watched Clarice's antics.

Several Nosy Nikis rushed out the yard door hoping they hadn't missed the drama that had caused such beastly joy. They saw Clarice jumping up and down like a PCP user about to do something insane or inhuman, and quieted their chatter at once. Clarice ignored them, finger combed her wild hair, stood completely still so she could feel every particle of her being and channel it for a singular purpose. Almost a dozen women walked out next to Patty and stared at her statue still form, and Clarice marveled at the hypersensitivity that allowed her to perceive them without looking in their direction. The channeling was coming to a critical mass, coiling, calm. A contained explosion.

BOOM! Clarice ran.

Every topographical aspect of the terrain could be felt through her thin soles. The patches of grass and clovers, the hard packed dirt and mounds and holes that were not an ideal running surface were intimately known by her Bob Barker's. Her toes were sophisticated sensors, inputting the rugged track data and instantaneously adjusting the height and length of her stride so that her feet were precisely placed with every step, propelling her as if she were running on flat ground. This extreme centeredness required a lot of effort, and it's a level of mental acuity she had only ever experienced after a dose of electrons.

She made a circuit and passed the group of women, which numbered around twenty now, and barely registered their presence. They were outside of her resolution, a blurring wall of graffiti in a subway tunnel. While she was on planet Performance, everything else existed in unconventional planes. Realities that flickered in and out, never able to tune in completely and distract her program. Some people practice meditation for decades to reach the Zen levels Clarice could attain with a mild shock and hard exercise. She knew she's reached that ultimate state when everything got slower as she got faster. She could see her thoughts and plan her movements by the millisecond, processing them accurately, in no hurry, because of the perceived slowing of time. She could throw punches faster, harder, and timed perfectly for a moving target. Her stamina improved from exacting rhythm on the muscles, contracting and releasing for optimal economy and output. Complex strategies, even mathematics, could be expressed in her head with ease. Focusing on healing could rid her body of cortisol and other stress hormones that impeded physical performance, literally healing her body with her mind. And, she could have rational, intelligent thoughts while simultaneously making her body run like a high-tech cyborg fueled by nitro.

Zen, baby. Sexy, funky Zen.

You should try it, I tell you, feeling like a pervert hustling a fetish.

Each lap measured about a quarter mile. Clarice was clocking them at eighty seconds. If her Bob Barker's didn't catch fire on the final sprint, she was pretty sure she would make two miles in ten minutes. She needed to do this every morning for a month, then up it to three miles. Add that to shadow boxing, mitt work and strength training and she'd be in fighting shape within six weeks. The problem would be maintaining that level of output without a trainer to push her. She was used to five or six fights a year, with intense training eight weeks before the bouts and light work the rest of the time. The MMA type business Clarice had been sucked into in the prison would warrant constant preparation, taking a serious toll on her body. From what she had heard, the women in the fight cliques fought every damn week.

How long could she handle that? How long before she injured more than her wrist and couldn't carry out her escape plan?

It wasn't as if Clarice could go see an orthopedic specialist about her wrist, or even a chiropractor for spinal maintenance. Any injury could prove catastrophic. Prison medical care was notoriously derelict. She needed to score a few quick knockouts, bet on herself every time, collect at least a grand in cash and get the hell out of here.

Yeah. That should just about do it.

Having cleared that burdensome hurdle, Clarice rehearsed thoughts for the future and became increasingly confident as the route solidified in the map of her mind. She had direction. She had ambition and physical ability. She glanced at Patty as she passed her and felt a warmth from her retarded cheering. She was doing jump kicks, clapping and singing an improv Shocker promotion in a horribly off-key bellow.

Clarice had support. She could do this.

The positive outlook coursed through her heated muscles as a shivering cool fire, tipping her past the sweat barrier as the supercharged power kicked in. Rivulets began streaming down her spine, slinging off her arms and legs. By the seventh lap Clarice was stealing glances at her shoes. She swore she could smell them burning.

The cluster of Nosy Niki graffiti blurred by in the tunnel for the final time, legs reciprocating from hips as torquey smooth as a Ducati V-twin as she blipped by them. She reveled in the burn, celebrating the exertion by digging deep to feel more of it. Reserve tank tapped, she powered into her highest gear, hair streaming out behind her ramrod straight. She floored it.

She clocked the eighth lap on her mental odometer and instantly focused on recovery. Walked with hands on hips, inhaling, holding deep breaths for several seconds while visualizing her leg muscles as workers that would calm and recharge if she petted them and praised the phenomenal stress they had just endured.

They burned like twin bonfires.

Her quadriceps and calves got the message. The blood receded, calcium ions settling down as the muscle cells cooled, adenosine triphosphate reuptake charging nerve plexuses for more abuse.

Clarice sighed in pleasure, the kind that comes only after experiencing pain.

New bullets in the clip, it was time to start shooting at something else. Without stopping, Clarice turned her recovery walk into a powerful lunge, fencing with stiff jabs for saber thrusts. Pivoting in increments, Clarice jabbed out a staccato clock pattern, reversed it, launched a series of hard body shots by dropping down and pushing forward off her toes. The grace and precision of the movement, the flowing speed that seemed boneless yet had the impression of great power at the same time, was like a dance, a violent tango with a phantom. The well-practiced shadowboxing drew startled expletives from the Nosy

Nickis, and enticed Patty to bust out in another THC-laced cheer.

Darting in her friend's direction, Clarice's thin soles shuffled over the grass too quickly to be seen clearly, punches blurring inches from Patty's head and body. Over and under combinations flew at her in a tremendous fury. Not one of them touched her. Patti grabbed at her eye, stomach, tongue sticking out in exaggerated pain, grimacing "Oh! Ow!" as Clarice used her for a target. Patty's comical expressions were beginning to break through Clarice's resolve, and she slowed as pleasure centers suppressed killer instinct. A smile crept onto her face.

Clarice pivoted away and chased her shadow across a patch of dirt for another twenty minutes, showering the dry areas with dark drops of sweat. Breathing fast, she dropped down without pause and started a set of pushups.

"Oh, hell no," Patty said, looking around at the other women. "I can do those. I be BOSS BITCH!" she roared, beating fists on her chest. The Boogerilla impression was spot-on, causing the crowd to erupt in laughter.

On her fifth rep, the Giggle God that Patty had summoned struck Clarice down, dropping her in the dirt. Clarice struggled with her laughter-weakened arms, planting toes and pushing out one more rep. Patty flopped down on a patch of grass, to the annoyance of several sparrows, and pumped out two pushups in perfect form. She stood, bowed for applause. It never came. Clarice took pity on her friend and gave a polite clap. She beamed at her.

A girl with her black and white pants rolled up above her knees, the one with the superb ass Patty had admired earlier, let out a musical giggle before dropping to the grass and attempting a pushup. The infectious energy she caught from them wasn't enough and she collapsed halfway through the rep. Clarice clapped for her anyway. It was a good effort. Women don't have the chest or shoulder muscles for pushups. If a girl could do one she was strong. Most of the male athletes Clarice had known could do almost a hundred without stopping. Clarice could do twenty-two before she had to do them off her knees. Clarice showed Patty's eye candy how to do them and her enthusiasm returned with another girlie chortle. She did eight pushups off her knees before her arms started wobbling, making her quit.

Clap-clap!

"You done?" Patty asked her. She picked grass from her shirt, checked her back pocket to make sure - no telling what kind of contraband was still there, walking over to her.

Clarice lay down on the grass and smiled up at her. The sun made Patty's blonde hair glow like a halo, which was oddly paradoxical when Clarice noticed her red eyes and devious expression.

"Nope. I need to borrow your legs," Clarice said.

"No prob. Just bring them back."

Clarice laughed. "Stand with your toes touching my shoulders so I can grab your ankles. I'll lift my feet to your stomach and you push them back to the ground. Hard."

"Gotcha."

After five sets of one hundred reverse sit-ups Clarice's core muscles were toast. Her shaking legs clumped to the ground and she looked up at the devious angel. Wiped sweat that stung her eyes. Dandelion and clover perfume filled her gasping mouth. "I'm done for today. Thanks," Clarice told her. Patty's face twisted with a skeptical smile. At that moment, she could have been on stage at any number of shows Clarice had seen while boxing in casinos around the world. Her goofy rubber face had a rare ability that world-class comedians would envy. It seriously enhanced the endorphin buzz that was kicking Clarice's ass from the workout. Clarice gave her a grin fit for a dental commercial. "You're looking at me like I just farted the alphabet," Clarice said. "What's the deal?"

"You're not done for today. Greenhorn."

"Yeah, so I'm green. Admittedly. Since you're such a pro at Convictism, why don't you be a dear and tell me why I'm not finished."

She reached a hand down to her. Clarice took it. Patty jerked her to her feet and looked at her with a serious expression. "The older black chick there is over the Vice Lord Flowers. They are allied with the Latin Queens. In Mississippi, anyway," she muttered, rolling her eyes. "The LQ leader is standing next to her."

Clarice looked at the Nosy Nikis and immediately noticed the group was arranged according to status. Clarice wouldn't have spotted it if Patty hadn't pointed out the two women of power. They were in the center of the group, terraced by what Clarice assumed was their lieutenants and foot soldiers. Security escorts, Clarice realized. They were all looking at Clarice and Patty.

"You think they want to cause trouble for me?" Clarice asked.

"I know they do. That little display of power you just put on demands to be challenged. Prison politics, Shock. Throw in the fact that you're one of Portsmouth's girls and it's business politics as well. You're the competition. And they know the stakes." She winked. "If it was me, I'd try to poison you, maybe get a group of chicken heads to jump you in the shower the day before we fought. Shit like that."

"You'd take me out like that?"

"Shit, baby. You? If we weren't tight you'd be one fucked up broad."

"Ah."

"But don't worry. I got your back."

Clarice absorbed what Patty said and attempted to concoct a countermeasure. Clarice hoped this wouldn't turn into a war, but was prepared to take it to that level if necessary. She was well-versed in high-stakes strategy and war tactics. Had to study it to make it in professional boxing. Her trainer, Eddy, handled the brunt of the negotiations, though there had been were many times when Clarice was put on the spot, targeted by shady promoters or casino CEOs, and had to do some serious maneuvering.

Those people were degrees above these women here, who were country bumpkins or street hustlers with no training, likely to use crude intimidation tactics. Threats of bodily harm. They might insinuate that Clarice's family were at risk...

Blah, blah, Shocker will walk right through them.

Well. Let's get this party started, shall we?

With her direction made clear, Clarice surrounded herself with a serene confidence that could say or do anything without fear of consequences. This attitude projected from her every angle and curve, every stride of leg and swing of arm. No nervous tics, no fidgeting hands, no adjusting of hair or clothes that didn't need adjusting. She looked into the eyes of the gang leaders in turn, walking in their direction. The foot soldiers, young thugs with permanent scowls and inferiority complexes, reluctantly allowed her through. She stopped a couple of yards from their alphas.

"Hi," Clarice said without her usual greeting smile. They looked at each other. Back to her.

"We meet at last," the Latin Queen said, a forty-something woman with a large button nose and gray streaks in her long dark hair. She spoke with a slight accent, but clearly, a woman used to authority. She waved Clarice closer.

Clarice didn't move. "Yeah. Nice to meet you. I guess."

"I'm Juanita. This is Yvonne," she said, nodding at the Flower leader, a late-sixties black woman with beauty marks covering her high cheekbones. She

wore a Dominican style shawl of yellow fabric on
her head. Clarice realized it was part of a lockdown
uniform and pursed her lips, impressed. Clarice loved
homemade garments. It was boss.

"I'm Shocker."

"We know who you are," Juanita said. Yvonne just
stared at her. The LQ said, "You may not be aware of
the assistance we have provided."

"I am. You're the one that got me the floorwalker
gig in lockdown. Thanks, by the way. That worked
out great." Yvonne smiled knowingly and Clarice narrowed her eyes. "What? You set that up?"

"No," Yvonne answered. Her voice rustled like dry
leaves. "But we had high hopes." She smiled again.

Conniving hag.

Clarice took a step forward and was stopped by
three women who grabbed her shoulders. As their
hands touched, Clarice ducked and pivoted in reflex, fast flowing movements that easily slipped out
of their grasp. They panicked. One pulled a knife.
Patty's hand flew down the front of her pants, upped
what looked like a large ice pick and ran toward
them. Without taking her eyes from the foot soldiers,
Clarice motioned Patty to stand down and wagged a
finger at the others with a smile. "Bad idea, ladies,"
Clarice warned them.

Yvonne started cackling. "Oh, I like this one," she
said. Her cackle turned into emphesymic coughs.
She pulled out a pack of cigarettes. Lit one. Juanita
frowned at her, though she ignored it. "You ladies
mind her words. Let her through," she said after re-

gaining her breath, blowing smoke over their heads. They moved.

Clarice walked up to Yvonne, trying hard not to snarl. "You like 'this one'? Well, this one doesn't like you," Clarice growled, then checked her anger. Emotions were counterproductive to her strategy. She needed presence of mind if she was going to survive here.

Breathe.

Center.

"I think you have the wrong impression, Shocker," Juanita said. She looked at Patty. "Maybe your friend gave you some misdirected information. Though she was right to assume it."

"Misdirected how?" Clarice wanted to know. She felt the woman was speaking sincerely, but she didn't relax her guard, peripheral senses tracking the hands of the scowling women to the sides of her. Patty absolutely vibrated with readiness, almost hopefully.

Juanita looked back to her. "We are not your enemies. On the contrary, chica. We have helped you and are obligated to continue the task. There are no ulterior motives. You are favored by El Maestro and La Familia, and we are loyal to them. It is that simple."

"Why?"

"Why what?"

"Why are you loyal to the Teacher?" Clarice said.

She looked at Yvonne, who shrugged and said, "She could find out easily enough. It's really public information at this point."

Juanita turned back to her. "We work together on various businesses. Dope, cars, women. Mostly. La Familia is a supplier and a fence. The Latin Queens can always find work when they get out. They make sure of it. So we always honor their requests." She glanced at Yvonne. "The Flowers are not Latina, but in here we are all Sisters. Everyone benefits."

"Let me guess. The Teacher wants you to help me live comfortably in here. Protect me, or whatever."

"Yes. But that's not all," Yvonne said. She flapped a hand at the other women. "Give us some privacy, ladies. You too, Patty." Patty glared, looked at her. Clarice shrugged and Yvonne put her shank away. Once everyone was out of earshot Yvonne motioned Clarice closer. "Come here, honey child," she rasped. Clarice stepped closer and could smell ashtray on Yvonne's breath. Clarice held hers.

"El Maestro wants us to help you escape," Yvonne said.

Clarice froze, breath lost from her words. Clarice recovered, put fists on hips, miffed at herself and that asshole Teacher for continually trying to manipulate her life. Who the hell did he think he was telling these gang leaders something that could get her in serious trouble?

They were obviously being secretive, but still. Nobody needed to know about that. Clarice glared at the two older women and said, "While I appreciate your honor, I don't need it. I have no intentions of escaping. And I'd like you to pass along a message to the Teacher for me."

"Okay. I can do that," Juanita replied, frowning in disappointment. "What is it?"

"Tell him I request another visit," Clarice snarled, fists flexing so hard they hurt. Knuckles popped audibly. They leaned away from her burning intensity. "So I can beat. His. Meddling. Ass."

Clarice turned on a toe and stalked off toward the zone door with white spots of rage blinking in front of her.

The dry rustling voice of Yvonne trailed after her. "Oh, I like this one!" She cackled.

Chapter XIII

South Mississippi Correctional Facility
Leakesville, Mississippi
March 2, 2012

The televisions sold in the prison canteen weren't very big. The flat screen was nine inches wide, five inches tall, and encased in clear plastic so shakedown officers could see inside it. Pegasus was the name brand on the sticker, right above an inspection stamp guaranteeing this product as one of China's finest.

Ace Carter's face showed he did not agree with the claim of high quality, and was offended by it. And the reluctant movement of his hands as he touched the plastic case indicated an ingrained loathing for inferior electronics. His hands were used to tweaking on more refined technology. This was an affront to their dexterity.

But another part of him, the louder, practical side that usually wore the pants and pushed the muscles, was happy to be doing something, anything, that would allow him to smell the electrons zipping around a heated circuit board again. Even one of poor quality. The hot carbon and polymer mélange, dashed with a hint of tangy ozone, was a scent with special meaning for him. It entered his nose and caressed his palate like a wine, sophisticated in its ability to make him aware of his potential-self. It retrieved memories of his most prestigious accomplishments, and inspired ideas, into infinity. The aroma was just so damn motivating.

He would free-base it if he could.

The TV's case was two sections held together by tiny pyramid-head security screws. Ace smirked at the steel fasteners, which seemed to respond to his condescension, twinkling like chrome under the fluorescent lights. He set it aside on the bed, squatted down on the floor and dug at a piece of concrete that filled a gap at the bottom of the wall. A thumb-sized rock came loose, revealing a hole with a long screw in it. He took it out, turned it over in his hand. A maintenance crew had left it after doing a job on a plumbing closet. Ace had grabbed it, recognizing it as raw material for a tool of some kind and cached it for a later use. The prudence paid off. It would make a perfect screwdriver.

He filed the head of the screw on a rough patch of concrete, carefully shaping it into a small pyramid. He then ground the sharp point off to a blunt surface, periodically testing the fit on the TV, molding the tool so it would lock into the security screws perfectly. Ten minutes of patient honing completed the task. He wrapped a length of string around the shaft for grip, started breaking the screws loose and had the TV open in about a minute.

"Security screws. Heh," Ace muttered, setting aside the tool and holding the two plastic halves open. There was a half-inch thick space between the LCD and circuit board. Perfect spot to stash contraband.

A stack of old science magazines lay on his bed. He set the TV on his pillow, began flipping through magazines and tearing out pages that had black ink covering large areas. He needed deep black colored paper for camouflage. He rolled two of these pages into tubes and measured them to fit the length of the LCD, rolled two more to fit the width. Each tube was about one-inch thick and showed the black ink on the outside.

Digging in his locker box, he grabbed an ink pen with Scotch tape wrapped around it, smiling as he recalled acquiring it from a captain's office. It was the first time he had stolen anything physical. All his previous thefts had been virtual: information from computers, servers, or databases from two dozen countries. Physical theft felt different only in that it was more risky, he mused.

He unrolled small sections of tape, using his teeth to cut them. Secured the tubes of paper to the LCD screen, making a rectangular box just big enough to hold the Mi-Fi router and iPod Touch.

Glancing around casually, he reached down the front of his pants and removed a sock that was cut and tied to his boxer's waistband, a pouch containing the Touch and router. He dumped them in his lap. Set them inside the TV. The fit was perfect, snug, and wouldn't rattle around if an inquisitive officer happened to shake it. He patted his babies with a pleased smile. Closed the TV. Attached tape on the bottom and top sectional splits. The clear tape was invisible on the clear case. An officer peering inside would only see black in the gap between the screen and circuit board, the paper having flattened out to fit the form precisely.

That's if they even looked, he thought. They might just glance at the front and back of the TV, satisfied with seeing the case clear of shanks and drugs.

"This shoddy reject is worth something now," he murmured, smiling down at his handiwork. He held it up to his nose, inhaled deeply. The breath he blew out was half sigh, half moan of desire. "Oh, yeah. That's that wacky tacky".

"You are out of control with that mess," Diamond said, rolling over on the bunk opposed to Ace, pulling down the sheet to free an arm. He rubbed his sleepy eyes, yawned like a toy dog, high-pitched and delicate. Stretched.

"You look funny without your eyebrows drawn on," Ace replied, sniffing the TV again.

"You can only dream of being this pretty," he lisped, flipping imaginary hair off his shoulder. "Picking on me to make yourself feel better won't change the fact that you have a sick fetish for electro-gizmo-thingamajiggies. Does your wife know?" He smiled, jerked the sheet off. Grinned when Ace turned away from the sight of his panties.

"She knows. She has her own, uh, sick fetish regarding electro-gizmo-thingamajiggies," Ace said, glancing over his shoulder and sighing with relief when he saw Diamond had pants on. Sometimes he would bum around in his panties for hours before getting dressed. Ace still wasn't used to that, and wasn't sure he ever would be. "Sick fetish. Heh. That's actually a pretty good description," he said, nodding at his friend. Looking down at the TV again, he made a real effort to put it aside. He couldn't do it. Sniffed it one more time, inhaling, sighing another half-moan.

"You just bought that. You planning on working on it already? I heard you sharpening something," Diamond said, pulling on a small t-shirt over his head. It gripped his torso and showed off his lean brown physique. He rubbed his flat stomach unconsciously, smoothing the shirt with feminine daintiness, looking at Ace curiously.

Ace pursed his lips and looked at his friend. Diamond was no tattletale, and out of all the thug boyfriends he's had, he only gossiped about their love life, never about his significant others' criminal activities. It would be better to tell Diamond now rather than him finding out later and being offended.

He already knew about the iPod and router, Ace told himself. And he'll eventually see me open the TV to stash them. He's my cubicle mate. It's inevitable. On the plus side, he can keep a lookout whenever I use them. I just hope the other two beds stay empty long enough for me to complete my preparations and leave. No one else needs to know...

He focused on his friend, reluctant to tell him about his hiding place. *Oh well. I don't plan on being here long enough for him to let it slip to one of his boyfriends, anyway.* Grimacing, Ace said, "I'm going to trust you with something. Please don't discuss it with your boy toys."

"Oh, right. Right. Like I'm gonna yell, 'Ace told me...!' in the middle of a blow job," he sassed.

The image he painted made Ace blink, bewildered, shaking his head to clear it away. "Um. That's not what I meant, exactly," Ace said, reining in a chuckle. "But you get the point. Thank you." He peeled the tape loose on the top of the TV, looking around to make sure no one was walking up on them. "Check it out," he invited, opening the case just enough so Diamond could see the stash spot.

Diamond sucked in a breath, stuck a bent hand to his chest. "My, my. Ingenious. You'd never think there's room for all that in there." He tilted his head. "What about the charger? Will it fit in there, too?"

"Yeah. But I already installed it in my radio." He set the TV down, grabbed a radio out of his locker box. Clear Tunes was stamped on the front of the clear plastic case, right over a small generic speaker. "I took the charger apart, and put the circuit board inside this piece of junk excuse of a radio. I wired it so it looks like it's part of the radio's circuitry. See?" He pointed to a tiny transformer on a one-inch square green board filled with tiny resistors and capacitors.

"I don't know what I'm looking at."

"Neither will the officers," Ace replied with a wolfish grin. "Electronic camouflage."

"True dat. How do you hook up the charger wire?"

"The headphone jack. I unhooked it from the radio circuit and spliced it into the charger's output. Look." He held up a short wire, one end a USB plug that fit the iPod and router, the other end spliced with a male headphone plug. "The charger is wired to this," he lectured, pointing at the female headphone plug on the radio. "It's only two wires, positive and negative, with 3.7 volts. Makes no difference what kind of plug is used, as long as it can handle the voltage."

"You are fierce with that shit, Ace," Diamond said.

"Thanks," he said, sniffing the radio.

"And sick with it."

"Thanks."

Sunlight was beginning to shine brightly through the windows on the east side of the building. Dust motes floated and blinked in the rays that entered the cubicles like long, narrow auroras. An officer walked down the aisles telling everyone to get ready for breakfast. Inmates in black and white or green and white striped pants gathered at the zone's main exit, eagerly waiting for the magic words that cued feeding time.

"Going back!" a lieutenant yelled at the hungry men, then turned and waved at the tower officer to open the door. The call was parroted by convicts down the line and shouted into cubicles with sleeping forms, guys averse to relinquishing the world of dreams and waking to another day of incarceration. Most were too drugged on psych meds, Benadryl, or marijuana to even budge an eyelid, much less actually consider the prospect of walking across the courtyard to the chow hall. A few made their own breakfast, lining up at the microwave to heat coffee, sausage and noodles, or simply sat on their bunks mixing powdered milk to pour over cereal.

Ace mixed dry milk and water in a bowl. Poured Raisin Bran to the brim and dug in, crunching and smacking with gusto. Diamond mugged him with a pooh-pooh face. Harrumphed loudly. Opened a compact and used the mirror to apply lip liner and pencil on his eyebrows.

Ace grinned and smacked louder.

"You eat like a dog," Diamond informed him. "And not even a cute one. A big, ugly, rude mutt."

"At least I eat. You bulimic prostitute," he mumbled around the tasty cereal. Soggy flakes fell from his lips, splashed in the bowl.

The pooh-pooh face appeared again. "Rude mutt."

"Bulimic prostitute."

A senior CO IV that didn't normally work in that unit stopped in front of their bunk beds. Tall with underdeveloped shoulders and a large paunch, he put his hands on his belt, pushed his chest out with authority. He demanded, "You two going back?"

"No," they answered in unison.

The officer looked at Diamond's makeup and tight shirt. Narrowed his eyes. "Better not be no funny stuff between you two. I don't condone homosexual activity on my watch," he said.

Ace choked on his cereal.

Diamond giggled at Ace, stood and switched his hips over to the officer. "Don't worry, big chocolate. Skinny white boys ain't my type," he said, inclining his head at Ace. He looked up at the officer with a sultry expression, licked his lips. "I like them black and strong." He looked down at the man's crotch, waggled his penciled brows. "And big."

Ace choked again, spitting out a raisin, spilling milk in his lap. The officer lost his authoritative attitude, backing away from Diamond with uncertain, frightened body language. Cornered prey. Diamond pursued him with a few switches and blown kisses, and he turned around quickly, walked away, shouting, "Going back!" in a screechy tone.

Smiling with satisfaction, Diamond watched the retreating man and dusted his hands. "Straights are easy to run off. We won't have to worry about him snooping around here again."

"That was awesome. You're my hero," Ace jested.

Diamond flipped imaginary hair off his forehead. "You can only dream of being this pretty," he lisped.

"Right on."

The zone cleared out and was once again quiet as the remaining men slept or silently ate or sipped coffee. A radio came on, broadcasting NPR national news at a low volume, muffled by the numerous box fans that pushed the humid air around.

Ace stood and stretched, put his bowl down, deciding to wash it later. He had a limited window to use the iPod and had a lot to do before everyone came back from breakfast. He opened the TV, removed his babies and glanced at Diamond.

"Don't worry, Mutt. I'll get on point," Diamond told him. He grabbed a Rolling Stone magazine and sat at an angle on his bunk so he could see the tower, zone door and aisles, gave a flamboyant gesture that took a moment for Ace to realize was a thumbs up.

Good to go.

Powering on the router and iPod, Ace opened the Safari app to log on to the Internet. He then opened a supplementary app, a Windows 7 program that had been modified for use on iPhones, his own software design, and used the Entanglement function so he could control a home PC. He went through various IP addresses he had memorized from his hacking days, hoping one of them was still operational. No luck. He logged out and racked his brain for new ideas. He needed more computing power. He could implement several scams to gain access to people's hard drives and processors, but he had made a promise to his wife to never take advantage of innocent people again. And he didn't have time for all that anyway. Such scams required constant monitoring, day and night.

"This sucks," he said to himself.

"What?" Diamond queried.

"I'm trying to find a computer to Entangle," he whispered.

"Ooo-kay," Diamond said, eyes wide, no idea of what he meant.

Selecting the Text Free with Voice app, Ace sent a message to a person he knew without a doubt would take care of business. But he was hesitant to involve Bobby because of the ramifications that could follow felony hacking and felony escape. It just wasn't fair to include people that could suffer consequences for your actions. Especially those that cared for you and would never tell you no.

Bobby certainly wasn't *expendable*, he thought. He has a wife and kids to take care of. If something went wrong, even a week in jail could prove seriously catastrophic to his household.

Well, we won't hack anyone innocent, Ace reasoned. *And I don't recall Clarice ever forbidding me from recruiting friends to help us escape from prison, even though it's technically illegal and sort of breaks my promise. Very illegal. And involves an innocent person.*

Dammit.

"I'll never win that argument," he said with remorse, smiling. "Still, though. If this isn't an exception to the rule, I'll just grin and bear her hooks and uppercuts."

"What's that?" Diamond questioned.

"I think I'm screwing up."

"Oh. I know the feeling. I use lube now."

"Nice."

Ace shook his head, refocused on the problem. The iPod seemed to burn his hands, waiting impatiently for him to make a decision. He reminisced about all the projects they had worked on together and couldn't think of a single time they hadn't nailed it. Bobby's competence was grade A. The intricate works he was capable of managing were far more complex than the task he planned now. In comparison, it was relatively low risk.

We'll just have to do this with perfection, he resolved, feeling reassured.

He sent Bobby a message that would leave no doubt to Ace's identity and the help he required, coded in case his wife was around. His thumbs blurred over the touchscreen.

Subject: Team Sanford and Son
Text: Sanford,
I need to borrow the Big Black Wrecker. I'm driving a Pinto in a NASCAR race. I can only make laps early in the morning or late at night. May need a big exhaust port, too, so I can evacuate this chamber.

The Message Sent indicator appeared almost immediately after he pressed SEND. Ace caught a case of the jitters while awaiting a response, suddenly second-guessing his decision to involve his friend. A feeling of déjà vu. He had asked Bobby not to visit or establish contact two years ago while he was in the county jail's pre-trial cellblocks, fearing his friend would inadvertently be targeted by the media or the

District Attorney. High-profile cases such as theirs were circuses that sucked in anyone with even inconsequential connections. Drama Bobby's kids didn't need to witness. Now that the media sharks had satiated their feeding frenzy on the shocking drug trafficking trial, and the subsequent conviction of a professional boxing star and her infamous hacker husband, and there was no chance of a new trial, Ace felt it was safe to contact him. He just hoped Murphy's Law didn't take effect somehow, show its ugly head and throw the proverbial wrench in the gears. If Bobby were arrested, Ace would never forgive himself. Neither would Bobby's wife, come to think of it.

Jeez, that's scary, he thought, picturing the woman coming after him. She was nearly as big as Bobby's six-eight, two-ninety frame, and would be on the war path. With Ace as the target.

"Nice," he breathed, then looked over at Diamond, hoping he would make another lube comment to distract his thoughts again.

Shuddering at the image of a squashed Ace bug under a giant woman's shoe, he stared at the touchscreen and was just about to send a disregard text to Bobby when a New Message popped up. He opened it with a twitching finger.

Subject: Team Sanford and Son
Text: Son,
The Big Black Wrecker hasn't raced since you left the Team. But she still runs. I can get her rolling in 15. How big of an exhaust port do you need? I can

help you evacuate King Kong if you want. Call me.
Sanford

A huge Kool Aid smile bloomed on Ace's face as he read the message over and over. Excitement and giddiness threatened to consume him, tearing his eyes, constricting his throat with a restrained shout of joy. He could see Bobby in his mind's eye sending the text, one giant paw stabbing the buttons on his dwarfed cellphone, the other hand holding a paint spray gun like it was a delicate toy. Sporting his blue camo Custom Ace outfit and standing next to a car he had just laid a coat of DuPont on with stupefying precision. The man was a god with paint and body tools, and Ace missed witnessing his skill almost as much as he missed Bobby himself.

Hand quivering with happiness, he dialed Bobby's number. Placed the iPod's ear buds in his ears and held the mic to his lips while it rang. The wire shook back and forth.

"Hello," Bobby rumbled in greeting.

"Sanford!" Ace exclaimed.

"Son!"

"Good to hear your voice, you big oaf."

"Good to hear yours, too, you skinny breadstick."

"I'm not so skinny anymore. Been getting my Jay Cutler on."

"Uh-huh. I'll believe it when I see it."

"In that case, I'll just have to show you. Soon," Ace replied. He grinned and clenched his fists to stop their renewed vibrating.

Bobby took a moment to respond, contemplating. "I guess that's why you need the Wrecker," he said.

"Yep."

"Can you operate it from where you are?"

"Yeah. Remember the iPhone apps I designed?"

"I still use them," he confirmed.

"When Windows 7 came out, I modified the software so Custom Ace employees could log on to the company's database via their phones. I had a copy of the software on an e-mail account that I downloaded on this iPod Touch. It works fine."

"Great. So you just need me to turn on the Wrecker? Anything else?"

"That's it for now. I have to break into the court system and fabricate a court order for transportation. Once I have a time and place, we'll work out the details."

"I'm game. Whatever you need," Bobby said with feeling, face turning serious. A rush of anger at his friend's predicament infused with love and loyalty, tensing his body. The phone's case creaked in his crushing grip. He tried to relax, took a calming breath. "Whatever you need," he promised again.

"Thanks. Hopefully, we can do this without hurting anybody."

"We'll see about that," Bobby said doubtfully. "Hang on for a few minutes."

He stepped out of the paint booth in his side yard, walked across the brick path that split the lawn in half and approached his house with wariness. He had to get to the computer without his wife seeing him.

She would immediately know he was up to something questionable if she found him booting up Ace's prototype computer, a machine that was designed and built by Ace in the prime of his former trade, and had been used only twice in the last four years, retired after Clarice and Ace started dating. Ace had asked Bobby to hide it before the police were able to thoroughly search their shop and home in Woomarket. It's mere existence on the property would violate Ace's probation sentence, five years he received from the Wikileaks bust, and would add time to his current sentence.

Chuckling as he remembered sneaking the huge computer out of Custom Ace, Bobby peeked into his kitchen window. He took a minute to admire his wife's backside as she leaned over to load the dishwasher. Walked quickly around the large brick house and entered the front door. Crept up the carpeted stairs, turned down the hall towards the spare room, his art studio/computer room.

The entry was imbued with odors of paint, mineral spirits, and the plastic and rubber scents of new electronic cables. Walking past a window that glowed with sunrise, he paused at an easel holding an unfinished oil painting. The depiction of children on a playground had been a work in progress for too long, and he wanted to kick himself for losing inspiration. But when his art mentor had been arrested, he simply struggled to maintain interest in painting anything other than cars.

"Clarice would kick my ass if she saw this," he murmured, smiling sadly.

Looking away from the canvas, he moved around it, growling away the maudlin feeling. Walked to a crowded desk in the corner, stared at the huge desktop perched on it. Black and muscular, like a beautifully ugly gargoyle, it had a presence that sang dark invitations and could justify any corrupt action, rewarding you with divine pleasure and power if only you'd turn it on and control the lowly mortals and their inferior computers. A different feeling of wariness suddenly overcame him.

The damn thing always managed to make Bobby uneasy, even though he had never actually used it.

The Big Black Wrecker was state-of-the-art components encased in black aluminum. The one petabyte hard drives and ultra-modified processor had enough speed to infiltrate and decode most secure databases, and could store decades' worth of information. The plasma screen was twenty-four inches with various ports and connections anchored in its black frame, and was coated with a thick layer of dust: the result of Bobby's wife's disinclination to go near what she adamantly considered "a tool of the devil." There was no way in hell she would clean it.

Attempting to smile at his wife's reservations, a disturbed look shadowed his features instead. He wiped a finger across the screen and sighed. Making sure everything was plugged in, he flipped on several toggle switches that powered up components foreign to him. The hard drives and plasma screen hummed to life, their own distinct high-pitched whistles slowly changing to higher frequencies that exceeded what human auditory systems could detect. The pump of the processor's water-cooled system kicked on loudly and Ace made a sound of longing. Bobby frowned, looked at his phone, stuck it back to his ear. "Excuse me?"

"That means it's ready," Ace said, clearing his throat in embarrassment.

"You heard that? You Spock-eared geek mother-fucker."

"I felt it. Like a baby kicking in its mother's belly."

"Don't tell me any more. I'm disturbed enough already." Bobby watched the booting data stream across the screen. Took a clean grease rag from a pocket, wiped the dust off. "You logged on yet?"

"Will be when we hang up."

"Go ahead, then. You said you can only drive your Pinto in the morning and late nights. Must mean you don't have much time."

"You're pretty sharp for an oaf painter."

"And you have a sporty mouth for a guy with no ass to back it up," Bobby shot back, grinning broadly.

"You may be right. Talk later?"

"Any time, my friend."

"Thanks. Call you tonight."

"Be safe." Bobby didn't bother to ask about Ace's illegal activities, or even worry about it being traced to his house. He knew Ace would cover his tracks.

He turned away from the Wrecker, intending to head outside and finish the customer's car in his paint booth. The sight of the easel and canvas froze his steps. Pursing his lips thoughtfully, he stepped to the painting and picked up a large wooden palette and tube of paint.

Ace set the iPod on top of his pillow, crossed his legs Indian-style, put the pillow in his lap. His index fingers jabbed the touchscreen's keypad without error, tongue creeping out the side of his lips, half-smiling, eyes alight as he lost himself in the virtual world. It was a lot like diving into an ocean, immersing himself completely in the Internet ether. He could picture the Big Black Wrecker's screen and keyboard. Feel the radiation from its processor and plasma screen and smell all the exquisite aromas of high-speed technology. He was only linked to the monstrous computer, though he felt like he was with it in person, inside it, one with the machine. Melded to it metaphysically, spirit flowing around and smiling a friendly greeting to every particle that traveled at the speed of light in its micro-circuitry. A part of the no-laws that governed quantum mechanics. He could see coding for the software of every website page he clicked on. See the digital Os and 1s that united to structure the program of the servers. His hair tingled almost painfully, and his smile faltered momentarily as he wondered if his head would catch fire from the unnatural thought processes. Kinetic scheming.

Deciding he didn't care, he would happily allow it to consume him, his smile resumed, brighter, with pure, irrational glee stretching his mouth grotesquely.

Diamond stared at his friend with concern. He had only seen psychotic killers and mentally retarded people wear the expression Ace had plastered on his angular face. A death's head grin. He checked the tower, aisles, exit door. Back to Ace. "Hey, Psycho Bill. You look like you have acid face. If you're holding out on me, I'm gonna be pissed."

When Ace didn't respond, Diamond rolled up the magazine in his hands and decided he'd throw it at the gizmo dweeb if someone came.

Ace browsed: www.courts.gov/ trial-courts/circuitcourt, attempting to find an optimal address to plan his escape from. He clicked on one he knew well, the Harrison County Circuit Court building, a large complex not far from Interstate 10. It showed a route that would provide a fast getaway, assuming everything went according to plan.

"It rarely does," he told the map on the screen. Opening another Window, he logged onto Google Earth and viewed the courthouse from a satellite view. Methodically committed the map to memory, a task that wasn't terribly difficult since his home had been in that county and he knew the streets well enough. *Yeah, this is the spot*, he determined, wishing he could print out a copy of the Earth View.

Logging out of Google, he defaulted to the government site once again and went through a list of judges. A flash of anger scalded his already simmering head as he recognized one. The Honorable Judge

T.W. Wallace had presided over their trial. He had sided with the prosecution on nearly every motion and objection, leaving no doubt as to his bias. Ace felt, no, he knew he and Clarice would have had a better than even chance with an impartial judge, one that knew what 'honorable' actually meant.

"Well, well. I believe it's time to restore your honor, Your Honor," he told the thumbnail picture on his screen. "You put us away. Now you'll let us out. How merciful of you, sir. Fuck you very much." twallace@courts.ms.gov was listed as the judge's email. Ace traced the address to its source by linking to the cookies in the servers, tiny packages of data that were left behind every time Wallace used his PC. The Big Black Wrecker's processing abilities and auto-decoding programs instantaneously showed Ace the judge's email password, IP address, home address, and a hacker's smorgasbord of personal information.

Grinning grotesquely once again, he Entangled the judge's computer and logged on to the court's electronic filing system, CM/ECF, and composed a transportation order for himself and his wife. He listed the order CC'd the Attorney General's Office for appearances, but didn't actually send it there; no sense telling the world about it. He linked Wallace's e-mail account to the iPod so he could monitor and manipulate any responses the judge might receive regarding the order. He and Clarice would be taken to court by armed guards one month from today.

Time enough to prepare resources on the street, he thought, mind double-checking the logic, seeing if he left anything out.

"Damn. Almost forgot," he muttered. "Duh." Copying the order onto another page, he personalized it for Clarice, typing in a message to give her a heads-up and let her know who had arranged the transport. She was certainly bright enough to understand the purpose of it, but he couldn't help throwing in a smartass remark, one that would give T.W. Wall Ass a coronary when he discovered it. She would get it through the prison's law library, unopened, unread. Perfectly secure. His fingers flew over the keypad.

Notice of Electronic Filing
The following was entered by Elephant Trunk Penis on 3/2/2012 at 6:34 a.m. C.S.T. and filed on 3/2/2012.

Case Name: State of Drunken Rednecks vs. Clarice Carter.

Case Number: Couldn't think of a clever 69 joke in time. Sorry. :)

Docket Text: Escape from the Planet of the Apes/Escape from the Prison
Planet!

The reference to one of Clarice's favorite songs, a number by a little known band called Clutch, would tickle her to death. Ace's chuckle started low and throaty, rising in volume and tempo as he threw his head back and bellowed in triumph. The mad scientist laugh totally freaked out Diamond, who squeaked and threw the Rolling Stone at Ace. It hit him in the head with a solid thump. He abruptly shut his mouth, looked at Diamond in shock, more from forgetting he was there than the knock on the head.

"Snap out of it!" Diamond shrieked. "You're creeping me out."

Ace blinked at him several times. Looked back down and quickly submitted the orders to the circuit court and MDOC Records Department, logged out. Put away the iPod and router. Set the TV in his locker box. He stood and coughed, embarrassed as he realized how caught up in the hacking game he had been. "Sorry. I get way out there sometimes," he said. Then revised that statement. "Uh. Well, every time. Thanks for checking me."

"Uh-huh." He eyed Ace warily. "Did you get what you needed?"

"Yep."

"What did you do?"

"Some light towing, a little wrecking."

"Towing?"

"With a Big Black Wrecker," was his mysterious response, adding a smile that was equally cryptic. And irritating.

Diamond harrumphed, threw his hands up and rolled his eyes.

Ace tried out his mad scientist laugh again. The job he'd just pulled off was only the beginning of many incidents that would warrant such laughter.

Chapter XIV

Central Mississippi Correctional Facility
Pearl, Mississippi
March 10 – March 11, 2012

Clarice's bra was a Bob Barker's piece of crap. The tag said it was made in Pakistan. Her mind couldn't help cuing sweat shop clichés with kids and old ladies laboring over sewing machines twenty hours a day for pennies. If someone told her the little bastard that made this bra was a terrorist infiltrator Clarice would believe them. This damn thing terrorizes her. It cuts and scrapes and makes her bleed as if she had been hit by IED shrapnel.

She lifted the straps off each of her shoulders, hissing at the blisters and raw skin that had accumulated from shadowboxing every day. And as for the underside of her boobs... The wire in the cups felt like warped barbed wire, grating her puppies in an attempt to make hot dogs. The wads of toilet tissue stuffed under there helped, but that just exacerbated the strap problem, throwing off the overall fit, and making her B-cups jut out like Clarice was a pre-teen trying to look busty for attention.

Visions of an evil, laughing, horned Pakistani kid would haunt her.

Sweat poured off her head, running down her hair, stinging the blisters on her shoulders. Clarice stood at a row of sinks running cold water. Dabbing it on her face and wounds. Patted dry with a towel. Clarice looked into the dented steel mirror and couldn't help smiling at the warped reflection of Patty sitting on a toilet behind her. She was singing a kid's potty song, peeing with such volume and force it sounded like a fire hose running under her. The stainless bowl and tiled walls reverberated the waterfall jam.

"That crappy singing doesn't come close to covering your peeing," Clarice told her reflection.

Patty's face distorted, elongated as she started singing louder for a moment. Stopped and stuck out her tongue. It looked ten-inches long. "Your crappy stuffed bra doesn't come close to giving you real boobs," she fired back, grabbing and shaking one of her double-Ds at her.

"Shut up."

The cold water was too much too resist. Clarice stuck her head under the faucet, soaking her sweltering neck and hair while trying not to touch her face on the dirty sink. The cold penetrated deep into her cortex, instantly clearing her thoughts, focusing her exercise-taxed equilibrium. The relief and recovery felt fantastic after several hours of training. Clarice toweled dry, pulled her hair back in a rough ponytail, secured it with a tie. Looked at her friend again, who was washing her hands in the sink next to her.

"Your wrist healed enough for tomorrow's fight?" she asked.

"Should be okay. I'll wrap it up tight and pad the knuckles before we go. Try to avoid head shots and use it for the body."

"Smart. Not many girls go for the body. They won't expect that. Most of these broads just throw a bunch of wild punches at the head." She held up her large fist, pursed her lips, examined it. "Including me," she mused. The knuckles were slightly misshapen, bulging from calcium deposits that had repaired damage from hundreds of hard blows in dozens of fights. "Nailing bitches in the head does hurt. Maybe I'll try some gut punches, too. Will you teach me?"

"Sure."

"Where's the best spot?" She pulled up her shirt to expose a pale white belly. Lifted her arms to stretch out the skin that surrounded her belly button.

She wasn't very fat, really. The muffin top was cute. Gave her warrior persona a little extra character.

Clarice pointed below it. "Anywhere below the belly button and above the hoo-hah is the best spot."

"The lower abdominals?"

"Yeah. The nerve plexus there is highly sensitive. There's not a lot of muscle protecting the organs. That's why you see boxers with thick padding around their waist. Even a light blow in that area will freeze up the diaphragm." Clarice smirked at her. "If your opponent can't breathe, she can't fight."

"If she can't huff, she can't scuff," she rhymed with a smirk of her own.

Clarice pointed between her breasts. "Right below the sternum and above the upper abs is another sensitive area. Best to hit that one at angles," Clarice advised, demonstrating by stepping to the side, holding an extended arm pointed at the spot.

"Got it."

"Lift your arms." She did and Clarice pointed below her armpit. "Another plexus is in this area, high on the ribs. If you can slip your opponent's punch and step on the inside while her -"

"Or his."

"Or his, arm is extended, you can easily tag this spot. Their lungs will feel like a grenade just went off inside them. They'll struggle to keep going. Fear floods their system a second later, and the fight's over with."

"Hell yeah. Then you can show off on them," Patty said, dancing around, winding up flashy punches.

Clarice smiled and shook her head. "You got it. Go Lucia Rijker on them."

"The Dutch Destroyer? Isn't she considered like the most skillful female boxer of all time?"

Clarice nodded. "She's the measuring stick."

"Hmm. Shame she retired before you could take her 'most skilled' title."

"Uh…"

"You gonna do a live demo for me tomorrow? Knock her out with a body shot?" she asked eagerly.

Clarice looked down at her wrist. Flexed her hands. Her smile turned wintry as she looked up at Patty. "I'm gonna Shocker."

* * *

The mop plopped wetly on the shower floor. The middle-aged Latin Queen blithely swirled it over the tiles, bobbing her head to the music blasting from a small boom box hanging from a shower head. Niki Minaj's sassy flow instilled swag in all eighteen of the women present. They stood against the walls of the twenty-by-twelve enclosure. Latin Queens under the shower heads, Flowers opposite them, and Gangsta Queens scattered around the empty guard tower, posted up at the entrances.

Captain Portsmouth stood with the G. Queens, smiling as Patty and Clarice approached. Her mouth was churning furiously. She took a Diet Coke bottle from her back pocket, spat in it. Thick, dark saliva skeeted from between her teeth, obscuring the plastic, draining slowly to the bottom. Clarice couldn't keep a look of revulsion from her face.

"Cream Tail," she greeted her with a disturbing smile. Bits of tobacco stuck to her large yellowish teeth. Clarice nodded, said nothing. The woman spared a scowl for Patty, looked back at her. "You is fighting the Suicide Bomber today."

"Suicide Bomber, huh? Boss fight name," Clarice said and snickered.

"She be the one on the end of the Flowers. The Muslim ho wearing the koofie," Porstmouth informed her, pointing down the line of women. A short, stocky, dark skinned girl wearing a white Islamic prayer cap, cut-off striped pants and a cute home-made tank stared back like Clarice had killed her dog. She was about Clarice's age. Deep-set dark eyes, wide nose, and wore a permanent grimace that looked distinguished from a hard knock life in a rough neighborhood.

Clarice smiled brightly, waved a silly hello to her. She lunged forward, cursing, and was held by several women next to her who looked in Clarice's direction with distinguished hard knock grimaces of their own. For good measure, Clarice gave them all a bright idiot smile, then tried to emulate their mean mugs. She liked the way it made them look, all tough, terrible and forbidding. "I have to get me one of those," Clarice said to Patty, pointing at her mimed thug scowl, like it was something Clarice could pick up at Wal-Mart.

She erupted with laughter. "You trying to make the Bomber explode before the fight starts?"

Clarice nodded. "Anger is great for energy. But it's uncontrollable energy, clouds judgment. If you get mad, you forget your fight plan."

She raised her brows, leaned away as if seeing her in a new light. "Pre-fight psych warfare, huh? Are you always such a devious bitch?"

"Nah. Sometimes I like to sleep."

Portsmouth walked into the middle of the shower holding a canvas tote bag. Took out a camcorder, USB wire, and a small Wi-Fi router. Plugged the assembly together, powered it on. A young, light-skinned G. Queen stepped forward and took the set-up from her. Portsmouth reached into the tote and pulled out a black ski mask, slipped it over her head. It emphasized her bulging forehead and wide jaw, which twisted and chumped incessantly. She dropped the tote, kicked it to a wall. Spat in the bottle again, the mouth hole catching a string of brown drool. Clarice shuddered. The Gangsta Queen held up the camera and zoomed in on her.

"Ladies and gents! Hoes and niggas of the Internet community! Welcome to another edition of Bitch Fight!" the masked captain announced grandly, bowing, twirling the spit bottle with a flourish. The women clapped excitedly, some with nervous excitement.

Clarice stood on wooden legs and watched the proceedings, stunned senseless. It was so unreal, so Hollywood fiction, it made her dizzy. There was no way all this had been going on without the authorities knowing.

Or being paid off, Clarice thought, turning to Patty with a beseeching look.

Patty explained, "The video is streamed live to a website. The girls' faces are automatically blurred by some kind of facial tracking program. The people watching have no idea who we are." She smirked. "Well, most of them. At least there's deniability."

"I'm familiar with the facial blurring tech. It's just so crazy. I can't believe where I am." Clarice paused for a second, frowning. "Why is she wearing a mask?"

"Insurance, I guess. She's a cagey hooker."

Portsmouth finished her spiel, then pointed at the Muslim girl. "Fighting out of the red corner, the short stack of dynamite you all know and love. The. Suicide. Bomb-errr!"

More clapping, though only from the Flowers this time. Caught completely off guard, Clarice realized Portsmouth was staging her fight first. And Clarice wasn't even close to being warmed up.

Uh-oh.

Stepping in place, Clarice began rolling her shoulders with uppercuts, quickly, loosely, trying to get some heat into her core, back, and neck. A body doesn't absorb impact well when it's cold. In boxing, getting 'caught cold' is an expression describing a fighter that got knocked out quickly from lack of a proper warm up. That's why you see boxers already pouring sweat before the first round bell rings. Clarice had to hurry and break a sweat, get some blood and neuro-chemicals flowing.

Turning to Patty, Clarice shadowboxed her smirking form. The Gangsta videographer turned the camera on her as Portsmouth announced her entry.

"And fighting out of the blue corner, the newcomer with great po-tential. The fierce and explosive, petite powerhouse you all know as the killer that knocked out our champion with a single punch. Niggas and hoes, I give you. Devil. Hands. Sally!"

Clarice spun toward the lunatic captain, flushing with more than enough heat to complete her warm up. Did she just say that? Devil Hands Sally? The unreal dizziness swept through her again, and Clarice invested all hope into this being a bad dream, some kind of subconscious illusion Clarice would wake up from any second now.

God, tell her this was a dream. This can't be real. The shower and area around it burst into a cacophony of laughing and clapping, and her fanciful hope of being in a Freddy Krugger dream shattered with prejudice. Patty was among the gigglers, of course. Hell, Clarice wanted to laugh herself, from the sheer ridiculousness of it. Clarice looked up at the ceiling in a *What Did I Do?* manner, quietly asking her maker why He was punishing her so severely. The petty sins she committed surely didn't warrant such a scandalous label. Clarice cursed, Clarice liked to beat up certain people, and, on occasion, Clarice had lusted on men other than her husband. She had even contemplated outright murdering numerous police officers. But even if Clarice had acted on it and killed a thousand of the badge toting pricks, she still wouldn't deserve the extreme punishment of being introduced as Devil Hands Sally.

Come on!

Snapping out of her grumbling reverie, cursing her luck, she rolled her shoulders again. Bounced on her toes. Looked over at her opponent with a neutral projection, plainly unconcerned about her abilities, knowing she would take offense and grow angry. She was obviously a hothead. She snatched the koofie off her head, revealing a men's style bald fade, lined neatly in the front. Mugged her, affronted. Portsmouth waved them to the center, put a hand on each of their shoulders. The camera focused on the three of them.

Porstmouth's mask churned. "Name of the game is Bitch Fight. Here are the rules: There are nam. I'll tell you when the fight is over. You two bitches give us a good show, now. Hear?" she demanded, half yelling, glaring at them in turn. We nodded.

The Suicide Bomber started huffing and puffing, psyching herself up. She screamed, "Allah akbar!" and raised her fists.

Portsmouth stepped back to a wall quickly, yelling, "Fight!"

The wondrous word triggered a lightning response from Clarice's calm, still body. Like a Top Fuel drag car waiting at the line and launching 7,000 hp at a glimpse of the green light, her left arm shot into Suicide Bomber's face, fist flexing, shoulder tightening as it flattened her nose. The speed of it baffled the girl, made her hands jerk up in response, autonomous nervous system controlling untrained arms, and Clarice threw a hard right-hand into her stomach, stepping forward and twisting her shoulders as fast as she could, punching through the target. Her fist sank so far in it felt like she hit Bomber's spine.

Both punches took less than half a second. The bomber doubled over, breath and spit driven out of her with such force it covered her face and arms, warm, wet, turning cool. The fight could have ended there, but Portsmouth was too slow to call it or wanted a more violent ending for her audience. Clarice glanced at her, boxing instincts directing her to the referee for a yay or nay, and smiled at her greedy expression. She wanted her to hurt this girl. Caesar gives a thumbs down. The fight junkie in her roared and stoked, dancing and shaking her ass in exuberance. Clarice flexed her mental fists and prepared to get another dose of the Feel Good.

A knockout was for the taking.

And a fifty dollar performance bonus to boot.

As the Bomber attempted to stand back up, Clarice stepped to her with her left foot, putting it down hard, transferring all her weight in that direction. Her left hook hit the side of Bomber's chin right as her foot planted, pistoning through as Clarice snapped her shoulders and thrust up from her toes. The girl's neck twisted sharply, eyes rolled, jaw slack, lips contorting as spit sprayed the women behind her. The Bomber didn't have a chance. Didn't even see it coming to try and block. All three punches hit her within three seconds. From the word "Fight!" to her laying crumpled on the floor took four.

You think she got caught cold? Amateur. Clarice shook her head.

The Gangsta zoomed in on the inert loser, up to her, the whine of the lens focusing audible in the stymied room.

Porstmouth finally took action, stepped to her, grabbing her wrist, raising her hand. "The winner, by knockout!" she bellowed, turning them in a circle to face the camera, jaw churning. "Devil. Hands. Sal-lyyy!"

No one clapped. Everyone just stared. Even Patty. Clarice had expected her to go full-retard cheerleader and blow the roof off with Sally silliness. Clarice looked at her friend and saw concern for her bordering on fear. Then Clarice realized she was snarling at her, mouth held grimly to show her canines, harsh and cruel and aggressive. Locked in fight mode. Even her fists were clenched, veins standing up, killer instinct that swelled her muscles, unwilling to regress, looking for any excuse to hang around just a while longer.

With a nearly painful effort, Clarice forced the fight junkie to become dormant once again, convincing her that she was assuaged for the time being, though she was ready to jump back to the controls at a moment's notice. Patty kicked back with an orgasmic grin on her lovely no-face.

Damn, Clarice loved that chick.

From snarling to eyes closed in pleasure, Clarice knew she looked like a psych patient. A wild cat with a belly full of cream, licking her chops.

Patty's wariness intensified, but she bravely approached and took her hand. "You okay, Shocker?" she said.

Clarice opened her eyes, smiling widely. "I lose it like this every time. Don't worry. You'll get used to it," Clarice promised. The look Patty gave said she highly doubted it. Cringing as a thought occurred to her, Clarice cursed loudly.

"What?" Patty asked.

"I didn't get a chance to bet on myself."

"That's too bad. I made two hundred dollars." She grinned, polished a chimerical apple on her shirt. Took a fake bite.

Clarice's snarl returned.

There were three more fights after hers. Thrashing, slapping, wrestling matches that you'd expect from tough country girls and back alley thugs. Though there were a few nice punches thrown from time to time. Even a knockout. Patty and Clarice watched with interest.

"I think I'm fighting her next weekend," Patty said, referring to a chocolate skinned Amazon that had scored the KO. She was as tall as Patty, but built more athletically, muscular arms and legs, big butt. Clarice looked at her torso, the origin of power, the first area she studied to judge a woman's potential. Hers was wide at the shoulders and thick at the waist. If she knows how to move her hips there will be plenty of pop on her punches. She would be a handful for any girl to fight. Even a pro. Clarice would give even odds on her vs. Patty.

"You can take her," Clarice assured her friend.

Patty looked at her, studying Clarice's face to gauge her confidence in her. "You think so?"

"You better believe it."

As soon as Clarice uttered those words, she thought of how many times her coach had looked her in the eyes and told her the same thing. The conviction, the ambitious fire stoked with over-confidence he gave her with that phrase and look projected from her now, instilling Patty with the boldness she needed to win.

She grinned fiercely and said, "I'll spank her ass." She knocked out an invisible opponent, bent her over a knee and proceeded to give her a loser's spanking. Several women saw it and broke out laughing. Clarice included.

"That's so gay," Clarice said.

Patty licked her thumb, jammed it in the phantom loser's rear. The laughing turned into choking hurrahs.

Captain Portsmouth approached them. "What you hens clucking about, huh? Come on. Show's over. Let's clear out of here. Everyone know what do to," she said, herding everyone out of the shower and on to the empty zone. Brooms, buckets of paint and paint rollers were stacked against a wall. Everyone grabbed an item or two, a prop to make them look like a crew that had been working in the empty building. A cover in case a warden or do-gooder captain happened to pop up on their day off.

The girls that had lost their bouts were the most injured. They wore paint masks or pulled the hoods of their jackets over their heads to hide any lacerations or swelling. One walked slowly, using a broom for a crutch to hide her severe limp. They all exited the building and headed down the maze of walkways to their own buildings.

Back in their cubicle, Patty and Clarice raced to undress and get in the shower. They both stank of sweat, paint, and that mélange of mold that accumulates in a grimy shower that hasn't been used in months.

Yolanda sat up on her top bunk, watching them. "Did y'all fight?" she asked.

"I didn't. Mine is next weekend," Patty replied. She jerked her head at her, grinning. "Shocker knocked out the Suicide Bomber in like three seconds."

"Shut up!" Yolanda exclaimed, mouth open. She finger combed her long dark hair, unconsciously picked at the acne on her slim face, adding to the scar tissue.

"It's true. Never seen anything like it. The video of Boogerilla getting her grill caved in didn't have shit on what happened today. If you go with us next week, you better bring some cash to bet on our cubie. She's a beast."

"Cool. I should have something by then. I'm supposed to do some tattoos tonight and tomorrow," she said importantly.

Patty gave her a knowing look. Clarice stuck a towel under her arm and said, "I wanted to talk to you about that."

"What, tattoos? You want one?"

"No. I'm a tattoo artist. I want to give you some tips."

"Yeah, right. Like you were a pro, or something." She rolled her eyes.

Clarice reined in the urge to slap her. Though just barely. It was quite a challenge. "Actually, I am a pro. I owned my own shop," Clarice said, half growling at her insolence. Freaking, mmm! Her mouth hung open again.

Before she could spout more idiotic disbelief, they were interrupted by two convicts stopping in the aisle in front of their bunks. Juanita and Yvonne both looked cantankerous, demeanors that fitted their positions as leaders of frustrating women. Since they weren't any bosses of hers, Clarice didn't care for their glares and stepped forward with a rebuke on her lips. Clarice pulled the towel from under her arm, squeezing it like a stress ball. Patty didn't care for it either. She reached down her pants. Whipped out her pick.

"There's no need for all that nonsense," Yvonne scolded Patty. She waved her arms wildly, frustrated as she stepped to her. Looked her up and down. "Come with us. We need to talk."

"Are you asking me or telling me?" Clarice wanted to know, matching her ill-natured mule look. "'Cause I'm not on your payroll, lady."

"Am I the only one here with any sense?" Juanita demanded, scowling at everyone. She sighed, gave placating gestures to Clarice and Patty. Nodded courteously to Yolanda, who watched the scene with her usual uncomprehending face. Juanita put her hands on her associate's shoulders and backed her up, moved in front. She tried on a smile, but knew it looked fake and dropped it. "Clarice, can we speak with you in private, please? It's urgent."

"Urgent for you or me?" Clarice demanded.

She glanced at Yvonne, who shook her head. Juanita grimaced, and Clarice could see she would tell her the truth, though reluctantly. "Urgent for us. It could hurt us. But it could help both you and us."

"I appreciate your honesty. I was just going to the shower." Clarice waved a hand at the aisle. The Latin Queen and Flower leaders preceded her, and Patty lunged forward to walk at her side. Clarice turned to her. "Give me a moment. I think I know what this is about."

"You sure?" Patty glared after the women, hand twitching at the front of her pants. She looked like a gunslinger about to draw.

Clarice gave a huge smile. "Positive. I'm not worried about those two. Three-second knockout, remember?" Clarice snapped a hook.

Patty pursed her lips, shrugged. "All right. But if I hear you cry out, I'm coming."

"That's so gay." Clarice snickered, turned and walked to the shower, leaving a giggling Patty and dumbfounded Yolanda staring after her.

The shower nearly sparkled, smelling of chemicals. One of the lights was shorted out, leaving the far corner in darkness. With shady business on their minds, naturally they migrated to the shadows.

"What's the deal?" Clarice said. "More BS. about the Teacher?"

"It's not BS," Yvonne spat. "El Maestro deserves more respect than that. He's jumping through hoops trying to help you, girl. No one's ever had his attention, personally, like you do." Her mouth puckered up like she had just swallowed a lemon War Head.

Juanita sighed loudly, pinched the bridge of her nose. "Ladies, please," she said. "We don't need to like each other. But we do need to be civil. We aren't a bunch of niñas in grade school."

"That's true," Clarice consented, ignoring Yvonne's quarrelsome manner. Yvonne was really pulling Clarice's strings, which was sort of unexpected, considering what Clarice knew of her and her remarks to her during their previous encounter. Something was seriously threatening them for her to act like that. People lash out when they are scared.

What devilment was the Teacher inflicting on them now?

Clarice focused on the Latin Queen as she began talking in a low tone.

"We know you said you didn't want any help from La Familia or from us," she said. "It's that we were sort of ordered to help you. We have an obligation."

"No, you don't. I don't want your help. That cancels the obligation."

"It doesn't work that way. Not for us." She sighed again. "*Madre de dios*. Please understand, when we get an order we are expected to report back that it was taken care of. If it isn't, we lose credibility. We lose business. It not only affects us, but hundreds of our Sisters."

"So what does that have to do with me? I'm not a Sister. I have enough problems."

"Well, honey, you're gonna have more if you don't work with us," Yvonne promised, eyes wide, jabbing a finger at her.

"Excuse me? I don't have to take this shit!" Clarice stormed, directing harsh eyes on her, Target #1. Fists twisting the towel like it was her neck.

"Yvonne! Please leave," Juanita said, stepping between them. Her face softened, looked at Clarice with a plea for peace. Clarice got a feeling that someone in La Familia had told the woman that she couldn't use violence with her. On the contrary. Recalling her visit with the Teacher, Clarice bet they were told to protect her from any harm. And Yvonne couldn't stand it. Her standard procedure of brute force threats was effectively taken from her. No wonder she was so flustered. She didn't know how to handle this.

Clarice checked her temper, tried not to mug Yvonne as she left. Couldn't do it.

Juanita sounded exhausted when she spoke again. "If you won't let us help you with escaping, at least accept this," she said, taking a cellphone and charger from her back pocket.

Clarice stared at it. Looked up to her. "That from the Teacher?"

"Yes."

"No thanks."

"Clarice, at least take this and make a call or two. Hell, throw it away. I just need to be able to tell La Familia you accepted it and it's out of my hands," she said, nearly begging. "I can't lie to them. I won't."

Clarice looked down at the phone again, attempting to process the situation from a more objective point of view. Anger was hampering her thinking and had thrown strategy under the bus. Several ideas occurred to her. Clarice needed a phone to organize her escape. Clarice had planned to use Patty's but now realized the authorities would be able to trace her phone if it was used for that. It was possible, anyway. The last thing Clarice wanted was for her friend to suffer unforeseen repercussions for something Clarice had done. Clarice could trash this deal once she had called a person or two and gotten things rolling. The problem was, Clarice didn't trust the Teacher. He was certainly a man with ulterior motives. Layers of them. He would be monitoring this phone account, know every number Clarice called or texted, every site Clarice visited on the Net. That alone was enough to make her tell Juanita to go sit on it.

But on the other hand, if Clarice didn't take it, she could possibly gain the enmity of several hundred hostile Sisters. For some reason, that thought didn't make her want to smell flowers and dance naked.

Well, Clarice really only needed to call one person. He'd take care of everything else. Being a 'former' organized crime affiliate, one of the few that never saw a day in court, he was skilled in evasion, and paranoid enough that there was no way anyone could monitor him.

That could work.

Clarice held out her hand. "All right. Tell La Familia you did your part."

"Gracias." Juanita beamed gratefully, perking up as she handed over the items. The two women nodded respectfully to each other and Juanita walked out of the shower. Clarice rolled the phone and charger in her towel, set it on a shelf next to her hygiene containers and got her butt under the water.

Possessing a cell phone in prison was a felony. Clarice would have to find a secure hiding place, make sure no Nosy Nikis discovered it. This was going to be a headache.

As Clarice washed her hair, she thought about Yolanda's stupid, incredibly irritating face and how hard it would be to keep her nose out of her business. Excedrin Headache #11,730,634.

Chapter XV

Juarez, Chihuahua
Mexico
March 18, 2012

"You will all kneel before me," Jimmy said to his pale reflection. His grating laugh morphed to wheezing, choppy coughs as he straightened his bowtie in the full-length mirror, head tottering with arrogance. He puffed up the handkerchief in the tuxedo's top pocket. Smoothed his thinning hair.

"You do look like a king," Hector said, standing behind him in a similar tux, dark hair slicked back from his chubby face. "Nice to be out of uniform, eh?"

"The police uniform is just a mask to conceal our royalty from those that would conspire against us," Jimmy replied with a British accent. He turned to look at his partner, lowered his voice. "I told you we'd get our due. Didn't I tell you? That greaser was our ticket."

"Yeah, Jimmy. You said it."

They left the spacious chamber, walked through a wide hall with marble tiles, Catholic statues, and colorful tapestries depicting the Virgin Mary in scenes of her storied life. The floor gleamed with dull orange spots of light, polished balls of fire reflecting from chandeliers hanging high above their heads.

Hector smiled down at his wing-tipped shoes, nodding as the heels tapped loudly, basking in the euphoric glow of success that the clothes and mansion imbibed. He never thought that he, a Chicano police officer, would be where he was today, a millionaire on the verge of retiring. And not even forty years old yet. He looked over at his friend and smiled, knowing all this wouldn't have happened without Jimmy. They had been through some rough patches together, surviving where others had broken or quit from the pressure. They had persevered, but police work and drug trafficking had taken its toll on them.

It was all worth it, though, he decided.

They emerged into another hall, this one even wider and more decorative, walked into the antechamber and stopped in front of beautifully carved double doors that opened on the ballroom. The fox head motifs above the door handles grinned at them.

The ceiling acoustics magnified Jimmy's wheezing coughs. He looked at Hector. "You ready?"

"After you, Señor," Hector responded, opening both doors at once for his partner.

The mansion's ballroom was cavernous. Murmuring conversations with margarita-laced laughter from over a hundred men and women floated on the cold circulating air. Cocktail glasses clinked on the upstairs balconies, evening dresses flashed waxed legs on the dance floor. Jimmy and Hector were greeted politely, but with reservation, the Mexican criminals of La Familia wary of the American police and reluctant to embrace them as full members of the organization.

El Maestro appeared out of the throng like an emperor, clearly in his element with a gorgeous Latina escort on one arm, bobbing her head to a Marc Anthony song that crooned from invisible speakers. People jostled to catch El Maestro's eye, which was focused on the policemen as he walked toward them, smiling warmly, elegant. Poised. A master of charm. He cleared his throat and everyone within hearing hung on his every word. "Gentlemen. It is a pleasure to see you again," he said. "I trust your accommodations are adequate."

"Si, El Maestro," Hector replied, smiling broadly. He bowed.

Jimmy just nodded absently, looking around at the beautiful cocktail waitresses and caterers. *It's like a damn Mexican Playboy Club*, he thought. *I'll score tonight for sure.* He rubbed his hands together.

El Maestro continued, "That is well, then. *Mi casa es su casa*," he said. "I will address La Familia in one hour. Enjoy your evening."

"*Gracias*, El Maestro," Hector gushed.

"Yeah. Thanks," Jimmy added, still looking at the women.

El Maestro ignored the discourtesy of the *gringo*, patted his escort on her hand. "Please excuse me. I must attend to some business."

She skimmed a finger along his jaw, bit her lip, with a seductive promise that said it was his loss. Watched him walk up the stairs greeting people and disappear through a door at the top. Two stern faced men with muscles too big for their suits stood guard outside the door. One of them put a finger to his ear, listened to a report over his earpiece. Said something to his associate. They both stared at the *gringo* policemen.

El Maestro walked into a small office with satellite communications equipment, several computers, and a bank of TV monitors on a wall in front of his massive desk. He took out his earpiece, pocketed it. Picked up some headphones, sat down and adjusted them over his head, positioned the microphone. "Report," he said.

Fifteen miles away at the ranch estate, Erik and Felix sat in a similar office inside the airport hangar. Their blue mechanic's coveralls were clean for a change, their freshly shaved faces shined under the drop ceiling lights.

Erik leaned forward, pressed the button on a microphone mounted to his desk. "Los policias gringos..."

"Practice your English, Erik," chided El Maestro.

"The American policemen haven't gone anywhere other than their chamber and the ballroom."

"Have they discussed anything suspicious?"

"Yes."

"Play it for me," he directed. He leaned back, frowning up at the monitors.

Felix had been listening to the exchange and hurried to pull up the security feed from the hidden cameras in Jimmy and Hector's bed chamber. He typed in commands on the keyboard, connecting the video to the mansion's security control room. The footage showed Jimmy standing in front of a mirror, posturing, while Hector stood behind him obsequiously.

"I told you we'd get our due," Jimmy said. "Didn't I tell you? That greaser was our ticket."

"Yeah, Jimmy. You said it," Hector replied.

El Maestro replayed the scene over and over, studying the mannerisms, tone of voice in relation to the facial and hand cues, word choice in relation to what he knew of their psyches. An expert in behavioral science, he could immediately discern that what they spoke of was an underhanded action that had elevated their status among La Familia. His frown deepened. Finally, he said, "They must be speaking of Jose."

Felix and Erik looked at each other. Erik said into the mic, "That's what we thought, too, El Maestro."

"Have you heard this 'greaser' reference before?"

"No. This is their first mistake. The bug we put in their patrol car didn't turn up anything useful before it expired."

El Maestro remained silent for several minutes. He said, "It isn't enough. Continue monitoring them."

"Si, El Maestro."

"What news of the lady and gentleman?"

Felix leaned forward. "The *gringa* is using the phone we sent to her through the Latin Queens. She tried to call her boxing *maestro*, but he didn't answer. That was her only call."

"Very well. Stay on it."

"Si."

"The gentleman?"

"We still can't track him on the Internet. Two days ago he did something impossible."

"Really?" Intrigued, El Maestro sat up, leaned forward. Stroked his chin beard.

"*Si*, uh, yes. Our server linked to his Mi-Fi router showed processing capabilities far beyond that of a Four-G network, and dozens of IP addresses popped up, claiming he was everywhere from New York to Macao." He paused for a moment, feeling a touch of superstition. "El Maestro, whatever he is doing, I could not imagine it. I showed the data to the maids and they were baffled, too. It was like he was using a supercomputer."

"Stimulating," he responded. *I wonder what he's up to*, he pondered. "Continue collecting data on his movements. Find someone who can decipher it."

"We will try. He really is like the Chupacabra of the Internet, eh?" Felix said. The three men shared a laugh.

El Maestro got back to business. "Stay with the lady. She will likely be the one to take point," he advised.

"Yes, El Maestro. When they escape, do you think they will go after the *gringo* policemen?" Erik said.

"That is entirely possible," he answered. "In fact, I'm counting on it."

"Oh," Erik and Felix said in understanding. They knew their boss wouldn't act on someone in the organization without absolute proof of guilt. It was a standard he made everyone uphold, a trait that set La Familia apart from the other cartels, which killed one another capriciously, based on paranoia without evidence. There had to be evidence, and none had been found to prove the American policemen had murdered La Familia's top lieutenant two years ago. They had been suspected from day one and thoroughly investigated. They were street smart, crafty enough that they might avoid punishment from El Maestro.

But the *gringa* boxer and her *chupacabra* husband had all the proof they needed to exact their revenge.

This thought passed between the mechanics with a glance. They grinned, knowing it would happen, one way or another. Pride swelled their chests as they became impressed with their liege's scheme.

Felix pressed the mic's button. "It is a fine plan, El Maestro," he praised, giddiness in his voice. "The *gringa*, she will take care of those *cabrones*."

Smiling, El Maestro said, "Don't count your chickens just yet. They must be caught, plucked, cooked, then put on a plate. We haven't even released the foxes yet."

"We will continue our efforts, El Maestro," Erik said. Then he remembered something. "The *gringa*, she is proving difficult."

"Yes?"

"The Latin Queens said she refused their help. She finally accepted the phone, but claimed she didn't want to escape. This is no good for our plans to transport her."

"I am not surprised. That will inconvenience us some, but don't fret. It is likely she has her own plan and doesn't want anyone to know about it."

"Smart *Señora. Hasta pronto*, El Maestro," he said. See you soon.

"*Hasta pronto*, Erik. Felix."

Removing the headphones, El Maestro leaned back to watch the policemen mingle in the ballroom. He had invited them to his city home for a party while they had vacation time. A gesture he did for all his security teams, lavishing them with all sorts of incentives and benefits as they enjoyed a week of life in a mansion. However, he had hidden motives for these two particular traffickers, hoping to catch them under the influence of alcohol or women and cajole a reference out of them concerning his friend's death. He would rather take care of them himself, in Mexico, than for the lady to take more risks on a mission for revenge.

Dismissing the police officers for now, he thought of Ace's use of some kind of serious computing power and wondered how in Mary's name he was able to do that from where he was in prison. "Simply amazing," he told the ceiling. "He should be working for me."

He couldn't figure out the how of it, but was sure of the why: hacking to organize his escape.

And therein lay another puzzle. *What did he hack into? How was he planning to escape?* It would be something very clever. Obvious to him, innovative to them. Something that would be stimulating to try and follow, see what happened.

Smiling pleasantly, he steepled his fingers. He loved puzzles.

Shutting down the surveillance monitors, he stood and turned off the lights. Left the room to give a speech to his beloved La Familia.

Chapter XVI

Central Mississippi Correctional Facility
Pearl, Mississippi
March 19, 2012

The cheap scent of generic laundry detergent pervaded the cubicle and aisle, a wet sheet throwing a mist over everything as Clarice shook it, popping out the excess water and soaking her arms and face. She hung it on a string tied between the top bunks. Walked back to the sinks to wring out another one. A small plastic waste bucket was on the floor, that she used to soak her clothes in. She rinsed them in a sink. Several pairs of socks, shirts, and underwear were stacked on a shelf above the row of sinks, waiting to be hung.

Clarice grabbed the last sheet out of the bucket, wrung it, rinsed it several times with hot water. Waiting on the sink to fill and drain took for-freaking-ever, and was killing her hands. She held them up.

The awful, swollen, wrinkled disfigurement from all the washing made them look like they were decomposing. Gross.

What Bob Barker hell was that detergent made in?

With everything on the line and billowing from her box fan, Clarice sat on the bunk and stared at her poor hands, trying not to cry.

"You look like that every time you do laundry," Yolanda said. She sat up in her bed, slipped headphones off her ears. The faint, funky sounds of Mary J. Blige squealed from miniscule speakers.

"You're going to have hearing impairment," Clarice told her, still pouting at her fingers.

Yolanda frowned at her radio, turned the volume down. Remembered her reason for talking to Clarice. "Why don't you send your clothes to the laundry? Hand washing takes, like, forever."

Clarice looked at her. "My clothes are white. I like them that way."

"Oh." She looked down at her dingy t-shirt, which was new but had been sent to the laundry. Once. Embarrassment slowly replaced her befuddled look. She hadn't been aware of her garment's condition until now. With all the dusty, unhygienic prisoners around here, Yolanda just blended right in, unaware, a product of her shabby environ and like-minded peers. Like everything else, someone had to point it out to gain her attention.

Clarice shook her head, continued her sulking, which was far more important than Yolanda's incurable ignorance.

"You two hookers look like you're rehearsing for an anti-depressant commercial," Patty announced walking into the cubicle. Her smile lit up the building. "I've got just the thing to turn those frowns upside down."

"What?" Yolanda said.

"Herbal Prozac," she said, holding up a bag full of weed.

"Shut up!" Yolanda exclaimed, clapping like a child shown a present.

Clarice smiled at the blonde giant. "No thanks, Patty. Are you sure you want to smoke today? The warden likes to do inspections on Mondays."

"Warden-shmorden," she dismissed, waving a hand. "This stuff is practically legal now. You telling me that fat-bellied, fat head, red-eyed secret smirking warden hasn't taken a few pulls from the bong? He looks like a veteran of the Munchie Wars. Probably has a five-foot pipe shaped like a big booty Jamaican chick." Her hands indicated an hour glass figure, super-sized bust and hips. "Come on, Shocker. Take a toke." Her waggling eyebrows and stupid grin did wonders for Clarice's mood.

"I don't know, man. I've never tried it," Clarice said, smiling, demurring, but without much conviction.

"Never?" Yolanda gasped. "Shut up."

"No, never. Dope and boxing don't mix very well. Neither does dope and running a business or raising a family."

"I don't know," Patty mused, fingers to her lips. "I have a kid. If I didn't smoke weed that little mother-fucker would have drove me crazy."

"So you're saying you're not already crazy?" Clarice queried.

"Well...Crazier."

Clarice laughed, thinking about all the times Nolan had made her feel like guzzling a bottle of booze from sheer frustration. She imagined weed would have the same alleviating effects, allowing a person to escape reality for a while.

Wouldn't that be great? To feel like she wasn't in prison, to experience freedom, even for a few hours, would be like a vacation. No fights, no escape plans, no ignoramus inmates or officers breathing stupidity in her face. No ugly Bob Barker hands. She could get high and laugh at all of it.

Suddenly, it sounded like a fantastic idea. She eyed the baggie in Patty's hand with acute interest. "Oh, what the hell. I'll give it a try," Clarice declared.

"Shocker, girl, you're gonna love it," Patty promised.

The excitement she exuded was infectious, and Yolanda and Clarice both giggled like kids on Christmas morning. Patty sat on her bunk and grabbed a magazine, put it in her lap, began breaking up a dark green bud with long pale yellow and red hairs that looked like little flags warning of extreme danger. The sheets hanging across the cubicle's entry blocked the view of the women walking through the aisle. Loud laughter erupted from the front of the zone, in the dayroom that by now was crowded with convicts of every race and personality, all ogling the men and hating the glamorous women on *The Bold and the Beautiful.*

Yolanda unplugged her headphones, allowing the radio's speakers to play out loud. Turned it up. Jumped down from her bunk, sat next to Patty. Grace Potter and the Nocturnals rocked their only hit, *Paris*, punishing the tiny radio, vibrating the bunk and making all three of them start doing the Pretty Girl Rock, snapping fingers, whipping hair back and forth. Cheesing like lobotomy patients.

The absolute abandon was beyond description. How was it possible to let go of so much, in here of all places? Megatons of stress and internal pressures lifted, and Clarice could have sworn she felt the bags under her eyes and the lines in her face just melt away. Troubles still randomly flashed through her awareness, mental Post It notes reminding her to stay prepared, seek opportunity – she couldn't forget her problems. But she could manage to enjoy the elation, which right now seemed on the verge of imploding deep in her belly, a warm joyous bomb of humor.

Clarice felt great in a bad place. And they hadn't even smoked anything yet. Just anticipated it.

Hello placebo-effect! Her new BFF!

A scratch of lighter flint. A squinted, puckered vacuum face from the Viking Princess, and clouds of marijuana smoke obscured her vision. It was wonderfully thick, almost tasty. It smelled sublime.

Even non-smokers and anti-pot folks could appreciate the aroma. It wasn't sweet or flowery, nothing that evoked terms like sexy or pretty. The pungent herb was an incense for unlocking creativity. Aromatherapy spurring ideas in great quantities, though almost too subtle to detect, while pasting an eye-squinting grin on one's face. It was tranquil and positive, and goddammit, *I-don't-know-what-the-hell-I'm-babbling-about-I-want-some*!

Patty turned her lobotomy grin on her. "I see you have contact already," she said with smoke drifting lazily out of one nostril. Then she started choking. Yolanda sniggered, shooting a ball of spittle to the floor. In the split-second silence that followed, Clarice was sure she heard that thing go splat.

Patty handed Clarice the joint as she was considering what was happening. She drew a blank. She looked at the joint in her hand. She pointed and laughed. They were already doing the same.

Clarice always imagined being cumbersome or nervous her first time, but that wasn't the case. It was much worse.

Simply put, it made her want to get tested for Down's syndrome. From the first hit, her thoughts and actions jumped timing. As she puffed on the weed she thought about her high school friends that tried to get her high at a Korn concert. For a second there she could even hear the drums and roaring crowd, growing louder, funneling a great hollow pressure into her head. It was dizzying, though pleasant. Then she realized that was just her galloping heart and lack of oxygen to her brain from holding a gallon of smoke in her lungs for way too long.

Clarice choked, dropped the joint on the floor. Coughing so hard the drummer did a solo on her boobs, ba-ba, ba-ba-boom, crowd roaring, turning to laugh at her, MWAH-HA-HA, filling her ears like huge, slow-moving waves crashing on a shore. The onslaught of cough-cramping pain, like that of being pepper sprayed, had never felt so pleasurable, so refreshing.

Gasping pathetically, but *oh-so-euphorically*, Clarice managed to pry open an eye. Her partners in crime were both doubled up over wheezing gales of something Clarice suspected to be laughter. Red faced, pointing with great merriment. Yolanda stumbled over to the joint, its ember burning at the halfway mark, picked it up. Hit it. Was seized by the Giggle God again. Clarice continued her own slobbering excuse for a laugh, though she had no idea what these other broads were so enthused about.

They were stuck laughing. On the level.

The concert and drums returned, really cranking in her head. Nodding, shaking, eyes-closed-head-banging. Her attention pounced on the radio on Yolanda's bed. Studied it. Swore it was playing some sort of bubble gum pop Katy Perry headache.

Where was the rock music coming from? No matter. Kept jamming it, grinning lobotomy-style, stupid-silly-giggly-girlie-freaky stomp the gas and haul ass...

I'm high!

Time and its unbending laws had no meaning on this plane of bliss. Exuberance was the Man around here, a big sonofabitch that bullied everyone into feeling good. *Feel like a boss, dammit. A queen. You have no choice in the matter. Float and cruise and be smooth, baby.* Clarice felt she could stand up and out-box anybody, fast as a shooting gun, pow-pow-pow her fists would hit their faces, relaxed and precise as she played with them, cat with a mouse. Warm, pulsing energy circulated down her arms and legs, up her torso like a powerful laser, a high energy beam blindingly bright, constantly changing frequency, growing more intense, louder, stronger, as the drug further consumed her.

What. A. Rush.

It plateaued after a time, no telling how long, leveling out on some function of cruise control Clarice had no control of, super-smooth-floating-smiling-slow-dancing-swinging-to-the-music. The drums and crowd simmered, allowing other senses to enter her awareness. Pop music invaded rudely. Clarice frowned at the terrible singing before recognizing the song as one she liked. Yolanda was just trying to tell her something in her irritating voice, ruining the melody.

"...Tattoos. You want to check out my gun?" she said.

"It's not a gun. It's a machine," Clarice responded automatically, as any serious tatt artist would do when their trade tool is denigrated. "If you're going to get serious about slinging ink, that's Rule #1."

"Machine. Okay," she said thoughtfully, head looking like it hurt from the lesson. Ingrained stubbornness fighting change. Or she was too plowed to focus.

Geez. This was going to hurt Clarice worse than her. And kill her buzz...

"Let's see it," Clarice sighed.

"All right." She opened her locker box, the corroded metal tracks grinding like fingernails on a chalkboard. Clarice's jaw tightened with the absolute weirdest sensation ever. Yolanda grabbed several wires, a pen, and an old Walkman-type tape player. The machine must have been dismantled and stashed so the parts looked like legal property. At least she had sense enough to do that. She began assembling it.

Snack wrappers crinkled behind her. Clarice spun around to find Patty tearing open a beef jerky, squirting a pack of mustard on the meat sticks. Eyes red, nearly squinted closed, her smile was lopsided, sloppy. "Practice safe eating," she told her, face turning serious. "Use condiments."

The Giggle God hit her with a combination to the body so hard that Clarice hit the floor, feet up, TKOed. Gasping in laughter herself, Patty handed her a meat stick slathered in mustard. Clarice took it. Forgot what was so funny. Took a bite. It dawned on her that she had become retarded.

"It's gross," Clarice mumbled around the food. Looked at Patty, eyes widening. "It tastes wonderful, though."

"Practice safe eating," she replied happily, licking her fingers.

Clarice sat up. Wiped the grease and safe condiment from her hands. Realized, too late, that Clarice he was wiping on her clean white shirt. Stared at the stains, horrified. Started giggling as her brain sizzled in an effort to work out that she would never get those stains out with Bob Barker detergent, and, *ohmygod*, she would have to spend money on a new shirt from some greedy, thieving, convict who worked in the clothes warehouse while restraining herself from knocking their teeth in, the extortionist bitch, and, oh-boy, wouldn't that be a headache? No, she'd think it was funny, like she did now, she was looking forward to it, and she wasn't really concerned with this because the stain looked just like Jesus...

Yeah, have you ever seen that, um, show where people had the Virgin Mary on toast and an Elvis mud stain on a shirt, just like this one, maybe it's worth money, though legally I can't keep it, being state property, and, oh well, why am I happy again, I think I should be depressed, or hitting something, a body, not a joint, my eyes are rolling back, what???

The poor shirt! Clarice decided just to give it to Yolanda. *She'll wear anything,* Clarice thought to herself, laughing.

What?

Rock music.

Keep jamming it, stupid-silly-giggly-girlie-freaky stomp the gas and haul ass... I'm retarded!

"No more drugs for this woman," Patty said pointing at her.

Clarice dragged herself back on the bed. "I feel like I drank a Homer Simpson potion," she croaked, cotton mouthed.

"D'oh!" Patty exclaimed. Clarice knew she'd understand.

A clattery racket behind them made her forget the slovenly remark Clarice had stashed somewhere in her misfiring head. The sounds were of a small motor powering metal over plastic. Clarice spun around expecting to see an elf doing some light weed eating around her tree, and was surprised to find a grinning Yolanda holding up her tattoo contraption proudly. The 3 volt tape player motor mounted on top of a Bic pen spun an out-of-round plastic wheel the size of a dime. A straightened paper clip attached to the wheel and pistoned through the center of the pen and out the tip. Old ink stained it from top to bottom, matching her dirty fingernails. The kindergarten-level engineering and unsanitary sight nearly triggered Clarice's gag reflex. The thought of that germ factory actually being used on someone…

Ugh.

Clarice snatched it out of her hand. Unhooked the batteries.

Yolanda scowled at her and screeched, "What's your problem?!"

"This is an abomination," Clarice said, mocking her screech. "Do you have any idea how dangerous this is? You should catch it on fire, then flush it down the toilet. It's a fucking biohazard, Yolanda."

"D'oh!" Patty chimed in, sucking down another beef jerky. Safely.

Clarice continued, trying not to laugh. She gave Patty a look that said, *This is serious, dammit.* Then looked back at Yolanda. "You were right. This is a gun. A freaking microbe gun. You are shooting your customers full of bacteria, maybe even a few viruses. Hell, they aren't customers - they're victims. Christ," she breathed, running a hand through her hair. Her OCD was really tweaking on her mind. It probably didn't help that she was completely baked on pot.

On the bright side, she felt no urge to hurt her cube mate, though she felt she should have, for having the audacity to show this to her with a proud smile...

For some reason, it all became very funny, and she didn't know what she was mad about or why she should be mad. The reason was right on the tip of her tongue, right around the corner from her sight. But she couldn't quite remember the reason she was looking for it.

Why are you broads looking at her like that?

"D'oh!" Patty trumpeted, glassy red eyes twinkling at her.

"You don't have to be such a bitch about it. Forget you, then," Yolanda sulked.

Clarice was pretty sure she was talking to her and accusing her of being the B word, yet she didn't have a clue why. Small black dots swarmed in front of her, frizzling, dancing like some kind of alien anti-lightning bugs. The drug wasn't through and swamped her with yet another wash of euphoria, warm vertigo that felt like she was knocked out on her feet even though she was sitting and nearly moaning from pure pleasure.

Her blurry eyes seemed to take years to re-focus. Yolanda, head down, looking ashamed about something, appeared to have lost the party fever that she so wholeheartedly supported only moments ago.

Geez, girl. Stop being such a buzz kill.

Clarice looked at Patty, shrugged. What's wrong with this turd?

She gave a slight nod, always a willing conspirator. "Here, you fat motherfucker. Eat something," she said, throwing a beef jerky and pack of mustard to Yolanda.

She caught it, scowled at her stomach. "I'm not fat," she argued, pinching her rail-thin torso. Her smile erased all signs of shame as she understood the tease. She loved how thin she was, and cheesed whenever someone commented on it. As usual, Patty's masterful use of vulgarity proved fruitful.

How many girls do you know smile after being called a "fat motherfucker"? That takes skill.

Um. Right. Skill. What skill? Damn.

Clarice kept losing her train of thought.

I think. Or I don't think. That's the point, right? Oh hell, I don't know. Why am I looking for the reason again?

The random turns of thought continued to elude and delude her awareness, pissing her off. She was thinking like a mentally challenged baboon... one thought after another, each deceiving her by presenting something more interesting than the last but just as forgettable. Something that grabbed her shuffling attention, something common and simple, yet complex. There was a feeling, a notion that an event was coming, a cycled incident that was routine and easy to observe, though it could prove harmful if undetected. There were signs that cue the incident, the presence...

Something that grabbed her shuffling attention, something common and simple, yet complex. A feeling, a notion that *oh-my-fucking-God-there's-the-warden*!

Instinct kicked in and Clarice dropped the contraband, nonchalantly moved away from it.

"Good afternoon. How are you ladies doing?" Warden Michaels said in a formal tone, back ramrod straight in his conservative white button-up and yellow tie. His eyes narrowed when they didn't respond. He stared at each of them in turn. Brows furrowing at the three sets of stoned eyes squinting back at him. Yolanda moved to set a towel on top of the tattoo machine, drawing Michael's attention.

"Hold it! Don't move," he commanded, pointing at one of the five officers behind him, gesturing for her to intercept Yolanda's endeavor to hide contraband.

As soon as the warden fixated on Yolanda, Patty eased away from her bunk and stood next to her own. Several more officers appeared like a gang of terrorists, all vying for Michaels' direction. He pointed to Patty, then Clarice, and the CO thugs moved to search them.

Patty wasn't going to submit quietly. She stepped up on her bunk, all over her goddamn pillow, the fucking slut, slapped her considerable backside and yelled, "Kiss my ass!" before jumping over the wall into the cubicle behind them. Her hard soled Bob Barkers hit the floor and squeaked like basketball shoes as she sprinted to the toilets, elbowing convict gawkers out of her way. She skidded to a stop in front of a vacant toilet. Flushed the bag of pot, snatched her phone and shank out of her pants and flushed them in quick, practiced movements that showed off her decade's experience as a convict.

The industrial toilet sucked down the major contraband like bite-sized snacks.

Two male officers rushed to grab her, slow and jerking from huge bodies unused to so much action. She allowed them to put her face down on the floor. Cuffed her. The warden walked up and looked in the toilet. Looked at Patty, mugging furiously. He didn't like being cheated out of a bust.

"That's okay," he told Patty with a look that said otherwise. Everyone had to look up at him. His head seemed to brush the ceiling, skyscraper high as his anger rose. His glasses and bald head glared rather than shined. "I've got something for you."

"Do we write her up?" inquired an officer.

"No. Spray her, then uncuff her," he growled, coldly settling the matter with illegal punishment.

A huge can of pepper spray was unleashed on her friend, whooshing like a fire extinguisher, covering her shirt, pants, tiles and the row of toilets with orange chemical. Patty choked until her throat stuck closed. Several officers ran off trailing their own coughs.

Paranoia had overwhelmed Clarice. This shit wasn't fun anymore. She knew it was just the weed impairing her ability to slow her heart rate and take charge of herself. But the presence of mind wasn't enough.

She had heard of people having a "bad trip" their first time getting high, though she seriously doubted that what she was experiencing was the same: a warden dictator and gang of correctional thugs terrorizing the party. This was insanity, live and in living color. Lots of unpleasant colors and discordant sounds. Sounds she could see were bad; colors she could hear were bad. She was too goddamn high and she hated it.

A mistake she would never make again.

From now on, she decided, she would stick to electricity.

Two female officers approached her, their looks turning cautious as recognition struck them, her reputation and capabilities at the forefront of their minds. They stopped several feet away, out of her reach.

"Offender Carter," one of them said, a tall, large woman with light brown skin and a horrible short wig. "We need you to kneel down and put your hands on top of your head, please."

The officer's shaky voice made her seem even more paranoid than Clarice, though that couldn't be accurate because the officer was able to talk. Clarice's mouth was so dry, so utterly out-of-order and disconnected from whatever pot infested section of her brain language came from, that she couldn't possibly reply to her verbally. She tried to think through the officer's request. Couldn't see why her arms and legs couldn't perform the task, and decided to give it a try, make it all look good for the warden so they'd leave faster. No sense going to lockdown for insubordination. Again.

As she knelt, Clarice looked over at the warden, who was scolding Yolanda for several superficial offenses and directing the COs to issue her Rules Violation Reports. The petty bastard worried about the wrong thing. There were folks around here being robbed and extorted, forced into sexual relations. And he's worried about *tattoos*? That wasn't his job.

It was hers.

The officers did a perfunctory search through their locker boxes and bunks, just randomly dumping paperwork out of manila envelopes and scattering hygiene products and clothes all over the place. Ripped down the clothesline, threw Clarice's clean whites and sheets on the floor. Patty's box was divested of several free-world ink pens and any extra clothes that exceeded the three-pair limit. The usual trifling shakedown harassment.

Another prison employee joined the party, though this one wore a bright floral print dress and a brighter smile with her limp. The old black lady looked like she could win a soul food cook-off with both hands tied behind her back. She moseyed up to her kneeling form. "Clarice Carter?" she asked.

Clarice nodded, afraid to speak, knowing her voice would betray her apprehension and attract the warden, like blood in the water attracts sharks. She desperately tried to gain control of her heart rate and work some spit in her mouth. Right now she felt that a prospecting pimp could own her for a bottle of lemon ice Gatorade. Or just a swallow of it.

The lady tilted her head at her curiously. "What's your MDOC number, honey? I have some legal mail for you."

Eyes bugging at her words, the anxiety attack took on a new form, a living being that rose high above her with deadly weight and shook her massive finger, warning her not to talk. *Just keep on panicking if you know what's good for you, sister.* Clarice stared at the lady like a carp out of water.

"That's okay, honey. Where's your ID?" she said, seeing Clarice was clearly upset about the officers tearing up the cubicle. Clarice nodded at her locker box. The woman waddled over to it. Squatted down and plundered through the trashed property until a driver's license-sized card with her butterface on it appeared in her hand. She read it, dropped it. She walked back holding out an envelope and document that Clarice had to sign to say she accepted the mail. Clarice scribbled out something vaguely like a signature. Accepted the envelope and renewed her *Apprehension Grand Prix* when she read the return address.

The Circuit Court? Could it be good news?

The law library tech shambled off with her cute grandma walk, wearing a sympathetic look for the harried inmates. After ripping open the envelope, Clarice forgot all about her and the search and the *hands on your head* order. A three-page court order unfolded in her hands. A transportation order from that cantankerous, biased, pathetic excuse for a judge, T.W. Wallace. Clarice read the contents quickly.

Elephant Trunk Penis? State of Drunken Rednecks v. Clarice Carter?

Clarice was thinking this was some kind of low-down attorney prank until she got to the Docket Text.

Escape from the Planet of the Apes/Escape from the Prison Planet.

Clutch?

It was Ace!

Her wonderfully ingenious husband with his mad scientist laugh and elephant trunk junk. Her desert dry red eyes threatened to well with tears. God, she had missed that brilliant idiot.

How the hell did he get them a new trial hearing?

This was no *Thinking of You* note. Ace was organizing an escape plan for both of them. He must have hacked into the court system, the crazy fool. He'd better not have broken his promise. *When is it?*

Clarice quickly ran her finger down the lines of "Judge Wallace's" order to find the date. "Monday, April twelfth," Clarice murmured, chest flushing with new emotion. It was far stronger than the anxiety. It clashed with it, denying negative thought chemicals and humping all the Feel Good stuff so that the irrational suspicions and trepidation instilled by the warden's show of power no longer mattered. Her THC clouded mind was once again locked into a definitive gear, heading through that dark and dangerous tunnel where only the ultra-determined can survive.

I will test my heart and succeed where others have failed. The end will justify the means: Freedom with my family.

Clarice shook her head, running that last thought again. What freaking tunnel? Clarice must have burnt something in her brain.

Crap. When does this stuff wear off? I'll kill Patty whenever I sober up.

Clarice focused on the documents again, rereading the important lines. All she could see was blah, blah, blah, her man was getting her out of here.

Yippee-kiyay, motherfucker!

"Offender Carter," the warden said behind her. "I don't care how big of a star you were on the street. You're just another number in here, you understand me? Get your hands back on your head."

"Yes, sir," Clarice managed, delighted to have spit in her mouth again. *Thanks, Ace. You'll get Extra Special Bonus Sex for that, just as soon as I see you.* The warden walked around and stood in front of her. Clarice folded the precious court order, pocketed it. Put hands on her head.

"Why are you smiling at me, Carter? Something about me that amuses you?"

276

"Not particularly, uh, sir," Clarice said, snorting back a giggle. Her cheeks heated with a blush. His heated with something else. Though Clarice didn't care. Clarice was leaving soon!

"You uppity folks never had any respect for authority. I couldn't stand it in the service, and I'll be damned if I stand for it in my own prison." He pointed to one of the COs, a dumpy lady that looked pretty much like the rest of the guards. She took ages to gain her feet, closed Yolanda's box and step-swayed over to stand in front of her boss.

"Yes, Warden Michaels?" she said, wiping sweat from her face and neck with a brown paper towel.

"Issue offender Carter an RVR for disrupting the orderly running of the institution, and another for refusing to obey a direct order."

"Yes, sir."

He walked off, waving for the herd of COs to follow. Does trailing their buck. The antlers that sprouted out of his head were nearly as funny as the short white tails twitching on the rear ends of the COs. The hallucination unleashed a wild chortle that made Clarice's temples throb dangerously. Three of the officers turned to look at her, two of them scowling at her evident humor at their expense, the other looking undecided about something. Possibly on the verge of calling the barbaric nurses that wield hypodermics full of Thorazine.

Clarice wiped off her stupid smirk. Patty was right - no more drugs for this woman.

"You all right, Shock?" Patty said, glaring at the COs, who turned to catch up to their group. "You look like you're a few laughs away from the crazy house." She began picking up her sheets, careful not to get pepper spray on them. Her shirt, hair and pants were completely soaked with the orange chemical.

"Yeah. Fine. I'm delusional and psychosomatic, but fine. You?" Clarice stood and coughed a little from all the pepper spray in the air.

"No sweat. I manage to get sprayed every six months or so. That stuff just clears my sinuses now. I put on the choke show for the warden's sake. Makes him feel like a big man when he gets to punish an impertinent hooker."

"What a life we have, huh? I've been sprayed half a dozen times myself. Doesn't affect my breathing or sight too bad now. Still cooks my skin, though."

"Broils it every time," she said amiably, lifting her shirt. Her skin was an angry red. "You never get used to that." She dropped her shirt, started cursing.

"What?" Yolanda asked, organizing her property. She paused and looked up at Patty. "Is it burning really bad?"

"Yeah, but that's not the problem. I had five hundred invested in that Motorola, and another four hundred in the weed. That swag cost two an ounce," she grumbled.

"Wow," Yolanda said.

"Ouch," Clarice sympathized. "At least you didn't get caught with it. No one went to lockdown for a change."

"Well, aren't you a pocket full of sunshine," Patty muttered. She sighed, then gave her a smile. "It's no sweat. I can hustle a few Johns and get back in the game." She opened her mouth, poked her tongue in and out of a cheek while holding an undulating fist to her lips.

Yolanda burst out laughing. Clarice just shook her head.

Chapter XVII

South Mississippi Correctional Institution
Leakesville, Mississippi
March 23-24, 2012

"Is this her?" Diamond asked, flipping through a stack of photographs. "She's cute."

"She is. But don't let the pretty smile fool you. My wife is no honeysuckle," Ace said. He sat up on his bunk, closed the computer science magazine on his lap and looked over at Diamond, who was studying old pictures of his wife and son.

"She was a boxer, right?"

"Yep. The boxer. She retired a world champion, number one on the pound-for-pound list."

"I'm not sure what that means, but it sounds impressive." He grabbed another photo, one of Nolan holding up a ratchet and socket with grease all over his little hands, beaming a smile only happy children are capable of doing. A magical moment in time a father could never forget. Diamond showed it to Ace. "Your son looks so healthy. I bet he misses you."

"Yeah," he sighed.

The buzz of the zone door made them look up and shake off the sentimental atmosphere. Several inmates in neighboring cubicles also paused in their activities, studying the five Latin Kings that mobbed through the door, their caution spreading throughout the entire zone. The sounds of fifty men moving around, opening and closing locker boxes, exercising, laughing and slamming cards on the tables were hushed as danger was sensed in the air.

"Those guys are Enforcers," Diamond whispered.

"What does that mean?" Ace said.

"Big trouble."

"Fantastic."

The LKs walked down the aisle mugging anyone who looked them in the eye. Stocky with matching buzz cuts and tattoos covering their bodies, the gang of young thugs swaggered directly to Ace and Diamond's cubicle. The one in front, who appeared slightly older and larger than the rest, locked eyes with Ace and scowled with menace. He halted the group at the cube's entry.

"Which one of you punks is Alan Carter?" he demanded. His four associates posted up behind him, arms folded over their chests. Two of them faced the other cubicles.

"I am," Ace said, perplexed. "What's up?"

"Don't be calling anyone a punk. White boy," Diamond spat.

"Shut your dick sucker, punk. Ain't nobody talking to you, you shitty leg queer. Why don't you go sparkle somewhere," the big thug said in a mock lisp, flashing his fingers to indicate fireworks.

Diamond's mouth worked back and forth, anger rising. His neck cocked. "You don't know me. I'll cut you –"

"Hang on, D," Ace said, standing and walking quickly between his friend and the antagonist. He faced the intruders. "What do they call you?"

"Death Punch."

"Oh, that's sexy," Diamond started.

Ace cut him off again, "Diamond! Please chill out." He looked back to Death Punch. "You obviously came here for a reason." He waved a hand at the other Latin Kings. "What's on your mind?"

"You. We want you to join us."

Heavy silence followed the statement. The hushed voices from neighboring convicts ceased as they overheard and quieted completely to hear more. Several box fans were turned off.

Ace's heart was pounding. He wasn't sure how to respond without offending anyone. His first thought was to say he was Caucasian, and not eligible. But looking into the face of a very white Death Punch stifled the remark. He glanced at Diamond, who had set aside the photographs and held something under his blanket.

Crap, Ace thought, grimacing with indecision. *I did not need this problem. I wonder what will happen if I refuse?*

"And if I say no?" he inquired.

Death Punch smiled. "There is no refusal. You join or you will get your ass beat every time a King spots you." The two LK subordinates facing them nodded their heads, grinning with anticipation.

Ace gulped. "Why me?"

"We know about you and El Maestro. The Teacher is our connection. You violated by dealing with him without going through us."

"But I didn't know –"

"Doesn't matter!" he exploded. He raised his voice so the entire zone could hear. "You have to be a Latin King to deal with La Familia. No one deals with them without our administration." He lowered his voice, glaring at Ace. "For some reason, El Maestro has chosen to help you personally. I have tried for years to get direct contact with him. I'm a Latin King! One of his followers. And he favors you? A peon? Not while I'm around."

"With that arrogant garbage, do you really wonder why El Maestro won't mess with you?" Diamond sassed. "I mean, seriously."

Death Punch turned, took several quick steps over to Diamond's bunk and slapped him in the face. The heavy blow cracked off the walls of the zone.

Diamond, no pushover, whipped a shank from under his blanket, stood up on his mattress and screamed a shrill challenge, waving the long sharp-

ened length of metal in front of him. He lunged toward Death Punch but was stopped brutally by a
punch to the side of his head, knocking him to the
floor. He cried out, elbows thudding hard on the
concrete, shank clattering and sliding over to stop
at Ace's feet. The LK who had punched him never
stopped moving forward and jumped on top of him
with more blows to the head, muscular arms and
shoulders churning as he pummeled Ace's friend. Diamond covered his head with his arms, curled up in
a fetal position, screaming.

Another LK joined his companion, adding two
more fists to the assault. A kick to Diamond's midsection cut off the screams.

Arms and legs shaking with fear, Ace looked back
and forth between Death Punch and his friend getting slaughtered. Death Punch grinned, nodded in a
way that said, See? This is what will happen to you.

Ace looked down at the shank, scared to death to
pick it up and commit to the fight. He had never been
a violent person. Never been in a single fist fight. He
was always able to out-think hostile situations.

Until now, he grumbled in thought. *I can't stand by
and do nothing while Diamond gets hurt. And hurt for
something I did.*

Visibly shaking, face pale, he focused on the shank
and asked himself what Clarice would do. She was so
calm and collected in situations like this.

She would probably hit Death Punch in his jaw,
then drop the others with body shots, he decided,

looking at all five bruisers as he imagined the Shocker would.

I couldn't do that if I was the star of a video game. "I'm going to die," he said, grabbing the shank with his left hand. From the squatted position, he jumped at Death Punch with his right fist balled up, throwing an uppercut in an effort to emulate what he had seen his wife do hundreds of times. The movement was awkward but effective, only slightly off-balance. His fist walloped Death Punch's chin, staggering him out into the aisle. Ace lunged toward Diamond's assailants with the shank slashing out before him. "Get back! Get the fuck off him!" he shouted, the blade whistling back and forth wildly, arm shaking. "I'll cut you! GET BACK!"

Startled by the unexpected attack from the computer geek, the LKs quickly jumped over the low brick walls to avoid getting cut, stumbling into the aisle and knocking their stunned leader to the floor.

Clanging keys and pounding boots stormed down the aisle. Lieutenant Cole jumped over a cubicle wall, knocking over a box fan, landed and blocked the LKs with his wide arms, right as they were mustering a counter attack, shanks in their hands, snarling at Ace and Diamond. Cole whipped a can of pepper spray from his belt, sprayed the five gang bangers until it emptied. They doubled over, dropping to their knees, coughing, sneezing, choking. As the thick cloud spread, convicts ran away from it, holding shirts over their nose and mouth, exiting on the yard.

Lieutenant Cole turned to Ace, who was helping Diamond to his feet, both of them coughing painfully, gasping for air. "Go!" Cole yelled at them, pointing at the yard door. He pushed the LKs out of the way so Ace could help Diamond through the aisle and out the door, into blessed fresh air.

They collapsed on the grass.

Several minutes later, the lieutenant walked out and approached them, scowling furiously. "What the hell was that all about?"

"They wanted me-" Ace began.

But Diamond clenched his hand, shook his head with meaning. "Those haters jumped on me. Ace got them off," he said.

"Uh-huh. Right," Cole replied. His attention riveted on Ace's hand. "Give me that!" He bent down and snatched up the shank. Surprise appeared on Ace's face; the blade was still in his grasp. Cole said, "You two are fucked. I don't think I can help you. The tower officer saw you fighting and called it in." He turned the weapon over in his huge dark hands. Tilted his head, listening to the radio. "ERT is already here."

At that moment, over a dozen officers in dark blue fatigues poured onto the yard, yelling for everyone to lay down on the ground. Huge German shepherds were straining from four separate leashes, barking, jumping at any prisoner that moved a limb. Cole nodded for Ace and Diamond to lay down. They did so, wanting no part of the killer dogs. ERT officers cuffed them, then escorted them to the other side of the compound to the segregation unit. They were placed in neighboring cells.

"Eww. This cell is nasty," Diamond complained.

Ace heard him through the vents above the door, muffled from swollen lips. "Yeah, mine isn't exactly the Trump Hotel either," he said, sitting on the mattress. His body still shook with adrenaline, but his heart had slowed. It was a sensation rarely known to him, a drained, hellish slowing of all functions. He absolutely could not believe he had attacked those guys. Remarkable.

Clarice will never believe this, he mused, shaking his head.

"Thanks, by the way," Diamond said. "I didn't think you would jump in."

"I didn't either," Ace admitted. "And there's no need to thank me. It's my fault they were there in the first place."

"I know that. But my smart-ass mouth is what got me into it."

"That's true."

The two friends were silent for several minutes as they contemplated their predicament, wondering if they'd be able to avoid further trouble from the LK Enforcers. Their pessimistic reveries were interrupted by the zone door slamming open, then closed. Two COs walked in and headed up the stairs, one carrying several bottles of chemicals and brown paper towels, the other holding documents with yellow carbon copy paper. The dreaded Rules Violation Reports. They stopped in front of Ace's cell first.

"You going to sign your RVR?" the CO said, a slim man in his early twenties.

"I've waited my whole life for this very moment," Ace responded. He took the proffered pen and scribbled his name in the blank designated "Offender's Signature," scowling at the label. His face deepened in displeasure as he read the report. "Wonderful. An assault charge."

"They'll never take it to court," Diamond said through the vent, signing his own RVR. "Them big folks don't care if we kill each other."

"That's sad."

"You want chemicals?" The other officer inquired timidly, a new recruit, nervous around two cons fresh off a knife fight.

"Definitely. There's probably a new species of bacteria waiting to be discovered in here," Ace said, taking the spray bottles and paper towels offered through his tray slot. "I can sense it growing." He soaked the entire cell, window, bunk, shelf. Passed the bottles back. Started wiping it up. The officers left.

Diamond started humming loudly, but squealed in sudden pain and stopped.

Ace laughed.

"It's not funny!" Diamond squeaked again, holding back a smile.

"It's either laugh or cry. Any chance we can get out of this by next week?"

"No way. A knife fight is six months in the hole. So you might as well get your lower back, or whatever you call that butt of yours, comfy over there."

"Six months?!"

"And that's only if we don't catch more RVRs in here. They hand them out like parking tickets in lockdown."

Oh no, Ace moaned in thought. *I still have to arrange transportation with Bobby before Clarice and I go to court. That's less than three weeks away. I can't do six months!* "Fuck."

"Well, listen to mister geek education curse like an alley whore. What's gotten up your electronic jock?" Diamond said, pausing in his cleaning to listen, concerned. "Don't sweat those Latin wannabes. We'll be ready for them next time."

"It's not that."

"Ooo-kay... You going to keep me in suspense? Or do I have to pry the business out of you?"

Ace looked around the cell, as if searching the cracks in the concrete and chips in the paint would reveal some kind of pattern of guidance, reading the fractal geometry like a shaman reads a toss of bones, seeking answers. Heavy duty cleaner filled his nose and prickled the back of his throat. He said, "I don't know if I should tell you."

"Really?" Diamond replied with a hand on his hip, the other waving a paper towel with attitude. "After all we've been through, you don't trust me?"

"I do. But you don't want to know about this."

"I'll be the judge of that."

Ace took a deep breath, making his decision. He needed a confidant. "Go to the back of the cell. There's a crack in our wall." He walked to the back corner and squinted through a slim gap between the cells. The light coming through dimmed as Diamond stuck his ear to the wall. Ace whispered, "I'm planning to escape."

"I take back what I said. You were right. I didn't want to know that."

Ace grinned. It was the response he had expected, and reassured him that Diamond could be trusted with this. "Too late, D. You and your smart-ass mouth."

"Screw you, rude mutt."

"Bulimic prostitute."

Diamond sighed. "All right. Anything I can do to help?"

"I don't know yet. I have to figure out how to get out of the hole first."

"Maybe Lieutenant Cole can help."

"He already said we were fucked."

"Then it will have to be a captain. The one over this building is that old drunk bastard, Bartleby."

"Captain Bartleby? I overheard some officers say he retired," Ace said.

"He tried, but rumor has it he couldn't get his pension yet because he's under investigation by CID," Diamond said, referring to the Correctional Investigation Division, a sort of Internal Affairs for MDOC.

"Maybe that's the doorway," Ace pondered out loud.

"What?"

"I was just thinking, if I can help that Captain get his pension, maybe he'll get me out of here."

"Us."

"Sorry. Us out of here."

"If it were anybody but you, I'd say you're living in a fantasy land. But your Macintosh-self just might compute a way to pull it off. He'll be around at shift change, I think. You have until then to come up with a game plan."

"Swell," Ace muttered. He felt exhausted, certainly not in any shape for this kind of scheming. As a general rule, he never made plans of any sort unless he was fresh, a habit he developed from working on computer projects worth hundreds of thousands of dollars, where any mistake could prove disastrous. He was obsessive about alertness on delicate subjects, and had integrated the principle into life in general. It was a rule he had trained himself not to break, though for some reason, the iron will that surrounded his standards was more flexible of late.

Well, I stretched Clarice's rules by involving Bobby. Too late to hold her snobbish nose in the air. For my freedom and my wife's, I think I can whip up a simple paradigm to manipulate the captain. In his position, it shouldn't be very difficult to appeal to his corrupt side. If I can get him the pension, he would do just about anything for her. He wants to escape this place, too.

Ace brightened at the thought, a trickle of energy reinvigorating his depleted mind. He looked around the cell with a new perspective.

"I'm gonna get some beauty rest. Holler if some juicy drama jumps off," Diamond said around a yawn, lying on his mattress and wincing, his entire body sore and bruised.

"I will literally holler."

Ace began pacing between the door and bed, one-two-three-four-five turn, one-two-three-four-five turn, knowing he had his best ideas while walking, wanting to keep his blood circulating to maintain his wits until Captain Bartleby showed up. Clarice's and Nolan's faces stayed at the forefront of his thoughts, constant reminders of his mission, his life's purpose, igniting a steady stream of excitement like the pilot light on a flame thrower. The flames were love, and his head and chest burned with anticipation of being with his family again. The emotional fire that had been so painful the last two years was now pleasurable, and drove him to overcome the predicament. He couldn't wait to feel the press of their bodies in a group hug, smell their hair and kiss their faces. Tell them in person how much he loved them and missed them.

He welcomed the burning pleasure and prayed to the physiology gods it never returned to the heart-crushing torture that had plagued him until recently. He finally suppressed most of it so he could survive as a convict. This was no life for a man with a family.

Hours passed. Ace paced. The zone door crashed open and two officers walked in, one holding a count roster. A brown-skinned man in a white shirt trailed behind them, slow, eyes red and blurry, deep-set in a mid-sixties face, scruffy gray beard as unkempt as his wrinkled pants and creased boots. His narrow hips and stick legs struggled to hold up his bulging stomach. Ace grinned as Captain Bartleby tried to keep up with his COs as they climbed the stairs, a bad punch line to a Mississippi obesity joke.

"Captain Bartleby," Ace said as the man peeked into the cell window. "I need to speak with you."

Bartleby's eyes strained to focus on the prisoner's face. "I remember you. You're Shocker Ares' husband. What the hell are you doing in lockdown, son?"

This is going to be easier than I thought, he mused, deciding to try and play on the man's affinity for boxing. "Had a little trouble with gang members."

"Yeah, it happens."

"You still watch the fights?"

"Hell yes. Friday Night Fights on ESPN tonight. Should be some decent matches. The women aren't as popular since your wife retired. Shame. I used to watch the Shocker on ESPN and HBO. Parked my old ass in front of the big screen with a bottle of cognac and hand down my pants. Like a black Al Bundy, or something." He laughed at his own joke.

Ace joined him, nearly giggling at the image his wife's fan described. "Wish I could watch with you. Sounds like a great way to spend retirement."

"Yeah, uh," Bartleby mumbled, wiping his bleary eyes. "Might be a while before I get to enjoy it like that."

"That's too bad. Trouble with MDOC bureaucracy?" Ace queried, seeing the captain was in a loquacious mood, hoping he would indulge his wont for gossip.

"Yeah. God damn CID investigation holding me up."

Yes… "CID, huh? I know some people there. Important people," Ace divulged, only half-lying. *I know their link and how to hack their databases, anyway,* he thought. He added, "People that can make things disappear."

The captain stared hard at Ace, suspicion noticeably whitening his eyes. He considered the prisoner's offer, then considered the prisoner himself. He knew Alan Carter and his wife were successful in business, with good reputations. As a fan, Bartleby had followed the trial and learned a great deal about Shocker's personal life.

They didn't get all that by doing bad business, he thought. *Illegal, perhaps. But not bad.*

If Alan can get that file…

"So your people can just, abracadabra, gone, huh?" he said.

"Something like that," Ace replied, staring back in earnest.

The captain nodded. "We might work something out, then. What do you want out of it?"

"Out."

"Out?!" Bartleby sputtered. "I can't get you out!"

"No. I mean out of lockdown."

"Oh," he said, relieved. "I can take care of that. You tell me when you've handled your end. I'll make some calls, and if it's all good, I'll sign your transfer."

"Deal," Ace said, smiling.

Captain Bartleby nodded, then hurried off and down the stairs to catch up to his COs. The zone door slammed shut behind them.

"Good news?" Diamond whispered through the crack.

"Yeah. It was almost too easy," he replied. *What the heck was I so worried about? I should have known it would be simple to deal with these corrupt officers.* "I have to hack into the CID database and look around for the dirt on Bartleby, then erase it."

"Should be easy enough for you. Let's just hope it's not a paper file."

"Crap. I haven't considered that. Are they that outdated?"

"Yeah. And lazy. One word: Mississippi."

"Crap," he repeated, mind racing. "I'll just have to try and see what happens. If nothing pops up then it must be in the paper files. I need my TV."

"Cole will be back in the morning. You already know he'll get it for you," Diamond said, curling up on his mat. "Wake me up then. I need like ten years of beauty sleep to heal all this shit."

"Good night."

Ace sat on his bed, lay down. Deciding he had made as much headway as possible for now, he fell into a deep sleep filled with short, flashing dreams of his family.

* * *

The following morning, Ace jumped out of his bed, startled awake by an officer pounding on the cell's steel door. He looked around wildly, eyes puffy, squinting from the rays of sunlight that lit up his face as he sat up. He slipped his feet into his shower shoes, stood and jumped again when he looked down at the tent sticking out the front of his boxer shorts. Grabbing his pants, he hurriedly tugged the ugly yellow material up his legs and tried to remember the dream that had produced such an impressive erection.

It was Clarice, he recalled. *She had me pinned to the bed with such strength I couldn't move. And her hips…*

Damn, it's gone.

His tingling, half-asleep arms told him he hadn't been pinned to the bed by his powerful wife. He shook his head, smiling. Walked to the door and looked into the dark, pleasant face of Lieutenant Cole, who smiled with something more than good morning cheer. Ace wanted to cross his legs.

"Wood morning," the lieutenant said.

"Um. Yeah. I guess it is," he replied uncomfortably. He looked at the ceiling and mouthed Why me? before standing closer to the door to hide the area of interest.

"What was that you told me about pitching woo on white boys?" Diamond lisped out the tray slot next door. "Now look at you. Hypocrite Cole."

Cole turned his bright smile on Ace's friend. "You're in a dangerous position there. All locked up in that tiny cell with nowhere to run."

"Whenever your black ass is ready," Diamond challenged.

Cole moved to banter with Diamond. Ace took a moment to do a few pushups, get circulating, then washed his face. He had a lot to do today. Hopefully Cole would get the TV for him presently, so he could get to work right away. If the hacking didn't pan out, he would have to find out who the convict clerk was that worked at CID and enlist his help.

He could probably get Diamond or Cole to do that. Between those two, they knew everyone in the prison.

Feeling energized from the much needed sleep, he hollered to get the lieutenant's attention. Cole and Diamond were engaged in a spirited dispute over who the greatest R&B singer was, and managed to make it a flirting contest, one topping the other with innuendos and hurtful comments.

"Hang on, Ace," Cole said. He looked at Diamond, grinned. "I'll be back to deal with you later, nigga. Why don't you go listen to your precious Alicia Keys? Oh, wait. You don't have a radio." He laughed uproariously at Diamond's spitting response, stepped over to Ace's door. "Hey, big guy. What's up?"

"I need the TV out of my locker box."

"All of your property was bagged, tagged, and stored in the property room."

"Can you still get it?"

"No problem. I have to go that way in a minute. I'll stop by here on the way back to my post. You worried about missing your soaps?" he said with a conspiratorial nod and smile.

"Yep. You got me. I'm a whining, crying, drama super fan."

"Uh-huh. I'll be back."

Ace had finished his workout by the time the lieutenant returned with the TV folded up in a blanket. "Are you the one that asked for the blanket?" Cole said loud enough for the guys in neighboring cells to hear.

"Yep. Thanks, Lieutenant Cole. It's cold in here at night," Ace said out the tray slot, glancing at the inquisitive inmates who were staring out their windows or slots. Several yelled that they needed blankets, too.

Cole rolled his eyes. "You owe me, big guy," he told Ace. He turned around and left to get more blankets, shouting at the men that harried him.

Ace unfolded the blanket and set the TV on his mattress. Opened it up and inhaled deeply, smiling at his iPod and router. He caressed them with a slow finger. Powering them on, he sent a quick text to Bobby asking for assistance with the Big Black Wrecker. Within five minutes, he was Entangled with the monster computer and tapped into MDOC's Correctional Investigation Division, searching through employee files for anything that had Captain Bartleby's name on it. Several files were found, all of them irrelevant.

"Son of a bad circuit," he cursed, logging out and making sure he left no browser history or cookies that could be traced.

Diamond's voice whispered through the wall. "Sounds like bad news."

"Yeah. It's a paper file. All the electronic files from SMCI are dated from last year. No new updates. Unfreakingbelievable."

"Lazyfreakingbelievable. Don't sweat it, Ace. I know one of the clerks there."

Ace perked up. "Figured you would. You think he'll help me?"

"No. But I know he'll help me. He's one of my Sisters," Diamond elaborated.

Ace wasn't sure what that entailed, but it sounded like something he should be happy about. "Can you get in touch with him today?"

"Probably. Pass the iPod over here. I'll make some calls."

"Geez. Does everyone here have a cell phone?"

"Epidemic," Diamond confirmed.

Ace put the Touch in a sock and stuffed it under his door. Slid it over in front of Diamond's cell. Diamond grabbed it and began calling his associates, talking with allusions only a life-long gay man would understand. Ace had to beat on the wall and holler through the crack for Diamond to keep his voice down. He was nervous about the other inmates hearing the obvious phone conversation and snitching. He went to the door and sighed with relief. Several convicts were shouting at each other across the zone, laughing about a movie they had seen. The noise was more than sufficient to cover Diamond's illegal conversation.

Diamond finished his chat and sent the iPod back next door, walked to the back wall and whispered, "I spoke to my Sister, Jazzy Thang, who gave me Twinkle's number. It just so happened Twinkle was on the phone when I called, talking to his man before he had to go to work." He gave a pleased squeal. "Perfect timing."

"Twinkle is the CID clerk?"

"Yep. He's going to stop by here in a few minutes, and claim he had morning sickness as an excuse for being late for work," he said, giggling. He pinched his tight stomach. "That slut probably is pregnant. I told him he should just call in fat."

"Either one sounds good enough for me," Ace said with raised eyebrows. "Thanks. What kind of person is Twinkle?"

"He does good business, if that's what you mean. Probably won't want too much for it."

"Probably?"

"Well, whatever he wants, you can do it, right? You're like the hacker extraordinaire, able to steal millions of dollars if you want."

"I can't steal like that. Anymore."

"Why not?" Diamond wanted to know, frowning.

"Promised my wife."

"All righty, then. No money. I'm sure there are plenty of other favors he'll want from you."

"Uh…"

"Not that, fool!" He laughed. "Like hacker stuff. Doctor some of his prison records. Get him an early release, or something. I'll talk to him about it when he gets here."

"Thanks."

Roughly an hour later, the zone door opened and a convict wearing green and white trustee stripes walked in. He was fair of skin and petite. His blonde hair was nearly white, cut stylishly for prison standards, short on the sides and back with long bangs that swept to the right just above his blue eyes. High cheekbones and small, feminine jaw, thick bottom lip that shone with gloss. He flounced up the stairs with a happy-go-lucky swing of his skinny hips and legs. Walked down the tier looking into cells, scowling at the men who offered rude comments, waving at those who whistled.

"I thought I was the only bitch in the building," Diamond said through his tray slot as the man approached. "Then you bring your Paris Hilton-looking ass on the zone."

"Diamond!" Twinkle greeted him, high-pitched, soft and effeminate. "Hey, slut." Unable to kiss Diamond's cheeks, he kissed the air in front of the window. "Hugs! What are you doing in here? I didn't get a chance to ask you on the phone."

"Well, Twink, let me tell you. You see, I got into it with these LK haters, and my friend Ace saved me…"

The two Sisters spoke rapidly, but quietly, for over twenty minutes, pausing only to laugh or clap their hands at humorous revelations. Ace paced his cell, letting his mind wander in no particular direction as a type of meditation. He certainly didn't want to pon-

301

der the lewd expressions that caught his ear from the camp next door. He heard a noise and looked up, stopped pacing, realizing the conversation had ceased. Twinkle smiled at him through the Plexiglas. "You must be the big hero," he said.

"Nah." Ace waved a dismissive hand. "I couldn't stand in the shadow of Mickey Mouse."

"Oh, and he's humble, too." Twinkle leaned back to look at Diamond. "Why are all the good ones straight?" he said rhetorically, then turned back to Ace. "My Sister here tells me we should do a little business."

"Can you get the file?"

"Yes, that's easy. The real question is, can you get into my file?"

"If it's on a computer I can," Ace replied, crossing his arms.

Twinkle grinned. "Lovely. Here's my info." He handed Ace a sheet of paper with his personal information and instructions on what he wanted done. "If anybody asks, I brought you a property receipt. That was my excuse for getting in here."

Ace accepted it with a nod. He recognized the handwriting as Diamond's, and determined it had just been scribbled down. "I'll get right on it," he assured Twinkle.

"Lovely. I'll stop by here this evening with the file. Diamond told me the business about the captain and I know just where to look for it. Don't worry. If the file and evidence is gone, so is their case. They'll forget about it. I've been working there for two years now, and I can tell you from experience it will work. Stuff goes missing all the time. No one admits it's happening."

"You'll bring me all the evidence they have on him?"

"All of it," Twinkle said. He waved at Ace and Diamond. Strutted off on his way to work.

Diamond banged on the wall. "I can hear that big silly grin on your face," he told Ace.

"It's so loud I need ear plugs," Ace said, cheesing like a chubby kid in a donut shop. He sat down and grabbed the iPod, Entangled the Wrecker once more. In a matter of ultra-processed minutes, he was clicking through the MDOC Records Department looking for Twinkle's file. He paused to study the sheet of paper Twinkle had given him, pursing his lips in thought as he read the request to erase a pending sex charge. He got a sinking feeling.

"This is going to be bad," he grumbled in prediction.

He found Twinkle's file and thumbed the screen to page through it, searching for the relevant crime. Several drug and solicitation charges popped up, spanning back ten years. When he found the sex charge, he nearly choked. Re-reading the screen his blood started to boil.

MDOC#:G9337
NAME: Derrick Patrick Nelson, AKA Twinkle
RACE: White
DOB: 05-15-1980

HEIGHT: 5' 5"
WEIGHT: 130
COMPLEXION: Fair
BUILD: Small
EYE COLOR: Blue
HAIR COLOR: Blonde
LOCATION: SMCI
PENDING OFFENSES: 1
CHARGE: Rape
DETAILS: Sex with a minor. Offender Nelson allegedly performed oral sex on a 10-year-old male before sodomizing him.
INVESTIGATION: Ongoing

"I'll murder that child molesting bastard," Ace growled. His neck and hands tightened in anger, shaking.

Diamond overheard and inquired through the crack, "Ace? You okay?"

"No, I'm not." He stood on wobbly legs and stepped to the wall. Took a deep breath. "Your friend Twinkle? He's a Chester." The words were spoken low, soft, but they carried a terrible weight.

"Oh, no. Dammit," Diamond breathed, face also pinched in fury. "That lying piece of shit. Ace, I had no idea. I'm sorry." He remembered the photos of Ace's son and a wave of compassion swept through him as he fully understood why his friend was so upset. He didn't know what to say. He felt at fault because he had been the one to introduce Twinkle.

Biting his lip, he decided to offer assistance for whatever Ace needed to do. "Ace? Ace???"

No response.

Alan Carter, father of a ten year old boy, began pacing again. A snarl had disfigured his face. A titanic conflict roiled among his thoughts, threatening to stab holes in everything he believed in and sabotage the entire escape operation. Every limb, every atom in his body screamed, demanded, that he not erase the child molester's file.

He deserves to be in prison! Ace's mind argued with him. He deserves worse than that. If you do this, he will get out and do it again to someone else's little boy.

It could be Nolan next time…

"No. No!" he shouted, fists pressed to his eyes in an attempt to erase the image. He stopped walking and took several deep breaths. Stepped to the sink and splashed water on his face. He had to shake off this madness and think about a solution. There was no other way to get Captain Bartleby's file in time. Without that he couldn't get out of lockdown and prepare for his escape.

I must get out of here, he thought. *I have to get Clarice out of prison. I have to acquire things for myself before they take her to court. Money, clothes. I can't run down the street in black and white stripes. Have to arrange transportation, identification, a place for my family to live…*

But I can't do any of that unless I do this first.

It was time to pay the Piper.

With utter disgust replacing the scowl, he sat down and palmed the Touch. Scrolled to the pending offense, erasing it. He then logged on to the Sheriff's Department in Twinkle's home county and deleted the arrest records before jumping on to the Circuit Court's database. He found the rape indictment and trial date scheduled in the court's docket, eliminating them and all traces that Derrick "Twinkle" Nelson had ever raped a little boy.

Suddenly dizzy, mouth filling with watery, salty saliva, Ace dropped the iPod and nearly fell as he stumbled to the toilet, grabbing the steel bowl with both hands and vomiting profusely.

The stench rose thickly in the cell.

"Ace!" Diamond yelled in distress, beating on the wall. "Talk to me, you geek. Alan Carter!" He was familiar with the coughing, retching sounds coming from next door and knew his friend was emotionally hurt. Tears ran down his face. He started sobbing. "Please answer me, Ace. I'm sorry."

The other men on the zone continued to yell excitedly about movies and Sports Center.

Chapter XVIII

Central Mississippi Correctional Facility
Pearl, Mississippi
March 23, 2012

Pop-BAM! Patty's left jab and right-hand smacked into the shower shoes Clarice held on her hands, thongs between the middle and ring fingers. Makeshift punch mitts that worked surprisingly well. The morning breeze chilled the sweat on her legs and lower back as they moved around the yard. Yolanda and a few early risers walked the perimeter in cliques of two or three, occasionally glancing at their workout session with interest or puzzlement, having never seen legitimate boxing drills before.

Patty noticed a girl watching her acutely, a young, trim thug that seemed genuinely entranced. Patty flexed her biceps like an idiot, grinning and nodding as if to say, *I'm that bitch.*

Clarice slapped a mitt on her shoulder to recapture her attention. "Point that shoulder at me," Clarice coached her, scowling. "You are right-handed. You want your left shoulder closer to your opponent so your jab reaches them faster. It's not a power punch; it's for speed. A range finder to set up your power shots. That leaves your right shoulder further away from your opponent. You want that right hand cocked, coming from way back there to build up velocity for power."

"I think I got it," Patty said, twisting her shoulders.

"Your left shoulder is pointed at me now. When you throw that right-hand I want your shoulders to completely switch places." Clarice demonstrated for her. "Thrust that right leg, straighten it so it pushes you forward, toward your opponent. Twist your hips simultaneously. All that energy is coming up your thrusting leg, torquing hips, transferring up into your twisting shoulders and into your right fist. Relax your arm for speed, then tighten your fist, arm, and shoulder right as the punch hits."

"So the right shoulder ends up in the front," she said to herself, extending her arm, looking down at her legs and hips. She smiled. "Got it. Leverage and weight distribution, right?"

"Right. We'll get back to that in a minute. Let's work on that jab again. You talk me through it this time."

She got in her stance, weight centered, on the balls of her feet. Toes pointed in Clarice's direction, knees slightly bent, her left shoulder towards Clarice, holding her relaxed fists up in front of her so her eyes had an unobstructed view. "I step with the left foot and jab," she said doing so. "Foot hits as the punch hits. Relax for speed, tighten up on the end of the punch."

"Put that foot down hard and fast. Bring your whole body forward explosively. Exhale."

She punched, stomped, blew out a short breath all at once. Then grinned at her. "Feels good. Tuck my chin, right?" She punched again, head slightly down this time so when her arm extended her chin fell in next to her shoulder, hiding it from potential counter punches.

"Looking good," Clarice praised, then quizzed her. "The chin must be protected, why?"

The blonde giant twisted her lips. "A punch to the chin sends a direct shock wave through the jaw into the brain stem. Which is what causes a knockout."

"And why must we exercise our neck muscles?"

"Shock absorbers."

"Yep."

"Hey, I get plenty of exercise for my neck. You should try my method."

"Really? What is it?" Clarice looked at her seriously. Patty held a curved hand to her mouth, bobbed her head up and down while poking her tongue in a cheek. Clarice waved her hands at her, giggling. "All right, all right. I get it."

"Oh, yeah! Feel the burn, baby." Patty flexed her neck, hard, veins standing out, eyes closed, face straining. Forcing her neck to work up and down with self-applied resistance. She stopped, grimacing and rubbing her shoulders. "Damn. That really is a good workout."

"I'll be sure to try it out on my husband," Clarice promised, shaking her head in wonder. "Let's get back to business. Throw fifty more jabs. Fast and in perfect form." Clarice held up a mitt. "Keep them straight. Get that elbow in."

The two women worked on boxing fundamentals for another half-hour, practicing the jab and right-hand before going back to one-two combinations. Patty's breathing became labored and Clarice called a halt.

"That's good work," Clarice said.

"You want to hit them again?" Patty offered.

"I'm good. I ran, shadowboxed, and hit the mitts. Two hours is all I'm doing today." Clarice dropped the shower shoes in the grass, grabbed a towel, water bottle. Wiped her face. Took a drink. "You ready for your fight tonight?"

"Oh, yeah." Patty's grin showed too many teeth. "You think I should try out my new jab?"

"Absolutely not."

"Huh?"

"Look, you just learned that. In a fight you'll perform from instinct. If we had a month to program your muscle-memory, we could make that jab and right-hand lethal. One session sure as hell won't do it. You'll just cloud your thinking by trying something new. A bad idea for any fight, especially with a dangerous opponent. Just go in there and do your thing."

She thought it over for a minute. "Makes sense." She watched Clarice toweling off, amazed at the striations and ripples in her arms, shoulders and legs. She shook her head. "Goddamn, Shock."

"What?"

"You're like the High Priestess of Gold's Gym. I'd give anything to look like that."

"Thanks," Clarice said, then drank more water. "Ah. You know, you could look a lot better. You have good natural proportions. Just need to shape it up. The boxing drills are a great start. But your eating habits..." Clarice raised her eyebrows and she frowned at Patty's stomach.

"I don't think I can give up the junk. I've tried." She patted her gut. "I like junk." They smiled at each other and Patty raised her eyebrows, in a parody of Clarice. In a confiding tone she said, "Have you ever been, you know, not-so-fresh downtown?"

Clarice burst out laughing. "Where do you come up with this stuff?" Clarice chuckled for a moment more, reined it in and put on her most sincere face. "No, Patty. I haven't. And there's never been another woman in the history of the planet with that problem. You, my smelly friend, are an alien."

"From the planet Vaginas Odoriferous," she said in robotic voice, doing a stiff, jerky hump dance. She paused and fanned a hand out in front of her with a Damn That Stinks expression.

"You are horrible," Clarice said.

They grabbed their things and headed back to the building. A hard gush of wind startled a flock of spar-

311

rows off to their right, blades of grass floating on the wind after them as they chirped and flapped away. Random drops of rain pelted Clarice's neck, arms, making her look up. Dark gray clouds cruised by overhead, a light sprinkle dispersing as a warning of the heavy burden about to be unleashed.

Patty elbowed her. "That's the girl I told you about," she said, pointing her chin at a convict walking out of their zone onto the yard. The girl looked around, spotted them, walked in their direction.

"The trustee from the clinic?" Clarice said.

"That's her. Helen Twelvetrees. Sexy bitch," she murmured. Noticing Clarice's sideways look, she stopped and said, "What?"

"Horrible," Clarice reminded her. A thought nagged her. "Helen Twelvetrees. Like the actress?"

"Who?"

"The chick in that movie with Clark Gable."

"Clark Who?"

Clarice sighed. "Never mind. No one watches the classics anymore."

They kept walking toward Helen and stopped in front of her. She was breathtaking, and Clarice suddenly sympathized with Patty's attraction to her. Her short, dark blonde hair was parted on the side to show off a perfect forehead, creamy white skin and pencil thin eyebrows. Her large eyes and full lips marked her as a walking estrogen pump. And her nose... boss. Not quite aquiline, not quite bulbous. Clarice loved it. She was taller than Clarice, athletic but voluptuous. She smiled and her eyes glittered knowingly, pleased with the effect she was having on them. When she spoke, her mystifying aura turned androgynous, which somehow only enhanced her allure.

Clarice swallowed, shifted uncomfortably.

"Patty," Helen purred.

"H-how's it going?" Patty stuttered, looking like she suddenly had two left feet and a tongue too big for her mouth.

Clarice grinned and extended a hand, shaking hers. "I'm Shocker."

"Helen. Pleased to make your acquaintance. I brought you something," she said. Looking over at Patty, her eyes turned even more sultry. If that was possible. "Your lovely friend here sweet talked me into 'borrowing' some items from my workplace. I didn't see you on the zone, so I placed them under your pillow."

"Thank you," Clarice responded. She turned to Patty for an explanation.

"Tattoo supplies," Patty replied, without taking her eyes off Helen. It sounded like taahoo splees. Clarice couldn't stop grinning.

"That's great. I already built a machine. I just need to make a needle and some ink. Would you like a tattoo as trade for the supplies?" Clarice asked Helen.

She shook her head politely. "No, thank you. I had an obligation to Patty. If you ladies need anything else, please don't hesitate to call on me."

"Sure. Nice meeting you," Clarice said, thinking how bizarre this conversation had been. Never in her prison life had she had met such a cultured person. (And never, now she came to think of it, had she accepted stolen property with such appreciation.)

Helen smiled and gave a quiet gesture of modesty, turned and sashayed back into the building. Patty and Clarice watched her walk away, mesmerized.

Clarice shook her head, hard, snapping out of her spell. She looked at Patty in a panic. "I need my man. Quick."

"Do you think her boobs are real?" Patty mumbled, still staring in the direction Helen had gone, memory burning bright with the image of her sophisticated air and sexy walk, her delicious lips.

Or maybe that was Clarice's memory. "Wow," was all she could say.

"Bet she got a boob job. But her lips are real."

"Certainly," Clarice agreed. "Come on. You can drool over her later. Let's go play with the tattoo supplies."

"Let's."

They hit the shower (a cold one, happily) and headed to their cubicle to see what kind of goodies Helen had brought for the planned tattoo operation. Lifting her pillow with a giddy, Easter-egg-hunt feeling, Clarice found a box of latex gloves, size SMALL, box smashed flat, presumably to fit in Helen's waistband for trafficking purposes. A large bottle of iodine, two boxes of alcohol pads and antibiotic ointment were tucked in next to the gloves.

Excellent.

The sight had a positive, but disturbing effect on her. She felt gratified, as she looked forward to indulging one of her life's passions. Slaking her artistic thirst was always motivating. At the same time, a deep sadness had settled in, an ugly undertone in a sunshine-filled picture, subtly reminding her of all the joys experienced at her tattoo studio, Tattoology, and underlining the loss of all that she had once ruled over. She had gone from owning a high-tech studio with four talented artists and hundreds of happy customers to this, a homemade machine and ink, with mediocre medical supplies stolen from a prison clinic. If she allowed it to go forward, the contrast would be depressing as hell. But being the glass-half-full *biatch* that she was, she managed to keep the dejection a mere thumbtack in her stomach, overshadowed by the ingenuity and artistic prowess she'd get to exert in the upcoming ink-slinging sessions.

Let's do some tatts, people.

The gloomy feelings suppressed, optimism regained, she glanced around to see if there was anyone besides Patty who happened to be looking in her direction. There wasn't. Clarice squatted down next to the head of her bunk and dug at the seam where the floor joined the wall. White caulking filled the gap. Last week, she had dug out the hardened putty and used the space as a stash spot for her phone, cash, and tattoo machine. To replace the caulking, she had crushed a bar of Ivory soap inside a Ziploc bag, then mixed in a little water until it was thick like Play Doh. It worked perfect to seal the hole. She pulled at the section of hard Ivory, popping it loose with minimal damage to the brittle soap, revealing a two-inch-by-five-inch space that was nearly a foot deep, as wide as the concrete wall. Moving her phone out of the way, she grabbed the tiny 3 volt electric motor and modified ink pen lying beside it. She replaced the false caulking and sat on her bed, excitement flooding her system in a way she hadn't felt in years. The unique euphoria made her toes tingle.

She was a little kid with new toys to play with. *Wheee!* Her heart sang.

Patty looked over at her from where she sat on her bed. Smiled. "Who's first?" she asked.

"You have a fight this evening," Clarice reminded her, smirking at the obvious disappointment. "You don't need an open wound on you. It could get infected."

"Tomorrow then?"

"Sure."

"That means Yolanda gets first dibs," she said sullenly.

"If she has the cash."

"I do," Yolanda said, walking into the cubicle. She sat next to Patty and smiled at the scowling giant. Her white Bob Barker shoes kicked back and forth several inches off the floor with girlish delight. She was rarely first in line for anything, and was determined to enjoy every second of this.

"You still want the pistol and roses?" Clarice asked her.

"Yeah," she said, rubbing the shoulder where she wanted the ink, grinning at Patty.

Patty snorted and scowled at her.

"Anything in particular?" Clarice said.

"Can you make it so the gun is shooting a heart-shaped bullet?"

"No problem. I have to make a needle. Will you burn the plastic?"

"Okay," she said.

Patty reached into her pants compartment and pulled out a Bic lighter, handed it to her. It was out of fluid, but Clarice didn't need it for a light; She only needed the flint spring, which she would use to forge a needle. She'd also use the fuel jet for a tip on the machine.

Removing the lighter's metal cap, she dismantled the striker wheel and carefully pinched the flint so the spring wouldn't launch across the room. She trashed the flint but kept the thin spring. Patty handed her another lighter, this one good. Clarice twisted up a three foot length of toilet paper and hung it over the edge of her bunk. Lit the end. A small flame kindled, about an inch high. The paper burned at a low temperature, just what Clarice needed to stretch this spring without breaking it.

Holding the spring pinched between both hands, she pulled on the ends until it lengthened as far as it would go, ruining the tiny coils. The tip of the flame beckoned to her, a challenge to test her skill on such a delicate working of metal. Frowning in concentration, she held one end of the spring just inside the flame, careful not to get too close to her fingers. The metal glowed a dull orange almost immediately, and Clarice gently pulled on the ends while moving the spring slowly through the flame, straightening it.

The trick was to keep the metal moving so it stayed a bright orange, the right temperature to get it pliable. If it stayed in the heat too long, turning bright red with a white corona, it would be way too hot, turning the metal brittle once it cooled. Clarice needed it straight, hard, but flexible.

Dexterity is the key here, people.

With the spring as stretched as a straight wire, Clarice grabbed the machine and juxtaposed the wire. The Papermate ink pen had one-and-a-half inches chopped off the end, an excess piece that made a perfect motor mount, bound to the pen at a ninety degree angle, just below the cut end. The one-inch-by-half-inch motor was secured to the mount with a rubber band, making the machine roughly six-inches long. Clarice measured where one end of the needle would insert into the motor's flywheel, and where the other end would poke out of the tip. Bending the flywheel-side of the needle at a perfect ninety degrees, Clarice held that section over the flame again, allowing it to heat to a red hot white so Clarice could break it easily once it cooled and tempered.

At the risk of looking unladylike in front of her peers, Clarice built up some spittle on the tip of her tongue, swiped it off between a thumb and finger. Extinguished the needle's crook, tempering the metal. It sizzled, but did not burn her.

In her mind's eye, she could see the millions of steel molecules dancing around, all excited in their party of heat, swarming each other, mixing, exchanging electrons like STDs. Then here comes the giant, the Goddess of Steel, and freezes the unworthy subjects in time once more by a mere glob of spit. Tssst!

Hee-hee. Make believe power is fun.

Clarice hissed a sizzling sound, a lopsided, slightly insane smile creeping up the side of her face.

Patty cleared her throat, and Clarice looked around at her, startled. Both of her cube mates stared at her, dumbfounded by her out-of-character behavior.

"Had to temper it," Clarice explained in defense.

Using just her fingernails, she carefully broke the brittle excess about a quarter-inch from the ninety degree bend, so the needle's end now had a small L-shape that would insert in the flywheel. Holding the other end over the flame, she held it there, gently tugging on the ends, until it reached the point of phosphorescence. The metal lengthened, stretched like hot taffy before breaking, leaving a tapered, sharp tip. Clarice trashed the excess piece of spring, blew out the flame and grinned down at her work.

Boo-yah! says the Goddess of Steel.

Clarice hadn't had the chance to play like this since 2010. But she hadn't lost her touch. She let out a sigh of relief that seemed to last ten minutes.

Yolanda paused in her task and said, "How'd you know how to do that?"

"I studied metallurgy years ago while training to be a metal fabricator," Clarice said, spinning the arrow-straight needle in her fingers. "This was child's play."

"Can you show me that? My needles look like... Well, they suck," she finished lamely, looking embarrassed.

Clarice looked down at what Yolanda was doing. "You need help with that?"

"Nah. I may not be able to make good needles, but I can make smut."

Yolanda had used toothpaste to glue two sheets of paper end-to-end, then connected those ends to make a cylinder. A convict "smoke house." She had taped two shaving razors together after removing the blades, and stood them up on the floor. Grabbing the lighter, she set fire to the plastic handles, hurriedly placing the smoke house over them and capping it with more sheets of paper. Black smoke poured out of the top before she placed several magazines on top to weigh it down, sealing the cracks. A trickle of smoke drifted out, but was sucked up by the box fan placed next to it, dissipating to only a slight foul carbon odor in the air.

We chatted for twenty minutes while waiting on the plastic to burn. Clarice cut several small squares from an old t-shirt, and placed them in a bowl of water, along with the needle, fuel jet, and the machine's needle guides. The guides, which were simply the tips out of ink pens, minus the ball points, inserted into an empty ink tube, one on each end. The assembly would slide into the Papermate to keep the needle from vibrating.

Clarice microwaved the bowl for two minutes, imagining tiny bacteria cartoons screaming as they died. Like on that Clorox commercial. The high-pitched pleas for mercy and responding deep voiced, god-like denial were absolutely necessary.

Patty cleared her throat again, looked at Yolanda, both of them flanking her at the microwave. "You should see Shocker after a fight," she said, twirling a finger next to her ear, making a cuckoo bird sound. "Looney Tunes."

Yolanda giggled. Clarice took her time scowling at them.

Back in the cubicle with the sterilized parts, Clarice assembled the machine while Yolanda checked the smoke house. It had quit burning, so she raised the cap, cut the paper cylinder and used her ID card to scrape up the thick soot from the floor, cap, and sides of the cylinder, forming it all into a single mound, chopping it into a fine powder. She held the ink precursor up to her, smiling proudly.

Clarice gave a big smile in return. "I can tell you've done that many times. Hardly made a mess," Clarice told her, taking the smut. "We will need another t-shirt."

"I have one," Patty volunteered. She opened her box, dug around, threw a huge shirt to her. "I was gonna make a loincloth and wear it for my next fight, but I see you need it more than I do." For some reason, her eyes seemed to turn brown.

"Shut up!" Yolanda exclaimed, smiling at the image.

"A fight costume?" Clarice inquired.

"Yeah. We need a new theme other than bitches in prison."

"But a loincloth? You going for a Raquel Welch look?"

"Who?"

Clarice sighed, "Never mind."

Opening her locker box, Clarice snaked her hand under some clothes, searched around and plucked out the item she was looking for. A red Coca-Cola bottle cap she had stashed for just this occasion. She swabbed it with an alcohol pad before pouring smut into it, filling the cap about three-quarters full. Grabbing another alcohol pad, she tore open the packet, twisted the gauze, and squeezed several drops of alcohol over the black powder. It broke down completely, melting into a thick ink. Using sterile water from the bowl, she dripped several drops into the cap to prevent the alcohol from evaporating and leaving the ink dried out. She held the mix up to the light, squinting at the texture to make sure no smut particles were floating on the surface, and to see if the ink was the right viscosity. It looked as thick as paint, a carbon smoothie thoroughly mixed and sterilized, courtesy of Helen's 'borrowed' alcohol pads.

She stirred it with a bobby pin, a buzzing, blenderish noise squealing out the corner of her mouth. *Hey, it was necessary.*

Patty and Yolanda snickered. Clarice mugged them, kicked her blender on HIGH.

Holding up the cap of ink, Clarice said, "Beautiful." Then she eyed Yolanda with her best *evil genius* face. Exaggerated brows. Super-gummy grin. "I'm ready to drill your ass now. You ready?"

Yolanda leaned away from her, rubbing her shoulder. "Uh, yeah. Guess so," she answered warily.

"Wash your shoulder. Lots of soap. Use your hand, not a cloth," Clarice instructed.

"Okay."

"Shave it first," Patty added.

"I don't have hairy shoulders!" Yolanda stormed, spinning on a heel and stomping off to the sinks. Her hand went to the dark fuzz on her upper-lip, and Patty burst out laughing.

Clarice's first convict customer returned to the cubicle, washed and ready for her tattoo, primly sitting down on her bed. Crossed her legs. She wore a type of anti-bullshit shield on her face, though it was an obvious struggle for her not to revert to the normal pout she expressed after being teased. She was learning, at least.

Patty and Clarice were in an obvious struggle as well, restraining themselves to hold in numerous remarks that would surely entertain them at Yolanda's expense.

As Clarice grabbed an ink pen and knelt next to Yolanda to begin drawing on her arm, she asked herself why she didn't feel like a bully for her lack of respect toward the young Ecuadorian. Patty must have had similar thoughts that sought justification.

"Stop acting like such a douche," she told Yolanda, hands perched on her knees, nose in the air to emulate Yolanda's snobbish posture. Flicked a hand at her. "I'm trying to be nice here, but you're just asking for it."

"Whatever," Yolanda sneered. But she relaxed, uncrossed her legs and watched her as Clarice drew a revolver on her Latin skin.

A douche. That's it. Patty had nailed it, and explained her lack of empathy.

Leaving a gap on the gun's trigger guard, Clarice sketched a rose vine through it so it tightened over the trigger, pulling it. Clarice continued with the vine so it wrapped around the butt and ended with a budding rose over the top and behind the hammer. Clarice dropped down below the pistol's barrel and quickly outlined another budding rose. Etched some action lines and smoke around the end of the barrel to indicate a bullet being fired, a heart-shaped slug that Clarice placed two-inches away and shaped so it looked like it had been fired at the speed of sound. The gun was positioned so it pointed upward, butt down, barrel directed at the top right of her shoulder. The roses filled the top left and bottom right sections, covering her entire outer shoulder and part of her upper arm.

"That's so cool," Yolanda said, looking at the customized bullet she had requested.

"That's fifty dollars," Clarice replied.

She frowned for a moment. "I got that." She dug in her pants, took out a wad of plastic. Unfolded it, handed her some bills that were inside. Settled her bottom on the mattress again, hands in her lap, still frowning.

"That's a five hundred dollar tattoo," Clarice pointed out, opening an alcohol pad. "You're getting a ninety percent discount." Clarice wiped down the two twenties and ten very thoroughly. Then put them away.

The corners of her mouth rose with her thick brows. "Awesome," she breathed, looking at her shoulder again.

"Wait until we get some shading on it. It'll look so realistic you'll be able to hear it shooting."

Yolanda turned to Patty and stuck out her tongue. Patty snorted in dismissal.

Grabbing the machine and bowl of parts, Clarice picked up the fuel jet, a brass cylinder about the size of a pen tip, and slid it into the business end of the machine. It fit into the Papermate's tip, the jet taking the place of the ball point, butting snug against the needle guide. A tight seal was necessary for the machine's suction and discharge of ink. The guide, being an empty ink tube, would fill with ink when she dipped the running machine in the cap. As she touched the tip to the skin, it would discharge its load, spitting out a thick black puddle for the needle to push into the epidermis, the outer layer of skin.

Clarice's fingers shook slightly as she grabbed the needle, nerves kicking in from the assault of exciting anticipation. Damn, she had missed this craft.

Loading the needle through the guide near the motor mount, she slid the former flint spring point first into the tube, bumping her finger along the body of the pen to jar the needle through the second guide. It poked out of the fuel jet and she clipped the needle's L-shaped end into the motor's flywheel, a circle of plastic smaller than a dime with holes for the motor's shaft and the needle. She gave it a spin with her finger. Smooth, noiseless inertia answered her touch, the plastic wheel spinning the needle like a piston of superior manufacture. It would run like a mechanically sound cream puff, zero vibration in the needle.

Her first homemade tattoo machine, and it was boss. She crowed her delight. "Please join me in a rousing chorus of *Who's yo momma?* followed by a hearty *Hell fuck yeah!*" She buffed her nails on her shirt.

"Shut up," Yolanda breathed in awe, eyes wide as she stared open-mouthed at her creation.

"It will run like a real machine," Clarice said, plugging in a power adapter, an adjustable power source they used for blow driers and curling irons. She set it on 3 volts and spliced the two wires to the positive and negative terminals on the motor. Switching the adapter on, she held the machine up horizontally in front of her eyes and let pride smack her around a little. Pride can be a heavy-handed SoB when he's been gone for a while. She wobbled with the fulfilling sense of achievement, the simple but slick engineering project in her hands threatening her ego with obesity. She blinked away the cerebral fat, reluctantly, and focused on the needle where it span, entering the guide.

From a side-view, the reciprocating shaft of the needle was so straight it looked like it wasn't even moving. Zero vibration.

Check.

Her eyes moved to the tip. The needle's point pistoned in and out of the tip with no flapping or variation from its course.

Check. The standard she was seeking.

Vibration, especially at the tip, will cause trauma to the skin. Potentially serious, bloody, painful, feels-like-an-amputation trauma that could get infected with such interesting critters as staph. Staphylococcus likes to attack skin and muscle tissue. It eats you. Such horrifying thoughts made her double check the needle's trueness. All those urban legends about penitentiary 'rip guns' tearing gory trenches and scarring people were real. Clarice had seen numerous victims here and when she was in the county jail. Your average convict, man or woman, doesn't possess the skills to build a quality, balanced machine. And their customers (victims) suffered for it.

But Clarice wasn't the average convict.

She adjusted the tip so the needle stuck out about 1/32", which was a good length for thick skin, such as a shoulder. She would use slightly less than that on thinner skin, like the inside of an arm.

She switched the machine off. Grabbed some gloves out of the smashed box. Patty had her phone out and began shooting a video as Clarice sat next to Yolanda again. "Shocker's a criminal now. Oh, yeah," she said, zooming in on her hands.

Clarice set a magazine on the bed, placed the cap of ink on it. Grabbed a square of cloth out of the bowl, a sterile wipe rag. "Criminal? Are you high?" Clarice said.

"You can't deny it now, Shock." She ticked off on her fingers holding the phone. "You've been fighting. Illegally. Now you're doing tattoos. Illegally. You're like a big walking felony these days."

"Uh-huh," Clarice replied, eyeing her warily. "Hand me that, please." She pointed to the huge t-shirt Patty had given her. As Clarice draped the would-be loincloth over her lap for an ink apron, she considered what Patty had just said. She knew Patty was only jesting, but at the same time the words rang true. Strange how she had never seen it from that perspective. Patty, being a career crook, didn't miss a beat. Clarice felt her actions were quite necessary, on par with her moral values and standards. Her personal beliefs. *The Right Thing To Do.* Though she was sure the so-called authorities that she'd come to dislike would say otherwise. Hell, at one time, not long ago, she would have said otherwise herself. Now look at her. Illegal fighting, smoking dope, planning a major escape. Her new BFFs were doing dinosaur time for violent crimes - Yolanda for armed robbery, Patty for murder, and Clarice felt that she fitted right in with them. Sisters.

The transition from law-abiding, criminal hating pillar of the community to where she was now on the other side of the fence was seriously disturbing. There was no line that divided right from wrong. No black and white. It was all shades of gray. And to all the people who might shake their heads in disagreement, all Clarice would want to say was that no one could grasp it till happened to them or their loved ones. Two years ago Clarice would have been shaking her head right along with them.

Clarice looked around the zone and wondered how many of these women were truly bad people, and how many were just victims of circumstances, playing the cards dealt to them.

How many of them would Clarice have convicted had she been on their juries? How many would she condemn now, with her new understanding of how things really were?

A glum feeling took hold of her.

Patty kicked her leg. "You're messing up my video with that ugly face. I was just fucking with you, girl. God. Next you'll be competing with Ms. Douche Ecuador here for the crown." She pointed her chin at Yolanda, who mugged fiercely. Patty recorded it. "Ms. Douche Universe," she laughed, shaking her head.

"You're right," Clarice said, perking up. "You're rude and crude, but right. Let's get this ink-slinging party started, shall we?"

"Let's."

Patty pressed some buttons on her phone and music began playing, a background jam for the tattoo video. *Closer* by Nine Inch Nails had all three of them humming passionately within seconds.

"*Help me get away from myself/I want to fuck you like an animal,*" Patty sang along with Trent Reznor, doing her (what else?) hump dance.

Clarice switched the machine on. With her left thumb and middle finger, she stretched the skin on Yolanda's shoulder, the latex gripping firmly. She positioned her other hand comfortably on the machine, as if holding a large, top-heavy pen. Dipped it in the ink. Gently pressed the needle into Yolanda's skin and began a line, starting at the bottom right of the piece and alternating up and to the left until she had everything outlined. It went quickly, only having to dip the machine a dozen times. She wiped all the ink from Yolanda's arm to reveal the fine black lines that made up the pistol and roses, coating the white cloth with a thick black stain. Clarice trashed it, grabbed another. Then reached for a packet of ointment. Squeezed some on a finger and slathered it on the girl's arm. She would periodically add more ointment to prevent the skin from becoming chapped, lubricating the penetration of the needle and alleviating some of the pain.

Yolanda gave a slight wince each time Clarice stopped and started again. Patty made sure to record all these signs of discomfort, throwing in the occasional sarcastic remark while grinning and humping her way through several songs by Jay Z and Dr. Dre.

With the outline complete and Patty taunting her to add detail, Clarice's hands worked with surgical precision, showing off years of experience, as she stretched the skin and shaded the dark areas with slow, deep circular motions, switching to shallow, faster motions as the machine ran out of ink and allowed for lighter shades. In ninety minutes, she had the revolver, both roses and vines looking like they belonged in the Museum of Modern Art.

"Shut up," Yolanda said, running her fingers over her shoulder. "It's not even red."

Clarice slapped her hand away. "It will be if you keep touching it. The bacteria on your fingers could cause an infection. Stop touching it," Clarice scolded.

Yolanda dropped her head and Clarice grimaced. Making an effort to un-bitch that lesson, she added, "Please."

Yolanda looked up at her gratefully. Patty snorted, and Clarice raised a hand to her in warning before she could comment on the douche pageant behavior. Patty snorted again, but kept her peace. Kept filming.

Grabbing the bowl, Clarice dipped a finger into the water and let it drop into the ink cap. Cut the ink at about a 1:4 ratio, ink-to-water. Tattooed correctly, it will heal into a pretty, smooth gray. Perfect for shadows.

Clarice dipped the machine in the new mix. Began adding shadows behind the rose petals and vines so that they became three-dimensional, looking as if they were situated just off the skin. Yolanda began squealing in delight, the mild pain of the needle long forgotten, the endorphins and joy from receiving her first professionally done tatt kicking her butt.

They were finished, and it looked boss.

Fifty bucks in two hours. Horrible by free-world tattoo artist wages, especially one of her caliber. But not too shabby for a prisoner. Now Clarice just needed more customers...

"That's so bad ass," Patty said with a touch of envy, watching her video. "You mind if I put it on YouTube?"

"No way. Are you nuts?" Clarice said, cleaning up her mess. "If someone recognizes us, we could get busted."

"That's the fun part."

"You are crazy." Clarice sighed. "But that's no excuse. The answer is still no."

"Too late!" she said, logging out. She stored the phone in her pants and gave a tough girl, brazened look that Clarice could only admire and giggle at. "Now the whole world will know of your sordid, slimy criminal activities, Ms. Devil Hands Sally." She made a face that reminded her of a campaigning politician lying to a large crowd and informed her, "Tattoos are dirty." As Yolanda and Clarice stared at the Thorazine candidate, she changed her act yet again, deepening her voice and projecting it, like those you hear on old religious movies. Like Moses in drag she intoned, "I have revealed you for who you truly are."

Her mouth hung open for a second. "You are high," Clarice accused.

"Lil' bit," she admitted.

"Think you're some kind of supernatural entity now? Wonder woman?"

"Termite."

"Who?"

"Termite. Like the insect."

"Um..."

"'Cause, you know. I eat wood. That's my super power."

Clarice's mouth fell open again. "Right. Gotcha." She turned away from her and mumbled, "How the hell do I keep walking into these lines?"

Clarice sent Yolanda to wash her arm and to advertise her work. She was more than happy to go show off and scurried to the task.

As Clarice peeked into her stash spot, the silver case on the cell phone caught her attention. She checked the time, looked around. Not much movement going on. And the officers rarely counted like they were supposed to, preferring to hang out in the hallways or towers and gossip. The chances of anyone catching her before she could hide it were slim. Maybe she could sneak a call or two before the traffic picked up. She grabbed it and her arm started shaking as she switched mental gears, as if the phone had some sort of physical power over her, snatching her out of her comfort zone and instilling doubt. She quickly analyzed the feelings, determining...Nothing.

She sat down, ran her hands through her hair. *Think woman. Why are you scared?*

All she could figure out was that she had become adapted to this place. It took some serious re-wiring to be able to deal with life as a prisoner. And when she held this phone, thoughts and memories of the free-world and all the people she loved and cared for clashed with the person she had become. Clarice hadn't seen or talked to her loved ones in a very long time. Would they know that she had changed? Would it matter? She told herself to keep hold of the stress shield she had built to keep from thinking about her husband suffering in prison and her son suffering without parents. But just touching the damn phone had caved in the shield, like the Big Bad Wolf blowing down a straw hut, jaws smiling, stepping inside, eager to molest her little piggy emotions.

There had been a similar, unexplained occurrence when she first got the phone. She had tried to call Eddy, but hung up before he answered. She told herself then that she had no plan so she didn't need to contact him yet. But that was just an excuse born of fear, she realized now.

She took several deep, calming breaths. Looked over at Patty.

Patty nodded in understanding. "I have to get drunk to call my kid," she said. "Nerves suck. If I call sober, I'm just reminded of how big of a failure I am and start crying. A half bottle of gin will fix you right up, though." She dug around in her locker box. Pulled out what appeared to be a bottle of Sprite, waggled her head in invitation.

Clarice smiled *no thanks*. "I'm good. Besides, I'm calling my coach, not Nolan. Not yet, anyway." The thought of Nolan's voice on the other end of the phone sunk in a little further, demonizing the butterflies in her stomach. The little bastards crashed around with spikes on sharp, leathery wings. Clarice eyed the bottle with more interest.

"If I call Nolan, I may have to take you up on that offer."

"Bar's open, babe," Patty said, taking a drink.

Clarice dialed Eddy's number and tried to will away the anxiety. What the hell was wrong with her? This was Eddy, her freaking boxing coach and mentor, for Christ's sake. She had no reason to be anxious. Yet she was.

And with no real explanation for it. Scared as crap.

She needed out of this place, ASAP, before any more irrational mental scarring took place. Pretty soon she woudn't want to talk to anybody out there.

The phone started ringing, rescuing her from herself. Eddy's baritone answered and tears leaked down her face.

"Hello," he rumbled.

"Coach!"

"Hey, darlin'! How are you?"

"Well, you know me. All sunshine and rainbows."

"Right. More like all left-hooks and elbows."

"Hey! I do not throw elbows," Clarice fussed, and they shared a laugh.

"I've been worried. They keep returning my letters, and I assume they restricted the phone since you haven't called."

"Yeah. They won't let me call or write – not you or my parents. I'm pretty sure that's against a few federal laws, but I'm in a no-win situation here. I've yet to make the warden's honor roll."

"I'll bet."

"Oh, by the way. Thanks."

"For what?" he asked. Clarice could picture his under bite sticking out, frowning, eyes beetled under dark, curly hair. Maybe a few random bread crumbs in his chin beard.

"For saving my dad. You flushed the evidence."

"Hey, don't thank me. Thank the prison industry for mandating such great toilets. I almost lost my arm when I shoved that phone down the drain."

"Yeah, right," Clarice replied, grinning ear-to-ear. Eddy's modesty was incredibly charming. They chatted about the fight game; he caught her up on their old associates and their current activities. Then they got to the business at hand.

"So. Are you ready?" he said, knowing Clarice understood exactly what he meant.

"Will be before the Big Day."

"When is it?"

"April second, at the circuit court."

"Hmm." He gave a thoughtful pause. "I won't bother asking how you got another court date. Or how you plan to get clothes and whatnot. What I am worried about is who handles the operation from this end. Do you have transportation arranged?"

"Nope."

"Good. Because I'm going to do it."

Clarice let out a relieved breath. "Thank you. Any chance you can do it without getting in trouble?"

"Sure, there's a chance. But that's not important. What's the worst thing they can do to me? Probation? Lock me up? Kill me? Oooh, I'm so scared," he said sarcastically. "I really don't care anymore."

"Coach, you are starting to freak me out here. You can't get in trouble for this! We can figure out something. Maybe just leave me a car somewhere."

"Don't fret, lass," he said. "You are too smashing for such ugly, dreary words." He dropped the bantering. "Listen. Serious business now. I'll take care of everything. I want to be there, outside the courthouse, in case you need me. I've done some similar jobs back in the old days. These things can get a little hairy. You'll be a fugitive amongst a hundred cops in the downtown area. They'll be on you instantly. You'll need someone to run interference. And believe me, darlin'. That's my specialty." Clarice groaned, but he continued. "You are risking your life. I'm way too old to worry about risking mine, so I'll be your insurance. We're family, Clarice. Family makes sacrifices."

Clarice groaned again, but it was less of a protest and more of a frustrated acceptance. He wouldn't take no for an answer. And she was shamefully glad, dammit. She told herself she shouldn't get too worked up about it. Eddy had been involved in serious crimes in the 'old days', and had worked for a few Italian businessmen on various projects that had become legendary. Things that would make a prison escape look like taking candy from a baby.

Still, though… Clarice held a daughterish fondness for the old dude, and it was hard to dismiss the protective instinct. He must have heard her thoughts.

"Shocker."

"Yeah?"

"I don't have anybody to take care of. Except you. No family that will miss me. Except you. I'm retired now, so it's not like I have a stable of fighters that will miss me. You're it. And, I'm doing this," he growled in his *I Am The Coach And You Will Listen To Me* voice.

"Yes, sir."

"Good. I need the excitement, anyway. I feel worthless without a purpose in life. This will get the ol' heart beating again." A knocking could be heard in the background. "Darlin'? I have company. Get back to me soon so we can go over the details."

"Thanks, Coach. Love you."

"I love you, too, darlin'."

He hung up and Clarice sat there with the phone still pressed to her ear for a moment, replaying the conversation and letting the paternal feeling he had bestowed dance over her. She wiped her eyes and stared at the phone's blurry keypad.

Whew.

She had missed that old man more than she thought. It was hard to believe he was retired now.

She'd have to grill him on that later. Probably been eating so much he has his own gravity by now…

"You look amused," Patty interjected. "Was that your coach?"

"Yep."

"He doing okay?"

"I guess. He's retired, which is a bit of a shock. He sounded really good, but I could tell he was bored stupid."

Her eyebrows jiggled. "What's he look like?"

"He's a young sixty. Big, dark, strong. Charming as hell when he wants to be, scary as hell the rest of the time."

"Sounds like my ex."

"The one you killed?"

"Yeah."

"Does that mean Eddy is your type?" Clarice asked with great amusement.

"Sure. Well, unless he has old man balls."

"That's gross. Stop it."

"I know, right? They hang down past their dicks. How is that even possible?" She scrunched up her face all innocent and inquisitive, a clueless teenager. Clarice was torn between laughter and gagging.

"Will you please stop? God! That's my coach you're talking about." Clarice closed her eyes and tried hard to shake away the disturbing image. Patty pointed and laughed. Clarice focused on the phone and guided her thoughts toward more important, genital-less issues.

Her former paint and body specialist came to mind. Bobby, the giant ebony muscle head that had proven his loyalty and friendship to Ace and her over the years. He was a resourceful, clever man, and could possibly offer some ideas or assistance for the escape.

On the other hand, Eddy wouldn't want her to involve anyone else. He would want to run the show solo, without interference from Bobby or others. So scratch that. She couldn't recruit Bobby for Team Shocker.

But she could recruit him for Team Ace.

She dialed his number and held her breath. The base of her neck throbbed as she listened to the ringing.

"Hello?" Bobby's deep basso answered.

"Bobby!"

A brief pause. "Boss? That you?"

"Yes. How are you, man? Your family well?"

"Yeah, everyone is fine. I was just thinking about you."

"Oh? You painting something on canvas for a change?"

"I did recently. A playground scene. Turned out well."

"Yeah?"

"Yeah. But that's not why you were on my mind. You ready for this?"

"For what?"

"Ace is on the other line."

Clarice couldn't respond right away. The implications were so vast and emotionally taxing that all she could utter was a strangled sound. Her chest and ears beat staccatos that nearly incapacitated her, lungs failing to remember breathing. Hands shaking. She moved several strands of hair out of her eyes while attempting to concentrate on Bobby's inquiring voice. Heart-tearing images of Ace in chains, screaming in a filthy prison cell, drove her over a cliff into a sea of grief. The pain was so strong she nearly hung up, unwilling to face it. A coward.

Could she talk to Ace without completely losing it? She wasn't sure that she could. And she didn't need any prison psych doctors cramming drugs down her neck or sticking needles in her ass for going into a rage and possibly hurting people. A most inopportune time to wig out.

Possibly, hell. If that did happen, she would most certainly hurt people. Peoples. Plural. Plurals. Lots of hurting.

But that's not as important as her fear of Ace sensing the change in her and not liking it. What the hell would she do then?

As her nose leaked onto the concrete, darkening the impoverished surface, Clarice fought her doubts and self-pity, drawing in every iota of her will to flush it away. Her manacled husband smiled at her, mouthing promises that everything would be okay. They'd be together again soon, and it wouldn't matter how much either of them had changed. She just had to fight for it, believe in it, put aside all emotion and deal with it like a warrior on a mission. Like the Shocker would in the ring. Cold-blooded. Ferociously clear-headed, as capable as a one-woman blitzkrieg, a think-tank devoid of outside distractions that would keep her from planning the kill. She couldn't allow fear for her family to get in the way. She couldn't let anything get in her way.

Eyes scarlet but drying, she tuned in to Bobby's concerned pleas for her to answer him. Cleared her throat and squared her shoulders. "I'm here," Clarice said in a surprisingly clear voice.

"You okay? I know this must be hard. You up to talking to Ace? I can give you his number so you can call when you feel better."

"No, I'm fine. I just had to collect myself. I had no idea you'd be helping him, though I should have. In fact, I was calling to ask you to do just that."

He paused and Clarice could sense his silent grin. "What makes you think I'd help that dweeb?"

"The threat of my straight-right to your ribs?"

"Ha! You know me too well, Boss," he chuckled.

"And don't you ever forget it."

"Hang on. I'll let the breadstick nerd update you on the plan." The phone clicked and Bobby said, "Boss? Here he is."

"Clarice?" Ace said.

The sound of his voice unleashed a massive battering against her volition once more, coming dangerously close to sabotaging her control, pummeling her with all those heavy, sharp feelings of love, hate, rage, that she had so cruelly suppressed only seconds

342

ago. The urge to throw the phone and start smashing everything and everyone in her sight was a blending of energies, all evil, coagulating into something tangible. The Devil was inviting her over to Hell for a bloody fist party, something the darker side of her would love to revel in.

The fight junkie tap-danced on cloven hooves, tail whipping around her blood drenched legs as she shook her ass and jabbed her rational self with a razor sharp trident. Her horns and teeth gleamed with firelight as she laughed uproariously. The bitch.

Clarice jabbed back, securing control. Sucked it up. Cursed her emotionally-wired x-genes and endeavored to speak to the love of her life for the first time in this new decade.

"Hi," Clarice said.

"Hi? That's it? No gushing platitudes for your loving, dearly missed hubby?"

"That's all you get, Elephant Junk."

"Ooh, I love it when you talk dirty," he oozed in his best sexy voice. It was so incredibly lame-cute. Classic Ace.

"Uh. I'll just set the phone down for a minute," Bobby interrupted, but they barely heard him.

"Well, I'm tired of talking. I'm an all-action kind of gal."

"Gee. I never would have known that if you hadn't told me."

"Such a big mouth for a little guy."

"I'm not so little anymore, I'll have you know. Uh-huh. Been working out like Schwarzenegger," he said, and Clarice could picture the idiot flexing his arm, one eye squinting, pulling up a side of his mouth in that sneaky, *Knows Stuff* look that she loved so much.

"Damn, I've missed you," Clarice gushed to her loving, dearly missed hubby.

He chortled. "I knew it! She couldn't take it. Had to indulge her inner drama queen."

"Is that a problem for you?"

"Not at all."

"Then respect your lady."

"Yes, dear," he said, huge smile in his tone. He sighed. "I was so goddamn nervous all I could do was joke. I've missed you, too. So much."

"There. Was that hard?"

"Uh. Yeah."

It was her turn to chortle. "For me, too."

We laughed together, then he said, "You sound good. But, um, different."

"Yeah," Clarice replied quietly. "A lot has happened." She frowned. "You sound different too."

He was silent for a few seconds, obviously having an Ace moment, lost in high-speed thought. Clarice shook her head, smiling, waiting. He snapped back to the conversation. "Oh. I hit a guy."

"No way."

"And I started swearing," he bragged.

"Oh, geez."

"I'm serious. Check this out." He cleared his throat. Deepening his voice, harsh and guttural as a ghetto thug, he said, "I'll blast your punk ass, bitch!" He cleared his throat again. In his very white, geeky normal voice he said, "How was that? Tough, right?"

Clarice answered him with gales of laughter.

"Hello? Hello?" Bobby said. "Is it safe?"

"Yeah, Bobby. We cooled it before any nine-hundred number action jumped off," Clarice managed through an aftershock of giggles.

"Ace couldn't handle phone sex, anyway," Bobby declared.

"Could too," Ace responded in a child's voice.

"Could not," Bobby played along.

"Could too!"

Clarice listened to her significant other banter with his best friend, feeling as if she were levitating off her bed. The three of them talking again, with such ease and comfort, with that familiar trust and understanding as if they had never been apart, was surreal. It was like they were at Custom Ace shooting the breeze while awaiting the first customers of the day, camaraderie of the highest quality, and light years different from what she shared with her fellow convicts. But similar in a way that she couldn't explain.

Clarice the Family Woman, the Retired Boxer and Business Owner, was a super-different chick from the skin and muscles that she operated now. Clarice the Convict was the person she had become, on the verge of running for her life to start a new one with her family, willing to break any laws to make that happen. Clarice the Convict was a whirlwind of strategy and action. A *take-care-of-business-with-an-S-on-her-chest* chick. Super Boss Lady.

"Excuse me," Clarice said in a commanding tone they'd heard on more than one occasion. They quieted. "Sorry to be the party pooper. You know I love you guys, but we have some business to attend before we get to play."

"Yes, dear."

"Yes, Boss."

She grinned fiercely. "All right, gentlemen. This is what we're going to do…"

* * *

After lunch several women stopped by to comment on Yolanda's shoulder and inquire about prices. By 4:00 p.m. shift change, she had knocked out three more tatts, totaling $150. $200, counting Yolanda's.

First up was a big girl with an engaging, sassy attitude that Clarice just loved. She plaited her hair and debated with Patty, loudly, about traditional hooker-John arrangements while Clarice immortalized her two daughters on her chest, two cute, plump faces above her heart with ribbons flowing around their cheeks, names in neat script on the ribbons.

$100. *Cha-ching!* went Shocker's cash register.

The second customer was a hard-core Gangsta Queen with boss dreadlocks and a permanent snarl under eyes that had seen too much misery for a twenty-year-old. She brought her radio and headphones. Bumped Lil' Kim while Clarice did her very first gang tattoo: a six point star with pitchforks and a little devil diva sporting an afro and holding a knife. Tatted it right above her belly button. When Clarice finished, the girl's responding smile completely transformed her appearance, and she suddenly looked her age, pretty and young rather than battle-wizened and hard, pleased with the trick shading that made the tattoo jump off the skin.

$50. *Cha-ching! Mo' cash fo' the stash*, as Patty liked to say after a day of hard work. Clarice was ready to admit that Patty's profession was much more demanding than hers. And much more profitable. But she felt absolutely no urge to compete with Patty's skills.

Clarice cleaned the machine for the third time. Stored it. Then she helped Patty prepare for her fight, which was scheduled for thirty minutes time. Clarice held the mitts while Patty gently, slowly started punching, warming and stretching her arms and torso before speeding up, increasing power. Patty broke a sweat and Clarice called a halt just before she fatigued. By the time they walked to the empty building where the fights were held, Patty's nerves would be primed and timed.

They left for their 'paint detail', leaving their IDs with the tower officer and walking out into the gorgeous evening. The sky was yellows and reds, the sun cruising toward the horizon, projecting darker reds and darkening clouds as it vanished. Bird crap covered the sidewalks and gave the place a manure smell, totally ruining the sight of the random flowers towering over grass that should have been cut weeks ago, still wet from an earlier rain. They tip-toed around the poop.

Entering the two-story concrete building they were supposed to be renovating, they encountered loud laughter and singing from cliques of girls standing around discussing the fights and their bets, rap music beating up some unfortunate generic brand radio. A few women were dancing, the smell of pot hanging in the air all around them. A pleasant change from the foul dung outside.

"That's good dope," Patty noted, her nose sniffing a sample.

"Focus," Clarice reminded her gently. She grumbled her assent.

The shower room was packed with the usual crowd, divided by gangs and sets, everyone loitering against the tiled walls, arms folded, game faces on. Captain Portsmouth stood at the center in front of a camera held by her GQ assistant. Ski mask on and churning as her jaw munched tobacco and she finished her MC work on the fight that had just concluded.

"Ladies and gents, hoes and niggas!" Portsmouth said, raising her arms to address the viewers. "Thank you for logging on to Bitch Fight. We hope you've enjoyed these great live matches. We now bring you the main event." She stuck her masked face into the camera and cocked her neck. "Two bad ass bitches that have thrilled you with their every performance..."

As she talked, Clarice hurriedly wrapped Patty's hands and wrists, binding the metacarpals so they wouldn't flex, solidifying her fists, encasing the wrists in layered support. Pulling a small comb from her back pocket, Clarice used it to stuff the ends of the wraps so they wouldn't unravel.

"Perfect," Patty observed, checking out her large fists wrapped in strips of sheet.

Clarice bumped her elbow. "Stay loose," Clarice suggested.

"Oh, right." She began moving around, breathing deeply, swinging her arms, punching slowly.

Clarice started to look around for Patty's opponent, the ripped Amazon, when a voice froze her spine.

"Sharp knife for a short life, Small Fry."

The familiar tone touched nerves connected to memories stored in the Extreme Danger zone. Instinct kicked in as Clarice spun toward Chiquita, rolling with a defensive move and taking the blow Clarice sensed coming on her shoulder. It was a slick maneuver, and saved her neck from being filleted. But one thing was sure: using moves learned for defending against punches wouldn't work out well when being struck with a knife.

The long, strong, dark arm of Chiquita blurred in her vision a millisecond before Clarice ducked and rolled and the flashing steel zipped through her deltoid like a ninja carving a turkey. Clarice roared in fury, darting backwards spry and fast, hands up. Her jab came alive all by itself, popping her attacker hard in the nose as her feet touched. Chiquita's knife arm never stopped moving. She reversed direction, the clear, shrill sound of steel whistling through the air as the blade arced back and forth inches from Clarice's upheld hands, twice a second.

Captain Portsmouth screamed belligerent threats at Chiquita, demanding that she stop this instant. Her words fell on rage-deafened ears. Chiquita's scarred, shining face was elongated with hatred, firmly gripped in killing mode, burping explosive snarls in time with her strikes, lips pulled back from large, horse-like teeth, shoulder muscles rippling with the violent movements.

The women surrounding them quickly cleared a circle, packing into the shower on one side and into the open zone on the other, getting out of knife swinging range. Clarice circled to her right, just barely evading the deadly weapon that sought her vitals with uncanny speed. The hand that expertly wielded the eight-inch shank feigned at her head, immediately following with a thrust to her abdomen. Clarice lunged backwards, right foot hitting and taking her weight, loading up like a spring, the blade flickering past, her arm scrubbing her ribs. In the blink of an eye, Clarice launched forward and to the side, propelling toward Chiquita's overextended body with twisting hips, rolling shoulders and a right-hand bomb that drove into her neck with horrifying force. Her fist tightened into stone, crushing Chiquita's larynx and battering her off balance as Clarice completely turned her shoulders through the punch, yelling a loud battle cry to boost the exertion. The roaring smack-crunch felt disgusting as Clarice sensed the damage it caused through her bare fist, but somehow gave her a supreme feeling of satisfaction, knowing she had just ended the fight with a single punch. She had been aiming for Chiquita's chin when she loaded up the shot, but felt some other force take over and guide it toward her neck.

Well. That's too bad, huh?

The impact tore a ghastly noise from Chiquita's opened mouth, spinning her around. She had enough left in her to counter as she staggered to maintain balance, slicing through Clarice's shirt into her lower ribs. Chiquita struggled to get a foot under her, stood with a hand on her throat, gasping for breath, furiously angry. She held her shank up again but made no move toward Clarice, paralyzed by her injury.

Clarice's shoulder erupted in fire, feeling like someone had impaled her arm on a lit blowtorch, deep-frying the tissue. The pain spread quickly, all the way to her finger tips and up into her cheek and scalp, pulling every available nerve-ending into the firestorm, a nuclear tail on a pissed off meteor. Clarice gasped but could hardly stand to suck in a breath after that. A moment later her side joined the party, igniting another fire ball that shot up her oblique one way, down through her hips and singed the hair off her crotch.

Felt like that, anyway. It was deep.

Portsmouth still cursed Chiquita, but was waving frantically at the GQ camera-woman to record the action.

Patty appeared behind Chiquita, brandishing her long spike, cocked back behind the deadly expression that was her face. Clarice waved and yelled for her to stop, but she was past the point of no return, bringing it down with all her weight behind it, sinking the shank into Chiquita's back up to the string-wrapped handle. The blow was gruesome in sound, the skin ripping rather than slicing clean, a wet, quick suction sound as Patty snatched her weapon back, blood splattering the ground, her pants, the brick wall behind her.

Chiquita crumpled to the floor, mewling in agonized, raging pain, unable to take a full breath or scream. She clutched her throat with her left hand, mouth wide open, the right dropped the shank and jerkily reached behind her to attempt the impossible task of staunching the hole high on her back. She flopped stomach down on the concrete in a puddle of her own blood that slowly spread out around her.

Because the whole thing from the beginning to end lasted maybe thirty seconds, everyone was still trying to process what had just taken place. Normally, when a gang member gets dropped by non-gang members, repercussions are enacted immediately. But Chiquita, being a Crip, a less common organization in this state, had no back-up present, so Patty and Clarice had no reason to fear immediate retaliation.

Patty nodded to Clarice, mouth a thin line, leaned down to clean her tool. Just casually wiped it on the back of Chiquita's shirt before sheathing it in her pants, her attitude that of an authorized peace keeper with no qualms about protecting the good citizens with ruthless barbarism.

"I...Get you," Chiquita gargled, one eye open wide in a glare at her giant blonde friend, the other closed tightly in pain. Blood foamed around the corners of her mouth and she started coughing up more of it.

Oh my God. She would have survived that throat injury. But not a hole in her lung...

"Her lung is punctured!" Clarice shouted, twisting around to the captain. "She needs help, quick!" The sudden turning of her head pulled on her wounds, tearing them. Clarice gasped. Blood leaked through her fingers. Clarice squeezed her shoulder harder.

Captain Portsmouth's masked head tilted sideways, and Clarice was reminded of a large black poodle thinking through a particularly difficult trick. "You and you," she commanded, pointing at two Gangsta Queens. She crooked her finger and they hurried forward through the crowd. "Get this stankin ho outta here."

"Where do we take her?" one of the girls asked.

"I don't care. Just get her stupid ass outta here, so we's can make this money."

Clarice stepped forward. "You need to get her to the hospital," Clarice said in outrage.

She stuck a hand up in front of her face. "Ah, hell nah, bitch. You be the captain now? Don't think so. I'm running this show, and ain't no Chiquita, Diedra, or Wynita gonna hold it up. We making this money, Cream Tail." She turned to her GQs. "I said get that ho outta here! Drop her somewhere she'll be found and don't let anyone see you. I need y'all back here ASAP."

They nodded, each grabbing an arm and dragging Chiquita toward the zone's main exit. Her shoes trailed blood as they scraped over the dusty concrete floor, their wearer nodding, unable to hold her eyes open as consciousness failed.

Clarice shuddered, suddenly cold. Closed her eyes. This was not happening.

"Are you okay, Shocker?" An aristocratic voice said, surprising her. It was completely out of place amongst the loud chatter of prison thugs all around them. Clarice opened her eyes and looked into the concerned face of Helen, who stood looking at her bleeding shoulder and oblique, eyes sad but intently studying the extent of the injuries.

"Not really," Clarice grumbled. "What are you doing here?"

She smiled. "Not a place you would expect to bump into someone like me, is it?"

"Nope."

"I'm here for the same reason as you: financial. I have some skill at first-aid, and, as you know, access to substantial supplies. Please." She motioned for Clarice to follow her. "Allow me to tend to your injuries."

A great sounding proposal. Clarice followed her to the other side of the room of empty cubicles, pushing through groups of women and stopping next to a pillow case with a small bulge in the bottom, which sat on the floor against a wall. Helen opened it, removed several squares of gauze, iodine, ointment, tape and anti-inflammatories. She handed her the pills. Clarice swallowed them dry. She gently pulled up her sleeve and cleaned the gash in her arm before closing it with steri-strips.

"These are not as good as stitches, which are what you really need. Though they'll keep it closed so it will heal with a minimal scar. If you tear it open again, it will have a large scar," she said.

"Fantastic," Clarice growled, knowing that with her luck, she'd end up with a Grand Canyon scar.

Helen smiled again. "I'll stop by later and give you some supplies so you can change the dressing," she said, taping ointment and iodine coated gauze over the steri-strips. "You must change them twice a day. More if they start to bleed again."

"Thank you."

"You don't have to thank me." She began cleaning the gash on her side. "You owe me twenty dollars."

"Ah. Right. Medic fee." Clarice gave a small smile. "Nice hustle. I could have gone to the clinic for free."

"That's true. Of course, if you had gone there, you would have been placed in lockdown on Protective Custody."

Crap. Clarice hadn't thought of that. Eyes wide with this new knowledge, she reached into her sock and pulled out a square of plastic with money in it. Happily paid the beautiful medic and thanked her profusely for her services. Helen said goodbye and Clarice went to find Patty.

Weaving through the crowd, conscious of bumping her arm, Clarice found her friend near the shower. Clarice stopped next to her, and they shared an odd silence, the kind that happens after a person shows a rare quality, that they are larger than life, proving imminent loyalty by aiding in a way above and beyond friendship. Strengthening the bond from platonic to familiar. Patty had just shown her she was willing to risk her life for her, had her back a thousand percent, a gesture of the highest respect. And Clarice had no idea what to say about it. One of those things where saying 'thanks' would only degrade the gesture, insulting the integrity of the bond.

Patty began to squirm and Clarice struggled with words so the odd silence wouldn't become uncomfortable.

"Well, that was fun," Clarice said.

Patty let out a breath and smiled. "Did you mean to hit her in the throat?" Her brows raised. "That crunch was so loud it had an echo. Like you smashed a can of Pringles." She winced, hand on her neck.

"It was an illegal punch," Clarice mumbled unhappily. Hey, Clarice was a pro. Clarice did not enjoy fighting dirty.

"What? Illegal? You're serious." She eyed her as if Clarice had just claimed President Obama was a transvestite. She saw Clarice was serious and burst out laughing. Several girls close by caught the giggling contagion, added their own tee-hee-hees, even though they had no idea what they were discussing.

"Look around you, Shock. Illegal my pimple covered ass. Ha!"

Clarice glowered, rubbing her stinging shoulder.

"Big ol' walking felony," she reminded her between giggles.

Portsmouth stood in the shower once again, waving her arms to direct the traffic. Everyone filed in, posted up in their reserved places. Patty nodded to her and walked up next to the captain, rolling her shoulders, and stared at her opponent, the Amazon, who stood on the other side, grim-faced, silent. Dangerous. Clarice stared, too.

The Amazon was about six-one, one-eighty-five. Her long, brown, muscular arms were eye magnets as she removed her t-shirt, revealing a modified bra that held her substantial bosom snug against her thick, cut torso. Clarice had known many female athletes, and few had abdominals that showed like hers, prominent, large and chiseled like a man's. Oblique muscles standing out between her ribs like thick fingers. Her legs were huge in the thighs, butt jutting out like the footrest on a Lazy Boy, black and white cutoff pants straining to cover everything. Calves slim, but strong, over long bare feet. Clarice did a double-take.

Eww. Put some shoes on, girl! That shower is filthy.

She untied the blue bandana on her head, handed it to one of her Sisters. Her short, wavy hair was masculine and very much added to the tough girl image conveyed by her facial features. Laila Ali came to mind, an Ali that had begun her career in inner city parks and alleys rather than in the top gyms with celebrity trainers. The formidable appearance was enough to intimidate most women, and probably a great many men. Patty's demeanor showed no signs of fear, only confidence, the comfort of being herself in a situation she knew well.

Clarice looked at the wad of money still in her hand with mixed, anxious feelings. Should Clarice bet on Patty? Would she be insulted if Clarice didn't? Clarice would give even odds on this fight, both fighters being completely unpredictable and inconsistent in their performances.

Dammit.

Sorry, Patty. I can't chance it. I'm too close.

Wincing, cursing, Clarice bent down and stuffed the cash back in her sock, adjusted her foot in her shoe. Stood up slower than her eighty-year-old grandma and watched to see how her dynamic BFF faired against the anti-Ali.

Captain Portsmouth chewed her cud, spat in a bottle and stuffed it in her back pocket. Twirled a finger at the camerawoman to start filming. She said, "We must apologize to the viewers for the delay. As you know, we's here at Bitch Fight are in a dangerous place, where anything can happen. And for being such loyal and patient customers, we will give you a free preview of that danger immediately after the show." She paused, and her ski mask did a weird, grotesque shifting backwards, her huge grin deforming her head and stretching the mouth hole into a wide oval. Clarice felt disgusted. She continued, "Ever see a knife fight between hard-core cons? They usually end badly…" She let that hang in the air for a minute, tantalizing, teasing the viewers' lust for violence. They would certainly hang around their computers after the show for that treat.

Portsmouth turned toward the Amazon, raised an arm in her direction. "In the blue corner, the fearless country girl with ham fists she knows how to dish. You niggas and hoes, give it up for the giant muscled hustler you'd love to see beat up your ex. I give you: Mocha. Blas-terrr!"

The Gangsta Queens cheered and clapped. The Vice Lord Flowers on the other side scowled and folded their arms tighter. Clarice just laughed.

Mocha Blaster? Come on!

Portsmouth needs her butt kicked for these ridiculous names. Still though, kind of made her feel better about the handle she put on her. Devil Hands Sally. Geez. Clarice would always resent her for that.

Yep. Butt kicked. All she needed.

MC No-Naming Idiot turned to Patty and introduced her. "And in the red corner, the wild white girl with no love for these hoes. I give you: The Blonde. Bomb-err!"

Clarice pursed her lips in approval. Now that was a cool fight name. And appropriate. Clarice yelled out a cheer, left fist raised high for Team Blonde Bomber. The shower was silent except for the movement of two dozen heads spinning in her direction, glaring at her. Clarice sensed silent eyes behind her as well, and Clarice made sure they all knew Clarice didn't care, glaring all around her to show her support for the underdog. Clapping from a single person began somewhere behind her, but Clarice couldn't see who it was when she turned to look. It was so polite and dignified that Clarice surmised it must be Helen. She grinned, turned back to the show, proud of Helen's courage to clap for one of three white girls present.

"This is the main event," Portsmouth shouted at the two warriors. "Fight hard. Hear? Let's get it on!" She stepped to the wall and the shower exploded in rumbling fist smacks, grunts and squeaking tiles.

Patty and the Amazon stood toe-to-toe slugging each other in the face as quickly as they could, feet planted, no defense or head movement whatsoever. Just pitching and catching, as they say in boxing.

As a boxer that specializes in not getting hit, the display was maddening to watch, irksome and highly disappointing. But from a purely entertaining point-of-view, it was kickass and definitely the sort of gladiatorial show fans would love.

Bitch Fight was raking in the Big Bucks.

A huge right-hand walloped Mocha Blaster in her eye, the pain startling enough to make her miss her swings and step back from the Blonde Bomber's assault. Clarice cheered louder, encouraging her friend to go for it. She did, crouch-walking in and thudding blows off her opponent's forehead, cheeks and ears. Just winging punches regardless of how they hit, sinking them knuckle-deep.

The Amazon took Patty's best shots, wailing an unnerving bestial howl and shook them off. Lunged forward to attack again, landing a right-hook to Patty's chin, the sound of it connecting loud, gasp-inspiring, a thick red stream of drool ejecting from her distorted mouth. The Bomber stumbled to the side, eating several more hard shots to the head that knocked her down, head crashing into the knees of a GQ. The Gangsta pushed Patty away roughly and Clarice shouted a challenge before pushing her way into the shower. Several GQs grabbed her arms, held her. Portsmouth waved a hand at her in warning. Clarice tensed, growling.

Fuck them! They couldn't hold her, couldn't stop her from helping her friend if she needed her.

"Patty!" Clarice hollered. She looked up, dazed but game. Waved her off and caught Mocha Blaster's long bare foot as she tried to kick her teeth in.

Clarice snatched her arms loose from the security hookers and clenched her fists, breathing faster, watching for anyone else who might molest her friend while desperately holding the fight junkie in her cage. The urge to cut loose was nearly overwhelming. There were eleven or twelve GQs in the shower and another dozen behind her. Clarice felt confident she could clock and deck three or four before they overpowered her – after which she might suffer a fate similar to Chiquita's.

For some reason, that thought didn't cause her to sing show tunes and do pirouettes. She grumbled an angry prayer, just in case, while eyeing the nearest targets.

Having friends can really suck.

Patty had caught the foot and shoved Mocha Blaster's leg, the force of it throwing her into the Flowers on the other side. They shouted angrily and pushed her back into the center. Patty gained her feet, raised her blood stained fists and screamed like a monster from nightmare. The Amazon answered with heavy, swinging fists, and they began another punching contest, looping wide, hooking blows at each other with total disregard for the damage they sustained to their faces and knuckles. Skin scraped on teeth and fingernails, noses, lips and cheeks split and gushed, swollen under sweat and tears of rage. The battle lust had utterly consumed them both. Demolition of their enemy and survival were all that mattered. It was anybody's fight at this point, the determined, murderous energy pulsing from the combatants, thrilling all who witnessed the phenomenal match. The punishment both women were willing to take awe-inspiring.

After two minutes of non-stop exchanges, they began laboring hard for breath, spit and snot blowing in a fine mist to mix with the sweat slinging off them. They tired, slowed. Patty grunted desperately, digging deep for more energy. Her heart was in it, but her burning shoulders had had enough of this shit. She ran out of gas first, and Mocha Blaster moved forward with punches that hit with painful slowness, loading up one right-hand after another. Patty crashed into the wall where Gangsta Queens had dodged out of the way. The Amazon's final punch had all her weight behind it, awkward, untrained and slow as hell, but it socked into Patty's ear with a crunch that was immediately followed by a reverberating knock as the Blonde Bomber's head ricocheted off the bricks, rendering her unconscious. She collapsed. The crowd of GQs clapped and celebrated, rushing their battered champion, Portsmouth and the camerawoman included, the cheers deafening in the confines of the shower.

Clarice ran to Patty, knelt down. "Hey!" Clarice gasped, holding her head in her lap. She mumbled, opened her eyes. Closed them. Clarice slapped her cheek. "Patty!"

She frowned, opened a groggy eye and glared at her. "Ask next time. Don't just shove my head in your crotch," she slurred.

Clarice sighed, relieved. "Sorry. Seeing you get knocked out got me so turned on I just couldn't help myself."

"Shit. Lost $300. You know how many blow jobs that is?"

Clarice laughed quietly, ignoring the warm ickiness that flowed down her arm from the ball of fire that used to be her shoulder. None of that mattered.

She was okay.

Chapter XIX

Juarez, Chihuahua
Mexico
March 25, 2012

"*Con permiso, Señor Felix*," the maid said, bending down to speak to the man under the truck. "*Tenga la informacion tu pedi*," she said, presenting him a thin manila folder as he rolled out on the creeper.

"*Gracias*, Eva," Felix replied, smiling at her with more than professional gratitude. She turned pink, giggled as he set aside a ratchet and stained the folder with black, greasy fingerprints. She inclined her head coyly, twirled around and worked her curves across the airport hangar, leaving her suitor with a wistful expression on his grease-dotted face. He shook his head and opened the file, careful not to stain the documents. Read the highlighted sections. He smiled in triumph. "Erik!" he yelled.

"Eh?" Erik answered from under a huge off-road truck thirty feet away. "*Que paso?*"

"*Tenemos que salir.*"

Erik gave a whooping cheer, tools clanging on the concrete as he dropped what he was doing to slide out from under the truck. The tiny wheels on the creeper squealed under his bulk. He stood, greasy face shining, smile bright and giddy. He walked over to his friend, who stood reading a file. "*Vamos encontrar los gringos?*" he asked, wiping his hands on a grease rag.

"*Si. Vamonos.*"

They hurried out of the hangar, walking under the Gulfstream jet and out into the arid, smoldering desert air. The ranch estate was bustling with activity. *Rancheros* rode around on horses or ATVs, yipping at the herds of cattle or guiding *burros* loaded with various supplies for desert travel, shovels and pickaxes clashing together like symbols in a band of neighing horses and barking Honda exhaust pipes. Chickens clucked in bad temper, forced to scatter from the path of the men, who held their breath as a gust of hot wind carried a strong scent of manure, thick enough to taste. The foul breeze subsided and they gasped with relief. Erik spat in disgust, kicked at a chicken.

The estate house loomed ahead of them, the Spanish villa roof tiles glowing bright red as the sun reached its summit, the stucco and brick walls providing shade for the smaller, similarly built building on its side. They walked up the brick pathway, stopped and knocked on the heavy oak door. Opened it when they heard their liege's invitation.

The cool air inside El Maestro's office was nirvana to the mechanics. They gave a collective sigh of pleasure, stumping the dust from their boots. El Maestro looked up from his desk in the center of the room. "Gentlemen. Please have a seat. I'll be with you presently," he said, typing quickly on a laptop. He finished, closed it. Entwined his hands and smiled with paternal affection at the men seated in front of him. "Report."

Felix glanced at Erik, who nodded. Felix said, "You asked us to find out when the gringos will escape. We tasked the maids, and they hacked the Department of Corrections to search for transportation orders. They found one."

El Maestro pursed his lips. "This maid. Would her name happen to be Eva?"

"*Si, El Maestro*," Felix said, blushing. Erik grinned.

"Very well," their boss said, also grinning. He enjoyed surprising his employees with knowledge of the estate relationships. He jotted down a quick note, set the pen down. "I'll see that she gets a bonus and some time off for a few dates with you."

"*Gracias, El Maestro*," Felix replied gratefully, his face flushed completely, eyes downcast in embarrassment. Erik laughed and slapped his leg. Felix handed the file over the desk. "Eva's findings."

El Maestro scanned the contents quickly, said, "Excellent. Well done, the both of you."

"*Gracias.* Do we get to pursue it?" Felix asked eagerly. He hadn't been to the States in years, and had many family members he wished to visit.

"*Si*, El Maestro. You say we-" Erik began, but was corrected.

"Said."

"You said we could assist the *gringos*. We know you normally have a security team-"

"That is true," El Maestro interrupted, holding up a placating hand. He looked thoughtful. "Because of the very personal nature of this operation, I will allow you to go. You gentlemen need a vacation, anyhow." He smiled at their enthusiastic response, looked down at the file. "This says the lady and gentleman will be transported to a courthouse on April second. I will grant you leave until the fourth of April."

"*Gracias, El Maestro!*" they exclaimed in unison.

He smiled again. "Since I'm in need of a break myself, I shall accompany you."

The mechanics glanced at each other. Felix said with concern, "But it could be dangerous, El Maestro. What if we-"

El Maestro held up a commanding hand, silencing any protest. "There is nothing to discuss on that matter. We'll leave immediately."

"Si, El Maestro." The men bowed and stood up.

El Maestro stood with them. "Have the maids appropriate our passports and relevant documentation for our alternate identities. You two handle the muni-

tions and transportation arrangements. I'll meet you
at the hangar in an hour."

"*Si!*"

"*Si, El Maestro!*"

Excitement tickling them inside and out, Erik and
Felix hurried out of the office and hardly noticed the
smell of dung in their urgent desire to get back to the
hangar and prepare for the mission.

Chapter XX

South Mississippi Correctional Institution
Leakesville, Mississippi
March 31, 2012

"I heard Captain Bartleby got his pension and retired," Diamond said. He stood, finished folding a homemade belly shirt, a match to the one he wore. Stored it in his locker box.

Ace looked up from the other side of their cubicle. Sat up, his bunk creaking a metallic complaint. "I was happy to hear it. Even happier that he kept his word and got us out of lockdown," he said. Closing the magazine on his lap, he rolled it up, strangled it, growling, "Happy, happy, joy, joy."

"What? Oh, get over it, mutt. You did what you had to do, and for a good cause."

"I know that," he sighed, dropping the unfortunate periodical.

"Then stop dwelling on it. You are so not cute when in bad humor." He paused, turned to Ace, lips pursed. "Let me ask you something." Ace looked him in the eyes. "Do you like feeling like that?"

"No. Of course not."

"Then refuse to." He snapped his fingers. "You can choose not to feel that way. Works for me and my super-confused feelings."

"Uh-huh. I can agree with that."

"What, that it works for me?"

"No. That you have super-confused feelings," Ace replied, looking pointedly at the panties Diamond wore. He snapped his fingers and cocked his neck to mock his friend. Diamond retaliated, grabbed some folded panties off his bed and threw them at Ace, who shouted and leapt off his mattress, feet thumping on the concrete floor, magazine fluttering up in the air, pages tearing.

"What are you two punks so excited about, huh? Playing a friendly game of Tickle Horny?" said a Latin King appearing in the aisle. His young pale face had tear drops tattooed at the corners of his eyes, and a five-point crown in the center of his forehead, ink blue and faded, art of such poor quality it looked like something you'd see in an ancient cave. Close-cropped blonde hair, a crooked nose that had seen one too many violations for un-Latin King behavior. More awful looking tattoos covered his arms and torso, which were out shape for one so young in a violent business. He poked his chest out and tried to make himself seem bigger, intimidating. "My Brothers are gonna smash you queers."

Diamond harrumphed, put a hand on his hip. "Little boy, you don't have any Brothers. They using you, and you know it."

"Fuck you," he spat, face scrunched and wrathful. Fists balling up.

"I'll pass, little boy. You're just the LK's scrub minion. Not worth my time. Anyway," he lisped, flipping imaginary hair off his forehead. "How much canteen do you pay your 'Brothers' every week? Huh, scrub?"

He worked his mouth in angry silence for an answer.

Another LK walked up, this one similar looking, though slightly more stocky, and Diamond hurriedly tugged on some pants in case he had to fight.

Ace smiled at his friend, and had the odd thought that he should have Latin Kings visit more often.

"*Amor de rey*," the newcomer said, entwining hands with his compeer, in the organization's handshake. He turned to look at Ace and Diamond. "That the guy that hit Death Punch? He don't look like he can hit that hard."

"I can't," Ace said. "I'm a peaceful guy." He threw up a peace sign, but his silly smile ruined the sincerity. He still felt satisfaction from decking that idiot.

"But I'm not," Diamond growled, anger beginning to contort his face. He glared at the two gang bangers until they squirmed, uneasy. "I could whip both of you little boys. How would you like that jacket on you, huh? Getting your ass kicked by a sexy black bitch like me."

They glared back in defiance, though faltered after weighing the risks and realizing their already precarious reputations were in jeopardy. *What if this homosexual did whip them?* their expressions said.

Ace tried hard not to laugh as they blew out dismissive breaths and endeavored a semblance of dignity as they walked off, chests poked out at anyone who glanced at them. Diamond's anger evaporated and he fell on his bed laughing, legs kicking up in the air.

Ace smirked at him. "You should be ashamed of yourself."

"For being so sexy I scare off little boys?" Diamond chortled. "Right. At least it got your mind off Twinkle."

And got you to put some clothes on, Ace thought, grinning. "They'll be back," he said, looking in the direction they went.

"Yeah. With boys I won't be able to run off."

The men on the zone staggered around making up their beds or heating coffee at the microwave, the strong bitter aroma of Maxwell House fueling the grumbling about going to work for pennies or nothing at all. Very few prisoner jobs in Mississippi actually paid anything, with the lucky, high salary earners only making about a buck a day, and the vast majority of workers being compensated for their hard labor with time off their sentences. Work for thirty days, get thirty days off. About a third of the convicts weren't eligible for Good Time. Consequently, none of the men were humming pleasantly with faces or gestures that indicated impatience to be at their cherished place of work.

With no job or Good Time eligibility to motivate him to find a job, Ace's work at present was figuring out how to get clothes, money, and a cuff key for the liberation attempt this coming Monday. He paced the cubicle while eating a bowl of cereal, thinking furiously through different scenarios, discarding, considering, discarding again.

Diamond's stomach growled loudly and Ace stopped, looked at him. "That thing sounds pissed off. Feed it something, for once."

"I'm good. The hunger pangs let me know I'm alive. They feel good, really."

"You need help."

"And you need your own business to mind, geek."

In response, Ace slurped up some cereal, smacking sharply, and smiled with milk-dribbling glee when Diamond shivered in revulsion. "What?" he said. He slurped again.

"Stop it."

"Huh?" Slurp.

"Stop!"

Slurp.

"Ugh. You are just gross."

Heavy boots clumped to a stop outside the cubicle. "Like you have room to talk," Lieutenant Cole said, stepping in between the bunks. His belt creaked as he placed his hands on his waist, staring at Diamond with dark, mischievous eyes that knew his secrets. Strong cologne wafted from his bright white shirt and barrel chest.

Diamond lowered his eyelids, long lashes shining with fresh mascara and homemade glitter. "Big, dark, and handsome," he murmured. "Too bad you're such an idiot."

"Uh. I can leave," Ace offered, setting his bowl down.

"Don't bother. I'll go. I need to talk to my Sisters and do something about those LK haters," Diamond said, standing. He shimmied into his flip-flops and brushed past Cole without so much as a glance. Strutted to the yard door and seemed to fade away into the morning sun beaming through the doorway. Dust motes and catcalls floated in with the chilly breeze.

Cole smiled at Diamond's magical wake, turned to Ace. "That time of the month?"

"I have no credible clue," Ace replied, stymied by his friend's super-confused feelings. He shook his head and focused on the man in front of him, anxiety and excitement fighting a confused battle in his stomach. Cole was just the person he needed to see. He walked closer, lowered his voice. "Can you, uh, help me get some things?"

"What's on your mind, big guy?"

Ace glanced around, then whispered, "I need a pair of pants, a handcuff key, and some cash."

The lieutenant's eyes bulged. He looked around quickly. Back to Ace. "You goddamn crazy-ass white boy!" He checked himself, lowered his tone. "Man,

you don't go around asking for those things like that."
He took a breath. "It's obvious what you want those
things for. And for that reason, because you are so
damn obvious, I don't want anything to do with it. I
won't risk trading this shirt for one like yours." He
pointed at Ace, scowling.

Ace dropped his head, embarrassed by his naïveté.
"I understand."

Another audible breath. "Here's some advice, big
guy: Ask for one item at a time and give excuses.
That way it's not so obvious. You don't want anyone knowing you plan to escape. Anyone," he emphasized, pointing again.

"I don't have time. I need everything now."

Cole grabbed his head with both hands, as if
a gigantic migraine had emerged inside his skull,
Godzilla rending Tokyo to shreds. He looked up at
the ceiling, pained, muttered to himself, "First he tells
me he's planning to escape. Then he tells me it's
going down soon." He looked at Ace, highly disappointed. "Don't tell me any more." He walked away
mumbling, shaking his head. Waved at the tower to
buzz open the exit. It closed heavily behind him, the
jarring noise like a bad omen to Ace, who had been
counting on Cole to help him.

He just knew Cole would help.

What the hell do I do now? he asked himself. *Who
can I ask?* He paced and let his mind go blank, allowing his much faster subconscious to sort through the
quandary. At the very least, he needed a key to remove his handcuffs and shackles. He could jump out

of the transport van and run down the street wearing black and white stripes. And he could survive without cash in the event things went wrong and he was unable to link with Clarice, forced to flee on foot through the city alone.

"But I can't run without a key…" he murmured in a trance.

Diamond's voice could be heard as he re-entered the zone through the yard door, shouting effeminately to several friends, flip-flops slapping his heels loudly as he hurried down the aisle and into the cubicle. "Ace!" he said excitedly. "I have great news."

Ace stopped pacing, focused his eyes. "Yeah?"

"Oh boy, let me tell you," he breathed joyously. He sat on his bed, crossed his legs at the knees. Perched hands on them. "I just had a meeting with three of my Sisters. And Princess Xena, over in unit twelve, told me Juicy Stuff used to be cube mates with a Latin King."

"So?"

"So, you didn't let me finish," he fussed, flapping a hand. He gave a big smile. "So, Juicy Stuff was giving the LK some juicy stuff, wink-wink." He giggled, kicked his legs. Settled down. "We got the dirt on those haters now. Sisters networking, honey!"

Ace caught on to the scheme and grinned. "This LK must be important to them."

"Supposedly, he's one of the highest ranking."

"Yeah, that could be bad for them," Ace muttered thoughtfully. He said, "Let me guess: If the LKs don't leave us alone, your Sisters will expose the guy and cause the entire organization embarrassment."

"That's the business! We'll rub it in good." Diamond held his hand up and Ace high-fived him with a laugh. "Juicy is on the way to talk to Death Punch now."

"Neutralize a threat with a threat." He shook his head in disbelief. "Now I'm caught up in prison politics."

"Be thankful you have a good diplomat on your side."

"I'll be sure to thank Juicy Stuff."

Diamond squawked, snatched a flip-flop off his foot, threw it at Ace.

"All right!" Ace laughed. "Thank you, my dear and queer friend."

"You're welcome," he replied smugly, flipping his imaginary hair.

Ace's smile faded. He cleared his throat. "Oh, yeah. I think I screwed up."

"Oh, pooh." Diamond frowned in a way that said he was having fun and didn't want to talk about screwups right now. He sighed theatrically. "What did you do?"

Ace knelt down next to him. "I asked Cole to get me a key, cash, and clothes," he divulged with a wince.

Diamond's eyes popped out so cartoonishly Ace swore he heard, AWOOGA! Diamond screeched, "You did what?!"

"Stupid, huh?"

"lil' bit." Big, long sigh. Flapped a hand. "Cole is good people, and will violate up to a certain point. But you should have known he wouldn't do that for you. Shoot, Ace." He rolled his eyes, crossed his arms and harrumphed.

"How was I supposed to know? He brought me the iPod and MI-Fi router. Why not the other stuff?"

"My, my. What a giant green horn you have sticking out of your head."

"Huh?" Ace touched his forehead, confused.

"You're green, dummy. There's a humongous difference between a convict wanting to chat on a cellphone and a convict wanting to escape."

"You mean a difference in possible jail time?"

"No. One is possible jail time if they get caught. The other is definite jail time. A lieutenant didn't get that rank by taking stupid risks. No one cares about prisoners having phones. Everyone cares about prisoners escaping. And people talk, as you know."

"I should have seen that. Dammit," Ace said heatedly, berating himself. He knew he had trouble understanding social situations that were so obvious to most people. He usually just laughed it off, accepting the eccentricities that plagued the ultra-intelligent. *This is no laughing matter, though,* he thought, trying to find the bright side so he could at least force a rueful chuckle. But all sides were swathed in deep, negative darkness. No chuckling allowed. He looked up at his friend. "Any ideas?"

"I don't know. I thought you'd hack something, create something with your MacGyver skills. Shit, man. You're the genius here. I thought you had it figured out."

"Well, I don't. I'm green, remember?" Ace sat on his bed, head down with arms on his knees, fists clenched in frustration. Anger at himself morphed into dejection, and tears welled as his throat tightened. He resisted the powerful self-pity, blinking his eyes rapidly, breathing deeply, aware that this kind of emotion was not constructive. He had to regroup, re-think everything.

Back to the drawing board. Son of a soldering gun.

"Can you help me get any of the items?" he whispered to Diamond.

Diamond, lips pursed sideways, deep in thought with a finger against his temple, said, "I believe so. Maybe." He twisted his lips around, began tapping the other temple. "Hmm... The pants won't be a problem. My Sister Tina can make those for a few dollars. But the key..." He mumbled for several seconds. Gasped when an idea struck, inhaled quickly with a face-splitting grin. "I think I know where I can get a handcuff key!" he blurted excitedly.

Ace shushed him. "Want to put an ad in the paper while you're at it? And you call me green."

He grimaced, bent a hand and rolled his eyes. "I'm slippin'," he lisped. He flicked a dismissive hand, whispered breathily. "Anyways, I know someone that works in the lockdown unit around those high-risk guys. They keep cuff keys on them at all times in case they have to take off their restraints for fights."

"I heard horror stories about that unit. Aren't they handcuffed to go to the shower and yard?"

"Yeah. The showers are basically one-man cells with a shower head. And their 'yard' is an eight-by-fourteen dog cage."

"Yikes." He cringed.

"I feel you. Solitary confinement is not for the weak willed. I wouldn't last a month in those conditions."

"Me neither. So you think you can get a key? What are they made of?"

"The hard plastic head of a Bic lighter is popular. They also use the valve stems on asthma inhalers, and even parts of razor wire. They make them long enough to open the cuffs, but short enough to keep in their mouth."

"That is really cool," Ace said, eyes wide in respect. "But at the same time, it's really terrible."

"No doubt. And they live like that for years."

"Yikes," he repeated. "So your friend can get you one? How much will it cost?"

"Not sure about the price. I am sure that I can get it, though." Diamond nodded at his friend. "Gotcha!"

* * *

In the cubicle behind them, a young, pale faced man crept away from the low brick wall after listening to the two queers talk about getting a handcuff key. He smiled and the faded blue tattoos on his face crinkled, skin abused by smoking and poor hygiene adding years to the youngster's appearance. The smile remained in place as he hurried back to his building to tell Death Punch about Diamond's plan to score a key, possibly for an escape attempt.

Entering his zone, he was greeted by two of his Brothers, who flashed hand signs and nodded in a manner to remind their subordinate of his place. Tattoo Face eased by the much bigger Enforcers, holding his breath to prevent choking on their foul body odor, looked respectfully around the cubicle they were guarding. Death Punch sat inside on one bunk, talking to that big, stupid queer, Juicy Stuff. Tattoo Face grimaced, a bad taste suddenly twisting his jaw. He waved to get his superior's attention.

Death Punch looked up from a heated discussion. "What the fuck do you want?" he demanded with a murderous scowl, obviously livid over whatever the homosexual had disclosed.

"Ah, I need to talk to you," Tattoo Face said, voice shaking. The Enforcers behind him snickered and he dropped his head, embarrassed.

"I can see that!" Death Punch roared. "That's why I asked you what the fuck do you want. Do you understand English, or did your fat mother not send you to kindergarten?"

The snickers became full-bellied laughs, causing Tattoo Face to jerk as if stung, shame darkening his entire head and neck in scarlet shades. *Damn, I'm gonna get taxed big time next canteen if I can't do something to look good*, he thought in terror. He sighed, closed his eyes.

Everything will be okay when Death Punch hears my news. I hope.

Opening his eyes, he cleared his throat and deepened his voice. "I have information that will help the problem with the..." He nodded at Juicy Stuff with meaning.

Death Punch got the message, scowling at Tattoo Face with a warning that said, *This better be good.* He stood and told Juicy Stuff, "Get out of here, bitch. I'll deal with you punks later."

Juicy Stuff stood up quickly, huffing. "Careful who you call a bitch, white boy." He waggled a finger of caution in Death Punch's face. "I've never been that kind of bitch." His tone and eyes intimated there was another kind, but it wasn't the subservient kind that Death Punch referred to.

Juicy snapped his fingers at the Enforcers, who jumped aside to avoid being touched by the homo, glancing warily at him as he strutted away with confidence.

Tattoo Face sat on the edge of a bunk, facing his superior. "I heard those two punks talking," he said.

"About what?" Death Punch asked, rubbing his knuckles ominously.

Tattoo Face recognized the signs of his boss wanting to hit something - or somebody - and scooted further back on the bed. "Escape," he managed to say without gulping.

"Huh?" He stopped rubbing his fist, stared. An evil grin slowly bloomed on his face, the planes rounding in genuine cheer. "Really."

"Uh-huh. Heard them talking about getting clothes and a handcuff key."

"For who?"

"Who?"

"Who's going to escape, you idiot?" Death Punch sighed, exasperated.

"Oh. Diamond. I think."

"You think."

"I'm pretty sure. He said, 'I know where I can get a handcuff key.'"

"Yeah, that sounds like he's planning to bounce. Okay. Good job. We can use that," he mused to himself, then said, "That punk Juicy Stuff needs his head busted." He bent a wrist, pitched his voice high and lisped, "Y'all LK haters better not mess with my Sister Diamond and his cube mate, or I'll tell everyone about y'all's boy getting his tally wacker wacked by this Juicy Stuff." He dropped his arm, grunted in disgust. The Enforcers laughed again. Death Punch glared at them. "That shit's not funny." They shut up. "We have to strip Pistol Pete of his flag and violate him for homo behavior. You think that's funny?" They refused to answer that. "Didn't think so." He glared again.

"That sucks bad, man," Tattoo Face blurted, shocked by the revelation. He knew who Pistol Pete was, and couldn't believe a guy like that, a high-ranking King, had sex with that, that thing.

Ugh. He frowned severely at the image.

"Yeah, it did suck. Literally," Death Punch stated. His subordinates snickered or frowned. "But it won't suck any more." He waved at the Enforcers. "Spider. Nickel Bag. Get your dumb-asses in here. We have business." They stepped into the cubicle and sat on the same bunk as Tattoo Face, flanking him, foam mat sighing under their bulk. "We're gonna drop a dime on those two punks. You feel me?"

"Drop a dime?" Spider said. "How does that work?"

"Tell on them," Nickel Bag clarified.

"Okay." Spider nodded. "But why say 'drop a dime'? I don't get it."

"Back in the day, pay phones cost a dime. People used them to call the cops," Nickel Bag said.

Death Punch's mouth hung open, bafflement freezing his expression as he listened in disbelief.

"Oh," Spider said in an understanding that rarely came to him. He frowned. "But don't pay phones cost more than a dime now?"

"Shut. Up." Death Punch growled through grinding teeth.

Spider continued his train of thought, fearing he was becoming confused and eager to prevent it. "Like, do they even have pay phones anymore?"

Nickel Bag laughed. Death Punch stepped forward and slapped Spider, then proceeded without wasting breath on explaining his corporal punishment. Spider wouldn't get it, anyway. "Spider, you will write a kite to the folks and tell them Diamond is trying to get clothes and a key for an escape plan."

"All right," Spider agreed, rubbing his cheek thoughtfully.

"That will put him in lockdown for a while. We can get to him in there, without interference from his butt-buddy, Lieutenant Cole."

"Good plan," Nickel Bag said.

"I know it is," Death Punch responded arrogantly. "We'll get Diamond out of the way so Ace won't have anyone to boost his nuts up the next time we try to recruit him."

"Boost his nuts up?" Spider queried. "Up where?"

Death Punch growled, shook his head. Nickel Bag laughed again.

* * *

As a rule, time in prison goes by slow. It was some kind of law of psychology, the relativity of perception; when there's not much to occupy your time, the brain senses the present as slow-paced, but will remember it as having flown by. When there's a lot going on, the brain senses the present as fast-paced, but will remember it as a snail's journey. Ace considered his perception of time as a prisoner as he paced the cubicle. His feet throbbed from the consistent ten hour walk, the cheap foam of his shower shoes smashed so flat the balls of his feet might as well have been unpadded.

The concrete hurt, but he couldn't stop, the feeling of life-changing circumstances on the horizon propelling him on. The feeling of *Something Has To Happen Soon.* An emotion that built up in his chest and throat, aching with energy, driving him to Do Something, *Think, dammit, because your instincts are screaming for freedom, a family to take care of. Better food and housing.*

You. Must. Have. This. Allofit.

Ace's biology tweaked and played con games with his mind, pushing him to panic, sacrifice, throw caution to the wind and do whatever it took to get free and pacify his ticking, beastly urges.

This nature of motivation is experienced by everyone who is imprisoned. Very few feel it so strongly they can't refuse it, can't just kick it to the side out of fear, procrastination, or any number of passive excuses. Ace felt it so strongly his teeth vibrated, a metallic taste of chemicals sticking to his palate and tongue, drugging him with non-stop energy to *GET FREE.*

He paced and pondered, rehearsing several scenarios for survival while awaiting news from Diamond, who should be returning with the key any minute now. The other men on the zone went about their menial jobs and routines in slow motion, it seemed to Ace. Though if he thought back to when he first began pacing, they seemed to lunge into hypermotion, fast-forwarding in comical movements, the sun's rays angling through the windows going from the walls to the floor and back in a matter of seconds, black and white pants blurring by, up and down aisles, off and on bunks like human tracers.

He remembered it as going quickly, yet it was all so darn slow.

"Hurry up, Diamond, before I completely lose my data base," Ace grumbled, raking hands over his short hair. He kept feeling pulses of anxiety as the image of his friend trafficking major contraband cut into his impatience to leave. The *Get Free* plan always found a way back to the forefront of his thoughts. At this point, Ace couldn't form the simplest of thoughts without handcuff keys jingling like wind chimes in his peripheral vision.

Diamond walked on the zone and waved thanks to the tower officer, a flirty gesture of appreciation for being allowed to leave the building in blatant disregard for security protocol. Stepped clear as the door shut. Walked in the direction of his cubicle on his toes, blithely humming a dance song, prancing, ecstatic over accomplishing his mission. He spotted Ace in his usual deep and contemplative pacing, mental hospital-esque, and decided to surprise the geek. He tip-toed up behind him. Pulled out a handcuff key and dangled it on the side of Ace's head. Ace glanced at it, recognizing it, Diamond was sure. Looked down again and continued pacing. Diamond made a noise of astonishment and Ace spun around to find his friend staring at him, an intent, concerned look on his face.

"Damn!" Ace jumped. "Why are you sneaking up on me?"

Diamond ignored the question, held up the key. "Just held this up by your face. You looked at it, Ace." His hands shot out to the sides, bobbed his head in a *What Planet Were You On?* expression.

"I didn't see it," Ace mumbled, though he thought, *I didn't think it was real.* He smiled cheerfully at his friend. "Let me see it."

Diamond handed it to him with a joyous smile of his own. "It's a real key. An officer was selling them to the high-risk guys."

"How much?"

"Twenty dollars. Cash."

Ace winced. "All I have is canteen."

"Don't sweat it, mutt. I took care of it."

"Well let me pay you back in canteen, at least…" he said, but trailed off when Diamond folded his arms and cocked a hip, the meaning a rebuke for attempting to denigrate his gesture of friendship, while, somehow, also reprimanding him for the offer of food to someone who doesn't eat. "Uh," Ace said.

"I said don't sweat it, dummy. All that matters -"

The zone door buzzed and slammed open, a train of officers pouring through it at jogging speed, heading straight for their cubicle. Ace had time to stick the key in his mouth before a captain, two lieutenants and five COs turned the enclosure into the inside of a clown car. They packed in between the bunks, grabbed Ace and Diamond roughly, without warning or explanation, and shoved them to the floor. Boots, keys, and mace cans on every officer creaked, clanging and thumping to emphasize their rude behavior.

The captain, a large black man that could have impersonated B.B. King, glared down at Diamond and drawled, "Offender Terrance Davis, I need you to hand over any contraband you have. If we have to look for it, we're gonna tear up everything on this zone." He pointed a threatening finger. "And everyone will blame you."

"I don't have any contraband, you old goat!" Diamond spat, dignified in denial even with his face pressed to the floor.

"Okay then. We'll do this the hard way," the Captain said, squatting down and sliding Diamond's shower shoes off. He stood and took a folding knife from his pocket, cut the foam flip-flops from end-to-end, dropped them on the floor like trash and pointed at his uncooperative prisoner. "I'll find it," he promised, then gestured to the COs. "Strip search him. Tear up everything."

The officers moved to do his bidding, faces grim and set on finding something illegal. When they made Diamond open his mouth so they could inspect it with a flashlight, Ace panicked and swallowed the key, mouth turned down severely.

This just keeps getting better and better, he thought sourly, watching two ham-handed brutes tear his mattress to tatters as he pictured the charming scene of retrieving the key in his gut. *What an adventure that will be.*

Both of them were told to strip naked and bend over, spread their buttocks while squatting and coughing. Ace did so, slowly, reluctantly, embarrassed and degraded like never before. Diamond, angry but not in the least embarrassed to be naked in front of so many men, channeled his disgruntlement into an offensive, bending and squatting like a stripper, coughing with a husky, sultry lisp that trailed off in a string of Ss. He succeeded in embarrassing all eight officers present. Several convicts witnessing the shakedown laughed so hard they had to sit down. One fell down. The captain shook a finger at Diamond, though he was at a loss for words.

They remained naked for over thirty minutes, Ace standing, Diamond forced back to the floor after his charade, as the cubicle was searched methodically, every crack in the bricks and floor probed with a fiber optic camera or stiff pieces of wire that the officers wielded in hopes of discovering a hiding place. The officer searching Ace's locker box picked up the small TV and examined it critically, carefully studying the circuit board through the clear plastic case, face intent on finding contraband he damn well knew was there somewhere. He deemed it legal, set it back in the box, began searching through Ace's clothes.

Ace sighed the breath he was holding, fighting to hold back an eight-hundred pound gorilla smile. A snicker escaped and he tensed again, relaxing when no one turned around to demand what was so humorous.

The officers began searching areas and items that had already been checked twice, glancing at their captain for direction. He waved his hands. "All right. Let's go," he growled. He pointed at Diamond, speaking to the COs. "Pack his shit up. Take him to lockdown."

"I ain't done nothing!" Diamond rebelled, still naked. Ace finished dressing and stepped forward to support his cube partner, but was grabbed by two officers who thought he meant to start trouble.

"You're up to something. And I aim to figure it out," the captain told Diamond. He looked down. "Put some goddamn clothes on." He glanced around, raised his voice. "Pack it up! Let's go." His protruding belly inhibited his planned badass exit from the cubicle, forced to wait on his COs, who sported even larger potbellies, to side-step out of the way, confused, cumbersome. More laughter erupted from the inmates.

Diamond was handcuffed and hauled off, his property rudely piled up on a sheet that was tied and thrown over the shoulder of a burly CO, books, paperwork, and personal items crushed and tearing inside the sack as he walked away. Ace stared after Diamond, wishing he could go with him, gratitude swelling his chest, demanding to be expressed. He's never had anyone sacrifice themselves for him like that. It was a beautiful feeling, a moment of heroism, one he would always remember and treasure.

The prisoners privy to the show determined it was over, returning to their routines. Fans were turned back on. Cards slammed and dice rolled once again. One convict remained standing, however, still staring in Ace's direction. Death Punch smiled, pointed a finger at him and pantomimed shooting a gun. Turned, walked off.

Realization hit Ace as if a bullet had really been fired at him. "That son of a bitch!" he said, fingernails digging painfully into his palms. He relaxed, ran his hands over his hair and immediately got an idea. "I have something for you, malware suckers."

He sat down on his mattress, grabbed the TV, opened it, powered on the iPod and router. Sent a text and waited on Bobby to crank up the Big Black Wrecker. Then he hacked into the MDOC commissioner's email account, sending out transfer orders - as the commissioner - that would get Death Punch and his underlings housed in the worst lockdown unit on the compound. The recipients would never question an order from the commissioner, and would hop like rabbits on meth to make sure the offenders were secured in the dungeon-like conditions their boss mandated.

Ace's thumbs blurred over the touchscreen, citing security concerns for gang activity, and recommended indefinite segregation. It would be months before any complaints from the LKs were seriously looked into. Maybe longer. Maybe never. Ace hoped for the latter.

Stashing his babies back in the TV, he smiled and decided to write a note to Diamond. News of the LK haters in the hole for duration would surely put a much needed smile on his face. *Did wonders for my mood*, he mused.

"Fuck with me..." He typed an imaginary keypad, spun it like a revolver and holstered it, hand landing on top of the TV.

As he lay back on his pillow, he thought of all the things, the nearly endless possibilities, that he could do just sitting there on his bed with an iPod and Mi-Fi router.

In prison, with mad power. I think I just had a cyber-gasm. He shivered, goose bumps tingling his arms, neck.

The smile and grandiose feeling of control was fleeting, however. He remembered the key. "Crap," he muttered. The single word brought a different kind of smile. "Literally."

Chapter XXI

Central Mississippi Correctional Facility
Pearl, Mississippi
April 1, 2012

Chiquita's death wasn't a big surprise. When word of it spread, Clarice had expected excited chatter among the women at the very least. Maybe a little outrage from the religious inmates that would never condone leaving a girl to die behind a random building. Or even some friends of the deceased coming out of the woodwork to seek justice or revenge.

Nothing like that happened. Nada. Zilch. No one cared. Not even CMCF administration. Just another gang banger they wouldn't have to worry about. Clarice was fascinated, though disturbed, by the lack of emoting, by the lack of correctional professionalism.

The image of Chiquita's whirring blade slicing through the air for her neck had haunted Clarice's sleep every night since the previous weekend. Being a stickler for good sleep (*and not getting any, dammit*) she was beginning to resent Chiquita's ghost as much as she resented the live version of the sorry bitch.

Leave me alone! Ugh.

Clarice rolled out of her sweaty, nightmare-soiled sheets, the warm, damp linen icky as it slid over her legs. Slipped on her shower shoes. Padded over to the toilets. Groggy, still half-asleep, she murmured a prayer which she hoped would get the sadistic knife maker off her back. *I mean, geez, girl. I tried to help. Go rattle your chains and blades in Captain Portsmouth's face.*

The toilet smelled awful, and Clarice could have sworn the surface of the seat had something moving on it. Chalking up the hallucination to sleep deprivation, she turned around and dropped her pants, naked white butt hovering over the rim as she held a squat and peed. The other women walking by to use the sinks or other toilets ignored her, and she ignored them, everyone used to the conditions that would embarrass those civilized, privileged folks in the free-world. Clarice washed up and walked back to the cubicle and grabbed Patty's foot, shaking it.

"Amugh," she said, smacking a big hand to her face to wipe up a little drool from the corner of her mouth.

Clarice smiled, seriously considering putting some shaving cream in her hand. "Get up, princess," she sing-songed. "Time to work out."

Patty answered her by breaking wind, groaned and rolled over, pulled the covers over her still-bruised head. Clarice laughed, noting the pile of snack cake wrappers on the floor next to her bunk. Patty had been depressed since losing to the Amazon, eating more and slacking in her hustling and other duties. But Clarice wouldn't let her skimp on the exercise. What kind of friend would she be if she did that?

Clarice punched her in the thigh, twisting a knuckle on the end of the blow, frogging the crap out of her.

"Get up!" Coach Shocker demanded.

"What?!" Patty cried, rolling over to face her, glaring. "I didn't sleep good last night. Leave me alone."

"That's because you ate a bunch of junk before bed. And you know damn well I'm not going to leave you alone. Get up, slut. We have to work out. Tonight you'll get to see the Amazon get her issue."

She opened her eyes wider, the cobalt blue irises brightening at the mention of payback. Her dry mouth clicked, "Oh, yeah." Threw the sheet off her. Stomped into her shoes, stretched arms over her head, yawning, groaning. "Okay. Let's go."

I should write a book on motivating people.

They grabbed their water bottles, towels and punch mitts, headed down the aisle and out on the yard. It was vacant.

Perfect. Clarice didn't feel like entertaining a crowd right now.

Spring was her favorite time of the year. Even behind all these fences she could appreciate the budding life that was evident all around them. The smell of flowers and foliage, up close and distant, of pollen being carried on the wind, mixing in the cool sinking currents before being carried away on the warn rising gusts that wrapped her hair around her face, strands stinging her eyes, which watered slightly from the direct breeze. Crickets clung to the tallest blades of grass in camouflage, darting away like tiny green missiles as the two women rudely interrupted their morning. The ubiquitous sparrows chirped short, sharp sounds, chasing each other across the yard and up onto the roofs of the surrounding buildings, flopping around in sand or puddles of water, whatever was available to improve their chances of attracting a mate. The feeling of life was in the atmosphere, ambient, fluid, enlivening Clarice's spirits, gasoline drizzled over the fire of her chi, so that it felt like the fourth of July in her stomach.

Ill with spring fever. *Hell yeah. Unbelievable that I could have this feeling in prison.*

The wind was strong, and would provide excellent resistance for their running. Patty's frowning mug told Clarice that she had the same thought, though she obviously didn't enjoy her legs burning like Clarice did. Even her walk was grumpy.

As they strolled the fence line for a warm-up, a different kind of pyrotechnics show erupted in the base of her core - anticipation of tomorrow's adventure. Between the weather and the prospect of freedom Clarice's body was stoked to super-human proportions, zinging with enough juice to power Biloxi. She felt light-headed, but in a way that enhanced coordination, eyes able to focus beyond her normal capabilities, seeing the grass and sky in rare detail. Her legs and arms positively hummed with strength, a feeling she usually only get after completing a training camp in preparation for a pro fight. She was peaking, body tuned to optimal physical and mental levels, nerves with hair triggers, ready to fire punches like an Uzi and move her feet like a cat with its tail on fire. Meow! Pow-pow-pow!

It. Felt. Good. Nobody could say otherwise.

She swigged a little water. Threw down her gear and elbowed the blonde giant. "Ready?"

"No," Patty grumbled, though she dropped her things on the grass next to Clarice's and nodded *yes*.

Clarice pretended to fire a starter's pistol and left her in the dust.

Patty, sprinting hard to get behind her, NASCAR draft-style, swatted at her jouncing hair and yelled over the wind, voice pitched like a commercial spokesperson. "Beautiful, bouncy, shiny! Bob Barker's shampoo gives you what you need to start the day off looking like shit!"

Clarice growled at the mention of his name, missing a step. Patty passed her.

That tricky hooker.

* * *

Investigator Collins was short with dark, nearly black hair. Wore aviator sunglasses over a huge nose. Thick mustache that would have contrasted with his skin this time of the year had he not spray-tanned religiously, bronzing his fit body to maintain the playboy image that set him apart from the local rednecks. He stuck one hand in his designer jeans pocket, the other in his black leather jacket. Pulled out a pack of Camels and a lighter. Lit one and eyed the crime scene through the smoke.

The afternoon sun had dried the dew on the grass. Dark, brownish blood flecked the ground and side of the building where the body had been left leaning against the concrete. Collins' eyes moved along the trail of week-old blood, wondering where the body had been dragged from. He doubted the resident CID department had thought to find out, or had thoughts that even remotely resembled detective work, for that matter. They didn't care about dead gang members. And that was precisely why he was here. As a senior investigator from the CID headquarters in Jackson, his boss had tasked him with solving a murder the locals were too uncaring or unskilled to puzzle out. There had been too many unsolved deaths lately, making the entire Correctional Investigation Division look bad. And concerned families and nosy media pests were putting heat on the commissioner.

"Idiots," he muttered.

"What was that, sir?" a CMCF investigator asked politely. He was also short and dark haired, though his appearance was far more generic. Khaki clothes and casual shoes off the racks in K-Mart. Small bulge in his bottom lip full of Skoal snuff. He held a note pad in his hand, the top page scribbled with doodles and meaningless notes, tapping against his leg while pondering why he had to accompany this Jackson prick on such a senseless job. *The nigger bitch is dead. So the fuck what?* He smiled at Collins again.

"Did you people follow this blood trail?" Collins wanted to know.

"What blood trail?" he said, peering at the ground in confusion.

Collins grunted in disgust, pointed at it. "See those brown dots? That's called blood," he said, school teacher to first-grader.

"Oh. No, we must have missed that."

"Uh-huh. Must have." He took a cellphone from his pocket, dialed his boss. Held the Samsung to his ear. "Collins. I found a trail of blood. The body had been dragged to the spot where she was found. Uh-huh. We'll need a dog. Yes, sir. I'll handle it myself." He hung up, looked at the other investigator. "What about the lab results?"

"Lab results?"

Collins shook his head, lit another smoke. This was going to be a long day, he thought in dismay. "For the DNA. The report said Chiquita Dinmore had someone else's blood on her. Surely the person that discovered that sent a sample to the lab."

"Oh, yeah. It should be in today."

"Good. Because that will tell us who the killer is."

The man nodded in understanding, still uncaring. The killer was just another gang banger he felt nothing for. *Bust them with the DNA evidence, give them a life sentence. Set them free. Doesn't matter. They al-*

ways come back to prison or end up dead. Why waste my time on them? He said, "You're right. We get DNA samples from every inmate when they are processed in." He sighed. "I'll call K-nine."

At least you ignoramuses do that, Collins thought, forcing a smile. He turned away before he said something unprofessional. Smoked his cigarette and tapped a $300 leather dress shoe while waiting impatiently for the K-9 unit to show up.

* * *

After lunch Clarice took a nap to recharge. They had gotten a little carried away during their morning workout, all jacked up on whatever it is that gives animals frisky fuel on spring mornings. They had driven their bodies through hours of boxing drills and strength training for the simple reason of just feeling like it. Clarice looked over at Patty. She was snoring.

During her nap Clarice completely lost the cheery spirit. Chiquita had left her alone, thank God, but a new nightmare had taken hold of her snoozing psyche. Nolan, her precious son, appeared to her crying, in danger, his small form curled up on an unknown floor while he bawled his little heart out. He even called out for his 'Mommy', which alerted her it wasn't just a dream. It was an insight. Clarice rarely had presentiments this strong, this maternal. So she listened to them.

Nolan was in imminent danger. Should she call her parents and check on him? If she did that, they would think she'd lost her mind in prison, and she wouldn't be able to help him. And it would probably tear her soul apart at the sound of his voice, sabotaging her focus to fight this evening and escape tomorrow.

She blew out a huge breath and decided on dealing with her son's safety tomorrow, blocking the issue from her mind.

Dragging sweaty sheets off of herself for the second time in a day should have made her disgusted. But she smiled down at the Barker's sweatshop products because she would never have to wash the mofos again. She flipped them the bird as if they were old man Bob himself.

Feeling her mood trying to bounce back as the terrible dream faded and thoughts of freedom once again drugged her, Clarice organized her scheming to determine what needed to be done before Shocker vs. Amazon this evening. She had to make a sewing needle, some running shorts, and a handcuff key.

All her life she had had access to quality tools and materials whenever she needed to fabricate something. Being in prison, she had to make everything, including her own freaking tools. A mere mortal would be at a loss as to where to start, what to use. As an experienced metal fabricator, *Improvisation* and *Innovation* were the names of twins who possessed her hands during times of forced creativity, magically conjuring skills that few humans contained. The twins believed they could construct anything, the arrogant pixies. Up to this point, that claim hadn't been refuted.

Today would be no different. They flexed at her.

The creative half of her brain became an inferno of all those groovy neurotransmitters and hormone releases that inspire and inspire and INSPIRE.

She searched around in her locker box, snagged a thick paperclip, one she had stolen from the case manager's office the previous week. Laughably, she had felt really bad for taking it. It was an opportunity she had to seize, she told herself at the time - also thinking she might get busted from the stupid guilty face she made after palming it off the lady's desk. Clarice wasn't exactly overwhelmed with pride at becoming a petty thief, but she just about managed not to confess or offer to handcuff herself before she left the office, and stashed the booty for the purpose of forging a sewing needle. She also had a sharp screw cached for the same reason, one she had removed from a light fixture with her fingers, shaking her head in disapproval of the poor maintenance and her continued trifling thievery. Because the screw could be considered a 'sharpened instrument' by shakedown officers, she couldn't keep it in her box. She squatted down next to her hiding place, picked the Ivory soap section out of the hole and fished out a small, shiny screw. Tested the point on her finger. *It'll do.*

Yolanda's long hair hung off her bunk as she looked down at her. "What's that?" the nosy creature asked.

Clarice sighed. She didn't feel like dealing with her. At this point, though, she guessed it didn't matter if Yolanda knew this particular secret. So she didn't try to block the view of her stash. Clarice nodded at it. "A hiding spot." Clarice put the Ivory caulking back in place, held up the screw. "And a punch."

"A punch?" Her face scrunched, having never heard of the tool. "That looks like a screw."

"Yeah, well, today it's a punch. I'll show you."

Clarice grabbed the Masterlock off her box, held it like a hammer in her right hand and took up the straightened paperclip in her left. Laid the clip on a smooth area of the concrete floor. Hammered out an end of it, flattening it. The softer metal yielded quickly to the stainless steel lock, smashing into a plane nearly three times its original width. She grabbed the screw and carefully placed the point of it over the center of the flattened area, and gently tapped the head of it with the lock, punching a hole through the end of the paperclip. She now had an eye for the needle.

"Whoa! Cool," Yolanda breathed.

"Mmm-hmm," Clarice answered absently, proceeding to the next step. Grabbing a large manila folder out of her locker box, she poked herself while unbending a staple from the thick paper. Got it out, stuck it through the eye in the paperclip so the hole would remain while Clarice rounded-off the flat metal.

Taking up the lock again, she held the clip to the concrete anvil and delicately tapped the flattened end around the staple as best she could. The metal began to round, smashing the eye closed, so Clarice removed the staple and filed the area on the concrete, grinding it smooth and round. Held it up, squinting with an eye closed. Light twinkled through the miniscule hole she had made.

Perfect. Now for the needle's point.

She measured by eye where she wanted to break the paperclip. Bent it back and forth until it heated and snapped. The creaking metal sounds she made, followed by a loud snap, were absolutely necessary for the process to work. She filed the broken end on the floor until it tapered with a rounded, sharp point. Held it up, tested it on her finger. It was two-inches long and could have come off the shelf in the sewing aisle.

I am the Goddess of Steel. Hear me ROAR…

"How…How'd you do that?" Yolanda asked. Her hair disappeared from Clarice's peripheral, replaced by legs that hung down and thumped on the floor. She knelt down next to Clarice, who had to lean away from her bad breath.

Clarice didn't have time for her, so she quickly recapped the process, a lesson Yolanda struggled to remember and would have pestered her about later.

Hee-hee. Would have.

Clarice grinned at her. *I'm leaving tomorrow!* she felt like screaming.

Yolanda smiled back until Clarice blithely shoved her out of her way and grabbed the jacket that hung off the end of her bed. It was dark blue with MDOC CONVICT heat-stamped on the back in white letters. About four sizes too big, which made the sleeves big enough for her legs. It wasn't the jacket

CMCF issued to her. That one, which looked the same, though was much smaller, was folded up under her pillow. This ginormous thing had been given to her by Juanita and Yvonne, the Latin Queen and Vice Lord Flower leaders who had refused to take her hints (and blatant, detailed notices) of not wanting their help. Apparently, they had heard Clarice was looking for some specific material for a sewing project and had assumed, correctly, what it was for. Frustrated, though unable to complain, she had accepted the oversized jacket and managed a gracious "Thank you" without gritting her teeth. The thin nylon would make do for her purposes. It wasn't as if she had time to shop around.

Clarice bit her lip, staring at the jacket in thought. She needed to remove the cushion from the inner sleeves, cut them to size for shorts, and measure and cut a section from the back of the jacket to make up the crotch and butt of the shorts. Then sew it all together.

Easy cheesy.

With no scissors or X-Acto knife around, Improvisation and Innovation decided a razor would do the trick. Clarice grabbed one from her locker box, popping the head apart with her teeth, ignoring the giggling dummy next to her who was endlessly amused by her un-ladylike etiquette. She removed a single blade carefully. Set it aside on the floor. Now she needed a template, a pair of shorts in her size to take measurements from.

She grabbed a pair of boxer shorts. Laid them on the floor in front of her. Took up the razor, piled the jacket in her lap, and quickly dismantled the thing at the seams, slicing the stitches to remove the cotton and polyester lining the sleeves, separating it from the outer blue material she would use. Proceeded to the back of the jacket, cutting around the heat-stamped letters to salvage a large, odd rectangle of material. Dropped that, picked up the sleeves, placing them over the boxers to determine where they'd go as legs. Cut them to size. Did the same for the other blue material, shaping sections for the front and back of the shorts, roughly, ending up with a diaperish design. A freaking smurf diaper.

Chuckling at the image of wearing this without the legs attached, her thoughts eventually jumped to a solution for holding them up on her hips. She eyed the elastic band on the boxers. It would do just fine to keep her pale cheeks from flashing motorists as she ran for her life in downtown Biloxi. She cut the waistband off the Barker boxers. Set it aside.

Lacking pins to hold the project together while she sewed, she decided just to use a quick stitch here and there. Taking up the remains of the jacket, her little fingers went about the challenge of removing enough individual threads to construct the shorts, pulling out segments two and three feet in length. Laid them over her legs, which were now folded under her, ankles aching slightly from the unforgiving concrete. She threaded her needle. Knocked out the place-stitching so that her smurf diaper had legs and a waistband attached. Began sewing.

It took nearly four hours, tedious work that made her hands burn with fatigue and her armpits sweat from concentrating on work she had very little experience with. But the result was well worth it. Not only did she accomplish producing an article that would contribute to her freedom, she also succeeded in boosting her self-esteem. She constructed the project successfully. That monstrous beast, Pride, hauled off and bitch slapped her.

Ah... Yeah.

She held up the shorts. The white boxer waistband sewn to the top looked like shit, but would be covered by her t-shirt in any case, concealed from the public. Clarice dropped her black and white stripes, balancing on one foot to kick them off. The accumulated heat of hours of sitting and working escaped, the cooler air exciting goose bumps up and down her legs. She frowned at some idiot that walked by and stared at her in her panties. Stepped into her new duds. Ran her thumbs around the waist. They were loose, not too baggy, with legs ending just above her knees. They fitted great.

Thank you seventh-grade home economics!

"You made workout shorts?" Yolanda asked.

"Yep. Exactly," Clarice answered her, grinning and posing. "It's going to be one hella-crazy workout, too."

"They look nice," Patty said from her bed. She gave her a sleepy wink. Sat up and looked around. "What time is it?"

"Almost six. We have to be at the spot in an hour," Clarice said, changing back into her pants.

"You fighting the girl that beat Patty?" Yolanda asked. Patty scowled at her furiously.

Clarice nodded. "Yeah."

"You don't look very worried," Yolanda observed.

Clarice looked into her eyes. "I'm not worried. I'll beat her."

She twisted her lips, eyebrows raised. Patty smiled. Clarice grabbed the jacket from under her pillow, looked at Patty while inclining her head toward Yolanda.

Patty took the cue. "Yo, Ms. Douche Ecuador. Put this muscle cream on my back. I'm so goddamn sore I can't even wipe my own ass."

"I'll do the cream, but not your ass," Yolanda said.

Patty turned so that Yolanda couldn't see what Clarice was doing, the cubicle filling with the horrible scent of Icy Hot as it was smeared all over Patty's back. Her skin, normally creamy white, looked yellow and light green in places where huge bruises were still healing, remnants of dark, angry purple and black wounds from the merciless battle a week ago. Patty grunted, sucked in a breath, winked at her as Yolanda cooed an apology.

Shaking her head, Clarice turned her attention back to the jacket. Made a small incision on the inside, slicing through the insulation in the back.

Folded up her newly made shorts and slid them inside the hole, unfolding them on the inside, flattening the material out so that the shorts couldn't be felt by any officers that came to search her before transporting her to court in the morning. Put a couple of stitches in the slit to close it. Refolded the jacket, placed it back under her pillow. Cleaned up her mess.

With escape clothes checked off her list, Clarice went back to her hiding place for what she hoped would make a handcuff key. The remains of the Bic lighter she had parted out to build the tattoo machine still had one useful part on it. Thank God she had noticed and didn't throw it away! Digging it out of the hidey-hole, she eyed the top of the lighter where the striker wheel, flint, and jet had been mounted, thinking the hole that housed the flint was the same diameter as the hole on a cuff key. As a mechanic, she had to be able to look at nuts, bolts, washers, et cetera, and know the measurements by sight. Years of experience enabled her to look at almost anything and know its dimensions. She was sure this would work.

Placing the head of the lighter on the edge of her steel bunk bed, she bumped her fist on it until it broke, a section of hard green plastic roughly three-fourths-of-an-inch square falling into her hand. She took up the razor blade. Carefully, methodically, she sculpted the excess plastic from around the flint hole, a hollow shaft in the center nearly a half-inch deep. The razor dulled, so she trashed it, grabbed another one. Continued the job, shaping a small square tab on the end so that she ended up with a tubular shaped deal with a tooth, just like a handcuff key.

Patty put Yolanda to work, continuing her ruse of being too beat up to function, conning their cubie into folding clothes and cleaning her bunk and locker box, effectively distracting the girl while Clarice handled her illegal business. Clarice didn't feel bad about the duplicity. Yolanda had seen her stash spot and shorts, but those were easily explained. A handcuff key in her possession wasn't something she could trust Yolanda knowing. Couldn't afford to risk her blabbing about it to anyone, even accidentally. So she remained out of the loop by necessity, thanks to the Viking Princess' skill in deception.

Not that Clarice actually needed to thank Patty for tricking Yolanda; the pleasure on her face was clearly all the thanks she needed.

Clarice left a small L-shaped head on the key for turning leverage. Trashed the razor and lighter scraps. Held up her handiwork. Pride gripped her in a bear hug, squeezing so hard she felt dizzy. The brute was on a roll today. She should quit enticing him before the bastard hurt her.

The tiny plastic key was small enough to keep on her and stick in her mouth should a shakedown terrorist team pop up. So she dropped it in her pocket, mentally checking it off her list. She was ready for tomorrow. Well, except for the money. She did the sums in her head. *I've about $500 from the two fights and tattoos. If - no, when – I knock out the Amazon, I'll* *have another $150. If I bet all $500 on myself, I'll total $1,150. That should do just fine.*

She thought of the possibility that things might go completely wrong so she couldn't meet Ace at the car, and might have to split up and run away by herself. A grand in cash would keep her from having to steal food or transportation, and from having to ask strangers for help. Her face would be all over TV. Not a good idea to show it to everyone, begging for help.

A debate between her friends brought her scheming to a temporary halt.

"I'm not rubbing your feet," Yolanda stated flatly, hand on an anorexic hip, looking at Patty's huge feet with revulsion.

Patty wiggled her toes. "But I can't reach them!" she whined, attempting to lean forward, groaning in pain, falling back on her pillow.

Clarice couldn't help it. She burst into laughter. They looked at her, Yolanda frowning, not comprehending the humor, Patty smiling so wide that the scabs on her mouth were in danger of tearing open. Yolanda turned back to the stunt master and Patty's delight flickered out of existence.

"Let's go. We're going to be late," Clarice said.

"All right," Patty said, jumping lightly to her feet. She put on socks and shoes without a single grimace or twitch of sore muscles, while Yolanda glared in outrage, mouth opened, closed, open, fists clenched in front of her. She growled loudly, stomped around in a circle.

Clarice laughed again.

"That's fucked up!" she sputtered.

Patty ignored her, looked at her. "Bring your phone," she said.

"For what?" Clarice asked.

"I want to get a vid of you beating that bitch to sleep. I loaned mine to an officer yesterday." Clarice looked at her questioningly and she shrugged. "They're shooting CO-inmate porn in A-building. They needed my phone's memory. Promised I'd be the first to see it."

"Ah. Um...Okay. You can use mine." Swiftly, Clarice went into the stash, grabbed the phone and handed it to her.

"Ready?" she asked her.

Clarice raised a fist. "I'm gonna Shocker."

Yolanda bitched about being ignored, but they ignored her, turned out of the cubicle and walked with purpose down the aisle, leaving a thoroughly slighted, stomping and fuming Yolanda behind.

"Why'd you do her like that?" Clarice asked, smiling and trying, unsuccessfully, to feel bad. "You could have handled that differently."

"That was a lot more fun. I like the girl, but she's a douche."

Couldn't argue with that.

They exited the building with their usual excuse, claiming to be on Captain Portsmouth's paint crew. A bright orange and crimson sunset painted the entire sky in spectacular fashion. The sidewalks were poop-free for once, and Clarice enjoyed the fresh air as it rapidly cooled, their shoes whispering over the rough surface of the concrete, resounding in the quiet, unusually deserted prison courtyard.

Before they reached their destination, two women appeared on the walkway, hurrying toward them. Patty and Clarice stopped, unsure who these women were or what they wanted. Patty reached down her pants. Clarice placed her right foot slightly behind her. The potential enemies clarified, becoming non-threats as they came closer: Yvonne and Juanita stopping in front of them.

"You're in serious trouble," Juanita told her without preamble.

"Huh?" Clarice replied, not exactly showing off her witty prowess.

Yvonne unstuck her puckered mouth. "They got blood off Chiquita," she said gravely. "You's the only other one bleeding there."

Oh crap.

Juanita stepped closer. "It's only a matter of time before they match it to the sample they took from you when you got here. We can't help you regarding that."

Ohcrapohcrapohcrap... "Then why tell me?"

"So you can adjust your plans, honey," Yvonne answered. "We is obligated to assist you however we can. This is all we can do." She nodded and walked between Patty and her. She didn't look back.

Juanita moved to follow her. "Suerte," she told her.

"Holy shit," Patty exclaimed.

"Yeah. Exactly," Clarice muttered, Googling her thoughts for solutions. Her cerebral search engine blinked *NO RESULTS FOUND, dammit,* so Clarice decided to keep moving forward, go with her plan until someone came to arrest her for murder. Even if they busted her tonight, Clarice reasoned, that wouldn't stop her from going to court in the morning.

"Doesn't matter," Clarice told Patty as much as herself.

"I hope you're right."

"Me too."

The interior of the building enveloped them with a warm, musty smell rather than marijuana this time. Patty cursed disappointment, but Clarice didn't mind. It vaguely reminded her of boxing gyms she had trained in, ones she thought were disgusting at the time but now dearly missed. She inhaled, a smile tugging her lips. Patty glanced at her in confusion.

A crowd of women could be heard in the distance, loud bantering, laughter and friendly curses that bounced off the ugly brick walls and paint splattered floor. Captain Portsmouth was the loudest, the first person that noticed their entrance. "You hoes is late," she said in her ever-charming manner, her mouth working a particularly large plug of chewing tobacco. She spat, waved for them to follow. "We gotta make this money. Hustle, Cream Tail! You up."

We trailed the idiot to the shower. A rap song filtered through the women's voices, one Clarice liked but couldn't recall who sang it. *"...I got five passports/I ain't never going to jail"* was her favorite part. A joint was lit somewhere, the scent alerting Patty, who stood up on her tippy toes, head scanning the crowd for the source of her Scooby Snack. Her nostrils actually flared, sniffing in different directions.

Clarice elbowed her. "Not yet. Wrap my hands first," she said.

"Oh. Right," Patty sulked, taking the rolled up strips of sheet Clarice handed her. She finished the job quickly and left to get the herbal monkey off her back, knowing Clarice preferred to be alone to get psyched, anyway.

The feel of tightly wrapped hands empowered her. Her body understood what it meant and responded accordingly. Her heart accelerated, muscles priming, vascular, simmering hotly from the abrupt influx of adrenaline. Her chin tucked. Her calves began pumping her feet off the floor. Shoulders rolled and fists flowed as she did her punching dance. Shadowboxing was so instinctual it was part of her autonomic nervous system, integrated from the factory, kicking in so naturally she questioned whether she was homo sapiens or homo buxis. Not human, but boxerman. A new species.

I was born this way.

Portsmouth cleared the center of the tiled floor, shooing the gang members to their designated walls around the showers. Looked at her watch. Pulled on her ski mask and turned to her Gangsta Queen camerawoman. "And, action!" she barked at the girl. "Welcome to Bitch Fight. Tonight you lucky folks are in for a special treat. We have two ruthless warriors..."

Clarice blocked out the annoying voice and focused on her opponent across the room. The Amazon stood barefoot among her Sisters, rolling her neck and shaking her arms. She glared at her, eyes deep, dark. Her chocolate colored skin looked darker than it did last week, a sign of working outdoors. She had been running. A lot, apparently, to get that shade for this early in the year. She knew extra stamina training was needed if she hoped to last long enough to beat Clarice. She had a fresh line on her men's haircut, skin shining from a combination of cocoa butter lotion and warm-up sweat. The broad looked dangerous. Certainly the biggest, strongest opponent Clarice had ever faced.

Clarice wondered how the Amazon perceived her.

"You shouldn't be fighting," a silky, estrogen-loaded voice said next to her.

Clarice turned to see Helen's breath-stealing smile and all the aggression she was trying to channel was zapped away.

Mother. Fucker.

"Hi," Clarice sighed.

"You are going to tear open your wounds again."

"That's great. I've always wanted to try the Bride of Chucky scar look," Clarice said, then shook her head. Said quietly, "I don't have a choice."

"On the contrary, my dear Clarice. You always have a choice. Simply ask yourself, *'Is this something that I need to do, or is it something I want to do?'*" she said, quirking a perfect eyebrow.

Clarice frowned. She had a point. It was a clichéd, duh point, but still an angle that for whatever reason Clarice hadn't been aware of.

Have I lost my fricken common sense, people?

Was she deluding herself, using the escape plan as a reason to say this was necessary? Was she fooling herself because she wanted to fight, to be involved in combat for the challenge, to satiate that pesky pugilistic junkie bitch that was her alter-ego? She could have done other things to make money. Why was she fighting for pocket change?

Helen's eyes *(light blue beautiful things, oh!)* penetrated hers, and smiled as if she had discovered some deep, morbid secret Clarice hadn't even realized she was keeping. Clarice shook her head, snapping out of her hypnosis. *What a terrible time for all this.*

"Who the hell are you?" Clarice said.

"I am just a person," Helen responded simply, managing a philosophical nuance.

"Well, I'm just a fighter. One that needs to win some money. I don't have time to psychoanalyze right now."

"You make your own luck." Helen reached into her pillowcase medical kit, removing a large roll of duct tape. "This will prevent the wounds from opening. Not exactly sterile, or even medical, for that matter. But there you go."

"I love you," Clarice said, rolling up her right sleeve. Helen laughed, a musical, lilting sound, like harp strings strummed with feather lightness, tender, sweet. *Makes my laugh sound like a gobbling turkey,*

Clarice thought. Helen cleaned her shoulder with an alcohol pad, drying the sweat. Unrolled a four-inch length of the thick gray tape. Pressed it firmly over the wound. Did the same for the cut on her side. Clarice thanked her.

"That isn't necessary. You owe me five dollars," she replied, holding out her hand, smiling her deliciously plump lips.

Clarice laughed. "You are good." She took out a wad of money from her pocket. "No offense, Helen. But you have to go away. You are very distracting."

"No offense taken."

"Would you mind placing a bet for me?"

"Sure."

"You going to charge me for it?"

She thought it over. "No. I'll wait until after the fight and charge you for nursing your fresh wounds." She gave a small smile, wiggling her fingers for the money.

Clarice laughed again. "Deal." Handed her $505. She disappeared and Clarice zeroed in on her job once more.

A casual glance at the yuckmouth captain would have been enough to put her back into a fighting state of mind. Having to look at that retard and hear herself being introduced as Devil Hands Sally?

Livid in 0.1 seconds.

"In the red corner, she packs dynamite in both hands." Portsmouth held her index fingers up on either side of her forehead like horns. "Devil hands.

She's fast with a fire in her ass! I give you: Devil. Hands. Sal-lyyy!"

Patty gave a big, loud, stoned giggle behind her somewhere. A polite clap from Helen. Clarice glared at the masked emcee. She hated that broad.

Portsmouth whipped a Coke bottle from her back pocket. Chewed. Spat in it. Pocketed it again. Turned toward the Amazon, waved a hand graciously. "And fighting out of the blue corner. The chocolate beast that has no cease! She quits when her opponent shits! Hoes and niggas, put your hands together for the Mocha. Blas-terrr!"

The tiled walls ricocheted claps and whistles from the nearly two dozen Gangsta Queens present. The Amazon was enjoying herself, soaking up the attention, taking small bows, raising her hands over her head and gesturing for more applause. Clarice concentrated on her torso, oblivious to the noise. Her abs were solid and not likely to give way to even her best shots. She'd have to catch her inhaling, when her abdomen relaxed, and time her punches to land at precisely that moment to freeze her diaphragm, preferably in the lower stomach between her belly button and hoo-hah. An illegal blow in pro fights, one she wouldn't have contemplated before now. However, in her present situation, in this prison shower facing a monster thug warrior, such strategic moves were fair game. Mandatory.

Looking at the Amazon's enormous head, Clarice recalled Patty's thunderous blows that just bounced off of it with little consequence, and decided the feeling of her much smaller fists on her cranium wouldn't be very pleasant. Fortunately, for the first time in her life, she was in a cheating mood, willing to fight in disregard to the boxing rules that normally governed her in this setting. Thoughts flashed back to bouts by the pioneers of women's boxing, Old School masters like Sue 'Tiger Lily' Fox, who knew all kinds of sneaky moves to beat far larger women, knew that ring generalship constituted all war tactics, and didn't mind stretching rules to do whatever it took to win.

Head butts were a foul notorious for sapping a boxer's energy. Clarice had seen many fights end badly because of them - always bad for the person on the receiving end. But that particular tactic wasn't for her, Clarice mused, rubbing her forehead, thinking through a list of boxing's dark art moves. Clarice once saw Christy Martin, 'The Coal Miner's Daughter', snap a quick uppercut into her opponent's extended arm, right in the elbow. It obviously hurt because the opponent wasn't throwing many punches after that, only eating them.

She looked down at the Amazon's knees. Another great target for that tactic. Clarice could easily drop down and stick a hook to the side of her patella. Hey, no one claimed any below-the-belt rules here. Or below-the-thigh.

Fair game. Hee-hee.

Portsmouth waved them to the center. Said something profoundly stupid that was supposed to threaten them into performing at their best. She yelled, "Fight!" and got the hell out of the way.

Her old pals Seek and Destroy knew their business well. Seek shot out like a bolt of lightning, jabbing the Amazon in her mouth before she could even raise her hands, which came up belatedly, in surprise, leaving an opening for her straight-right.

Body moving forward after the jab, Clarice thrusted explosively off her back foot, throwing Destroy into the Amazon's stomach, sinking a solid blow into her waistband, exhaling, tightening fist and shoulder as it hit. Pivoted to the left, ducking her responding, wild swings. The Amazon backed up, startled and confused by Clarice's speed, grunting angrily because she got hit and couldn't hit back. Raised her fists together below her chin and slapped a bare foot forward on the tiles, swinging for Clarice's head, a looping punch Clarice weaved under and countered, tagging another right-hand to the Amazon's body. Pivoted to the left again, circling behind her.

In four seconds, Clarice had landed three punches to the Amazon's zero. They were ineffective other than rousing the onlookers. The GQs roared at her wrathfully, dissonant anger in stark contrast to the women on the other side. The Flowers cheered her on, swinging arms to imitate the calculated punches Clarice had nailed their enemy with. The small enclosure made it seem like the cheers and jeers were from a much larger crowd. There was nothing like an enthusiastic fight audience to motivate Clarice with gladiatorial zeal.

The frustrated Amazon lunged at her with two straight, fairly quick punches. Clarice blocked one with her left hand, slapping it aside, the blow stinging her palm. Slipped her head to the right to avoid the next one, aware of the limited space behind her while dialing in her range in front. Clarice couldn't back up any further, and had to prevent the Amazon from pushing her into the wall of her Sisters. The Amazon's leg moved to step and Clarice instantly threw a fast one-two at her head, not caring whether it hit, making her pause to block. The Amazon's hands came up, but Clarice weaved out over her front foot, loading up a left hook, thrust up from the toes while torquing her shoulders and converting all that leverage and energy into fuel for the hook. Her left fist hit the side of the Amazon's knee with a loud smack. The woman screamed in outrage, stumbled to her left, trying to regain balance. Clarice jumped all over her, lambasting several combinations to her head and body, driving her backwards so that she never got her footing. The Amazon's hands waved erratically, unable to catch or block most of Clarice's shots. Her lip and eye caught the worst of it, splitting, bleeding, raging hot breath all over her face as Clarice weaved under her arms on the inside, tagging her ribs with thudding, hollow sounds. The woman hit the floor.

The Amazon was a brick wall. Strong and hard. Clarice's hands hurt already, and she hadn't done any real damage yet, just managed to anger the Amazon. Clarice backed up to recover her breathing, having the presence of mind to know how hard she had been throwing her shots to compensate for her size. At once, the Amazon got up. Limped forward, shook out her leg. Clarice felt something wrap around her shoe and pull her backwards. She looked down to see the hand of a Gangsta Queen jerk her foot from under her. She fell forward, hands hitting hard to catch herself. Looked up in a panic and a very manly foot blurred into her face.

Whack!

Dizziness swamped her. Black dots and swirls of red invaded her vision. Hands gave away, elbows thumping to the ground like a drunk kicked out of a bar. The cursed hand let go of her foot with a 'cracker-ass ho' thrown in for good measure. Instinct saved Clarice's head from a future MRI scan, taking control of her arms to roll her out of the way of the Amazon's lunging heel strike. Her heavy leg rammed hard into the concrete inches from her head, a blow that would have fractured her skull had it hit.

Clarice's mind, full of those lovely fight-or-flight chemicals that allowed her to perceive in slow-motion, noticed with an odd detachment a puddle of blood with a tooth gleaming whitely at its red center. Right next to her heel.

A tooth. An incisor to be exact.

Her tongue flickered to a hole in her mouth, warm, salty blood flowing from the gap in her upper gum.

That stinking bitch knocked her tooth out! Her front tooth! Oh, hell no...

Rage and violence are two sides of the same coin. One can turn the other if the critical mass is reached, perpetuating a cycle that can be hard to stop. You get mad, you hit something. You hit something, you get madder. Emotion linked to action, action linked to emotion. Losing a tooth would definitely get the cycle going.

Clarice jumped to her feet with ire boiling in her irises. Ducked a punch, hit the Amazon in her nose.

Got madder.

Span around and pelted the GQ that had tripped her with a four-piece combo, punctuating it with a devastating hook to her fragile chin, knocking her out cold.

Stupid, interfering tramp. Clarice rolled her shoulders.

Got madder.

Pivoted one-hundred-and-eighty degrees, crouched, sprang at her nemesis with ferocious killer instinct, tapping into a source of energy that could only have come from Hell. Demonic fire trailed her double right-hand, exploding sickeningly as it hit the woman's face, splitting her cheek. Feigned a left, reset her shoulders and nailed her in the chin with an overhand right, elbow coming off her rolling hip, a 100mph fast ball bomb that hit and flung her into the wall of Vice Lord Flowers.

Clarice got madder.

She bounded off the women, crying out shrilly as she swung back in desperation. Her intense focus, compounded by the raging blood lust, saw the Amazon's punches as slow, cumbersome things that she easily slipped and countered, loading up a fast, chopping uppercut that she threw from the shoulder, connecting on the Amazon's extended arm at the elbow, fist tightening and going through her arm. A loud pop followed. The Amazon shrieked.

Clarice got MADDER.

The Amazon's right arm was useless; she flailed at Clarice with the left, throwing front-snap kicks at her midsection with her good leg. Clarice pivoted, easily knocking aside the Taekwondo moves with her forearms, eyeing the woman's grunts, which were huge and loud, making the Amazon's breathing very visible. When she inhaled again Clarice was already ripping into her ribs, left hook plunging into her slack core directly over the liver, right-hand following a split-second later, sinking into the soft area above the pubis. Her diaphragm failed. Her eyes popped. She blacked out, dropping to the floor, injured knee and elbow knocking against the concrete with gruesome effect, surely making the injuries worse. Clarice spun in a circle looking for something else to hit.

Clarice got MADDER.

The Gangsta Queen whom Clarice had knocked out about eight seconds ago was still sprawled on the floor, her friends standing over her, fuming, trying to wake her, pumping themselves up to jump on Clarice for transgressing against their Sister. After the Amazon hit the floor with finality, the avenging tribe yelled curses and battle cries, rushing Clarice, with their slim girlie arms, unaccustomed to fighting, windmilling in the air all around her. Clarice ducked, blocked, pivoted, charged into the weak sluts with hard accurate punches that made them cry out after the cracking impacts, dropping two of them. A blonde Viking warrior appeared in her peripheral, huge arm cocked behind her coming forward to slug one of the women next to her, battering her to the floor.

Chaos ensued.

Clarice barely felt the fists that connected with her face, back, legs, boobs. She moved among the contenders with a murderous glee, power coursing through her and into them in the form of pounding, exploding fist grenades, busting eyes, noses, lips, ribs, swinging into the melee with everything she had. She fought for her husband and son. For her freedom. For her family's future. She couldn't be stopped. Tears ran down her face, mixing with hot, splattered blood, the red essence of war coating her arms and staining her shirt, the sight, the color and smell, further igniting the killer instinct that utterly controlled her.

Barking dogs and loud men's voices sounded from the front of the building, noises that should have set off alarm bells in her head. Portsmouth darted away, snatching the camera from her assistant. A fist smacked into her cheek, and Clarice turned to see an officer, a huge woman in a blue ERT uniform, draw her fist back for another shot at her. Clarice pivoted to direct her fury at the new enemy, but was tackled and thrown to the ground by two men. Her head cracked against the cement.

Ow.

A sound like several fire extinguishers discharged at once filled the shower. A thick, orange cloud of pepper spray covered everything, everyone, choking and blinding inmates and officers indiscriminately. Dogs barked and growled. Officers threatened everyone to get the fuck down, now, swatting prisoners here and there with sticks, stomping a few with Hi-Tech boots.

Everyone got down.

The two brutes holding her canceled out any link that remained between her madness and her fists. The bump on the head certainly took some of the fight out of her, as well. The fight junkie got back in her cage, and Clarice went limp as the combat lust faded, leaving her more exhausted than she had ever been in her life.

A voice used to authority pierced the throng. "Where is she?"

"Over here, Mr. Collins," the woman who had hit her said.

Clarice's eyes were closed tightly, painfully, from the thick chemical. She struggled to open one. Focused on a leather dress shoe that stood next to her face.

"Offender Clarice Carter. You are under arrest for the murder of Chiquita Dinmore."

Clarice gasped a response that sounded like "Ackah," and shut her eye. She realized she had just lost all of her money and her phone, as well as being caught on a murder charge. She sighed.

Is her life one continuous party, or what?

Part III

Chapter XXII

Biloxi, Mississippi
April 2, 2012

Clarice was a criminal. By this stage, no other term could possibly describe her.

Two years and twelve days ago, she had been a law abiding family woman with businesses and employees and a mountain of responsibilities, none of which was felonious, or even a misdemeanor. Since then, however, she had assaulted officers, fought in an illegal fight ring to win illegal gambling money, performed unlicensed tattoos, committed larceny against her prison case manager (a lady Clarice actually liked). Then she was arrested for murder. She was really only an accessory, but she didn't see herself giving up her friend Patty in exchange for a lighter punishment; she saw herself getting a life sentence. And now, for the grand finale, she was about to engage in felony escape.

What in God's name happened to me? For crying out loud, people. The worst part is, it's not over. There's no telling how many more laws I'll break before it's all said and done.

Clarice sighed, shook her head. She hated thinking about the unknown.

When the transport van entered Harrison County, she took the shorts out of her jacket. The courthouse in Biloxi was only about fifteen minutes away, maybe less than that. The guy driving held such things as speed limits in low regard. Clarice looked up at the two officers in the front: two older black dudes working their eight hours so at the end of the day they had a bucket of chicken and a six-pack to put on the table. The passenger was sleeping. The driver, wired to the gills on Red Bull, hummed along to an R&B slow jam. Clarice liked the too-slow, too smooth music for one reason: it would provide cover for the noise she was about to make removing her chains.

Hum that song, baby.

The steel grate separating the front seats from the passenger seats cast a grid of shadows over the vinyl benches, her face and arms. The sun looked so different this close to the Gulf. So much better. Clarice had missed it. This would be the last sunrise she would see from behind a steel cage. Her oath on it.

Her tongue darted around her cheek in search of the hard plastic key, momentarily aborting the mission for a swipe at the gap in her grill. All night she had been tonguing the damned hole where her tooth had been. Her face hurt from the five-hundred smiles she had tried in front of the steel mirror, hoping to find an angle that wouldn't make her look so, so...*Hag*. Her eyes were still red from hours of pouting, dry-crying herself to a sleep that came and went in three seconds.

Losing her front tooth really bothered her.

Clarice inhaled slowly, deeply, to quell the rage and misery that threatened to bubble up again. Got the key. Spat it in her lap. Glanced at the officers, who were clueless as to the ruckus she was about to kick off.

Let's do this.

The cuffs linking her hands to the waist chain came off easily. She stuck her thumbs inside the chain. It had just enough slack to slide over her hips. She lay down on the seat. Slipped the chain off, carefully holding the cuffs so they wouldn't clank against the chain. Pulled it over her shoes, and, oh-so-gently, set the restraints on the seat. Leaned down and unlocked her shackles. Again, the key worked perfectly, effortlessly opening the leg manacles. Clarice set them on the seat as well, the links tinkling faintly.

"What are you doing back there?" the driver asked. Clarice froze, heart lurching in her chest. She held her breath.

Should she play asleep? No. Talk to the guy. She wasn't doing a damn thing. She'd swear it.

"Just lying down. My back hurts," she said.

"I'll bet. You look like you've had a rough time of it."

"You have no idea," she muttered.

"You hungry? I'm stopping at McDonald's after your hearing."

"No, thank you. I had the continental breakfast before we left the hotel."

"Ha! Good one."

He began his caffeinated humming again and her sphincter unclenched, releasing the fear that had gripped her.

Wouldn't it just suck if I got busted before I even had a chance to run? Whew.

Clarice had been locked down after the fight ring was busted and they arrested her for murder. She was in a yellow uniform for the fifth or sixth time. She couldn't remember. Didn't care. She slipped off the pants, slowly, pulled on the shorts and put the pants back on over them. Dug around in her crotch to find where the ends of tape holding the cellphone stuck to her skin. Pulled it loose, wincing at the hair that came off with it. Not from the pain; from the length of the hair. There was a wildebeest in her drawers.

Gross.

Patty's advice to hide it there was spot-on. Odds were, an officer patting a woman down wouldn't get too close to the hoo-hah, having an aversion to sticking their hands in such an intimate area. Clear tape was wrapped around the phone. Clarice peeled two sections loose, leaning over to break it with her tooth. Cursed as air sucked in through her gap. *Ugh.* It felt like an icicle driving into the hole.

Stupid Taekwondo kick.

With the tape dangling from her fingers, Clarice picked up an end of the shackles and taped it to her ankle, wrapping the tape around her sock. Did the other side the same way. Pulled her pants legs down over the rigged deals. When she climbed out of the van the officer – if he even looked - would see the chain stretched between her legs and assume the shackles were secure. The jacket, zipped up, would hide where the waist chain should be, and Clarice would simply stick her hands in her jacket pockets to hide where the cuffs should be. All she had to do was get out, reach down and snatch the taped chain off, and run like a bank robber.

A shiver passed through her. That thought was too close to home. One of these officers could start shooting at her as if she really were pulling a bank heist. She had read somewhere that they couldn't shoot at escaping prisoners anymore, unless they were attacking the officer. But Clarice doubted these guys wanted to lose their jobs over her. They could make up whatever story they wanted. With her history of tussling with COs, who wouldn't believe them?

What a fun thought. Fun, fun, fun.

The van exited off Interstate 10, tires humming louder as they slowed and turned, fading, the pitch becoming higher as they gained speed again, a background rhythm buzzing along to the R&B. Seeing the beach and water again was painful, unexpectedly so. Fortunately, the view was limited to only seconds before they turned and headed into downtown Biloxi. The streets all looked the same, seemingly unchanged since the last time Clarice cruised them. As nostalgia was not on her To-Do list, she couldn't enjoy the sights of her home town. They were minutes away from action. And she was ready. As ready as a scared to death girl can be, anyway.

She looked down at the phone in her lap, a small, sad smile forming at the memory of Patty giving it to her this morning.

"You need it more than I do," Patty said, her voice distorted through the vent, locked in the neighboring cell.

"Then why do you sound so reluctant to give it to me?" Clarice asked.

"Because. I just remembered how many blow jobs that thing cost me." She sounded positively woeful. "I still owe a few."

Clarice shook her head, smiling. "You are a good friend. I'll pay you back when I get settled."

"If you get away."

"I will."

"I've heard that before."

"Not from me."

"True." She yawned. "It's like three A.M. I'm about to pass out. You take care, Shock."

"You, too. I love you, Patty." Her voice broke. Goodbyes are the pits.

"Now, now. Don't get all mushy and shit. Go handle your business. Take care of your family and forget all about this dookie hole."

"I will. But I won't forget you."

436

She sniffled, whispered, "I won't forget you either, Shock. Good luck."

Clarice promised herself that wouldn't be the last time she spoke to Patty.

Taped to the phone was $300. Clarice had no idea how her friend had acquired another phone, cash, and tape, and she didn't want to know what she did to get it so quickly. That's what she told herself, anyway. After they were interrogated by CID and locked down, two male officers, and one female, had shown up at *chez* Patty for one hell of a party. Her ears were a little raw from cramming them full of toilet paper to block the noise. Noises. Weird ones.

Remember that when you discover video files on the phone. Do not watch them...

CID investigator Collins was a real piece of garbage. Apparently, because he was slightly smarter and better looking than the locals, he thought that entitled him to an Asshole license. He had arrogantly swaggered around the table Clarice sat behind, using words three-feet long in an attempt to impress her, get her to bow to his superior will and confess. It didn't work. His long line of smooth crap was not in the least convincing. Clarice was so exhausted from the fight that she had nodded off, bored stupid by his questioning. He had got frustrated, stormed out with a pack of smokes in his clenched hand. Clarice had taken a peek at the notes he left on the table. Next to her name was written: "Cold. Street wise. Without remorse."

Whoa. Never in a million years would Clarice have imagined seeing those words applied to her. It would have stung if she weren't so numb and tired.

Anyway, he gave up. Said he'd see her in court and had officers escort her to lockdown. *The weak quitter.* One of the ERT officers had offered to persuade Clarice into confession, but changed her mind after an associate pulled her coat tail and whispered Clarice's name.

Yeah, lady. You know the rep. Clarice had poked out her boobs, stuck her nose in the air.

They hauled her self-important, disdainful butt into a cell and unceremoniously dumped her on the bed. Clarice stood and mugged them, eternally grateful that she didn't have to fight them. They slammed the door.

Yeah. I thought so.

The van hit a huge pothole, rattling the suspension and cheap interior, jarring Clarice back to the present. The courthouse came into view, a two-story concrete and brick building that took up the entire block. It was bumper-to-bumper with police, sheriff's deputies and highway patrol cars hogging most of the space. There were a few vans present, similar to the white one Clarice rode in, differing only in the correctional institution names stenciled on the sides. They had to stop several times to allow officers to escort their prisoners across the street, or a random law enforcement vehicle to pull in or out. The officer driving cursed as someone stole his spot, waking his colleague. Clarice couldn't make out his words.

Her legs shook. Visibly. She flexed them, pumping in a little blood so they wouldn't be so stiff after the long ride. Then she twisted at the waist to loosen her back. The passenger threw up his hands, frustrated that they couldn't find a parking space, waved to suggest that they drive around to the back of the courthouse.

Uh-oh. That wasn't in the plan.

Clarice powered on the phone. Sent a text to Eddy: Parking in back.

Pressed SEND and flexed her legs again. Twisted. Breathed.

Okay, Clarice. Get it together, dammit. You can do this.

"Please don't let anyone get killed today, Lord," Clarice prayed. "I just want to be with my family."

The prayer did absolutely nothing to make her feel better. If anything, her damn legs shook even more. The van puttered around the block to the street behind the courthouse, which had much less traffic and people. They found a place to park. The gear shifter clinked into PARK. The passenger yawned, stretched his arms. They opened their doors simultaneously, the passenger stepping over to unlock the side doors so Clarice could get out. The doors unlatched, creaked open and cool air blasted her face, pulling loose a few strands of hair from her tight ponytail. She stood and baby walked to the step of the door, careful not to pull the shackles loose. The man held a hand up to her, but Clarice ignored it, kept her hands deep in her jacket pockets, jumped to the ground, both feet hitting together, knees nearly buckling, weak and shaky. She looked at the officer, hoping he wouldn't notice her heart trying to do a Michael Jordan jump out of her throat. He nodded, closed up the doors. Turned to walk around the front of the van, joining his co-worker, expecting her to follow.

They forgot to guard me!

She reached down and snatched the shackles off, threw them clanging down the street and took off at a dead sprint. Both men shouted. She heard their heavy boots running after her, sounds muffled from all the blood rushing through her ears. The pounding cardio pressure was so high it inhibited her performance. Her legs, normally as eager as a race horse's, struggled to thrust her forward, saturated in terror chemicals. The thick jacket resisted the wind, slowing her badly. She unzipped it, slung it off while barely hanging on to the phone, instantly feeling lighter, relieved, picking up speed. She made it about a hundred yards from the van before risking a glance back.

Both officers had stopped fifty yards behind her, doubled over with hands on their knees, hacking up phlegm, breathing laboriously after running harder than they'd ever had to as adults. One of them yelled, "Stop!" and pulled his weapon.

A shot followed.

The .40 boom sounded like two, three shots as the report echoed off the buildings on both sides of the street. The bullet ricocheted into the row of cars that

Clarice ran next to, metal screeching, denting, paint scraped off loudly. People shrieked.

Clarice was one of them.

Scared or not, her legs caught another gear. She could feel the fibers deep in her skeletal muscles really grab and pull, engaging more than ever before, throwing her into an explosive sprint, and...

Ohmygod.

Being shocked had nothing on being shot at. The level of muscle recruitment and speed that followed was beyond description. It was god-like. Think of the strongest, most skillful super-hero chick out there and multiply her by a thousand.

Clarice could have beaten her retarded with a flick of her pinky nail.

Momma likes this long time.

The fear vaporized. Clarice smiled maniacally.

She turned right, dodged two cars that slammed on the brakes to avoid crushing her. She waved as if they were courteous motorists allowing a pedestrian right-of-way. Kept up her speed. A small black Vespa carrying a huge man appeared behind her on the sidewalk, an Italian motor scooter Clarice recognized as Eddy's. The one he used to ride behind her during roadwork for training camps. Her coach wore his USA Team jacket, an open-faced helmet, dark sunglasses and a huge grin. Her heart sang at the sight.

She turned her attention back to the path ahead of her and managed to run even faster.

Cars and people were everywhere. Numerous sirens sounded behind her. An old lady shambled out of a coffee shop and pointed at the girl blurring down the street in prison yellow, shouted something about 911 to whoever manned the shop's counter. Clarice turned left.

A row of trucks presented the opportunity Clarice wanted. Without slowing, she jumped into the back of a large green Chevy, hurtling the bedrail as if it were the fence around the high school stadium that she used to vault, clearing it like it wasn't there. Crashed into the bed, shoulder taking the impact, rocking the suspension sharply, shocks squeaking. Frantically, she tore off the yellow pants, adjusted the waist of the shorts. Jumped out. Eddy handed her a helmet and she straddled the seat behind him. He gunned it, the bike took off, making 20 mph in as many seconds.

Traffic was no match for a Vespa, able to bypass everything by simply driving between cars or down the sidewalks. Biloxi police were everywhere, but they were looking for a prisoner running in yellow, not two people on a scooter. They drove right past three cops on foot before some busybody broad came out of a store and yelled, "There she is right there! She was in the back of that green truck!"

Stupid Good Samaritans.

The woman pointed at Clarice, looking at the officers that swarmed the intersection, waving her damn hands in all directions to make sure they got the message. They did.

Christ. To think that could have been me a couple of years ago...

Clarice wanted to deck both the woman and her old self.

"Hang on, darlin'!" Eddy yelled, twisting the throttle to its stop. The little two-stroke engine, already struggling under Eddy's bulk combined with Clarice's buck-thirty-five on the back, grunted out exhaust notes so cute and pet pig-like they would have caused a fit of laughter under different circumstances. They accelerated to a ferocious 35 mph, turned a corner on tires too small for so much weight, drifting slightly, and were blocked by two police cars. Eddy hit the brakes, back tire squealing to a stop. Four cops got out and stared at them, drew their weapons. Hurried toward them.

Oh boy. Not good.

Clarice looked behind her. Threw off the helmet, a useless disguise now. No cops were trailing yet. What could she do?

Eddy tossed his helmed as well. "Run, girl! I'll take care of these rooty-poots," he said.

"But, Coach!"

"But nothing, girl! Get your butt moving. Now."

"Yes, sir."

Clarice was about to pivot and flee when a freakish sight froze her feet. A huge black dude, a bodybuilder with a "Where's the Beef?" t-shirt stretched over his enormous chest, appeared behind the four cops like a bear towering over far lesser mammals. Another man tailed him, a slim, geeky looking guy with short brown hair, a white shirt and black and white striped pants.

Bobby and Ace! What the hell?

The former paint-and-body specialist of Custom Ace snatched up one of the officers and slung him into his partner like a rag doll. They hit the pavement hard, their gear and boots impacting loud enough to be heard over the traffic.

Ace spotted her and ran through the confused officers, past Eddy. Stopped in front of her. "Hey," he said breathlessly.

"Hey," Clarice replied just as winded, though from the sight of her husband, rather than from running.

"This is kinda fun, huh?"

"Sure."

"Run, girl!" Eddy said again. Then he stared down the two officers that remained on their feet. Lifted his considerable fists in a posture very familiar to him. He stuck out his under bite in a smile and told them, "I may be a little old, but we can rock and roll."

Clarice grabbed her husband's hand and took off. Clarice heard Eddy's shoes scramble over the street too quickly for a man his size and age, followed by two loud, crunching blows and gasping cries of pain from the officers. The lovely sound fueled their escape.

They rounded a corner, completely off the plan now, unsure how to make it to the car on the next block. Heard footsteps behind them. An officer, running at full speed, attempted to cross the street to get behind them. He never saw the car that hit him.

A late '80s Camaro full of teenagers hit the policeman at roughly 40 mph, more than twice the speed limit. The unfortunate lawman crumpled the hood, fender, busted the windshield and caved in the roof, flipping awkwardly over the car and onto the road. He got up, surprised that he could, and shouted at the car. It hit the gas, tires chirping, speeding away from the cop they had just rammed and nearly killed.

Ace and Clarice looked at each other and burst out laughing. Then they ran again.

Car engines and sirens raced to the block behind them. The disturbance caused by Eddy and Bobby must have attracted every cop in the area. The men they so easily took out probably keyed their radios in a sheer panic, calling in everybody and their daddy to stop those two wrecking machines. The distraction wouldn't last long. They needed to get to their getaway ride and boogie, ASAP.

They ran past two streets full of people, several of them shouting and pulling out cellphones when they saw them. Clarice glanced at Ace and her eyes popped at the sight of his yellow pants. No wonder they didn't look like a happy couple out for a morning jog. They wouldn't make it to the car before 1-800-CRIMESTOPPERS got a gazillion calls and police surrounded them.

New plan, then. They'd steal a car.

"Come on!" Clarice said, turning into a large parking lot full of cars, one with relatively few people.

"Where are we going? The car is that way," he said pointing west.

"We'll never make it. A dozen people back there saw your pants and called 911."

"Dammit. I wasn't able to get pants. So what's the plan?"

"We'll steal a car."

His eyebrows shot up. "Really? Wow."

Clarice scanned the area. No one was looking at them so she grabbed his arm and darted into a row of cars. Squatted down. They sat on their haunches, panting, looking around. Every car and truck that she could see was a potential ride to freedom. The Ford Fusion in front of them, the Kia Optima behind them - didn't matter which one they chose. Clarice had the schematics of their ignition systems in her head. She'd worked on cars for years.

"The Kia," Clarice said. "Get in."

"Why the Kia?" he said, opening the passenger door.

"I don't like Kias."

"Oh, yeah."

Sitting in the driver's seat, Clarice leaned down and stuffed her phone in a sock, using some of the tape still stuck there to secure it, berating herself for not sewing at least one pocket into her shorts. Quickly she opened the glove box and pushed the button to open the trunk. Ran around the rear of the car and lifted the spare tire cover, grabbing the tire iron. Slammed the trunk. Jumped back in the car, butt squirming into the seat and telling her this ride really sucked. She frowned unhappily, looking at the steering column. She could rip open the plastic casing and bust the ignition lock, twist two wires together, touch another one to the positive lead to start the engine and give this little Korean POS hell. Would only take a minute.

So why was she hesitating?

She looked around the interior, mind flashing back to a customer, an endearing family man that had brought in a car just like this to her shop. He had been so stressed out about the vehicle breaking down, worried he'd miss his daughter's soccer game. Clarice sympathized, having a kid of her own and knowing exactly how worrisome extra-curricular activities could be. So she repaired the Kia within an hour, jumping the man in front of several other customers, going completely against shop policy. When she told him his car was ready, he got tears in his eyes and grease on his shirt when he hugged her.

Could she steal that man's car?

Ace looked at her steadily, his *Knows Stuff* smile turning up a corner of his mouth, squinting an eye. He put a gentle finger on her cheek and wiped the tear that drag raced down it. "You can't steal a car, dear," he said softly. "Remember the oath you got all Custom Ace employees to take?"

Clarice sniffled. "Something about no malicious acts against peoples' cars because they are potential customers, pride and loyalty to the profession, et cetera."

"Yeah. Ethics blow, huh?"

"Totally," Clarice replied and laughed.

"So, fearless leader. What now? No one will offer us a ride while I wear these," he said, pinching his pants.

A police car drove by slowly, the officer intently searching both sides of the road, parking lots. Ace ducked down, cursed.

Her eyes narrowed. "I can't steal this person's car," Clarice growled. "But I sure as hell can steal his."

"Huh?" Ace peeked over the dashboard at the cop, who turned into the lot across the street.

"Open the trunk," Clarice said, getting out of the car. She reached back in and grabbed a pair of sunglasses out of the console, put them on. "Stay here."

"Yes, dear."

When Clarice got the tire iron from the trunk, she saw some clothes in plastic dry-cleaning bags. She opened the deck lid again, replaced the tire tool and rummaged through the business suits and dresses, deciding she could take a few items and live with herself. Found a jacket and fur hat for her. Put them on. A pair of pants that should fit Ace. Shut the trunk and threw the slacks to him before running across the street to flag down the police cruiser.

Running, she thought what it would be like if she stole some family's car and ended up crashing it or causing extensive damage. As a mechanic shop owner, she had sworn to preserve civilian cars, not destroy them. Even with her recent criminal mentality, she couldn't bring herself to do that, not even to gain her freedom. She couldn't hurt innocent people in any way. This cop and Ford Police Interceptor in front of her, on the other hand, were a completely different story. He wasn't innocent; he was the ENEMY. He gave his word and signature to do war against law breakers, knowing the rules of the game. With her vast dislike of po-lice, Clarice had no qualms about engaging him. In fact, she looked forward to it. She'd trick him out of his car, knock him out, and take his ride.

Yeah. Simple plans always work best.

The policeman stopped when he saw her running toward him. Clarice was confident the hat and glasses, plus the fact that she was running towards him rather than away, would be disguise enough. She flapped her arms like a damsel in distress, really projecting the act. Screamed, "Help! Police! I've been robbed. Oh, please help me."

The man jumped out of the car quickly. Clarice fell down at his feet, sobbing.

"Oh, my God," she cried. "They jumped me and took my car. Help me please!"

He grabbed under her arms, stood her up. "Ma'am, are you hurt? Do you know who took your car?"

"No," Clarice said, looking up at him, blood turning cold as she zeroed in on her target. The guy's chin and jaw looked like they were made on a German tank assembly line. Her eyes moved down to his thick vest, armor that would make her hardest body punches feel like tickles. A real sob came out and he patted her shoulder, got on his radio to report the crime.

Clarice sighed. This was just not her week.

She took off the hat, glasses and jacket. Dropped them and rolled her shoulders, then looked down at his crotch. Her primary target.

She tried to say something between sobs, choking out a shaky whisper. He leaned down and asked her to repeat it. She leapt up, grabbing the back of his head with both hands, bringing her knee up into his face, banging it hard between his eyes. It smacked solidly and he cried out, startled, grabbed his face with one hand, pepper spray off his belt with the other. But her feet were already planted on the ground again, and he had no chance to act before Clarice propelled forward with four quick, straight punches into his balls. Bam-bam-bam BOOM!

He doubled over, roared once and backhanded the crap out of her. His arm, nearly as big as her leg, hit her in the side of the head and knocked her on her ass. She squawked when her butt hit the pavement. He dropped the can and lunged at the crazy bitch attacking him, hurt but not crippled by the knee to the head and combo to his man parts. He forgot all about pepper spray procedure in his enraged determination to hit her back.

As all ladies should know, ball shots have that effect on men. They are a capital offense. A wise woman would learn from Clarice's mistake and use something a lot bigger than her fists if she ever tried it. Would make sure the guy went down for the count. Otherwise, he'll turn into the Incredible Hulk and try to smash her.

Clarice gained her feet, ducked two swings that would have knocked out *all* her teeth, as his huge arms literally whistled through the air. She pivoted to the right and threw a left-hook, then a right uppercut to his jaw. They landed like slaps on his massive head, sending jolts of pain down her arms. Barefisted fighting is so not fun. Ouch.

I didn't really think this through, did I?

A crowd of people were accumulating around them, with more people running out of the strip mall businesses to see the show. Most of them cheered on the cop, though a few, some young Asian thugs, were cheering Clarice. She rattled off two quick combos to his head, able to hit the lumbering man at will, dropped down for another shot at his groin, nailing him with a hard right, eliciting a mere grunt for her effort. This behemoth wasn't very impressed with her work.

She took a quick glance at the police car. The door was open. Engine running. Maybe she could jump in it and take off. No, he might be able to run across the street and catch Ace getting in. Couldn't risk it. She had to stop this guy.

Now.

Clarice thought of the most dangerous, hurtful place she could hit him. A rabbit punch. A hit in the back of the head where the spine joins the skull, directly impacts the brain stem. It's devastating, potentially causing permanent damage, even death. Looking at the size of this dude's skull, Clarice doubted her little fist could kill him. Hell, without hand wraps, she'd be lucky to make him dizzy enough to get away. Nothing for it but to do it, she guessed.

She feigned a jab to make him jump, bring his hands up. Ducked under his arms to get behind him, pivoting, quickly planting her back foot and stepping forward hard and fast with her left foot, bringing an overhand right haymaker off the hip, throwing it with a roar of exertion, tightening fist, shoulder, aiming at a spot two feet on the other side of his head. It hit the back of his neck with tremendous force, breaking her hand and knocking him to his knees, spitting, expelling his whooshing breath. The Asians cheered uproariously, laughing and applauding, one of them filming the scene with his phone. Clarice groaned, clutching her hand under her boobs. It was numb now, but she knew it would be on fire in a moment. *Super-duper.*

The officer shook his head, started to get back up. Clarice fumed, incensed that she had broken her damn hand and still hadn't stopped the guy. Calmly, angrily, she walked up to him, drew his stick from his belt and whopped him in the head, in the exact same spot her punch had landed. He fell on his face, unconscious, breathing raggedly. A shocked silence overcame the crowd. Clarice hefted the stick and grimaced at them, shook the weapon at the Team Law fans. A dozen people raised their hands and backed up. She spun on a toe and ran for the police cruiser, dropping the stick, hard wood clattering on the pavement as she slammed the door.

The array of electronics on the dash and console were a little intimidating. This was the new Taurus Interceptor, the Crown Victoria's replacement, loaded with state-of-the-art tech unfamiliar to her. She shifted into DRIVE and stomped the gas pedal, deciding Ace would be the one to disable the GPS locator. The 365 hp V6 responded with gusto, shooting her out of the plaza, through the intersection, into the parking lot where Ace crouched next to the Kia.

He jumped in. "Do you have to turn everything into a big production?" he teased. "Gosh. You crowd-happy drama queen."

Clarice bumped her hand, which made her glare at him. "I'm not a drama queen!"

He flinched. "Okay. Sorry. Why are you yelling?"

"I broke my fucking hand!"

"You want me to drive?"

"No!"

"Will you please calm down? Stop yelling at me."

"I'm sorry!" Clarice yelled at him.

Several squad cars and a Jeep Cherokee with K-9 UNIT painted on the side skidded into the plaza across the street to rescue their fallen comrade, the sixth one down so far. Clarice muttered a thanks that no one had been hurt too badly, yet. She adjusted the seat to reach the pedals better, used her left hand to shift the car and hit the accelerator. Steered out into the street and floored it, heading back to the beach for a quick loop around I 110 into D'Iberville. The seats made straining noises every time they were pinned back from the g force.

Oooh...Baby. It'd been too long since Clarice had felt that blissful sensation!

Her butt squirmed deeper into the seat, happy with the power making it vibrate. Her hand loosened on the wheel, in the way a sword master grips a sword looser in order to work it faster. Her focus turned to speed vision, looking where the car was about to go rather than where it was going.

Ace fastened his seatbelt.

"Unbuckle, love. You have to disconnect the GPS," Clarice said, hitting the brake before a curve, gassing it again. Passed a trio of cars on a double-line.

"Yee-haw," he said without enthusiasm, nervously watching the road. Clarice knew he had always been terrified of her driving - today it would likely turn his hair completely gray, the poor thing. Clarice bet his gonads had migrated north somewhere, though he was overcoming his fear and reluctance, sticking his head under the dash and starting to sort through the wiring harnesses.

"Yee-haw, indeed," Clarice agreed, turning a corner so fast the car got sideways, fishtailed with smoking tires before straightening, catching traction, engine bellowing as first-gear wound out through the RPM range.

Ace made a girlie noise.

The rearview mirror showed several police cars of various agencies on their trail. No telling how many would be waiting ahead, blocking intersections, setting out road spikes. Her criminal persona whispered in her head.

You can't outrun police radios; you have to out-think them.

Their only hope was to devise a plan that would shake the pursuers so they could hide before they got a helicopter overhead. Otherwise they were screwed, hardcore with no lube.

That thought was cut short as they blitzed through an intersection, losing the tailing cops and picking up three more. The highway patrolmen turned in behind them, sirens and lights blazing. Clarice looked at the dash, anxiously, searching for the switch to turn on their light bar and siren so the innocents in their path would have a warning.

Couldn't find it. Couldn't take her eyes off the road to keep looking.

"Ace! Where's the switch for the lights and siren?"

His head popped up, arm following. He looked once and hit the correct switch, snorting disappointment at her. Went back to work under the dash. *Smart-ass geek.*

Traffic looked really thick up ahead, stop lights and tail lights flashing red as far as Clarice could see. She slowed, began weaving through cars like cones on a slalom course. Had to drive up onto a sidewalk at one point, blaring siren and blinding lights making people dart into stores and out of the way. The highway patrol followed, easily keeping pace with her.

She needed to get to roads with less traffic, ones she knew well enough to really maneuver on, shake these bastards.

She looked up at the street signs that flew by, barely able to read them at this speed. Turned a corner. Recognized the one she wanted and turned a hard right onto Big Ridge Road. Stomped the gas, transmission downshifting, car leaping forward. The twin-turbo Ecoboost's dual exhaust rumbled furiously off the buildings, houses, and huge oak trees they passed.

Ace came up from the floorboard, cheesing beautifully, holding a harness plug in his hand. "Got it," he bragged. "Shorted out the locator, and fried the computer so they can't track the IP."

Clarice looked at the navigation and computer monitors, a faint burnt wire smell invading her nose. The screens were black. She gave him a quick smile. "That's my man. Now be a good boy and buckle up. Latch mine, too, please. This is going to get quick and dirty for a few minutes."

"Yes, dear."

A neighborhood came up on their right, and the idea she had floating around in her head fully surfaced, ready to implement into action. She locked up the brakes, turning a dizzying right, let off and got back into the throttle, turning into the residential area with a power-slide, rear tires boiling smoke, painting the entrance with black marks thirty-feet long. Zoomed around several curves, turned down seemingly random streets. The troopers followed, but were fighting out of their weight class and fell behind.

Her eyes moved from the mirror back to the road. Clarice grinned insanely and shouted, "You motherfuckers can't drive!"

Ace grabbed the *Oh Shit* handle above his door and squeaked a very mousy sound.

Clarice turned down another street, which was short and intersected with two other roads, houses on every corner. She stomped the emergency brake to sling the rear-end around without affecting her steering, released the brake and hit the gas in one motion, the car sliding into someone's yard and taking out their mailbox and trash can before hitting the pavement again, accelerating, tires roaring for grip. The move was executed to near perfection, evoking a bazillion goose bumps up and down her arms and breasts.

"YOU MOTHERFUCKERS CAN'T DRIVE!" Clarice bellowed in challenge, cackling. Ace turned very pale, woozy looking.

The three cops following them didn't know these streets and obviously lacked the drifting technique in their driving repertoires to pull off that turn at that speed. The first two patrol cars skidded sideways up into the yard and kept going, crashing into the house, taking out the entire brick wall with booming destruction, one car hitting behind the other. Dust and grass flew in all directions. The third cop had slowed enough to miss hitting his buddies, tearing deep ruts in the lawn as he turned to chase them.

"That was Hollywood material," Ace breathed, turning to stare behind them.

"Two down, one to go," Clarice said, jaw locked in concentration. She used the palm of her hand to spin the wheel left, right, left again, racing through the neighborhood. The car behind them kept pace, attempting to catch up. She slowed, allowing him to stay close, hoping to block his view from the trick she had in store up ahead.

A group of children playing in the street ran into their yards, waving at them as they went by. Ace and Clarice waved back. They were really cute kids.

Clarice turned down a cul-de-sac, a dead end road with empty lots and a huge ditch deep enough to prevent anyone from driving through to the next block.

Ace panicked. "This is a dead-end!"

Clarice started to pat his leg and bumped her hand, lighting it up and pissing her off. "Who's driving this car?!" she screamed.

"You are. Please don't scream at me."

"I'm sorry!" she screamed at him.

Burning, broken hand. Gapped grill. Eye swelling shut from that backhand earlier. Exquisite joy from racing to freedom with her husband. It was like she had nuclear PMS, emotions fusing and fissioning. If she had a mood ring, it would be glowing like the sun, about to explode from the confusion.

The dead end approached. Clarice let off the gas, glanced in the mirror. The cop was close enough so Clarice hit the brakes, turning slightly to the right so his bumper would ram the corner of their car, spinning them around as he plowed by. He hit them, they spun, he passed and Clarice hit the gas again so that they did a complete three-sixty, ending up behind him, her left hand working the wheel with precise coordination. She floored it and rammed into his still moving car, pushing it into the ditch. Let off and hit the brakes. The patrol car's back tires came off the ground as its nose hit the bottom of the ditch, crunching the hood and busting the headlights. The highway patrolman jumped out of the wrecked car, boots landing in water. He kicked around madly, fell down on the muddy bank, cursing them.

Ace laughed and clapped, leaned over and kissed her cheek.

Clarice stuck her head out the window, shook her good fist at the guy and trumpeted, "Yeah! One hand on ya, biatch!" Clicked off the lights and siren. Turned them around and left celebratory black marks in their wake. She steered back onto Big Ridge Road and headed for a quiet spot she knew next to a bayou so they could hide for the night. Turned on LeMoyne Boulevard, not far from Ocean Springs.

They turned into another neighborhood, this one mostly woods and empty lots, the result of a big hurricane that had wiped out the entire coast almost seven years ago. Some big casino corporation bought everyone out after the storm, giving most people a really good deal for their land near the water, which is where they needed to build casinos in this state. For whatever reason, they never did anything with the purchase. Clarice was glad, too. The marsh and bayou in this area was gorgeous. Would be a shame to see it ruined and replaced with more gambling barges and hotels. There was enough of that around already.

As they cruised a narrow lane next to marsh land and pine trees, Clarice began to relax. The unique smell of the bayou plants acted as aromatherapy for the anticlimax, unwinding her after the death-defying roller coaster they just rode. She drove them into a thicket of bushes and trees, not caring if they got stuck in the soft pine straw-topped mud that crunched under the tires. Killed the ignition. The engine ticked and hissed in relief. Mockingbirds cawed, and a blue heron flapped gracefully from the trees onto a muddy bank. Small aquatic critters, likely frogs and baby mullet, splashed in the water only yards in front of them.

It was nirvana.

Clarice turned to see how Ace was doing and they got a good look at each other for the first time since 2010. His hair had never been that short before, but it looked good, made his new muscles look even bigger. His unreal blue eyes sparkled like sapphires, clear and mesmerizing. A five o'clock shadow covered his jaw and neck, rendering his angular face rugged and incredibly sexy.

Clarice touched his chin. "You look delicious," Clarice said huskily.

He gave a huge grin, blushing, ears turning red. He leaned back and took her in. Looked at her ugly Bob Barker shoes, homemade shorts, beginning to make a pooh-pooh face. Eyes widening in alarm at her broken, deformed-looking hand tucked under her boobs like Clarice had a nerve disease. Swollen eyes, scabs on her nose and lips. His eyebrows were nearly in his hairline by the time he looked in her eyes again.

"You look, uh, great, dear," he said, nodding sincerely.

Clarice smiled...and he jumped back, hitting his head on the door pillar.

"What the short-circuit happened to your tooth?!" he sputtered.

Clarice started crying. She realized she had unconsciously kept her mouth closed when facing him until now. She pictured what he saw, a swollen, scabbed Butterface with a gaping black hole in her smile, and cried harder.

"It's okay, Clarice. We'll get it fixed. Don't worry about it." He hugged her, stroking her hair, kissed her forehead, cheeks. He knew she liked that, knew exactly how to calm her. Clarice got a hold of her pitiful weeping, turned her face up to his. He kissed her with such tender passion her toes curled and her muscles melted into putty, all the pain and stress evaporating. Somehow, she managed to put her arm around him and kiss back. Ten years later, they decided they were animals that needed oxygen, came up gasping.

"Wow," he said.

"Exactly," Clarice agreed.

He put a hand on her cheek and Clarice winced. "Sorry," he murmured. "From fighting?"

"Smiling."

"Smiling..." he breathed, confused, but not thrown off his current mission. "So. You, uh, wanna do it?"

Clarice giggled an affirmative.

He said, "I had a homosexual cubicle mate and was afraid to ever, you know, relieve myself." He chuckled. "My balls are big."

Clarice laughed, lifted an inflamed brow. "Sounds like a problem we should take care of. I hope you don't mind." Clarice gestured at her legs and lady parts. "I didn't have a chance to wax before our date. My apologies."

He looked down at his lap, his pants bulging, suddenly five sizes too small. Looked at her and smirked. "Yeah. Like that's a problem."

They kissed again, and he helped her get her shirt off, becoming immobilized when he saw her shoulder and side.

"Duct tape. You're duct taped," he said, dumbfounded.

"Bondage. Does it turn you on?"

"Like a Cray supercomputer."

Powerful stuff.

The critters around the car were unconcerned with their gasps and cries of pleasure, engaged in similar spring time mating rituals of their own.

Chapter XXIII

Biloxi – Ocean Springs, Mississippi
April 3, 2012

If you Bing the word "hummer" all manner of results pop up. Some expected. Others, not so much. The pictures and instructions you would like to keep your children from seeing entered Clarice's mind as she lay on the back seat of the police cruiser, half-dreaming, half-awake, aware of Ace on top of her, something vibrating pleasantly in her nether regions.

Clarice stretched, groaning delightfully at the feel of his comfortable weight. Smiled and whispered, "Ace. Babe, I have to go pee first."

"That's not me," he mumbled, sniffing, lifting himself off of her, cool air sucking away the heavy mix of their scents. "But I like the way you think," he said, then nibbled her ear.

Clarice swatted him. He opened the door and Clarice helped him out with a less-than-polite shove of her foot. The dork laughed, bare feet crunching in the weeds, naked derriere glowing bright white as the sun hit. He turned around, scratched his luminescent no-butt. Proceeded to relieve himself. Clarice grabbed his pants off the seat, moving her legs off of them, and fished her phone from under her. Checked the screen. It was Eddy!

"Coach?" Clarice answered, voice croaking, mouth as dry as the small beach visible behind Ace.

"Hey, darlin'! You miss me?" Eddy said, baritone straining the tiny speaker in her ear.

"What happened? Is Bobby okay?" Her heart raced, heating her cheeks. Reality slapped her fully awake, and she cringed at how much trouble she had gotten her friends in. "Please tell me he got away, too." Clarice put it on speaker phone.

"Sure. He's fine. Well, other than suffering a minor indignity of having to ride on the back of the Vespa."

"You guys got away on that thing?"

"Yes," Bobby's deep voice rumbled, echoing in the quiet of the wooded shore. "Because I sacrificed and rode bitch," he boasted proudly.

"You gotta give it to him," Eddy said. "Riding behind a guy like me is an image killing bullet to your manhood. He took it surprisingly well."

A monstrous growl made the speaker squeal, click, hum loudly before returning to normal volume.

"They got away?" Ace said, eyes wide, smiling. "Hey Bobby. Eddy."

"Hey, Ace. How are you two making it?" Eddy said.

Her man looked at her and glowered. He complained to Eddy, "All she wants to do is cook, clean, and have sex." He sighed loudly, rolled his eyes. "It's so annoying."

"I'll bet," Eddy replied, a paternal smile in his tone.

"I don't believe it," Bobby said in snobbish disbelief, his basso making him sound ridiculous.

"Believe what?" Clarice said.

"That Ace knows how to have sex."

"Do too," Ace said.

"Do not," Bobby argued.

"Do too!"

They stood there laughing at the phone for a moment, listening to Eddy and Bobby do the same. Then Clarice said, "How did you guys get away? I thought for sure the police had you surrounded."

"They did," Eddy answered. Clarice pictured him elbowing Bobby and grinning. "But the old man still has a few tricks up his sleeve. Your pal Bobby is fairly capable as well."

"Yeah," Bobby said. "After we dropped those four dingle berry po-lice, Eddy convinced me to ride trick on that little motor bike and we hot-tailed it outta there. They couldn't follow because of all the traffic. We hid inside a store - Eddy actually drove us inside the store - where we were directed to a wine cellar by an Italian gent older than God. The cops did a routine search and questioning around the area, but nobody had seen anything, certainly not two huge, angry cop-killing maniacs on a clown bike."

"You hid in a store?" Clarice said, baffled, giggling at the image of their five-hundred-plus pounds on the Vespa, steering up into someone's business for a surprise visit and plea for help.

"Yeah. A deli. I know a guy," Eddy said, reticent. "Forget about it."

"You always know a guy," Clarice said in wonder.

"Forget about it," he agreed. "By the way, I clocked you at fifteen miles per hour for an entire mile. Correcting for speedometer error, I'd say you ran a consistent thirteen miles per, and that's a -"

"Four-and-a-half minute mile," Clarice breathed in disbelief. "That's sexy."

"Yep. A new record for you, Shock. I've been contemplating how to implement all this into a training regime. So far, I can't think of anything without cops and bullets. Any ideas?" he said only half joking.

Clarice spun to Ace, eyes alight, expression that of a teenage girl who has just spotted the latest popular skinny jeans on sale and must have them now. "We're getting a gun!" Clarice said excitedly, squealing.

"Uh…" he said.

"How'd you two love birds make it to Victory Lane?" Bobby wanted to know. "Who got hacked, who got knocked out?"

Ace crossed his arms and glared at her. "Clarice has been keeping secrets from us. She wasn't in prison! She was on some planet where they metamorphosed her into a biomechanical demon race car driver. Her reflexes aren't human. She was so in tune with this cop car it was as if she had been practicing high-speed chases every day - with cerebral implanted Bluetooth controlling the car's ECU."

"Please geek-down your answers, buddy," Bobby jabbed at him, then said to her, "Like riding a bike, huh, Boss?" He laughed, then mused to Eddy, "Her most radical driving, and the bread stick nerd survived it."

From his tone, Clarice knew he and Eddy were sharing a look, frowning their *Not Bad* expressions. A few mutters of respect for her adrenaline-shy hubby.

"You're still in the police car," Eddy stated, voice turning serious.

"Yes," Clarice said.

"Is it hidden?"

"Should be good for a day."

"I'm on my way to get you."

"We need clothes and food."

"What do you need?" he queried.

"Navy blouse, pencil skirt, open-toed sling backs and a lobster salad," Clarice replied without hesitation. "And a portable shower. If you spot something feminine, bring it." Ugh. Clarice couldn't wait to shake off the masculinity of prison.

"Double that order," Ace said, curtseying as if he had a skirt on.

Clarice eyed him warily and mouthed, "Were you the gay cube mate? Or your friend?"

He stopped posing, stuck his tongue out and shook his penis at her. Grabbing his pants, he put them on, making sure Clarice saw his movements were manly.

"So peanut butter and jelly with sweat pants and a side order of hand towelettes," Eddy said. "Thank you for choosing Fugitive King. Please drive around to the window."

"I want fries and a divorce with that," Ace added. "I'm citing 'irreconcilable driving differences'."

"He screamed like a girl," Clarice informed them. Eddy merely chuckled. Bobby sounded like he was choking to death.

While they waited on delivery service from Fugitive King, Ace and Clarice walked down to the water. Held hands and sat on the sand bar, fully exposed in all its smelly glory, low tide waters lapping gently against the small beach and bank connected to it. An early morning fisherman motored his skiff out around the marsh islands a couple hundred yards in the distance, sea gulls hovering over him, man and boat silhouetted from the rising sun 93,000,000 miles behind him.

Ace gripped her hand. "Should I moon that guy?" he said.

Clarice looked at him, shocked, and gasped, "No! What's wrong with you? Act your age, dude."

He just smirked. Stood and offered her his hand. Clarice took it and gained her feet. He bowed and kissed her fingers.

Then they turned around and exposed their glowing rear-ends to the fisherman.

A faint, gruff bark of laughter floated to them over the water. They turned back to the bayou to see the man waving at them.

"We should host Good Morning Mississippi," Ace said sagely, buttoning his pants.

A growling, high-end race engine boomed from a down-shift, reverberating throughout the streets behind them, grasping her attention. As the vehicle neared her pulse quickened, and Clarice recognized the exhaust notes of her Snarling Darling, the 427 cubic inch hunk that had been the love of her life long before she met Ace. They walked up the embankment to the police car and her 1959 El Camino pulled in behind it, Bobby behind the wheel, teeth bright white in the dark interior. He killed the ignition and the atmosphere around them sighed, relieved of the monstrous combustion waves her baby panted at idle. Another vehicle followed, a red late-model Toyota truck, Eddy's work horse. They got out and smiled at her gushing antics.

Clarice approached Camino like it was a dangerous beast that used to be her friend but hadn't seen her in a while. She held her breath, ran a finger lightly down the red and gray fender, over the sleek door, appreciating the lines that flowed perfectly into the side of the bed. Inhaled the carbon vapor heat and high-octane fumes emanating off the undercarriage and polished aluminum wheels, like the musk of a barely tamed wild animal. She shivered in ecstasy.

"How?" Clarice whispered. Her truck looked exactly as she'd left it. She couldn't believe her eyes. She assumed it had been seized along with everything else.

Bobby said, "I managed to sneak it away. The police never had the chance to inventory Camino or the Wrecker." He sighed. "Those greedy pigs took everything else, though. All they left was some random tools they must have felt were of no value to their so-called drug-related property seizure." He shrugged. "Sorry, Ace. Couldn't get the Dodge Ram."

"You could have gone to jail," Clarice fussed, hugging him.

He squeezed back. "I had to get it," he said, iron in his voice, while managing an apologetic glance for his frowning friend.

Clarice hugged her coach. "You bring clothes?"

"Potato sacks and rope belts," he said, handing her a plastic grocery bag. Noticing her hand, he grunted, gently grabbed it, pressed around the bones and knuckles, nodded to let her know it wasn't too serious. Wordlessly, he took a roll of tape from his jacket and taped it up tight. It felt better. Clarice smiled thanks.

She opened the bag, threw a pair of gray running pants to Ace. Got the other pair for herself, putting them on quickly, unconcerned about the men seeing her in underwear; they'd been a part of her life long enough to have seen her in less. Took out the Saran wrapped sandwiches and opened one, stuffed half of it in her mouth. The white bread melted, giving way to the most delicious PB&J she'd ever had. She opened a bottle of lemon ice Gatorade, sipped, cringing as the cold hit the back of her throat.

She moaned with pleasure.

"Hey! Don't start without me," Ace said. She threw him an orgasm sandwich and Gatorade.

"Have you thought about what you want to do next?" Eddy said. He leaned against his truck, hands in pockets. Bobby leaned next to him, watching Ace devour his food like a starving wolf, smiling.

"Yeah," Clarice said. "We need to get IDs, get Nolan and leave the country."

"Just like that," Eddy said. "Hmm."

"Yeah. Just like that," Clarice said scowling.

"So you're not using the IDs the Teacher made for you?"

"Not likely."

"Didn't think so." He smiled. "What about the twenty grand?"

"I'll give you the names of women who helped me on the inside. I want it put on their inmate accounts."

"Donate the Teacher's filthy drug money to charity," Eddy said, writing on a note pad. "Names, please."

Clarice gave him Patty's, Juanita's, and Yvonne's names. Thought about it and added Helen and Yolanda. "Put ten thousand on Patty's, split the rest between the others."

"Sure. Anything else?" he said amiably. There wasn't a single thing Clarice could say, do, or ask of the man that would ruffle him.

"No, that's it. If I need a box of steaks, a five-O-one-C-three charity, or a hit man, I'll call you."

"You do that," he said seriously.

"Ace and I will get IDs and money. We'll disappear and get in touch when we get settled."

Bobby shifted uncomfortably. He said, "I know you, Boss. You sure you're not going after those police and forgetting to tell us about it? I've never known you to let a slight pass. Those two bacon factories ruined your life."

"Thanks for reminding me," Clarice grumbled, but nodded to validate his point. "Honestly, I haven't thought about revenge very much. Everything was put into getting out. If something happens and we decide to get some payback, I'll be sure to tell you guys."

"Promise?" Bobby said.

"Promise."

"Hey," Ace mumbled around his second sandwich. "Don't I get a say?"

"No," Bobby said.

"Yes. Of course," Clarice said, mugging Bobby. Turned back to Ace. "What's on your mind?"

He swallowed a huge bite, chugged some Gatorade. Burped loudly. "We should give those police crooks a taste of their own medicine."

"How so?" Eddy said. They all turned attentively to her husband.

His sneaky-cute *Knows Stuff* smile appeared. "Revenge hacking."

"Um…" Clarice said.

He looked at her. "I've done a lot of hacking to get information, but it was always for profit. Just recently I hacked to get revenge on these Latin King thugs that harassed me and Diamond." He told them about the gang bangers and the incident with them snitching on his cubicle mate, who took the fall for the escape plan. Ace had hacked into the commissioner's e-mail account and composed transfer orders that got the LKs locked down. "The same concept can be applied to the cops that set us up," he finished.

Eddy and Bobby looked at each other and frowned. *Not Bad.* Clarice liked the expression and frowned it at her man. He nodded importantly.

"What about our son? We need to be with him," Clarice said, rubbing her shoulders. "I had a bad feeling that he was in danger."

Everyone looked at her, an uneasy sensation spreading through their group. They knew how seriously she took her intuition, and knew how uncannily accurate her premonitions were.

"He's okay, Shock," Eddy said quietly. "I saw him yesterday. He's fine."

"He'll be safe at your parents' house," Ace assured her, walking over to rub her arms. "We need to tie up all our loose ends before we're ready for him. Before we're ready to start over." He stroked her hair and Clarice nearly purred. "What if we get a thousand miles away, make it to a beautiful place, but we can't enjoy it because we hate ourselves for not getting justice? You know that's what will happen."

Clarice grabbed his face in both hands, rubbed his prickly cheeks and stared into his determined eyes. "Where'd all this confidence come from?" Clarice squeezed one of his biceps. "New muscles, new courage. What happened to you in there? Your balls are bigger than mine now." Clarice kissed him, ignoring Bobby's snickering behind them. "All right," Clarice said decisively. "Let's take care of business." Clarice shoved Ace out of her way and took several steps over so she could face the three men at the same time. "Their names are Jimmy Wallace and Hector Valasquez. They work for the City of Biloxi Police Department. What else do we know?"

"They also work for the Teacher," Eddy added. "Probably as an escort for drug trafficking. That means not only do they have police resources, they have cartel resources as well. And money. They're well paid."

"A stash of it?" Clarice asked, remembering her hidey-hole and the illegal money she had in it. A few hundred or a few million, She figured anyone with illegal cash would need a hiding place.

Eddy perked up. "Absolutely. They'll have a spot." He chewed on that for a moment. His brows lowered, eyes darkening. With an evil smile he said, "What's the worst thing you could do to those guys?"

Her grin mirrored his. "Take their money."

"Yeah!" Ace exclaimed. "They've risked their careers and ruined lives, probably murdered people to get it. Means the world to them."

"Let's catch us some little piggies and rob their bank," Bobby rumbled, chest flexing excitedly.

Ace grinned at his friend. "Is the Wrecker online?"

"And open for business."

Ace took an iPod and Mi-Fi router out of his pocket. He noticed her questioning look and said, "A gift from the Teacher."

"He sent me one, too, but I lost it in a fight." He returned her inquisitive look, but Clarice waved him off. "Long story. Can the Teacher trace that router?"

He glared at her, insulted, grimaced as if to say *please.* "Not to worry, dear. I've taken measures to evade their amateur tracking skills," he said, powering on the devices and sniffing them in turn. He inhaled deeply, huffing the electronic fumes like a teen sniffing White Out, sighing with rapturous emotional excitement.

"You. Fucking. Geek." Clarice deadpanned. He looked up at her, having forgotten she was there - high on his toys and the promise of hacking challenges. She leaned over and stole a sniff for herself. Sighed in pleasure.

Bobby trotted over on eager feet, joined their addict circle. Eddy stared at them like they were revealed as extraterrestrials.

"It's a mechanic thing," Clarice told him.

"If you say so," he replied, holding his hands up.

Ace Entangled the gargantuan computer that resided at Bobby's house and was through the BPD's firewall in minutes, scrolling through alphabetically listed police employee files. He found their marks, their photos popping up on the small touchscreen, the four of them muttering various curses and angry animal noises at the sight of the enemy. Eddy wrote down the patrol car's number, and their home addresses. Ace's thumbs blurred over the screen and he found the make, model, and tag numbers for their targets' personal vehicles. Eddy took note. Ace back-tracked out of the system, covering his tracks before logging out and powering off the devices. Pocketed them.

Clarice looked around at her team, eyes stopping on Eddy. "Coach, you've dabbled in this type of work before. What do we need to do?"

"Chart their daily routines," he replied instantly. "We have to track their movements: know where they go, how long they stay there, how often they go. The works. In the old days we used manpower. We had a guy at every conceivable spot the mark would go. Nowadays, with technology, it's so much easier. Anybody can acquire tracking devices cheaply, and simply place them on the mark's person, their car, and follow the blinking lights on the screen," he said, pointing a thick finger at the iPod.

Not Bad frowns all around.

"Do you have any tracking devices?" Clarice asked Eddy.

"No."

Ace held up a finger. "I have an idea. We can use cellphones."

"Phones?" Bobby said. "Good idea. Even the cheap ones have GPS."

"Exactly," Ace confirmed. "We can get several from the Dollar Store and plant them on their cars." He held his toys up. "I can activate the GPS setting on this and follow those assholes' every move. I'll keep notes on their movements."

Sounded great to her. Clarice said, "Gentlemen. We have a plan. Bobby, will you get the phones, please?"

"Sure, Boss."

"Coach, if you'll accompany Mr. Carter and me, we'll need your assistance in scoring some IDs."

"Just point the way, darlin'."

Clarice turned to Mr. Alan "Ace" Carter and her heart thudded warm tingly waves through her chest and down her arms. He finished tucking in his shirt, noticed the effect he was having on her. He tightened an imaginary tie and said, "How do I look?"

Clarice looked down at his ragged Bob Barker shoes, a match to her own, riddled with holes and cracks. At the stolen baggy slacks and prison-issue t-shirt that, combined with the style of shoes, made him look like a broke-ass skateboarder. His expectant face, scruffy and dirty from the previous day's tribulations, looked stressed and in dire need of lots of sleep, especially after the party they threw in the police cruiser to celebrate their getaway. Clarice had never seen him look so rough. And yet, she'd never seen him look so breathtakingly handsome. She told him so.

Sort of.

"Your picture should be on gay money," she said.

He affected a blush. Bobby snickered. Eddy slapped his leg and barked a quick laugh.

Clarice waved at her coach. "There's a shotgun and two bulletproof vests in the trunk," Clarice said, pointing at the cop car. "You think we'll need them?"

His smile vanished. He looked at her seriously and said, "I hope the hell not."

* * *

The Department of Motor Vehicles in Biloxi was in a typical city-owned building, a small bricked affair with landscaping and gardening so lackluster it served no discernable cosmetic purpose. They drove past a parking lot full of teenagers' first cars, the lucky permit applicants gleefully skipping and smiling or dragging feet and frowning, expressing the outcome of their tests. Several highway patrol cars were parked near the end of the building. A state trooper stepped out of his cruiser and scowled at Camino, who's illegal-in-most-states exhaust snarled wicked staccatos off cars, buildings, and didn't stop disturbing the peace until the sound waves dissipated over Biloxi's back bay waters up ahead. Clarice waved at the man, drill sergeant-esque in his trooper hat and erect posture, tall boots. The sorry bastard just scowled even harder, but he dragged his eyes away from the hot rod violating the noise ordinance, turned and marched into the DMV.

Clarice looked at Ace, sandwiched between the bucket seats, leaning more to her side because of Eddy's wide, unyielding shoulders. "You think we need a more nondescript car?" Clarice said.

He shrugged. "Couldn't hurt. Being fugitives is a learning process, huh?"

"You better believe it," Eddy answered. "You can make all the plans you want, but they rarely go off without a hitch."

"Murphy's law," Clarice uttered.

"Right," Eddy agreed. "Whatever can go wrong, will." He smiled secretly. "It's a good thing you have an anti-Murphy expert on the Team."

"Oh yeah?" Clarice said, looking at him.

"Yeah. I asked Bobby to get Camino's tag registered in the name of one of the IDs the Teacher sent you. So you at least have a legit license and tag if you get pulled over." He dug in his jacket, handed her a fake license with her picture on it.

Clarice quickly memorized the name, Patricia Stevens, remembering it as one Eddy had mentioned at visitation. Put it away. "Thanks for telling me." Clarice gave him the Stink Eye. "When did you do that?"

"Months ago," he said in a mystical voice, one with great foresight. "You're welcome."

"Let's go over the plan again," Ace said, flexing his fingers in anticipation.

"Hang on, cyber cowboy. Let's find a place to park," Clarice said.

They turned onto the road next to the bay, and Clarice took a moment to appreciate the sparkling surface of the water, refracting the sun in blinding patterns of white, blues, and grays, pleasing but hard to stare at. A salty breeze flowed into the window, cool with a hint of the oak trees they parked under. She turned the key off. With the Snarling Darling napping, they could hear other cars, people's voices and the wind beginning to whip up on the waves to their right. Simple sensations she used to take for granted but now cherished.

She sighed at the same time Ace did. She looked at him and they shared a knowing smile. She said, "Okay, hotshot. This is your show. Run it."

He pecked a kiss on her nose. "I love the way you boss me to be a boss."

Eddy held up a finger and opened his mouth, but shook his head instead of elaborating. "Nah. Too easy," he said, jaw sticking out at Ace in a mischievous smile.

Ace ignored the humor, and Clarice recognized it was because his eccentric personality didn't quite grasp it this time. It was odd; he could be the funniest man on the planet one minute, then the next minute not understand that he was being teased. He was a weirdo. But he was her weirdo.

He said, "I can hack into the DMV's computers from here. But because of the way their system is set up, it will be a little tricky for what we're trying to do."

"How so?" Eddy inquired.

"There are probably six or more computers behind the counter. I have to take control of one to print out the IDs. You will have to tell me what computer I have control of, then distract the employee so I can use the computer to upload our info in the system. The

screen will show several Windows opening and closing, and all kinds of data typed in. If they see that,
they'll shut the system down and likely search the
area for the hacker."

"That would suck," Clarice muttered, showing off
her superior powers of observation. She felt she
should at least contribute that to the operation.

Ace continued. "Then, you'll have to tell me what
printer I have control of, do more distracting so you
can retrieve the IDs."

"No problem," Eddy replied, getting out of the
truck. He pulled a Bluetooth jawbone from a pocket,
affixed it to his ear. Got out his phone and dialed her
number, stuck his hands and phone in his jacket.

Clarice answered the call, put it on speaker. "We're
good," she said.

"Yep," Eddy said, voice vibrating her hand through
the plastic case.

Ace scooted over into the passenger seat, closed
the door. "I need twenty minutes to get us some social
security numbers," he disclosed. "I'll have that done
before you make it to the front of the line."

"Make it quick," Eddy said. "There's a lot of people in there, but I don't plan on waiting in line." He
turned and took his time walking on the side of the
road back to the DMV, waving at a duo of kids with
their mom, scowling at law enforcement.

Ace already had the Touch and router out, powered on and Entangled with the Big Black Wrecker's
awesome processing power. Clarice leaned over and
watched him break into the Social Security De-

partment. In minutes the worm programs run by the Wrecker penetrated multiple firewalls, swatting aside 128 bit encrypted passwords to gain control of the system's executive functions. He found the section where S.S. numbers were updated, began searching through numbers that began with 404, apparently planning to establish their identities as having been born in Kentucky. He found two available numbers and entered them into a different section of the database, covering his tracks as he backed out. On the iPod's screen, the cursor blinked in a slot labeled NAME.

He looked at her. "How about I name you and you name me?"

Clarice laughed. "Sure. Why not? How about Hugh Jackman?"

He leaned away with a *Yeah Right* look. "Please. Have you seen my ass?" He blew out a cynical breath. "As if Hugh Jackman could compare."

"George Clooney?"

He chose not to hear her. "Okay, Miss Anastasia Jade Crawford. You are now alive. Happy Birthday."

"Okay, Mister Julian Longshank Mitchell. You are now alive and living as my boyfriend. We getting married any time soon? I want to out-do our previous wedding." Clarice preened like she had on a gown. "Big plans, baby."

"Great," he drawled, not meaning it. He frowned. "Longshank?"

"Code for Elephant Trunk Junk."

"Ah. Clever. You named me after my penis. I should have named you Hooker. You know, after the punch."

Clarice hooked him, confirming that she did in fact know, but didn't necessarily agree.

"Ow. See? Fitting." His thumbs raced over the touchscreen. "We'll have to file an application to get the S.S. cards once we get settled. I'll do a similar job to get us birth certificates."

"Sounds good."

"You two ready?" Eddy rumbled over the speaker.

"Just a minute, please," Ace replied. His eyes widened in concentration, reflecting the iPod's light, tongue creeping out the side of his mouth. He found the Wi-Fi network for the DMV and ran a program to hack the security code. Noticing her curious look, he told her, "See those numbers?" The screen showed several sets of numbers changing from hundreds into thousands. "When they reach five-thousand, we'll have the password."

Not Bad, Clarice frowned at him.

The five sets of numbers reached their marks and Ace said, "I'm in. Eddy, I'm going to move the cursor on the computer screens one at a time. Tell me when I have the one you want."

"Okay," Eddy murmured quietly.

Ace thumbed something on the iPod, then, like Homer Simpson spotting a cupcake, he said, "Mmm..."

"Mmm, what?" Clarice said.

"Mmm-hmm, mmm-hmm," he answered as if he had the cupcake in his smiling mouth.

"Mmm-hmm," Clarice agreed, even though she was completely befuddled by what was lighting up his hacking pleasure centers. He looked like he was on some kind of master of puppets trip. It was positively adorkable.

Right or wrong, geek or freak, you have to stand by your guy, right?

"Not that one," Eddy whispered, then chuckled. "You just erased something this lady typed in. She looks puzzled."

"Whoops," Ace said without much sincerity. He typed some more.

"Stop. That's the one," Eddy said. "Hang on."

"Roger that," Ace replied.

"Who's Roger?" Clarice said, knowing he'd say something about the origin of radio communication interjections, or some brainiac crap. Before he could answer, a sound like someone hitting their head on a brick wall thunked over the speaker phone, and Clarice realized the background noise filter on Eddy's Bluetooth must have been damaged along with the person's noggin, allowing them to hear whatever her coach was up to.

Eddy bellowed, "This man needs help! Somebody call an ambulance! He's having a heart attack!"

Whoa. This could get interesting. Clarice held the phone closer.

A commotion strained the speaker: Shoes tapping rapidly on tiles, rustling clothes, and several women's concerned voices vied for dominance of Eddy's earpiece. The noise faded suddenly, and

Clarice pictured her coach nonchalantly easing away from the scene, walking to the counter to view his prize of unmanned computers.

"Ace. Take off," he said, a hint of pleasure in his tone. "You have about five minutes."

"Taking off," Ace responded, thumbs typing with phenomenal coordination. Clarice leaned over to see what he was doing. The screen showed he was simply typing in the fabricated names and stolen social security numbers. He clicked on the iPod's menu and went through a file of photos, scrolling through several family portraits of him, Nolan, and herself. Sensing her bewilderment, he said, "I had these stored in the Cloud. Will only take a moment to Photoshop in a blue background so I can print them on our licenses."

Clarice kissed the side of his neck. "You brilliant man." He blushed a lovely scarlet, the hair on his arms standing up in excitement. His thumbs caught another gear.

"Excuse me, ma'am," Eddy said to someone. "Is there an ambulance on the way?"

"Yes, sir. I'm sure they will be here shortly," the lady said, faint and nasal, nearly robotic sounding over the phone.

"That's not good enough!" Eddy exploded, emphasizing it with a heavy fist slammed on a counter. "Hurry, Ace," he muttered, then screamed at the poor employee again. "That man is dying! Get the paramedics here, lady!" He paused for a second, chuckled, said in a normal tone, "Okay, you have a few more minutes."

"Won't need them," Ace said. "Look at the printers. One should be flashing."

A moment later Eddy said, "Uh-oh."

"Uh-oh what?" Clarice said tensely.

"The lady whose screen was erased earlier? She was the only one left behind the counter after the poor gentleman had a coronary, and she just happened to be looking at that printer when it flashed. She has a real suspicious look. Crap. Now she's checking the computers."

"Uh-oh," Ace agreed, nervously flexing his fingers, indecisive.

"Do something, Coach," Clarice insisted. Her knuckles turned white from gripping the phone.

A tense, thoughtful pause later, Eddy said, "Print them."

"What? Where?" Ace queried, thumbs hesitating over the keypad.

"Just print them!" he stormed. The phone made a staticky, scraping sound, and Clarice recognized it as Eddy's massive paw snatching the Bluetooth out of his ear and shoving it into his pocket. A second later the call disconnected.

Ace printed their licenses. They looked at each other and said in unison, "Uh-oh."

They turned to look at the DMV right as the fire alarm went off, steel bells clanging with incredible racket, echoing up and down the busy street, startling several sea gulls that were scavenging in front of Camino. Half a minute later Eddy appeared on the road, hands stuffed in his pockets, walking at a pace that made him look like a citizen fleeing a potential fire rather than a criminal that had just pulled off a major felony. The street and parking lots filled as people hurried out behind him.

Clarice started Camino and watched the mirrors for signs of pursuit, blood pressure spiking as she anticipated another race with the cops. Ace pocketed his babies and scooted over. Eddy got in. Calmly shut the door. Clarice popped the clutch, chirping the Mickey Thompsons in the hard packed sand, resisting the urge to open up the throttle, steered around an oak tree, sliding sideways up on the road, and decided to take the scenic route next to the bay. Checked the mirrors again. No cops.

Dammit. Maybe next time…

A cool salty breeze filled the interior and seemed to force the three of them to relax. Eddy sighed. "Well. That was my cardio exercise for the week. I'm getting a little old to be pulling jobs like this."

"But you're so good at it," Clarice said, glancing at him with a quick grin. Clarice noticed him look at her missing tooth again, yet he still neglected comment. And she loved him for it.

He grinned back. "True. Odd to hear you condoning my illicit talents, but no less true. Here." He tossed their IDs to them.

"What was that head-hitting-a-wall sound?" Ace asked.

Eddy looked at him. "That was a head hitting a wall. I had to knock somebody out."

"You punched an innocent person?" Clarice exclaimed.

"No! There was a guy sleeping on a bench. He woke up when they called his number. While he yawned and stretched, I looked around to make sure no one was paying attention, then smashed him into the wall with a shoulder." Clarice looked at his choice of weapon and winced at the huge slab of muscle that must have crushed the man. Eddy shook his head, continued. "I made it look like I was catching his fall. His chest compressed. Because he had been sleeping, circulation to his head wasn't very good. You know how that feels. He passed out, and I screamed bloody murder."

"He hit his head," Clarice said frowning. "It sounded like a rap song bass note."

"It wasn't that hard," he argued. "I got the job done, didn't I?"

Clarice looked down at her new ID. Anastasia. Hmm. It was a pretty name. She could get used to that. "Yes you did. Thank you." Clarice looked at Eddy again as a thought burned for an explanation. "Fire alarm?" she asked.

"Skills," the old guy bragged.

Clarice sighed. "Good enough for me."

"Where to next?" Ace said.

Clarice looked at her hands on the wheel, fingernails filthy and chipped, one swollen and purple. At her face in the mirror, scabbed and peppered with small bruises, hair oily and oh-so-ugly. Clarice could smell the grime and old sweat sticking to ev-

488

ery inch of her body, and suddenly felt embarrassed. Disgusted with herself, angrily so. She showed her husband an expression that made him flinch.

"I still have to freaking go pee," she told him.

"Oh." He held up an empty Gatorade bottle, waggled it with a stupid grin. "Porta-potty," he said.

Eddy added his two-cents. "I'll sing Pavarotti to cover the noise, darlin'."

Clarice growled. They laughed.

They needed to get away from Biloxi, and since Jimmy and Hector lived in Ocean Springs, Clarice headed in that direction. A quick jaunt down Interstate 10 and Highway 90 and they pulled into Wal-Mart's parking lot. Found a spot close to the road in case they needed to leave quickly and parked Camino. Killed the beast and looked at her guys. "Where are those towelettes?" Clarice asked. "I'm going to clean up and put on some makeup so nobody thinks I've been battered by my old man."

"Heh. Like I could even hit you," Ace mused.

Eddy smiled at that. "You'd certainly have to pack a lunch if you ever tried." He handed her a large stack of hand wipe packets.

"We don't need to be seen together," Clarice told Ace. "I'll be back."

"Yes dear."

She walked into the store feeling like a hobo. The nice little old lady that greeted customers at the door put a hand to her chest and appraised her ragamuffin appearance. She wanted to ask her to leave. The vagabond feeling intensified. Clarice ignored her and the urge to reassure the store executives that she had money.

She walked with affected purpose to the hygiene section. Grabbed a small bottle of Pantene shampoo. Deodorant. Toothbrushes. And Colgate whitening toothpaste. She remembered seeing the commercial for this stuff from prison and couldn't wait to try it. Her poor teeth had suffered through two years of generic prison-issue garbage, and it showed. A lap through the makeup section to grab foundation, powder, and some lip gloss was like walking into a tractor beam. Some kind of artificial super-gravity tried to hold her there. It was really hard to just stroll away from that Cover Girl and Maybelline heaven, the hardest part being to forego mascara and eye liner. But Lord knows she didn't need black streaks running down her face or into her eyes during the upcoming mission. Sighing with regret, she hurried to the clothes section before her larcenous hands betrayed her and she started pocketing eyelash volumizers.

The sight of blue jeans cheered her considerably. They were cheap brands, but jeans were jeans, really, and her legs and booty ached to feel denim again. She found a pair that wouldn't quite cut off her circulation, found a butch pair for Ace. Headed to the shoes. Grabbed a pair of low-quality sneakers, green and pink, that looked like $200 Nikes compared to the Barker's Bitch Chicks Clarice had on. Found a manly pair for Ace. Some socks and underwear, as well. T-shirts. Fast-walked to the checkout counter.

"Hi," the cashier said, a pleasant twenty-something girl with short brown hair and glasses.

"Hello," Clarice said.

She tried not to look at her too hard, but couldn't help a furtive glance and comment. "Rough night?" she said.

"Yeah." Clarice waved a hand. " I escaped prison. Beat up a cop and stole his car. Then I had to out-run three highway patrolmen, making them crash so I could get away. My husband and I celebrated with hours of sex in the police car afterwards." Clarice sighed dramatically. "Rough hardly describes it."

She laughed loudly. "Sounds like someone has been playing Grand Theft Auto." She handed her the change. "Have a nice day. Try not to hurt any more cops," she tittered.

"I'll try, but I won't make any promises." The girl giggled again. Clarice waved and headed to the re-stroom.

Well, it's official. I'm going to create my own video game.

Squatting down to peek under the restroom stalls, Clarice determined the room was empty. Locked the door. Hurried to a toilet and cleaned the seat with a hand wipe. Plopped down, groaning with a mix-ture of pain and relief, peeing so loudly she became worried other shoppers could hear it. The alleviation was dizzying, pleasurable, and she wanted to sit there for a year or two and write a poem about it - *TMI* - for her admiring audience, but instead she got up and went to the sinks. Stripped off everything and scrubbed down with one towelette after another. She thought about just hanging her ass over the sink, but changed her mind when she looked in it more closely.

Ugh. It looked worse than a prison sink.

Dressed in jeans, fresh underwear, socks and shoes, Clarice washed her hair, enjoying another wave of pleasurable alleviation. Dried it with the sweat pants. Finger combed it into a ponytail. Put on a shirt, a white Hanes.

The foundation swirled on smoothly, covering the abrasions and contusions. A dabble of powder blended it all together, giving the pigment a more natural tone. A touch of some deodorant on her hairy pits, some lip gloss on her kisser, and Clarice felt like a woman again. She smiled in the mirror. Flipped the bird at her gapped grill and brushed her teeth. Trashed the institutional shoes and underwear on the way out.

Good riddance Bob, you sadistic goat. Her hair, teeth, boobs, butt, and feet won't miss you.

The parking lot was sparse, and Camino's beauty could be clearly seen at the perimeter, the red and gray paint and polished wheels sparkling as though her love was the winner of a car show. Her hips swayed a little more than was proper and she picked up the pace, eager to get back behind the wheel, plastic bag in her good hand crinkling faster, bumping her leg.

A large Rent-a-Center moving truck was creeping past her ride, the driver probably drooling over Camino's boss presence. The truck rolled by and a scene from her nightmares appeared behind it. Ace, Eddy, and two cops were rolling on the ground in a death struggle, grunting, cursing, grinding elbows into the gravel and fists into each other. The cops tried desperately to get them into academy-trained choke holds. A goddamn Fugitives vs. Police MMA matchup.

Oh. My. God.

How did they find them so fast?

Clarice dropped the bag and sprinted across the parking area, nearly colliding with a car that, fortunately, had a driver with enough awareness to hit the brakes. Weaved through a pair of ugly-ass Toyota Priuses, hurdled the hood of a Cadillac and did her damnedest to kick the head off the shoulders of the cop pinning her husband down.

The field goal kick wasn't how Clarice planned on breaking in her new shoes. They certainly sustained some wear as Clarice put on a burst of speed and struck the man in his cheek, shoe compressing, bending her toes back, ball of her foot plunging deep into his face.

Whop!

The prick in blue hollered in surprised pain, losing control of his hands, rolling as Ace shoved him over, climbed on top and began raining blows on the cop, skinny arms a windmill as he yelled a battle cry.

In the seconds it took all this to happen Clarice recognized the chubby face of Hector Valesquez, the SOB they were after. A quick look at the huge turd

Eddy was wailing on told her it was Jimmy Wallace, SOB #2. It was freaky.

It was scary.

They found us. Here. How?

Clarice grabbed her wet hair and looked around in a panic for the backup they surely had, finding none, not even their patrol car. That doesn't mean they didn't have pals on the way.

They had to go.

"Ace! Eddy! GET IN THE TRUCK!" Clarice screamed, dashing to Camino. Opened the door, jumped in, started it. One of the cops shouted something that was distorted by the loud exhaust. Her guys piled in, Clarice gunned the Snarling Darling, dumped the clutch, boiling the tires and shifting into second as they caught traction, shooting them out onto the highway. Several cars locked up their brakes, laid on their horns, swerving to avoid them. The three of them were panting, them from fighting, her from fear. Clarice kept an eye on the mirrors, eventually letting off the gas when she felt comfortable that no one was following.

Eddy said, "They tracked us somehow. It must be the phones."

"Why would the Teacher want to help us escape only to have us arrested again?" Clarice said.

Eddy thought for a minute. "I don't know. How else could they have found us?"

"I have a sophisticated program set up to deter and attack any device that attempts to track my router. No way it's mine."

They looked at her.

"I got my phone from Patty, my best friend. She had no connections to the Teacher. And there's no chance she would work with the police, especially against me."

"You sure about that?" Eddy said skeptically.

"No. I'm positive." Clarice scowled at him.

"Let me see it," Ace said. He grabbed her phone from the console under him, removed the battery so he could read the IMEI and SIM numbers. Powered on his iPod and Mi-Fi. Clarice glanced at the touch-screen a few minutes later and saw he was hacking into some aspect of the Verizon network, searching for signs of a trace.

"It's been compromised," he said quietly, not looking at her.

"Uh-uh. No way Patty would turn against me," Clarice argued.

"Well, she did, Shock," Eddy said bluntly, his tone suggesting he'd been around long enough to not be surprised by a friend's betrayal. He grabbed the phone, tossed it out the window.

Patty...How could you? What did you get out of it?

The highway's intersections were filling with rush hour traffic, slowing them to a crawl. And Clarice was glad. She no longer had the focus for driving fast.

She was sick to her stomach.

* * *

Jimmy raged at his three foes escaping in the hot rod. "You can't run from me!" He coughed several times, ears vibrating painfully from the bellowing exhaust so close to his battered head. "I'll get you!" he promised.

The El Camino raced away with a booming roar, tires burning, squealing for traction as it zipped out of the parking lot onto the highway, brakes and horns blaring from other motorists. The two patrolmen stood up on cramped legs, arms shaky, drained of energy, breathing ragged from fighting with the fugitives.

Hector wobbled, held his arms out for balance, fighting vertigo and nausea. "Jimmy, I think I have a concussion." He held a hand to his jaw, gently pushing on the swollen cheek. Winced at the pressure building in his throbbing head. "She kicked me in the face. Hard."

Jimmy looked at him, coughed. "Yeah, you don't look so good." He felt his own jaw, wondering how the hell he was still conscious after that man had bludgeoned him with sledgehammer fists. *I knew I could take a punch*, he thought. *But those were fucking mule kicks.*

He rubbed the back of his neck, regretting having left his taser in the car. Made a mental note to stop and purchase some Tylenol.

"What do we do now?" Hector said.

Jimmy looked in the direction the El Camino had gone. "We track them. As long as they have that phone, we can follow them."

"I don't think it's a good idea to try and capture them like that again," Hector said, limping after Jimmy, heading back to their patrol car parked on the other side of the store. Several vehicles passed them, Wal-Mart customers and kids staring at the two policemen who had obviously just been in a bad fight. "Tell me again why we did that?"

Jimmy glared at him and accused, "You screwed that up, not me."

"Hey! You said to grab the skinny one. I did that. How did I screw that up?"

"You were supposed to cuff him then help me with the big one."

"The girl showed up and kicked me!" Hector argued, becoming upset, head pounding sickeningly. "I'm hurt."

"Yeah, well, you should have been faster. None of this would have happened."

"That guy was stronger than when we arrested him two years ago, Jimmy. And that other guy, whoever he was, fought like a professional. We didn't have a chance. Why can't you admit it was a bad idea?"

Jimmy stopped and stuck a finger in Hector's face. "It was a good idea! You fucked it up. I don't have bad ideas, Hector." He grumbled unintelligibly, rubbed his neck, started walking away from his intimidated partner.

We'll just shoot those motherfuckers on sight next time.

He had planned on capturing the couple and inter-
rogating them, make sure they haven't done or said
anything that would harm him. All this time they had
been in prison, he had worried their case would be
overturned, some unforeseen evidence popping up
to free them and bust him and Hector. *Killing and
burying them would nip that in the bud, though*, he
thought, smiling.

He looked at Hector, thinking how sad it was that
he couldn't tell his only friend and partner what he
planned to do because the man was too weak to handle it. The gutless man was still seeing a nut doctor
from when they killed that greaser Jose years ago.

Sad. He grumbled again.

They made it to the cruiser. Got in, groaning stiffly.
Drove around the store and turned west on the highway.

"Can we call it in now?" Hector said from the passenger seat, a note of pleading in his voice.

"Hell no. We're not even in our jurisdiction. I told
you. We catch them and keep it quiet. This is personal."

"Whatever you say, Jimmy," he replied miserably.

This was a monumentally bad idea, Hector thought.
*I should have reported the fugitives as soon as they
spotted them, had the entire force surround them, send
them back to prison.* He looked at Jimmy. *Where
they'll be safe from you*, he thought in dismay.

Why did Jimmy want to catch them anyway?
It couldn't be good, whatever the reason. Jimmy's

gung-ho, take-it-personal approach was going to get them in serious trouble. Get more people hurt.

That girl and her husband haven't done anything to us. We screwed them. How could he get that twisted? Why?

Hector shook his head, regretting it, groaning as pain swamped him, making him dizzy again.

"Are you checking the signal? Where are they?" Jimmy demanded.

Hector checked the computer screen on the dashboard, which showed a map of Ocean Springs and a red dot for the location of Clarice Carter's phone. He said, "We just passed it."

Jimmy's head whipped around, searching for the El Camino. "Fuck, fuck! They figured it out and tossed the phone. Fuck!" He gave a frustrated cough, pulled out an inhaler. Took several puffs. Slammed his fists on the steering wheel.

Hector said timidly, "So that's it, I guess. Can we let this go? We tried, Jimmy."

Jimmy glared. "Not yet. Patty Sullivan knows more. We only had to threaten her kid and she told us about the phone. If we take her kid, she'll tell us more." He coughed, puffed on the inhaler, eyes darkening on his pale face. "Oh, yeah. She'll tell us. She knows where her friend is going. Women tell each other everything. Especially women prisoners."

"You want to kidnap her daughter?! *Madre de dios,*" he nearly whimpered. He crossed himself, said a prayer for the girl, knowing it was futile to try and dissuade his psychotic partner. He couldn't believe how far out of hand this situation had become, and he hoped to God the girl wouldn't get hurt.

He leaned his head against the door, listening to it pound a millisecond after his aching heart.

Chapter XXIV

"…And I couldn't get my handcuffs off because I had to swallow the key. So when I got out of the van and this slab of meat," Ace jerked a thumb at Bobby, "saw I was still in restraints, he just walked up like a stereotypical robber and asked the officers escorting me for a light. He hit them with, what do you call these?" He held his arm up horizontally and punched.

"A hook," Eddy supplied.

"He hooked both of them in the jaw before they could even answer the question." Ace looked at Bobby with exaggerated adoration, held his hands over his heart. "You're my hero."

If Bobby had lighter skin, he'd have been blushing. He remained quiet, embarrassed, heroism not being his thing.

Eddy laughed. "I love it! So he took their keys and uncuffed you. Where's the key you swallowed?"

Ace dug in the collar of his shirt, pulled out the key on a string tied around his neck. "Came out yesterday. Finally." He wiped a hand over his forehead. "Whew. Had me worried."

Clarice walked over to Bobby, hugged his neck. Kissed his cheek. "Thank you," she said simply.

This time Clarice could have sworn he had a pinkish hue.

Cool.

Clarice looked at Ace and folded her arms. *I did that, not you,* her demeanor said. She buffed her nails on her shirt.

The sound of children laughing joyously made her step outside of their tent. The Gulf Islands National Seashore Park was lush with flora and fauna, adults, kids, animals and trees flourishing vibrantly in the spring sunshine. Song birds jammed in the ancient oaks, while their raptor cousins glided on the salty winds, diving among the camp sites for left behind picnic scraps, hurrying to scavenge the morsels of potato chips and bread crumbs before raccoons grabbed them.

In the camping slot next to them, a little boy and girl of about the same age, possibly twins, chased one another around their smiling father, who stood at a barbecue grill cooking some kind of aromatic meat while keeping a watchful eye on his progeny. Clarice watched the beautiful brats with a sad smile, feeing

502

an irrational jealousy of their dad. He looked so damn content.

When would she get to see her son play like that again? Would this ordeal ever end, or would they never see another time of comfort and security?

There were no guarantees living as fugitives. No certain answers.

Tears threatening to well, she turned and strolled over to her truck. She and Bobby had executed a quick sanding job on it the day they were found by the cops. It didn't take long to cut down the glossy, lovely red and gray to its primer base, matte gray with specs of bare metal here and there. Poor Camino. It looked depressed, a feeling Clarice could relate to. The only thing that kept her frown lines from becoming permanent was knowing how much fun it was going to be to paint her baby again.

Glass half-full, and all that optimistic shit.

Opening the door, Clarice sat behind the wheel. Squirmed, sighed. Looked at her hand, which felt nearly healed wrapped in an ace bandage and splint. Even her shoulder and oblique felt mended, the duct tape having been replaced by real dressing. The week at the park had gone by with decent progress. Bobby had picked up several phones, wired extra batteries to them, and planted them on their marks' cars so Ace could monitor their movements. They had new clothes, plenty of food, and Clarice even got to enjoy some leisure time in the local nature trails with her honey. Ace was scared of birds, Clarice was scared of snakes, so their hormones were checked, severely, every time they attempted something in the woods other than hiking.

Stupid wildlife.

Still though, it was pleasant, an extraordinary experience full of sentiment, nostalgia and appreciation, a welcome contrast to the hell they had escaped from. Ace and Clarice were reinvented, they decided. New People. Therapists say married couples must reinvent themselves every few years if they want the relationship to remain strong, long-lasting. Well, now. Clarice doubted their adventure was what they had in mind, but whatever works, right?

"Shock. You need to see this. Ace thinks he found their stash spot," Eddy said, ducking back inside the huge tent.

Clarice hurried back inside their nylon fort. Ace, Eddy, and Bobby sat in lawn chairs with their arms resting on a small plastic table in the center, huddled around Ace's iPod. A car battery under the table connected to a power inverter with phone chargers and a droplight plugged into it, wires strung haphazardly, the light hanging from the center of the tent's domed ceiling.

Clarice stepped behind Ace and put her hands on his shoulders. Looked at the touchscreen and note pad in front of him. "What's up, babe?" she asked.

"Their routines are fairly consistent throughout the week," he said, flipping through his notes. "Based on the number of times they've stopped at each destination, the length of time stayed, and factoring in their relative connections to the destinations, I've formulated an equation that gives odds on where their stash -"

"No math, please. Just the results," Clarice said, patting his arm.

He dropped his head momentarily in disappointment, sighed. "Oh, all right." He closed the note pad and said, "I mapped their patrol route. They leave their homes, report to the station, hit their beat, then back to the station before going home again. That's most days. However, twice this week their route changed. They traveled the entire length of Harrison County from the southwest corner to the northeast corner, way out of their jurisdiction."

"That must be to escort traffickers," Eddy thought out loud.

Ace nodded. "On both occasions, after they returned to the station for quitting time, they didn't go home. They went to this address here." He pointed at the screen, showing them a point on a street map of Fontainebleau, an area right outside of Ocean Springs' city limits, on the Gulf. Google Earth showed the address to be a small house trailer.

"Did you find out who owns it?" Clarice said.

"Yeah. Lindsey Slater."

"Is she connected to them?" Eddy said.

"Nope," Ace said confidently.

"How do you know that, breadstick?" Bobby rumbled.

Ace looked at his friend, radiating a smart-ass grin. "Because my geek Kung-fu is strong, you meathead. I hacked into the bank and real estate databases associated with the trailer and property. That should have led to all sorts of info about Ms. Slater. Bank accounts, social security number, job, et cetera." He looked up at her. "Lindsey Slater doesn't exist."

Clarice grinned and kissed his upturned face. "Those idiots weren't slick enough for my man."

"You're my hero," Bobby gushed, hands to his heart. He stood and crushed Ace and Clarice in a hug. Eddy whooped out laughter, voicing the positive excitement they all felt.

"Gentleman," Clarice said after Bobby allowed her to breathe again. "Let's get us some payback."

"Literally," Ace said.

Eddy stood and shadowboxed a few combos. His underbite jutted out wickedly. "Let's do it."

* * *

Camino roared down Beachview Boulevard, the main road leading into a huge neighborhood called Gulf Park Estates. Ace, in the passenger seat, kept checking his iPod's GPS app to make sure their cop buddies were still elsewhere.

"We're good," he said. "They are on this side of the bridge, but that's just for their lunch break. They'll be back on their beat in thirty minutes."

Clarice nodded, glanced at the rearview mirror. Eddy and Bobby were following them, the Toyota's V6 straining to keep up with her 580 hp. Grinning, she opened up the throttle a little more, blasting by the rows of houses fast enough to shake the trees, flowing over the lovely hills that made up the

506

road, legs tingling after each crest, stomach dropping thrillingly.

A bridge and marina appeared up ahead and she slowed. The dank, muddy stench of a bayou at low tide pervaded the truck, reminding her of the first night back together with her husband in the stolen police car near the marsh. To her, it was the scent of victory, of perseverance, the fierce desire to fight for their right to life and happiness, freedom. And she'd forevermore associate the smell with romance reunited. Not that she'd go out and search for a bayou mud perfume, mind you, but she'd been seriously considering buying a place near the marsh.

Do they have bayous in Brazil?

"Take the next left," her navigator said as they rolled over the bridge.

"Crap," Clarice muttered. The turn was immediately after the bridge, and she was still going entirely too fast. Downshifting quickly, she hit the brakes, mind connecting to the machine like it was another appendage, visualizing the huge Brembo calipers clamping the carbon fiber pads on the vented rotors, the instant friction hot enough to make the steel glow orange. Shifted into second, let off the brake and got back into the throttle, earning a squeak from Ace as she took the turn with the hope that no other cars happened to be there. It was incredibly stupid on her part, though Camino didn't mind a bit, his NASCAR-like suspension a fiend for such maneuvers. They roared sideways, her grinning, Ace ululating, and were off like a rocket down some road called Simmons' Bayou. Eddy's truck turned in behind them at a more sensible speed.

As advertised, the street twisted and turned right alongside of a narrow bayou. House trailers prevailed throughout the area, with tall pines and numerous types of hardwoods in full bloom somehow making the little trailers seem more homely than Clarice would have imagined.

"That's it. Pull in there," Ace said, pointing at a lot on their left.

She turned into the gravel driveway. Parked. Got out. The trailer was smaller than the others, maybe two bedrooms. Brown and white. Overgrown grass and weeds around the wheels under the home and on the quarter-acre lot indicated that no one lived here. No cars, no shed or items in the yard. Not even a single old flower pot. No life.

Lazy, sorry-ass cops. The neighbors should complain.

Eddy and Bobby pulled in, got out and walked up to them, both of them scanning the other residences for signs of being watched.

"Looks okay," Eddy stated cautiously. "Let's take a peek." He had a crowbar in his hand, holding it with a familiarity that didn't surprise her in the least. The trailer's door was locked. It took less than a second for Eddy to wrench it open with the tool, the thin metal protesting like a scream suddenly cut off. They all looked around prudently. No one appeared at their windows or challenged them. They walked inside.

"It's empty," Clarice said, looking around at the thin carpet and cheap paneled walls, brown and white like the exterior. Stale air and mold offended her senses as she walked into the kitchen/dining area, began searching through the cabinets, finding only several large rolls of plastic wrap and clear tape.

"Appearances can be deceptive," Professor Eddy lectured. He hefted the crowbar, stepped to the far wall in the living room, and, after only a brief inspection of the panels, stabbed the tool into a seam, popping the thin wood loose with ease. He snatched the entire section off, the tiny nails ripping out of the studs with mouse squeals, cracking the panels. In between two studs from the floor to the ceiling were stacked bundles of cash wrapped in plastic. "Who's your daddy?" Eddy told the money.

Her eyes bugged out. That was too easy. "How'd you know to look there?" Clarice said.

"Skills," he boasted, then gave in to her imperative look. "There were scratches on that seam. The other seams were smooth." He shrugged. "Hiding money in the walls of a trailer is nothing new. It's overdone if you ask me. Cliché." He grabbed a bundle, trying to peer inside the plastic. Unable to see the money clearly, he bobbed his hand up and down, weighing it. "Fifty K stacks," he pronounced with surety.

"Nice," Bobby said.

"Holy crap," Ace mumbled. Clarice just smiled.

The mountain of treasure held them spellbound for an undetermined amount of time, each of them sorting through various fantasies they planned to indulge with their newfound wealth.

Ace brought them back to reality. "Uh," he said, looking at the iPod. "Guys, they're coming. Fast."

"What?" Bobby exclaimed, moving to look at the touchscreen. "They must have had a silent alarm."

Ace nodded, went to the busted entry and studied the doorway. "There's a magnetic sensor imbedded in the lock plate," he informed them.

"How much time do we have?" Clarice said, knowing he could extrapolate an accurate window for them. Eddy and Clarice began digging the money out. Clarice piled it in his arms like firewood. He carried it out to his truck.

"Maybe five minutes," Ace said warily. "They're really moving."

"Five?! Dammit!" Clarice cursed, turned and tore the money out of the wall, twisting around to stack it onto Bobby's arms.

"I should have anticipated an alarm. Duh," Ace said apologetically.

"Stop being a sorry motherfucker and help!" Clarice yelled, throwing several plastic bricks at him. He fumbled her passes, picked them up and hurried outside.

After six armloads, the stack was only halfway gone. They needed another three minutes, at least, to get it all loaded in the truck. "We're not gonna make it," Clarice told Eddy as she filled his arms again.

"Yes we will," he replied. "Tell Bobby to drive my truck. I'll keep them busy while you guys finish. Circle around and pick me up on Beachview, at the marina." He ran outside, spilling several bundles on the way down the steps. Ace picked them up, ran after him.

Anxiety filling her, Clarice looked out the door, planning to tell her coach to just forget it. They'd take what they had and leave. Eddy, digging in the tool box in the bed of his truck, pulled out a shotgun, bulletproof vest, and took off running down the street. "What are you going to do?" Clarice hollered after him.

"Just get it loaded and meet me at the docks!" the stubborn bastard yelled back.

Bobby and Ace rushed back inside and the three of them divided up what was left. Stumbled out to the Toyota, stuffing the cash behind the seats. The king cab was completely filled, the bundles towering over the headrests, brimming over between the seats, random stacks like giant fallen dominoes on the console and passenger seat.

Before they could pile in the last of it, the distinct sound of a Ford Interceptor engine froze them in their tracks, racing around the curves of the neighborhood, tires protesting angrily to show the mood of the cops headed in their direction.

Clarice ran out to the street like a big dummy. "Where's Eddy?"

Her question was answered by a shotgun going off like a bomb on the quiet road, the explosion echoing out over the wide marsh, followed by a car crashing just as loudly. A few seconds later a gun fight broke out, two pistols popping like fireworks compared to Eddy's booming shotgun blasts. The instant war zone scared the bejesus out of Clarice. One gun shooting at her was a rush. But two held by pissed-off cops that knew they were being robbed for millions?

Clarice decided Eddy's plan was fine.

"Let's go! Bobby, take Eddy's truck. We have to circle around to the main road and wait for him at the marina," Clarice said, jumping into Camino's pilot seat.

"You're the boss," Bobby agreed, already in the truck.

They drove through the maze of streets, dodging dogs, slowing for kids, trying not to stare with dumbfoundment, and an odd admiration, at the redneck yards filled with old project cars, trucks, and junk. Made it to the main road and sped to the marina, pulling over in the parking lot of what looked like a store that had been washed away, the foundation the only thing left.

Clarice stared at the mirrors, waiting for Eddy to come trotting over the bridge. "Please, please, please," Clarice prayed. "Come on, Coach."

"There he is!" Ace said, pointing to their right.

Clarice looked over to see the old man limping out of the marsh, soaking wet, gun in one hand, bulletproof vest strapped over his enormous torso like a child's life preserver. Apparently, he had foregone the convenience of the bridge for a refreshing swim across the bayou. It had psyched her out - and no doubt did the same to the crooked piggies.

Eddy lumbered over to her window, wet shoe prints trailing across the street and parking area.

512

Squished to a stop. "Hey," he gasped, breathing laboriously.

"Hey yourself," Clarice said smiling.

"Did I ever tell you I'm too old to be pulling jobs like this?"

"Sounds familiar, yeah."

"Well darlin', I take that back. I'm not too old; I'm too archaic. That run and swim nearly killed me." He gasped, leaned on her door.

Bobby drove up next to Eddy, opened the passenger door. "Need a ride, stranger?" he said.

Eddy turned to look at him, back to her and Ace. "Sure. But if any of you claim I'm your hero, I'm breaking your ribs."

They laughed. He got in the truck. And gunfire opened up on them.

The unexpected assault of bullets ricocheted all around them, dislodged rocks from the lot and peppered their tires and undercarriages. Clarice shifted into first with a shaking hand and stomped the gas, zooming out onto the road, stealing a quick look at the rearview. Hector stood at the center of the bridge, Jimmy several yards behind, kneeling down, both pointing their weapons at them while putting in new clips of ammo.

As Clarice took the first right to get out of the line of fire, a fresh barrage lit up the street around them, bullets whining this way and that like the sound effects in a John Wayne movie, a single slug pelting into Camino's tailgate.

Pwack!

Clarice felt it through the wheel, through the shifter and pedals, as though a part of her had been hit.

"Those fuckers shot Camino!" Clarice raged, shifting gears hard, turning left to circle back to Beachview.

Ace looked like he wanted to say something to comfort her, but couldn't overcome his need to stare at the road, hold on for dear life, and accentuate her mad woman maneuvers with effeminate cries of fear. What her man didn't know was his cute, anxious shouts were all the comfort Clarice needed.

Clarice whipped Camino back onto the main road at ludicrous speed. Ace squealed and gasped. Clarice felt better already.

Bobby gave the Toyota hell, actually keeping up. Clarice guessed that Eddy was cursing his driving skills while dodging bundles of money being flung all over the cab.

Bundles of money...

They'd done it. They got their ass! It was a dream come true, sweet justice.

Score one for the Good Guys! Well. Sort of good.

The Gulf Islands Park wasn't far. As they turned into their campsite the rush of surviving the dozens of bullets fired at them was displaced by another, more pleasant effect of adrenal overload: Knowing that they beat their enemies in the worst possible way. They took from them the very foundation of their corruption, the carrot that motivated their jackass personalities. There's no telling how many years of illicit, bloody, immoral danger they had suffered through to get that much cash. Clarice wished she could see their faces when they saw that big hole in the wall where all their twisted dreams used to be, knowing who took it and why.

Hell, I'd trade the cash to voyeur such priceless expressions.

Clarice giggled and clapped.

Ace felt it, too. "Celebration to come!" he gloated.

* * *

The trailer door was wide open. The metal around the knob and deadbolt were as warped and torn as the lock plate. A mockingbird landed on the roof, staring down at the two cops with a curious condescension that did justice to its name. Jimmy and Hector stared at the damage, at the magnetic sensor that had triggered a useless alert to their cellphones. Wordlessly, they walked inside, lacking sensation, knowing what they would see, unable to fully process the ramifications just now. Stopped in front of the gaping maw that had been their safe, now raped and devoid of their hard-earned fortune.

Fury, black and malevolent, challenged Jimmy's beta-blockers. "That cunt," he spat hotly.

"Yeah," Hector agreed numbly. He stared at the hole that had contained his dreams, his family's dreams, eyes unfocused. Lost.

Jimmy looked around the floor with jerky movements. Stuck his head outside to search around the steps, through the tall weeds, hoping to find a plastic bundle, at least one, that had been dropped in haste.

No luck.

"That cunt," he cursed again.

"We have to go, Jimmy." Hector shook his head, the consequences of their wrecked patrol car and shootout sinking in. His hands shook with his voice. "Did you hear me? We have to go! The Sheriff's Department will be here any minute."

"Shut up, shut up!" He coughed. "I know that. Let me think." He stomped around the living room at an awkward pace, his weight booming on the hollow trailer floor. He said, "We'll have to take a car from one of these trailer trash idiots around here. Then we have to figure out where that cunt and her fuck buddies went."

Hector's eyes watered. He didn't want to go after them, didn't care about that filthy, life-ruining money anymore. But he also didn't want to flee to Mexico broke, a criminal and fugitive without resources, knowing this was probably a best case scenario after this mess. He closed his eyes, tears streaming silently, afraid for his family's future without that money, afraid for the little girl Jimmy had taken from a school playground, who must be cold and hungry and scared in that tiny room...

He looked up at Jimmy and whimpered, "Can we please let the girl go? It's over, Jimmy."

"No!" he roared, turning and shoving Hector into a wall with a crash, caving it in. He grabbed Hector's collar with both hands, banged his head on

516

the wooden panel, his wheezing breath hot as he growled, "It's not over yet, Hector. Oh, no. This game is just getting interesting."

"But Patty didn't know anything. She tried," he whispered in terror, bladder threatening to void. "You said you'd let her go if Patty talked. She tried, Jimmy. She told us everything she knew."

"Fuck her and the kid! They're trash. Unimportant. What matters is finding Clarice Carter." He let go, paced again. "This is end-game, Hector. Us against Everybody. We won't be able to explain the car crash and shootout. Traffic cameras will show us racing through Ocean Springs, out of their jurisdiction, in pursuit of nothing. Dispatch wasn't notified. We'll be prosecuted if we go home or to the station, which means we can't report the El Camino and Toyota to get help finding them. And that wouldn't work anyway, because one of those goddamn trucks is full or our cash!" he ranted, pointing a finger at his co-conspirator. "That's our money! I'll be damned if BPD confiscates it. Fuck them." He raked his fingers through his thinning hair. "We'll get the cash and head to El Maestro's place in Juarez."

"But where are they, Jimmy? We can't just Google her. How are we going to find them without BPD resources?"

"Google her?!" he stormed, face changing shades of red, purple. "I'll bend her over and Yahoo! the cunt. The solution is simple."

"It is?" Hector said meekly, his whole body shaking.

"Yes. We took the wrong kid. When we went through the Carter's file the other day, I saw a report that said they have a son. He lives with the cunt's parents."

"Santa Maria," Hector breathed when he realized what Jimmy meant.

Jimmy grinned unpleasantly. "Patty's daughter will have a playmate soon. That should make you happy. Let's go."

As they walked out of the yard, a small yellow station wagon pulled up to the driveway, window rolling down. A bird-like lady with snow white hair in curlers and coke bottle glasses looked at the policemen with sincere concern. "You boys okay?" she said. "That was some wreck back there. Heard a lot of gunfire, too."

"We're great, just great," Jimmy said, coughing. He opened her door. Grabbed her shoulder with one huge hand, leaned over and unbuckled her seatbelt with the other. Jerked her out of the car.

She fell on her hip, crying out in pain. "What?! OH-ahh!" she shrieked, curling up in a fetal position.

Jimmy shoved Hector around the front of the car. "Get in. We don't have much time."

Hector stumbled around the vehicle they were carjacking. Opened the door. He looked over the roof at the poor old woman. "I'm sorry, ma'am," he said lamely, getting into the passenger seat.

The petite lady, pride hurt more than anything else, managed to sit up. Her lips twisted in anger.

She flipped them off. "Fuck you!" she screeched at the crooked bastards as they sped off in her new Subaru.

Chapter XXV

Ocean Springs – Vancleave, Mississippi
April 13, 2012

It was 4:00 a.m. and her husband sang an oldie to her with comely ugliness.

"Even though we ain't got money / I'm so in love with you honey," the idiot crooned.

Clarice blushed. "You're drunk," She told him when her love-distressed brain started working again. "Swear to God. We do have money."

"That's true," he said, agreeing on both accounts, drinking straight from a bottle of champagne. He gave her a stupid, lopsided grin and slurred, "If you do a strip tease, I'll decorate your panties with Benjamins."

Tittering, Clarice said, "You left 'drunk' in the rearview mirror, pal. Plastered is the avenue your inebriated ass is driving on now." Clarice pointed up to the drop light, dimmed by her underwear wrapped around it, hundred dollar bills sticking out like leaves on a hanging plant. "We already did the strip tease."

He blinked, remembered and smiled again. This dude could not hold his alcohol. "Superrrb," he declared. He twirled the bottle over his head and tried a sexy, conspiratorial voice. "Then this must be the VIP Room." He reached for his fantasy stripper and fell over, tent floor rustling.

"Must be," Clarice laughed. Leaning back on their pallet of blankets, Clarice checked her watch again, a cheap lady's Timex Eddy had picked up for her along with various other commodities, including the wine that gave Ace memory lapses and her teenage giddiness, before he and Bobby left to attend to their personal agendas.

Clarice glanced at a stack of newspapers on the table. They had their mug shots all over the front pages, of course, but were deficient in pics of their accomplices. The authorities, by some stroke of auspicion, had been unable to identify Eddy and Bobby. None of them were sure if that would last, so Ace kept monitoring the law enforcement databases so he could intercept any information some helpy-helperton citizen may provide that could lead to their arrest. So far, he hadn't had to erase a single tip; the tips listed weren't accurate. Eddy's omerta code wouldn't allow him to admit it, but Clarice suspected the Italians in Biloxi made sure the business owners and patrons around the area of their escape kept their mouths shut.

Connections rock. Even criminal ones. Who the hell am I to judge? That ship has sailed, people.

"Hey," Ace said, poking her with his foot, nearly falling over again. "Did you meet any Sisters in there?"

"Yeah. You too, huh?" Clarice sighed. "I swear, the first day I walked on the zone, a group of hard core lesbians mean-mugged me while *Welcome to the Jungle* played in the background."

"Me too!" he exclaimed. It came out as meee toooo! He hiccupped.

"You were sized-up by lesbians?"

"Uh-huh." He thought hard for a minute. "Well. They were gay and wore panties and makeup. They looked like lesbians. And they were Sisters. So, same thing, right?" Hiccup. "All very confusing to me."

Clarice laughed then smooched his cheek. "How about some music?"

"Sure."

Setting down the bottle, he crawled to the back of the tent, his bony naked ass pointed at her, inciting a giggle attack. Grabbed his iPod off the table. Ten seconds later *Barracuda* by Heart rocked the tiny speakers, filling the tent with surprisingly crisp sound. The bass and full-range projected clearly because of the stillness of the park outside. He crawled back to the champagne, took it in both hands and finished off the bottle. Burped. With a sloppy smile, he looked at her and said, "Hey. This could be your theme song."

"Right. I'll need one for my video game."

"Video-deo game?" Hiccup.

"Yep. It's gonna start out with this chick, whose addicted to electric shock, gets set up by two crooked cops and goes to prison. She fights a bunch of COs, then gets involved in a fight ring to win money. She'll do a few tatts for variety. Gets cut by a psycho, loses a tooth. Kills a prisoner or two. Then, for the final level, she'll escape to get revenge on the cops and reunite her family," Clarice concluded, the idea going from a joke to a potentially serious venture. Clarice frowned. "I'll call it, *Shocking Circumstances.*"

"Nice," he slurred. He looked at her seriously, trying in vain to keep his eyes focused. "And I will buy a copy and play it," he promised.

Clarice beamed at him.

"Since you have a million dollar" - hiccup - "future in the gaming industry, you would be wise to consult a master of the craft."

"You want to bring Nolan here?" Just saying his name got her really excited. Damn, Clarice missed him, and would love to hear the little dude lecture her about games.

"Yeaaah." Hiccup. "Superconductor, yeah."

Clarice pursed her lips, looked at her watch. "I bet my dad is up already. I could ask him to bring Nolan for an hour and leave before sunrise. Can you take the tap off his phone?" Clarice inquired, knowing the U.S. Marshalls would be monitoring every house and phone connected to them escapees, especially her parents' place.

Ace gave her his signature please look. "You insult me, my dear."

Clarice thought for a moment. Her dad would have to drive around to see if he had a tail, then park and catch a cab to their hideout. It wouldn't take long, and Clarice had faith he could pull it off; he'd want to make up for the phone smuggling debacle.

Feeling a rush and light-headedness that had nothing to do with the champagne bubbling in her tummy, she nodded to him. "Do it."

Her face was going to be smile-sore again, but for a good, non-tooth-missing reason.

Weeee!

Twenty minutes later, beginning to feel impatient, Clarice told her unusually slow geek hubby, "You should be arrested for drunk hacking."

"I know. I'm sorry. My thumbs won't cooperate. Keep pushing the wrong keys." He held up a finger, which wobbled like the rest of him. "Never fear, dear. I shall prevail."

By some virtual magic, he isolated her dad's cellphone GPS signal, linking it to a program that blocked the feds from using their own triangulation programs, then connected her dad's number to an Internet phone service Ace had set up with voice encryption.

"Done," he boasted, attempting to twirl the iPod like a six-shooter and holster it. He dropped it, stared at his electronic weapon. He murmured, "HUI."

Hacking Under the Influence. Adorkable.

Clarice grabbed the device from him, put the earbuds in and dialed her father's number for the first time in years.

He answered after the first ring. "Yes?" he said shakily, a tone Clarice remembered hearing after he and Mother had been arguing.

Attempting to assuage his mood, Clarice loaded up some sweet daughterly love. "Hi, Daddy!" Clarice gushed.

"Clarice!" He sobbed. "My Lord, it's Clarice," he said to, presumably, her mother. Sniffed. Spoke to her again. "You must know. I'm terribly sorry, honey. We could do nothing to stop them."

A really horrible feeling, as big as an elephant, sat its tonnage on her chest. "Know what? Stop who?" Clarice said slowly. Ace picked up on her mood immediately, looked at her without crossing his eyes. Clarice said, "What happened, Daddy? Are you and Mom okay? Where's Nolan?"

"They took him," he whispered, and Clarice knew exactly who he meant. He sobbed again, her mother doing the same in the background.

The jubilant, warm atmosphere in their tent became cold and dark in a span of seconds. Her broken hand was the first to start shaking. Then her arms, legs. Her voice quavered as she looked at her husband, the father of their kidnapped son, and informed him, "They took Nolan."

Ace's face flushed a deep red, heart beating visibly at his neck, lurching in anger. Fear pushed the alcohol out of his system. With a pained, sober look he whispered, "My son..." He stared off into space, analytical mind automatically racing through possibilities for a solution.

Clarice focused on the phone again, a smoldering anger overcoming her fear, giving her resolve. She took a deep breath and felt a monstrous influx of energy. Pure, raw maternal instinct, empowering her with the strength to lift a car or break through walls to rescue her child. The iPod's case cracked in her crushing grip. "Tell me everything that happened," she growled.

The phone made a noise like it changed hands and her Mom said, "It was those policeman that arrested you. I wasn't sure at first, but remembered them after they had left." She paused, struggling for composure. "They came here in uniform like they were working on a case, and claimed Nolan may have witnessed a crime his teacher did at school. I wanted to help, of course, so I went to get him. When Nolan walked to the door, they just… just took him."

She let out the most pitiful wail Clarice had ever heard, renewing her own river of tears. She wasn't in any shape to be methodical, to retell the incident with clarity, so Clarice had to be strong for both of them and tried to walk her through it.

She put the iPod on speaker and asked gently, "Mom, did they say where they were taking him?"

"No," she sobbed miserably.

"Make any demands, like a ransom?"

"Yes. The big one started screaming like a maniac, saying that he wanted his money back." She sniffed. "What money, Clarice? Did you take something from them?"

526

Clarice couldn't answer. She looked at Ace, both of them staring wide-eyed, with fear, with shame, at their ignorance.

Boy, did they screw up.

How could they tangle with professional crooks and think there would be no repercussions? They had shown them their treacherous abilities before, at their arrest and trial.

They were wet-behind-the-ears amateurs going up against seasoned pros. It had never occurred to either of them that the crooks would take their kid. They had stupidly assumed the fight would remain between them. Turns out, not everyone thinks as they did. Those guys had completely different standards.

And we should have known that. I should have known.

Stupid.

Ace was suffering with the same thoughts. "We didn't consider all the angles." He shook his head. "We messed up. We could have protected Nolan and your parents before taking the money."

Clarice nodded, throat tightening. It took all her will power to refrain from punching herself in the face. How could she have been so blind and selfish? What kind of mother and daughter was she, not to consider the welfare of her loved ones before doing something that put them in danger? The worst part was, she had a warning. She knew Nolan was in danger, a premonition that had hit her like an incendiary bomb over a week ago.

Why didn't she listen to it? Make the others listen?

"Because I'm a big, fat, stupidhead," Clarice muttered in disgust.

Ace crawled over and hugged her, the tears streaming down his face mixing with hers.

Clarice's mother brought them back to perspective with a glimmer of hope. "I just thought of something," she said, voice breathy with emotion, becoming tense with a eureka moment. "I saw their car. You know cars, Clarice."

Clarice sat up straight. Eddy had wrecked their patrol car. They must have stolen a citizen's car after the shootout. She seriously doubted they would attempt to use their personal cars; internet news said they were wanted for questioning. No way they went home after that mess at the trailer. They'd be in the stolen car. Maybe Ace could track it…

"What was it?" Clarice said.

"A yellow Subaru Outback," she replied confidently. "A station wagon, or crossover, whatever they're called now. A new one."

The woman was no mechanic, but she enjoyed reading car magazines as if she were one. Those old *Hot Rod* and *Motor Trend* mags were the reason Clarice got interested in all things automotive. Clarice told her, "Great. Maybe we can find it." Clarice looked at Ace.

"I can," he said. "Probably, if we hurry."

Clarice squinted at him in thought. Looked at the iPod. "Mom, we have to go. We'll take care of this, okay? Stay home and don't call anybody else. I'll contact you as soon as possible." Clarice hung up before she could question their plan or inquire about the money again. Jumped up and tugged on some jeans and a tank. Socks. Shoes.

Ace dressed, then grabbed a loaf of bread and began cramming slices into his mouth to soak up the alcohol. He mumbled around the food, "We have to go to Bobby's house."

"Why?" Clarice started throwing everything on top of a blanket and rolled it up like a sack.

"Bandwidth. I need to use the Big Black Wrecker in person for this job. Entangling it won't work."

Crap. "Bobby's wife won't like it."

The thought of the beastly woman obviously gave him pause as well. His eyes widened. "*Whoa.* I forgot about her." He sighed. "I hope she'll play nice."

"She will. For Nolan," Clarice said without much conviction.

"Good. Because there's no other immediate way around it."

Why does life have to be so hard?

* * *

Going to Bobby's house was dangerous. There was only a slim chance the feds were watching it, but it was still a chance. One they shouldn't take. One they had to. The way Clarice saw it, this was just one more Bad Idea checked off on a long list of STUPID ones she'd shopped for in the past few months. *In for a penny, in for a pound, right?* And for Nolan, she was willing to go in for a gazillion pounds. All kinds of STUPID on a list as long as it needed to be.

Bienville Place was a quiet middle-class subdivision packed with huge houses and tiny yards. It was too early for anyone to be outside, or even at their kitchen tables enjoying their first cup and a paper. Camino's ungodly engine changed all that.

The roaring, snarling exhaust blasted off the pretty homes with deafening effect, the lack of space between houses amplifying the rude awakening as Clarice drag raced through the center of the neighborhood, a few bedroom lights flicking on as they passed.

Normally, she'd have driven slower, with a healthy respect for people's privacy and peace, keeping the noise to a minimum on general principles. But today wasn't normal; it was a crisis. So she really didn't give a fuck about upsetting anyone.

Suck on my 580hp alarm clock, yuppies.

Bobby's house looked like all the others. Two stories. Brick, white vinyl siding. Big windows and a manicured lawn. It differed only in that he had two lots, the extra space a work area with his boss garage and paint booth sitting proudly atop a high foundation, like some kind of mechanic's temple, a Mecca for gearheads to go to for meditation or prayer to the Grease God.

Clarice pulled into the driveway in front of the garage, drove around the paint booth to hide Camino. Killed the engine. After racing several miles with ear-busting noise, the silence had a faint, high-pitched whistle blowing annoyingly in her ears. Ace stuck a finger in his ear, wiggled it. Clarice held her breath and waited for the feds to surround them.

Minutes later, Bobby appeared in front of them, dark face and bare muscular torso camouflaged in the darkness. Teeth and boxer shorts bright white. "What the hell, Boss?" his deep voice grumbled.

Ace and Clarice got out, gently shut the doors, a too-little, too-late effort to be quiet. Clarice walked up to Bobby and hugged him. "They got Nolan."

He tensed up, squeezed back. "You mean they kidnapped him?"

"Yeah," Ace said, anger dripping from his words. "But we're going to find him. We need to use the Wrecker."

"You got it," Bobby replied. He turned around and looked up to his bedroom window, sighed heavily as the light turned on. His wife peeked out at them. "We might need helmets. When I told Pearl I was helping you, she hit me with a Louisville Slugger."

"She hit you with a bat?!" Clarice said.

He waved a hand like it happened all the time, no biggie. "She's a headstrong black woman. I've been hit with worse."

Sheesh.

Clarice looked at Ace. He licked his lips nervously.

"Come on." Bobby waved for them to follow him. He spoke as they walked. "Pearl told me earlier she knew you'd come here. She heard Camino and woke me with her *I Told You So* look." He chuckled, glanced back at her with a grin that glowed in the dark. "The entire neighborhood probably heard you coming from a mile away. I'll go upstairs and keep Pearl busy while you guys use the computer. Just hurry. And be quiet. If she hears you in the house, she'll go nuclear and murder all of us."

"Gotcha," Clarice said.

Ace gave a thumbs up.

Getting killed by an angry wife and mother would be a slight inconvenience right now, Clarice felt.

Guess I'll just add it to my STUPID list and go shopping.

As they went through the front door, Bobby hurried up the stairs, the carpeted steps strong enough to take his weight without creaking, an addition Clarice suspected he'd installed to better his chances of sneaking around. They followed a moment later, reaching the top and heading down the hall on tiptoes to the studio/computer room. Stepped in, shut the door.

An impressive clutter of stereo equipment, tall speakers and well-used desks made up the small room. The desk to their left held Bobby's desktop PC, a regular set-up like most people have. It looked like a Ford Pinto compared to the Ferrari Enzo on the desk to their right.

The Big Black Wrecker was awe-inspiring. Freaky, alien in appearance, like some kind of futuristic tech you'd see in a sci-fi movie. The plasma screen lit up the room, screen-saver playing out a Bugs Bunny and Elmer Fudd cartoon, framed by handcrafted black aluminum with connectors and wires for very modified and confusing components sticking out from the sides of the monitor, running out of sight. The rectangular hard drive towers, also black aluminum, hummed with a distinct feeling of power, their turbine-shaped vents and cooling fins somehow terrifying and comforting at the same time. It was hard to look at. The thing's capabilities were scary to ponder for very long. But those same capabilities were what got them out of prison, and, hopefully, would be able to find their son.

Clarice felt like she should kneel in its presence, afraid, yet consoled.

Ace nearly ran to his old love. He caressed the monitor, whispering a greeting, fondled the giant hard drives and other components with a very disturbing intimacy. Sniffed it several times. "I missed you," he said.

Clarice shook her head and turned to look at the easel and canvas to her left, in front of the room's sole window. Bobby had done a kickass job on a playground scene. The oil painting depicted a swing set and monkey bars with fantastic strokes. Children were playing, scattered throughout a grassy park with sandboxes and short trees, oblivious to the perils of the world. She resolved to give kudos later.

Her serene art critique and Ace's perverted reunion were interrupted by a sassy, very loud and forceful voice screaming at her disobeying husband.

"Bobby Lee, I told you to stay out of it!" Pearl yelled, only slightly muffled even though there must be several walls between them. "What about our children, huh? What are you gonna tell your daughters

533

when their father's in jail? You hard-headed fool! How you gonna change Tamika's diaper with hand-cuffs on?!"

The lecture continued with one bombing scolding after another. Clarice cringed, picturing Bobby standing there with his head down, afraid to wipe the spittle off his face. At the same time, She felt terrible for endangering Bobby's family. She understood Pearl's fear for her kids. Bobby was the provider, and she was an angry mama defending her babes, aggressively persuading their father to stay out of trouble so he'd be around to help raise them.

She was expecting to hear a few smacks or breaking furniture, so she was stymied when Pearl abruptly quieted. Clarice listened intently, confused, looked at the window and thought she should open it in case the good woman had only paused to find her bat. Ace's fingers on the keyboard were the only sound for several minutes. Then the door opened and Bobby walked in, nodded an affirmative to her, Pearl barging in behind him. Clarice looked at the woman's hands and relaxed when she saw them empty.

Pearl walked up to her, stopped, looked at her hard, with fierce, determined eyes, tearing slightly. She hugged Clarice with great strength and whispered in her ear, "We must climb the highest mountains and swim the deepest rivers for our children, Clarice. I know you will. I know you will, too, Ace," she said stepping back and nodding to him. He nodded back. "I wish I could help, but I have my own to care for. The best I can do is loan you my husband." A tear spilled down her round cheek. She raised her head high, a six-three, two-hundred-and-seventy pound woman that managed to look regal even without her wig, in a bathrobe. "Please bring him back in one piece. Good luck to y'all." She patted Clarice's arm, turned to Bobby and snapped, "I'm taking the kids to my mother's!" Shoved him out of the way. Stomped heavily out of the room.

The three of them looked at each other and gave a collective sigh.

Bobby said, "I had to clamp my hand over her mouth to get her to listen about Nolan." His chin came up. "Her sweet side came out after that. She simply demanded that I stay out of jail, then demanded to speak to you, Boss."

"I never doubted her compassion. I'm grateful to her," Clarice said gravely. Turned to Ace. "Yo, Doctor Frankenstein. Can your monster do the job?"

Ace nodded, still thinking about Pearl, sat back down in front of his creation. He eyed the screen and said, "There are several traffic cameras they passed going to and from your parents' house. Most Subaru Outbacks are gray or white, so the yellow was easy to spot. It looks like they headed east on Highway Ninety, then north on Fifty-seven. I assume that because they never passed the cameras in Gautier."

"Vancleave, huh?" Bobby said.

Ace looked dejected. "Not many cameras going into Vancleave. It's still pretty rural in that area."

"So, what, that's it?" Clarice said, turning into Ms. Bad Bitch before everyone's eyes, directing unreasonable anger at him for poor work performance. "That's all the Wrecker's got? I thought you said you could find them."

He looked at Bobby, at her, discomfited. Quietly he said, "I'm sure I can find them. But I have to tell you guys something first."

Clarice just looked at him. He had a confessional look that she'd only seen once before, when he told her he had been a hacker for Wikileaks. Only it looked worse this time. A lot worse.

Bobby recognized it, too, shifting with his own discomfiture.

"Well? Let's have it," Clarice said, making a rolling motion with her hand. Pointed at her watch.

The numerous buzz-click-hum noises from the Wrecker lent an eerie resonance to his words, like he was about to reveal he was from the future and terminators were real. "Do you know what a botnet is?" he said.

Bobby shook his head in the negative. Clarice shrugged.

"I used to be a terrible person," Ace said. He took a deep breath, ran his hands over his face. "But I didn't even realize it at the time. I was caught up in the thrill of climbing the Internet mountain. There are realms of cyber power few people know about, and even fewer - one in a billion - know how to achieve. Immense power that corrupts, changes people." He stared at her. "I achieved it."

Okay. Now he was scaring her. "What, exactly, is a botnet?" Clarice wanted to know.

"A supercomputer made of PCs and laptops." Clarice just stared. He continued. "I designed all kinds of Trojan horse software, ads that promised free merchandise if you clicked on them, and mass emailed millions of them. Daily." He looked up at them, determined to lay it all out and face their judgment. "The ads had a virus that infected your PC or laptop so that I could borrow its processing power. There's an enormous amount of time that goes by when your computer is on but you're not using its processing power. I infected countless systems. One-point-eight million connected PCs has enough processing power to equal one of the five most powerful supercomputers in the world." He paused, and Clarice saw it was because he regretted telling them his darkest secret. It gave his next revelation boss gravitas. "The last time I checked, in two-thousand-and-nine, there were over twenty million connected to my botnet."

Her eyes threatened to launch across the room. Bobby sucked in a breath and whistled.

"I had control of anything I wanted. Government databases. Bank accounts. Satellites. I even played with the Mars Rover. Drove it around the alien planet like a radio-controlled car." He looked her in the eye again. "I could have forced entire countries off the Internet if I felt like it. I was drunk with power. The King of Hackers, a cyberspace deity. No one knew who was doing it. It was my own personal universe. I lived on Seven-Up and pizza, never showered or left home. All I did was play God, manipulating millions of lives at my whim. It was insane."

Bobby looked at his friend with a new respect. Clarice looked at him as if seeing him for the first time.

Who was this man she had fallen in love with and married?

I mean, holy-freaking-Jesus, people. He is truly one scary dude.

Force entire countries off the 'Net?

"It's a good thing I met you, Clarice," he said, smiling wanly. "There's no telling how far down that path I would have gone. I was a six-pack of Seven-Up and two pizzas away from becoming a Marvel Comics super villain. I was untouchable."

Clarice walked over and took his hand. Kissed the back of it. Rubbed his long fingers. In a tender voice she said, "I just touched you." He smiled. "That means you're not that person anymore. That's in the past. I know who you are now, and who you want to be." She grinned. "I told you before we started dating that I would kick your ass if you ever started hacking illegally again. Do you remember that?"

"Uh. Yeah," he replied uncertainly, leaning back, pulling his hand loose.

She leaned over, kissed him a wet smack on the lips and said, "Well, fuck that. Forget I said it. I don't care how many countries you force off the Internet as long as it gets our son back."

"Yeah, baby! Do it, Ace!" Bobby cheered, pumping a fist over his head.

Ace sighed in relief, and Clarice wondered how she'd have taken this news a couple of years back, when all her morals were still intact and she didn't have a dozen felonies under her belt. He gave a wicked grin, spun around to work his magic.

Logging on to some website in a foreign language, possibly Cyrillic, he gave his customary lecture to keep them non-geeks appraised of his activities. They pretended to understand all of it.

He typed and spoke almost absently. "Back-end servers control the botnet and automatically re-encode their distributed infection software every thirty minutes, for new transmissions, making it difficult for anti-virus vendors to stop the virus and infection spread. The location of the remote servers which control the botnet are hidden behind a constantly changing DNS technique called Fast Flux."

Clarice thought she'd got the gist of it. "So there could be millions more computers infected since you last checked, and there's no way the cyber authorities could trace or counter it."

"Right," he confirmed, fingers blurring over the keyboard, typing in code to access servers. "If a security firm tries to investigate any aspect of my botnet, an experienced DDOS, distributed-denial-of-service, automatically detects their debuggers and fights back, attacking the security firm, and really inconveniencing their system for a while." He chuffed with amusement. "It punished them every time. Eventually, the firms get scared and quit snooping."

There went her eyes again.

Ace cackled in a way she'd never heard before. It made her shiver, though not unpleasantly. His talent was what first attracted her to him, after all. All this talk of power was wrong, but nothing convinced her libido of that.

He continued, "Dozens of firms have tried to disinfect my network, but there is no command-and-control point, so they never made any progress. They'd recover a hundred thousand, and I'd infect twice that amount. Heck, my baby kicked them out and disabled their networks. Ha!" he cackled again.

His baby...

Now Clarice know where that mad scientist laugh came from. He was mad. And Clarice found it sexy.

She stroked his hair. Bobby snickered.

"You said you can control satellites?" Clarice queried.

"Uh-huh. We'll need a good one to find them." He leaned his head back, looked up at her. His smile showed too many teeth. "I can do better than 'good.' Only the best for us, dear."

"You sweet talker, you."

After fifteen minutes of Ace's unintelligible mutters, non-stop pounding of keys and moan-squeak-hums from the Wrecker's processing, he stopped with his jaw on the floor, bug-eyed. "What the fried microchip?!" he gasped incredulously.

"Um. Problem?" Clarice said, squinting at the meaningless code on the screen.

"No," he whispered, thoroughly delighted. He stroked the screen. "You see that? It's so beautiful."

"See what, you Wheat Thin?" Bobby said, also squinting at the Wrecker.

He sniffed a tad of condescension at them. "The numbers, of course." He pointed at the gobbledy-gook. "This is big. BIG. This much data... Wow. There must be over fifty-million connected. With this much bandwidth, spread through all those countries, I could collapse the world economy, start wars, steal trillions of dollars and give it to the poor. I could, I could..." He cackled. "I could do it with half that much bandwidth! Hoo-hoo-hoo, Ha-ha-ha!" he trumpeted, totally madcap.

"Should I hit him?" Bobby asked her.

"Not yet." Clarice sighed, grabbed Ace's shoulders and shook the hell out of him. "Earth to Megatron, put your cyber penis away. You can play with it later. You need to stay focused here."

He looked at her with crazy eyes. "This is an historic moment, Clarice. The world has never seen this much power, computing or otherwise. The possibilities-"

"Hit him."

Pap!

Bobby jabbed Ace in the side of the head. Held his fist up and threatened another.

Ace blinked in surprise. "Why did you hit me?" he screeched at his friend.

Clarice answered him. "Because I don't need any more guilt on my conscience right now." She held up her own fist. "Look, Ace. I understand the overwhelming pull of power you feel right now. It's like

541

sticking a pipe, lighter, and slab of crack in front of a dope fiend and telling them not to smoke it. I can relate, trust me. You just have to fight it, believe that you can control it. We are here for support, just like you were there for me when I needed you." He knew about her inner fight junkie, and had witnessed first-hand how hard she had to struggle to control the berserk bloodlust that overcame her after past pro boxing matches.

His brow furrowed. He nodded, relaxing. He re-asserted control over his emotions. It was a visible transformation, and Clarice couldn't help thinking about his super-villain comment earlier.

Bobby and Clarice dropped their reality-checkers.

"Sorry," Ace muttered. "Once a hack head, always a hack head." He laughed ruefully. "You never recover; you either go to jail, start working for the government, or your skills surpass the chances of getting caught. But you'll always be a hack addict."

"I could break your hands," Bobby volunteered.

"Wouldn't work. Even if you broke my spine, I'd just type with a stick in my mouth, or something. Have a mouse implanted in my brain."

They burst into laughter, and the optimistic drive of their team returned.

Ace went back to work, claiming he'd need time to recruit his 'zombies', PCs not-in-use, before tackling the U.S. Navy's satellite system.

As the first hint of the sun on the horizon made the window glow, someone knocked on the front door.

They froze, listening, surprised and indecisive. They knocked again.

"Who the hell?" Clarice said anxiously. If it was the cops, they were in a bad spot to run from. Walking to the window, Clarice took a quick peek, seeing only the side of the neighbor's house, a thin strip of grass in between.

"I wasn't expecting anyone," Bobby said. "Stay here. I'll take care of it. If you hear fighting, run to my room and go out the window."

He disappeared and they heard laughter downstairs. He returned a moment later with Eddy. Her coach swaggered in and hugged her with one arm, the other holding a box of pizza. "You okay, darlin'?" he said solemnly.

"We're making progress. How'd you find out?" Clarice said.

"Your fathered called me. I rushed to the park, found you already gone, so it was only logical to come here next."

"Where'd you get pizza this early?" Ace inquired. "I used to eat it every day and could never find it for breakfast."

"I know a guy," Eddy replied. "Forget about it. Dig in." He set the box down on the desk to his left, pushing aside a keyboard and bric-a-brac.

Ace jumped up, looking like a slobbering dog as he happily pranced over to the food. Opened the box. Sucked in a breath, eyebrows climbing to his hairline. Four semi-automatic handguns, black steel, polished and gleaming with oil, were positioned like slices of pizza around clips of ammo in the center. He frowned severely, turned to glare accusingly at Eddy.

"No Scooby snacks," Eddy said cheerfully. "Just business packs."

"Right." Ace grunted. "Great. Just what I need. I'll probably shoot myself trying to load one."

"We'll get to that." Eddy waved a hand nonchalantly.

Ace moped back over to the Wrecker, sat down and typed with strokes that let the room know what he thought about being pizza-teased.

Eddy shook his head, looked at her. "Catch me up."

Clarice took a breath, leaned her butt against the back of Ace's chair and said, "Pearl clobbered Bobby with a bat for helping us escape, but said she's cool with him helping us get Nolan back." Bobby's eyes shone with pride. Clarice smiled at him, looked back to Eddy. "Ace is an evil super villain with control of the world, but we won't allow him to play with his Megatron penis until we take care of the kidnapping business."

"Bobby punched me," Ace grumbled, stabbing several keys loudly.

"Good," Eddy said. He looked at her with a neutral expression, not doubting what Clarice just divulged, just completely unaffected by it.

Grab your dictionary. Look up 'imperturbable'. You'll see a huge guy in a U.S.A. Team jacket, underbite jutting out as if seeking something to excite him.

Clarice continued her briefing. "Since the cops didn't leave a way to contact them, Ace checked traf-

544

fic cameras and determined they went towards Vancleave. He's going to borrow a Navy satellite to find
them."

"Good," Eddy repeated. He crossed his arms, looking thoughtful. "Odd that Jimmy and Hector neglected to leave instructions for the money to be
traded. That shows that Jimmy, the obvious leader, is
having some serious mental issues. He's likely paranoid about you guys finding evidence that would
prove he set you up two years ago. And there's no
telling what kind of stress the Teacher's business is
putting on him. That really worries me."

Clarice's face fell. "You don't think he'll hurt
Nolan, do you? Surely, they'll call my parents and
arrange a trade. They'll want the money back."

"A rational person would. But this guy has made
some really bad calls. He's unpredictable." He paused,
frowning. "I understand why they made a deal with
Patty. But why jump us at Wal-Mart? They had the
advantage, a tracking device they could have followed to a far less public place. Then they took the
kid, an action that took forethought, yet they didn't
arrange a drop." He shrugged, spread his hands.
"None of it makes sense. There's no telling what
they'll do next."

"Why don't we ask them?" Ace growled. He
cracked his knuckles, swiveled around in his chair,
looking at each of them in turn, projecting the most
vehement mug Clarice had ever seen on a human being. It was wolf-like. Talk of his son being killed without a good chance at ransom ignited a fervid energy

within him. The evil super-villain morphed into an evil super-father, one those cops would regret messing with. His sneaky *Knows Stuff* smile appeared, constricted with inner pain. "Why don't we just call those burnt transistors and ask them?" he spat.

"You know their number?" Bobby asked.

"I will. Observe." He jerked his head at the computer, swiveled back around. They crowded behind him. The screen showed a satellite view similar to what you'd see on Google Earth, but in shades of green, grays, and black. Night vision, seen from really high above a dark, heavily wooded area. Ace began a techno spiel. "Dimension recognition software found them relatively easy. It's sort of like facial recognition, but for cars, buildings, city skylines, et cetera."

"I saw a smart phone commercial that advertised that. All you had to do is take a picture of a building and it would tell you where you were and give directions. Is that the same thing?" Bobby said.

"Similar, yeah. I entered the dimensions of a late model Subaru Outback and scanned the entire Vancleave area. Fortunately, few people drive Outbacks in that town. Look here." He pointed to a wooded area alongside a river, the Pascagoula, Clarice thought, and zoomed in on the car they were looking for, parked on a dirt road next to a small houseboat. He changed the resolution to visible light and they could just barely tell the car was yellow. The road snaked through thick woods that flanked a tall bridge, one Clarice recognized, having driven over it before, long ago. Several other houseboats lined the river's banks, some right next to each other, most hundreds of yards apart.

"How do you know they're there?" Clarice said, trying to contain her excitement. They had the bastards' ass now!

Ace held up a finger. "The human body produces electromagnetic waves in the form of infrared light. Heat. It's measurable. Adults give off a larger signal than children. Let's take a look." He typed and zoomed in on the roof of the houseboat. The resolution was unreal, showing the individual seams in the corrugated steel roof and cabin, the forty-foot pontoons on either side of the craft holding it afloat in the dark water. Ace typed, switching the frequency back to thermal imaging. The scene changed tones, the boat, water and dock darkening to nearly black, while several spots of color appeared ghost-like inside the boat's cabin, dark red that concentrically faded to orange with faint yellow outer rings, indicating the bodies' cores and the heated air around them. Two big spots, two little spots.

Two little spots...

"Oh my God," Clarice breathed.

Eddy grunted, said quietly, "Does Patty have a kid?"

"A daughter," Clarice whispered. Her hands started to shake.

"Then she didn't betray you. She was trying to protect her kid."

547

Bobby, on the verge of hyperventilating with rage, left the room to cool down, likely thinking about his own daughters. Ace snarled. Eddy looked thoughtful.

Clarice was bombarded with a mix of emotions, a concentrated surge of energy that was hard to sort through without screaming. For a second, relief that her friend hadn't sold her out for her own benefit felt great. Then the evident kidnapping of her child unleashed a deep, broiling fury and hatred that made every vein in her body throb, pulse madly under her skin. Fear for the kids.

They must be frightened beyond reason, traumatized.

A fresh bombardment hit her, this time visually, pictures of their kids crying pitifully, curled up on a cold floor of that boat while Psycho Cop and his thug partner...

Broiling fury.

She lost consciousness. When she came back to, Eddy was screaming at her, pinning her to the floor, his great strength and weight struggling to hold her arms behind her head while he sat on her legs.

"Shock! Get yourself under control, girl!" he bellowed. "You're not going to help those kids by breaking your hands on the wall. Save some of it for the mission."

Gasping with feral snarls, Clarice felt her senses begin to return as she focused on her coach's face and Ace's above his. The white ceiling beyond. A metallic, electrical taste coated her mouth. Adrenaline. A lot of it. Stiff carpet pricked the backs of her ears.

Her hands pulsed with power, the right one throbbing as inflammation set in to renew the aching of metacarpals. She kept taking deep breaths, but couldn't get the tension to leave her arms. They just wanted to punch something, somebody. Preferably, a cop. Or cops.

But not the walls, dummy, she told the crazy broad in her head. The fight junkie had come out of her cage, released by the visions of the children, and she couldn't remember it. A moment later her dynamic alter-ego relented, she relaxed, and Eddy let her up. Looking around at the destruction she had inflicted on Bobby's sheet-rock, Clarice winced. There must have been twenty fist-sized holes, and several giant ones, between two walls in a corner. Pearl would hit the fan when she saw this.

Clarice decided not to visit for a while.

Eddy eyed her warily. "I'd forgotten how strong you are," he said. "You were like greased lighting. You were slipping… weaving under my arms like a mongoose. I couldn't catch you by myself." He held his ribs and grimaced.

"You punched me," Ace complained, also holding his ribs. "I hope you feel guilty." He limped back over to the Wrecker, shaking his head.

Whoops…

Bobby stood in the doorway looking at the damage. He tisked her. "You should have come outside with me," he said wryly. "Feel better?"

"Much. Thanks for the use of your walls." Clarice raised an eyebrow. "I think I'm getting my period, so there's no guarantees it won't happen again."

"That's wonderful." He held up a fist, knuckles skinned, bright pink splotches on dark skin. "I'm feeling a little PMSed myself. Let's take it out on the cops next time."

"Deal." Clarice smiled, feeling in control once more. Fist-bumped her bloody knuckles into his.

Eddy clapped a hand on Ace's shoulder. "Before your wife destroyed two perfectly innocent walls and assaulted two perfectly innocent bystanders, you said something about calling those goombas."

"I did," he confirmed, typing. The screen changed back to visible light, with a type of shooter's bull's eye appearing in the center, flanked by numbers that indicated range and frequencies. "Cellphone antennas transmit and receive constantly to communicate with the towers. The phone doesn't even have to be in use, just on, for the signal to be intercepted. I beamed a laser frequency probe down into that boat and picked up a signal, which is radiating from the smaller of the two big infrared signatures."

"Hector," Clarice said.

"Yep." He highlighted a long number on the screen, punched a key to open another Window. Entered the number in some other system Clarice was clueless about. A search sequence began, ending in seconds, showing a new number in a box labeled RESULTS. A cellphone number. "Voila," he said smugly, cracking his knuckles.

"Nice trick," Bobby said, frowning *Not Bad* at Eddy. Ace waved a hand. Nothing to it.

"You okay to call them?" Eddy asked her.

Clarice narrowed her eyes. "You bet your ass I am. Where's the money?"

"Close. In a safe place."

Clarice nodded. "I don't want anyone getting hurt. We'll try to do this the right way and make a clean trade. Everyone agree?"

Ace and Bobby nodded. Eddy looked skeptical, but nodded anyway.

"I believe they'll want to ensure they get the money back. I'll tell them the only way to do that is by giving us the kids, unharmed," Clarice said mostly to herself. "They shouldn't be worried about the feds being involved, considering they're dealing with fugitives. I have to make them believe they won, and that we're leaving the country after all this." Clarice closed her eyes. Took a calming breath.

I can convince them. I'm sure of it. This is just a business transaction. I've negotiated with crooked idiots before.

She opened her eyes. "All right. It's time to take care of business."

Ace handed her the iPod with an encouraging smile.

* * *

The houseboat rocked every time another boat passed by on the river, the small waves created by the wake crashing against the pontoons, causing Jimmy to stagger around the cabin, off-balance.

"Dammit, dammit!" he spat, catching himself on a wall. He looked out of a window and glared at the small fishing boat speeding away, the family in the craft illuminated in yellows and oranges as the sun began to rise over the dark water. "I hate boats. This is your fault, Hector. We should have gone to the hunting camp."

Hector looked up from his seat, one of the four chairs around a small wooden table, two of the chairs holding the little girl and boy they had kidnapped. The bags under his eyes puffed out when he talked. His voice was raspy from stress, exhaustion. "There are hunters at the hunting camp, Jimmy. They couldn't have brought the *niños* there."

"Well, if I get sick you're gonna have to answer for it," he promised.

Hector ignored the threat, too tired to care. In a grating, but pleading, tone, he said, "We need to call them."

"I'll tell you when we'll call them." He glared ominously. The children flinched and whimpered. "You got that? I'll tell you. I have to figure out how to do this without the feds interfering."

"They're not involved. Clarice and Alan are fugitives. They wouldn't have called the FBI."

"They are! They are involved!" he exploded, eyes rolling wildly, his manic, pale and sweaty face contorted. "You don't think that cunt's parents called them as soon as they left? Bet your greaser ass they did."

Hector shushed the weeping children. The girl, an eleven-year-old with plump rosy cheeks and long, curly locks of blonde hair, curled up in a ball, hugging her knees. A stream of urine ran from her filthy sundress down the leg of the chair, pooling on the floor beneath her. Hector noticed, smelled it, closed his eyes, laid his head on the table. A new level of dread consumed him. He fought it, and bravely murmured, "Please calm down. You're scaring the *niños*."

"Fuck the kids!" he shouted. He pulled his gun, pointed it at the girl. "I'll shoot this pissy little bitch and toss her in the river."

The boy stood up, angular face scowling in anger, fear. His long dark brown hair stuck to his sweaty forehead, his tear-stained face. He walked in front of the girl. "Leave her alone!" he shrieked. Tears ran down his face afresh. He balled up his fists and looked the monster in the eye. "My mommy will come for us. She's a champion fighter and will kick your ass!"

Hector stopped breathing. Jimmy jerked as if slapped.

The girl opened her eyes to see the gun pointed at them and started wailing, her normally musical voice streaked with terror, incredibly loud inside the small enclosure.

Hector scrambled out of the chair, pushing it clattering to the floor as he lunged between the gun and the children. He held his hands up and panted, "We need them. We need them, Jimmy! To get the money, remember?"

"We don't need them!" The gun shook in his hand, knuckles white, showing through nearly translucent, bloodless skin. "They're just in the way." He waved the gun around, scrunched up his face and mocked a child's voice. "I'm hungry. I had to go to the bathroom. My mommy will beat you up." He stared harshly, stabbed Hector in the chest with the pistol, thundering, "AND THEY PEE ON THE FUCKING FLOOR!"

Hector kept glancing at the gun's barrel, an enormous black hole of death, and felt like adding to the puddle on the floor. This is it, he thought. He'll kill her and the *niños*. Throw them in the river for fish food. And they could have lived, he mused, mind and body numb, beyond terror. They could have gotten the money back, let the kids go. And left the country for a better life...

Jimmy's hand continued to shake. Hector's body mirrored it.

Jimmy bared his teeth, straightened his arm...

A nano-second before Jimmy decided to kill everyone a phone rang. He blinked in surprise, almost pulling the trigger. Hector jumped as if he had. The ring tone, a dramatic yet uplifting Avril Lavigne pop song, was ridiculous to hear under the circumstances. It continued to jam, Ms. Lavigne demanding to know *why you always gotta make things so complicated*, exorcising some of the smothering negative energy that

possessed Jimmy, Hector, the kids. A positive hypnosis.

Hector hurriedly took advantage of his partner's
confusion. Gently he said, "I think that's good news
calling. We should answer it, and get our money."

Jimmy lowered the gun. "How do you know
it's about the money?" He coughed several times.
Blinked in confusion.

"Alan Carter. He's a hacking wizard. Tracing my
cell would be simple for a man of his skills." Hector
looked at his watch. "It couldn't be anybody else."

Jimmy licked his lips, and Hector saw the old
greedy, cash-hungry gleam return to his eyes. "Answer it. Put it on speaker."

Hector let out a breath. Motioned for the boy to sit
down. Dug in his pocket for the phone, said a quick
prayer to the Virgin Mary and a special thanks to
Avril. Flipped it open. "Yes?" he said.

"I have a proposition for you guys," Clarice Carter
said clearly.

Nolan heard her confident voice and drew strength
from it. He leaned over and whispered to the girl, "My
Mom is coming for us. Don't worry."

* * *

"One last hurrah. That's it. After this you can stick
a fork in me," Eddy said. "I'm done." He continued
wrapping her hand, his nimble, agile movements uncanny for such large fingers.

"Gotcha, Coach," Clarice replied, smiling at his
complaining tone, humorous because it conveyed an

eagerness to see some action. "You know you don't have to do this. Right?"

He paused mid-wrap, eyes wide in feigned shock. "What a verbal kick to my manhood. Darlin', you know I have to do this. I mean, I care nothing for you or the kid. That's not why I'm going." His bull-dog grin flashed. "I need a new story to tell the fellas at the gym. I'm supposed to be a man's MAN. I need some good macho gossip."

Clarice pursed her lips. "Wrapping my hands with brass knuckles is a good opener."

He grunted agreement. Finished taping her left fist. Slid a six-ounce brass knuckles over her right fingers, which were wrapped in gauze to cushion the metal from impacting on her flesh. Held it snug and began winding the long red hand wrap around her hand, knuckles, between the fingers, pulling tightly before leading the wrap around her wrist, back around the hand again. The excess was com-piled thickly at the base of her hand, supporting the eight tiny wrist bones, reinforcing where they ad-joined the radius and ulna. He slapped her wounded shoulder, his usual signal of completion, and Clarice shrunk back involuntarily. A tearing, burning sensa-tion zipped up her neck, telling her the cut had re-opened and *why the hell are you slapping it like that?!*

Helen's warning about keeping the wound closed floated through her awareness a second before pic-tures of the Grand Canyon did. Huge, serrated, jagged cliffs of red. Clarice looked down at her freshly duct taped shoulder, a softball-sized muscle bulging out of her black tank top. Her delts used to ripple and glow, her best upper body features, gorgeous in their symmetry. Now one was scarred. And it wasn't one of those cool wicked-shaped deals that people admired. It was FUBARed. Ugh.

I'll miss you Perfect Shoulder.

Shrugging it off, she looked at her hands. They felt... Deadly. But... Sexy. Powerful.

The weight and shape of the gleaming brass knuckles jutting from both fists was enough to make her shiver at the thought of the damage they could inflict. The brass combined with professionally wrapped, hard-as-brick hands with her skills?

Whoa, scary-sexy-power.

All she needed to do was get within punching range of those cops...

"Are we ready?" Bobby asked. He and Ace sat in front of the humming Big Black Wrecker, Ace staring at the monitor, Bobby watching Clarice watch her hands. He seemed uncomfortable, and she realized the homicidal smile on her mug was the likely culprit.

She looked at him and inclined her head toward Eddy. "Cue cliché."

"I was born ready," Eddy provided. He looked hard at each of them. "But you two aren't. I'll be back." He left the room and returned a few minutes later with two bulletproof vests and a black, tactical pump-action shotgun. The items they had taken from the police car. He handed a vest to her. The other to Bobby.

"But there are four of us," Clarice said, accepting it. Eddy nodded.

"I'm not going," Ace said. Eddy nodded.

"Um. Why?" Clarice said.

"I have to keep the Navy out of their satellite. There are about a hundred Navy Intelligence officers trying to break back into their system right now. If they do, they'll see what the satellite is surveilling and send everybody and their momma to that houseboat."

Eddy nodded.

Ace looked at the 9mm Glocks in the pizza box. Back to her. "You guys are the combat warriors. I'm the computer warrior. I would be a liability running around with a gun."

Eddy nodded vigorously.

Clarice felt relieved. At least Ace would make it out of this. "You're right. Your strengths are here. We'll need you to be our eyes, tell us where the cops and kids are in relation to our positions."

"Not a problem." He handed her the iPod and Mi-Fi router, pointed to a phone mounted on a wall. "You have earbuds. They have Bluetooth. We'll do a conference call."

Eddy nodded again.

Clarice smacked her coach in the arm. "If you knew all this, why not say it?"

He looked down his nose at her, a man of infinite wisdom. "I find that the best teaching if often done by allowing the pupils to come to the answer on their own." He looked around at everyone, showing teeth. "I was confident you kids would work it out."

Clarice growled at his stupid smile. "Bobby and I get vests because we have family, huh?"

"Correct. Family and bright futures."

Scowling, Clarice wanted to smack him again. She understood his reasoning, to give them the available protection because he saw their lives as more valuable than his, but she didn't have to like it. She gave him a quick, hard hug. Pushed him away and grabbed the pistols out of the box. Handed two to Bobby, with four clips. Started cramming clips in her jeans pockets.

Grabbing a pistol in each hand, she held them up, looked around at her team with narrowed eyes and said, "I love you guys."

Quiet, powerful determination gripped their faces as they left the house.

* * *

The thunderstorm swept through Vancleave with little warning. Thick, roiling, lightning-filled clouds completely covered the sky, dark and ominous specters that capriciously destroyed homes, forests, and flooded rivers. The roaring wind pushed the storm north from the Gulf of Mexico, covering southern Mississippi entirely.

The Pascagoula River seemed especially incensed, the violent currents and wind damaging enough to make most people evacuate the areas by the water.

Men scrambled to get their boats loaded on trailers, jumping at the claps of thunder and shrieking at the bolts of electricity as they raced away from the boat ramps. Docks and sheds were secured. Families ducked branches blown free of severely swaying trees as they crossed their yards to their vehicles, on the way to higher, safer ground that wouldn't flood.

Not everyone had the option of leaving.

"Shut up, shut up! I told you, Hector. We're not leaving." Jimmy pointed and sneered at his partner. "Just sit your scary ass in that chair and keep those damn kids quiet."

The boat moved up and down and to the sides, faster, higher, as the height of the waves and speed of the wind increased. Water leaked in from the roof here and there, and a bellowing roar filled the cabin through the thin walls like an air raid siren, moaning up and down in pitch, making it necessary to talk loudly to be heard.

Hector beseeched his old friend. "We have to get off the boat! Please, Jimmy." Lightning flashed right outside, windows beaming blindingly, the accompanying cannon boom shaking the walls, chairs, and everyone in the cabin. The kids screeched in new terror. "Please, Jimmy! We'll sink or get struck by lightning!"

"No! Not yet. Stop whining, will you?" He stomped around without balance, catching himself on the walls. Coughed. "Won't be long now. I'll get the rifle and hide in the woods. When they approach, you go out to meet them. When they hand you the money, I'll take care of the rest and we'll get out of here."

Hector thought fast. "I'll take the kids out with me. They'll want to see they're okay before trading. That's what she said."

Jimmy's face twisted, teeth bared in a snarl. "NO YOU WON'T!" he shouted. "Fuck her! Those runts stay on the boat. We're calling the shots, you got that? Not them! You tell that bitch to give us the money or we'll kill the kids. Period."

Hector looked at the frightened children, huddled together on the floor, and thought of his own *niños*. Three of them. They were younger than these two, even more vulnerable. The thought of them being kidnapped by a monster like Jimmy made him choke out an anguished cry. He took a deep breath, collecting himself. His eyes moved to his gun, still in its holster on his police-issue belt. They had discarded their uniform tops after jacking the old woman's car, but had no other changes of clothes yet. The white shirt, bland and meaningless, seemed to take away the power he felt when wearing the whole uniform. He looked down at his half-uniform, his pants and boots, feeling like half of a man.

He looked at the gun again.

I could shoot him, he realized. *I could shoot Jimmy. Then the kids would be safe. And I could get away from all this. Just take her family and go.*

With the money...

He raked his hands through his thick, dark hair and could smell the greasy fear in it, a ubiquitous cloud of paranoid perspiration that seemed to coat everyone and everything. Jimmy began another crazy tirade. Hector ignored it, waiting for him to turn around again so he could draw his weapon.

Heat, an inferno of fear, engulfed his stomach and spread down his limbs, a poisonous, nauseating rush that zapped his energy and made the paranoid sweat pour from his face onto the table, darkening the wood. He put a hand on the butt of his gun, hand shaking slightly faster than his knees. Looked up at Jimmy, vision blurred. Waiting on the moment.

It came.

Jimmy turned to look out the window, at the shore, and Hector's courage failed completely. He let go of the gun, turned his head away from the children and vomited profusely on the floor, spatter going in all directions, specs appearing on Jimmy's pants, boots. The kids moaned loudly, the boy gagging, coughing.

Hector laid his head back on the table with a bubbling sigh. Wiped his mouth.

Jimmy looked at his boot, shook off the vomit, face and neck flushing with rage. "Oh, god-DAMN!" he shouted, booming lightning and bellowing wind accentuating his fury. "VOMIT. JUST LIKE THE FUCKING KIDS, HECTOR!" He growled a beastly, insane noise, punched a wall, caving it in. Stomped out of the room. Shouts and furniture breaking in the bedroom could be heard before he returned with a long rifle in his hands. He adjusted the strap over his head, aimed it out a window to check the sight on the scope. He lowered the weapon and glared at Hector. "It's show time. Are you too sick to handle this? Do I have to do it myself?" He pointed the rifle at Nolan.

Hector's head came up and he nearly vomited again, a new wave of dizziness swamping him. He stood as quickly as he could, blacking out, white spots in his vision, made it around the chairs to stand in front of the kids. "I'll do it. I'll meet them and make sure they have the money." He held his hands up, face bloodless from the nausea, looking down the barrel of a gun for the second time today.

His stomach heaved. He choked it down.

"Damn right you will. Then you get the cash and get the hell out of my way. That cunt has to pay for what she did to us. All of them have to pay!"

Pay what? Hector thought. *What have they done?*

Dismayed, shamed but angered by his cowardice, he found the strength to get his legs working again, taking one last look at the children before following Jimmy out into the hellish storm.

* * *

Just. Freaking. Perfect.

As soon as they left Bobby's house a spring super storm showed its ugly head and chased them all the way to Vancleave. Peeking out of the Toyota's king-cab window, Clarice couldn't see a damn thing except for lightning in distant clouds, luminous jagged lines of current that reminded her of her old mouthpiece, pink with white lightning teeth.

Eddy drove over the bridge they had reconned with the satellite, turned off on a dirt road, steering them through thick sand and mud that made her glad she hadn't brought Camino. The ground clearance was much taller on this truck. The V6 roared and grunted valiantly, powering them through the sludge like a reliable old tractor, the ruts testing the tires and suspension, rocking the three of them side-to-side.

They parked by one of the bridge's huge steel pillars. Sat for a moment, listening to the rain and wind batter the trees and bushes around them. The river was just ahead. Clarice could smell its muddy rage, struggling to contain the obese currents the tempest forced upon it. The shape of the tumultuous river was apparent from the banks of sand, the tall grass on either side of the boat ramp, and the towering pillars that rose out of the water like unconcerned statues to connect to the bottom of the bridge.

With visibility at maybe twenty feet, she couldn't actually see the water. She hadn't seen sheets of rain like this since the last hurricane hit. The weather certainly seemed appropriate for the situation. It would help their mission, hopefully, by allowing them to move around unseen. But the danger of a thunderstorm had always been like an evil foretelling to her. Like when an animal senses bad weather coming and doesn't question the urge to flee to safety.

I mean, has anything good ever happened during a raging t-storm? Besides that. Geez, people. Get your minds out of the gutter.

"Is this Bluetooth waterproof?" Bobby asked no one in particular. "I just got it. Would be a shame to short it out." His enormous frame caused substantial distress to the passenger seat as he shifted around, shoulders so wide they touched the door on the right and butted Eddy's shoulder on the left. He fiddled with the earpiece, frowning.

"I hope you kept the receipt, because we're about to test that bad boy," Eddy replied, also adjusting a Bluetooth in his ear.

"Ace? You have everyone connected?" Clarice asked. She put the iPod and Mi-Fi in a Ziploc bag, stuffed them in a front pocket. The ear bud wire ran under her shirt, under a piece of tape stuck to the top of her boob.

"Yes, dear. There's a little static because of the storm, but I ran the signals through a program that will clean it up and make sure we don't get disconnected," he said. "How's your end?"

"I can hear you."

"Testing," Eddy said.

"My penis is bigger than yours, Ace," Bobby said. "Testing."

Ace replied with an appropriate *My Daddy Can Beat Up Your Daddy* retort.

Bobby grunted and looked at her. "We can hear each other just fine, Boss."

Clarice rolled her eyes. Made sure her guns were loaded. Safeties on. Flexed her brass-knuckled fists, Seek and Destroy, feeling the scary-sexy-power once more, though it was touched with something else. Some other, hyper-infusion of primal, raw force. Being this close to Nolan really brought home the danger he was in. It was one thing to feel anger at him

565

being kidnapped while in the security of a home. It was quite another to be right at the place where her son was being held, about to take action to rescue him and make motherfuckers suffer for it. That protective, maternal drive gave her more confidence in her abilities than she'd ever experienced before. The emotions rendered a resolve so complex, so energy dense, that she knew without a doubt she could punch holes in anything that got between her and the kids.

Whoa, scary-sexy-mommy-power. Talk about thriving under pressure.

Eddy cleared his throat. Clarice looked up to see them staring at her, coach pursing his lips in thought, Bobby cautiously regarding the manic shine that had frequented her eyes too often of late. Clarice flexed her fists, nodded to them. They climbed out into wet sand that covered their shoes, clothes instantly soaked. The men could stand up straight, but Clarice had to lean into the wind, squinting her eyes so she could look in the direction they needed to go. They walked to the back of the truck and lifted two military duffle bags out of the bed, fighting with the straps, shouldering the money. They trudged off down the road that curved into the woods near the river, spreading out to make themselves harder targets, Eddy on the left by the turbulent water, her next to the woods, Bobby stepping as sure-footed as a panther in the center, guns in hand. Clarice expected to smell horse shit and see the sign for the *OK Corral* any second now.

The rain was relentless. The wind was worse. Small branches, twigs, and sharp-edged grass constantly hit them, a flora fusillade that lacerated her arms and face. If she wasn't already seeing herself like the Bride of Chucky, she'd probably have bitched about it.

Snapping wood that sounded like heavy footsteps coming at them caused Eddy to whip his shotgun around, move quickly in front of her. Bobby and Clarice froze; Eddy aimed his Glock at the noise with a snarl.

Ace gleaned their apprehension and reassured them. "Don't worry, guys," he said. "The targets are still two-hundred yards ahead. I doubt they have friends with anti-IR suits hiding in the woods."

"I bet the Teacher has employees with suits like that, for trafficking. Maybe they're pals with Jimmy and Hector," Eddy muttered, voice distorted by the wind but clear over the phone. His eagle eyes peered into the dark brush, sweeping the gun back and forth, distrustful.

"Maybe," Clarice said. "But I have a feeling the Teacher would be aware of his crew helping these guys and would put a stop to it. For whatever reason, he's been helping us and not them. And kidnapping parties aren't his thing."

"Doesn't seem to be his style," Eddy agreed. "Still, though. Prepare for the worst, et cetera." He put the shotgun's butt on a shoulder, crouching and pointing it like a soldier crossing into unknown enemy territory.

Which is precisely what we're doing, dummy, Clarice notified herself, lifting her own weapons. Switched the safeties off.

"Hector is moving your way," Ace said excitedly. "Fifty yards, straight ahead."

There was no pause or hesitation of any kind at this revelation. They shared a scowl from the same cookie cutter as they picked up the pace, eager to do battle with the men that had screwed with their tribe and held the next generation hostage.

A terrible gust blew in from their left, pushing her sideways, a curtain of rain following it. Hector appeared from behind the sheet of water, his t-shirt and uniform pants stuck to his square body, gun in his hands held up with professional experience.

Clarice screamed and almost shot him.

He screamed and almost shot her.

"WAIT!" Eddy thundered a fraction of a second before death flew from their weapons. His authoritative baritone froze everyone in place. Their eyes had no choice but to glance at him. "Let's stick to the deal," he growled, eyes dark, deep on his frightening face. "Two kids for two duffle bags."

Hector looked at her warily, unwilling to lower his gun as long as Clarice glared at him with murderous intent. He swallowed and told her, "Miss Carter, your friend is right. I want to -"

BOOM!

As if wielded by Thor, a hammer wielded slugged her in the chest, propelling her off her feet, into the mud, as if she were just another leaf on the wind.

She landed heavily on her back, a wet splat, arms and legs flailing. The gunshot reached her ears briefly before the storm absorbed it, wet sand squishing in her ear canals, hair, lungs unable to suck in a breath. She must have blacked out because her vision and hearing were cut off for a moment.

Her sight returned. She raised her head to see Eddy diving on top of her right as the sniper fired again. The bullet that had been meant for her head penetrated his side with a gruesome blow, deflecting off of ribs, spine, coming out the other side to punch into the ground next to her face. A whoosh of hot blood sprayed her in the eyes and mouth.

Eddy lay on top of her, twisting around painfully. He rolled on his side and got her legs out from under him, one arm still holding the shotgun, the other curling her up so he could shield her with his body.

Another bullet hit him in the back.

"Coach!" Clarice gasped, wiping blood out of her eyes.

"It's okay," he said grimacing. "That one hit the money."

Clarice noticed the straps still on his shoulders and thanked God he hadn't dropped the duffle bag. He might have been willing to be a human shield, but Clarice preferred the Benjamin barricade. Pain suddenly flared up from under her left boob and Clarice cried out, the numbness leaving to let her know that even with a vest on it hurts like a mmm to get shot.

"You all right?" he rasped. Another bullet hit the duffle bag, this one emphasized with a distant shout of insane frustration. More gunshots cracked in the woods next to them.

"Think I have a broken rib or two." Clarice shook her head. "Forget that, Coach. You're the one dying here."

"Yeah. How inconvenient, huh?"

"We have to get you to a hospital." Even as Clarice said it, she realized it was futile.

He shook his head ruefully. Let go of the shotgun. His hands tried to staunch the wounds on both sides, frantic, panicked movements that made him gasp in pain.

Eddy was the toughest person Clarice had ever known. Seeing him so vulnerable, in such excruciating pain, cut her to the core. She was no expert on trauma, but she knew enough to tell these gunshot wounds were fatal, and her beloved coach would be dead in a few minutes. She didn't know how to react to it. Calling an ambulance was senseless. The nearest hospital was too far away. She had no idea where the sniper was, and rashly leaping up for revenge fire would only get her killed. *John Waynette* she was not.

She turned so she was face-to-face with him. Put her hands over his to add pressure, ignoring the biting agony in her chest. Water pooled between them, the road flooded enough to be a river on its own, the stream a dark red immediately around them and fading to pink as the blood spread further out. Thunder boomed loudly, making them flinch, anticipating another bullet. When nothing happened, their senses returned to each other.

Eddy looked into her miserable eyes and smiled. Blood coated his teeth, ran out of his mouth. "I can't tell you how proud of you I am," he whispered.

"No," Clarice said, pressing on his wounds harder. She pleaded. "Don't do this. Stay with me, Coach. Don't die on me." Tears poured down her cheeks, warm on cold rain.

He let go of his sides. Gripped her hands. Pulled one to his lips and kissed it. The water became darker and Clarice whimpered.

"It's okay, darlin'. I've done everything I wanted to do. I had a great life." He squeezed hard. "I even had a daughter, a special girl that made my life worth living. You gave me purpose. I would have died of boredom years ago if I hadn't known you." He chuckled, coughed, and blood started flowing out of his mouth without cease. The sight of it caused her to sob uncontrollably. He laid his head down in the mud, eyes closing involuntarily. With a great effort he whispered. "I would have done this again. For you." His eyes opened again, his Grip of Death making her knuckles smash painfully against the brass. "You must...Be prepared to...Sacrifice...For your children...Always."

Clarice squeezed back and blinked furiously to clear her eyes. She managed to stop sobbing. Eddy took several more uneven breaths. His body went slack, eyes closing for the last time. Hands opened, dropped, splashing in the crimson water.

He stopped breathing.

"Coach?" Clarice whispered. She shook her head, muttering, "No, no, no, no..."

She wept for her coach. Her friend and mentor. Her second father. An unknown amount of time went by before it dawned on her that Jimmy and Hector could show up any second to finish her off. Bobby, wherever he was, might not be able to keep them from getting close to her. She needed to get her butt in gear and take care of business. Eddy's last words were still resonating in her thoughts, and Nolan's precious face manifested in her mind's eye, renewing her strength. Her purpose.

Renewing her rage.

She leaned forward and kissed Eddy's forehead. Body vibrating with rampant energy, she told him, "Thank you. For everything. You will be avenged." She kissed him again, then dug in his jacket for something he always kept on him. A roll of athletic tape. Stuck it in her pocket, wincing. She looked around for her pistols, but couldn't see them anywhere. The shotgun was handy so she grabbed it, peeked over the top of Eddy and the duffle bag.

And nearly lost her life.

The rifle boomed and the bullet hit right in front of her face, fibers from the heavy canvas bag blasting into her eyes, momentarily blinding her. She dropped down again, panting, heart racing wildly.

Holyfreakingjesus.

Ugh. That mother-FUCKER!

She looked over at the nearest tree to see how far she had to run. There were several small pines about thirty feet away. Even if she could make it to them without falling in the mud or taking a bullet, they wouldn't provide enough cover. She peeked around Eddy's head and spotted a huge oak tree up the road, maybe forty-five feet. There's no way she could sprint-hobble to it without getting her head blown off.

She needed help.

She patted her ears, grabbed the earbuds that were hanging limply from the tape on her boob. Blew the water out of them, the mic. Put them in, astonished that they worked.

Apple products are the shit. Was Steve Jobs one bad dude or what?

"...He's to your left, behind a thicket of brush. Twenty-five feet," Ace informed Bobby. "Jimmy is still in the same spot. He took another shot at Clarice."

"I'll circle back to help her," Bobby said.

"You do that," Clarice said.

"Clarice!"

"Boss!"

"I knew you missed me."

"Are you hurt?" Ace said, worried, relieved.

"Broken ribs. I'll live."

"Eddy?" Bobby asked anxiously. He'd undoubtedly seen Eddy take the bullet that would have killed her, fatally wounding himself.

"He's dead," Clarice said tonelessly.

Bobby cursed proficiently. Ace picked up on her lack of emotion and remained quiet. She could sense his concern for Eddy, but knew his anxiety about her going all *Resident Evil* was far greater. He had a pretty good idea what she was capable of when pushed to the point of rampage.

Fortunately, they didn't get time to think about it any further.

"Uh. Jimmy is trying to flank you, Clarice," Ace said.

"Good. Which side?" Clarice peeked around Eddy's feet, seeing only the sandy bank sloping down to the river, a few large pine trees, hoping to spot Jimmy's humongous// head so she could put some buckshot in it.

"To your left. He has plenty of cover. You probably won't be able to see him."

"I'm almost to you, Boss," Bobby said, voice breathy from jogging.

"Bobby. Stop there and fire straight at the river," Ace said.

"Roger that. Boss?"

"I'm ready."

Gripping the shotgun, Clarice got her feet under her and tensed to scramble for the oak tree. Bobby's Glock opened up, measured shots that cracked a hundred feet down the road in front of her, answered by Jimmy's booming rifle. Clarice stood, staggered out into the open, shotgun aimed where she thought Jimmy would be, pulled the trigger. The tongue of flame visibly heated the rain into steam, recoil bucking the barrel up, kicking the gun's butt back into her sternum, causing her to yelp. It felt like a knife was stuck in her boob, digging in further with every step, the agony intensified every time she inhaled.

She bent forward, lowered her elbows, attempting to ease the pain enough to make the tree without passing out. She stumbled through several pools of muddy water, climbed precariously over rows of gnarled, twisted roots. Made it to the oak. Leaned her back against its trunk, kneeling down, panting. The huge branches and full bloom of leaves above her head acted as a natural umbrella, creating a pocket of calm in the storm. Clarice sank down on a root the size of a park bench, grateful that her ass was out of the water.

Bobby plopped down next to her. "Heya Boss."

"Hey."

"Hurt?"

"Yep."

"Help?"

"Sure. Take this." Clarice leaned the shotgun against the tree, handed him the roll of tape. Unstrapped the vest. Laid it aside. Tried to pull her shirt off. She couldn't get her arms over her head, and squealed painfully when Bobby grabbed the tank top and finished the job.

"You look bad, Boss," he said, whistling.

"Thanks." Clarice buffed her nails on her bra. "I'm thinking of launching a blog on fashion."

He looked at the gap in her smile, bruises radiant on her face, arms. At her duct taped shoulder. His brows furrowed uneasily at the huge purple and red contusion centered under her left boob, skin inflamed all around it. He looked up at her and smirked. "Zombie fashion?" he said.

"Yeah. Cute, right?"

"Maybe. Unless you puncture a lung."

"Guess we'll find out when I start coughing blood bubbles." Clarice hit his shoulder. "Come on. Tape me up. I'm still in this. There's no stopping now."

"You're the boss."

Clarice lifted her arms as high as she could, exhaling completely. When her diaphragm compressed, she nodded and Bobby quickly wrapped the tape around her torso, layering it thickly under her breasts in a four-inch strip that covered her upper abs. The pain lessened immediately. She could breathe without wincing, and her arms could move without her chest feeling like baby back ribs being ripped apart on an Applebee's buffet.

The wonderful magic of Eddy's tape. She took the roll back, eyed it sentimentally before pocketing it. She put her shirt back on.

"You good?" Ace said.

"All peachy, and shit," Clarice confirmed.

"I'm glad. Because three more goons just entered the game."

"Uh-oh."

Bobby tensed, grabbing his pistols. Put in fresh clips. Clarice grabbed the shotgun and jacked a round in the chamber.

"Where?" Clarice demanded.

"On the river. They're racing toward the houseboat in one badass cigar boat." He clucked his tongue.

"The boat has sophisticated stealth tech. I was lucky to spot it. They are wearing anti-infrared suits. These guys are serious business."

"El Maestro," Clarice growled. "Looks like I was wrong about him."

"Yeah." Ace cleared his throat. "I have a way to help, but I can't do it until you have the kids and are ready to leave."

"Um..."

"No time to explain."

"Understood." Clarice looked at Bobby, fierce, mad as hell. "For Eddy and the kids," she snarled, standing up. She took off, running in the direction of the houseboat as fast as she could, shotgun pointed in front, stumbling occasionally on the treacherous ground. She didn't make it fifty-feet before Jimmy's rifle roared and she realized her dumb ass had left the bulletproof vest under the tree. The bullet burned audibly through the air next to her head, hitting a dozen branches ahead of her before finding something solid enough to stop it.

Spotting a log tall enough to shield her, she dove behind it, crashing through a dense huckleberry bush that added another bazillion scratches to her zombie fashionista look. Landed in soggy pine straw, unripe green and red berries raining down on her, one landing in her mouth as she opened it to squawk indignantly. She ate it.

"Don't move, *chico!*" Bobby shouted, his overwhelming basso straining the earbuds. Her ears vibrated painfully. "Put your hands up and keep your

Julio Caesar Chavez-looking ass right there." He took a breath, then said, "Boss, I have Hector at the boat."

"On my way."

Damn. I should have just taken the road like he did.

Clarice lurched to her feet, somehow feeling more energy and wondering if there had been pixie dust on that berry. Capturing Hector had raised her pain threshold. Bio-potions ran unchecked through her vengeful-geared mind and flesh-hungry fists. It was yet another flavor of aggressive motivation, riotous, inspiring violent intentions.

She couldn't feel the brush that gouged her cheeks, neck, scraped hard against her arms and legs as she plowed through it, determined to reach Hector, water flinging off whiplashing branches in all directions. She made it to the road, turned right and saw the houseboat, the Subaru, Bobby in a shooter's stance, both guns pointed at Hector, who stood on the boat's deck, hands up.

In her blind frenzy Clarice had lost awareness, particularly the ability to pay attention to her husband coordinating the operation. Bobby glanced back at her, his apprehensive eyes telling her it was too late. They were in lethal danger.

Her A.D.D. ears woke up.

"Clarice!" Ace shouted. "Dammit, look to your left!" She didn't have time to turn her head before the bullet hit her.

Jimmy, standing in the middle of the road fifty yards away, rifle aimed and leading to compensate for her running, calmly shot her like he would a deer.

The large caliber bullet hit her arm, left shoulder imploding as the humerus shattered, shards of bone ripping through muscle, rotator cuff, like grenade shrapnel. She span sideways, nearly toppling, stabbing desperately at the ground with the shotgun to keep her balance. Her momentum was enough to keep moving forward. She crashed behind a magnolia tree, face in the sand and roots, taking the fall on her right shoulder, busting open the wound there. Her legs stuck out in the road.

Jimmy fired again, the heavy round feeling like a missile thudding into her left thigh.

"RAH!" Clarice hollered as her entire leg and ass was deep fried in nuclear lava. Her jaw locked up, torso twisting, writhing legs squirming for cover. She got her legs drawn in, gasping, the pain too much to voice.

Bobby spun away from Hector and fired at Jimmy. "You goddamn hillbilly punk!" he roared, both Glocks spitting 9mm fury at the bastard, several rounds finding their mark before he ducked out of sight.

Two seconds after Bobby turned, a hesitant Hector pulled his weapon and shot Bobby, point-blank in the ribs, an area not covered by the vest.

"No!" Clarice yelled, the effort cut short by her flaring wounds.

Bobby staggered to the side as if someone had landed a good hook on him, turned halfway around and fired at Hector's dodging, scrambling form. Stopped when he realized the kids were on the boat. He looked over at her, a pained, apologetic expression that stayed on his face as he collapsed. His tall, heavy body fell like a sequoia, striking the water-filled ruts with a splash. He took in ragged breaths, unconscious but alive, face just above the water.

Clarice ground her teeth. Balled up her functional fist and punched the magnolia. The broken bone reminded her eloquently that the hand was hardly "functional," and she cursed, rolled over on her back, panting.

"Clarice!" Ace screeched in her ears. "Bobby! Someone answer me."

"Bobby's down. I'm hit in the leg and arm," Clarice rasped. It dawned on her that now her other Perfect Shoulder was FUBARed.

"RAAHHH!" Clarice screamed.

"Bobby..." Ace breathed.

"He's down, not dead. Yet. I'm in no shape to help him at the moment." Clarice growled, winced, sucked in a breath. "Where's Target Number One?"

"Lying on the side of the road. Hector is inside the boat, in the same room as the kids," Ace said, tone shaky.

"Great. Right where I want them."

Clarice lay there gasping for a minute, looking up at the dark sky and rain streaking down, pelting her in the face. She was pretty sure she could summon up the energy to get up and hold the shotgun long enough to shoot Hector. But she couldn't do it if she bled to death.

Sitting up, she managed to tear off her tank top, ripping it into two pieces. She folded each section into a square, planning to use them as compresses. Took the roll of tape from her pocket. Pulled a length loose with her tooth. Placing a square over the wound in her leg, she carefully, shakily, proceeded to wrap tape around it until she thought it was tight enough to stem the bleeding. Biting the roll, she unwound another length of tape. Tore it off. Placed it over the second square of shirt. She had nothing to dry the blood and water to ensure the tape would stick, so she just put the compress on there, the strip of tape holding it long enough so she could wrap the remaining tape around her arm, under her pit, over the top of her shoulder. Clarice could feel the bones grinding together, tearing through muscle and tendons.

It hurt sooo bad.

"Crap," she spat, lying down again, exhausted from the effort.

"You okay?" Ace gently inquired.

"Oh, yeah. I'm farting petunias here. Hector still inside?"

"Uh-huh."

"What about the Teacher's boys?"

"The cloud cover is too thick. I can't see in the visible light spectrum very well, only thermal. I tried, but couldn't see where they put ashore. Even the best radar systems in the area couldn't detect their boat."

"And they're wearing anti-infrared suits?"

"Yeah. I won't be able to see them if..." His voice broke, and Clarice pictured him furious. He spoke faster, with angry passion. "You can bet your sweet butt I'll keep looking, though. If I see them, I'll cook their ass."

"Barbecue them good. I could eat," Clarice replied, having no idea how he planned to "cook their ass." Clarice smirked, feeling humor that was likely due to shock. "All this rescue and death stuff has given me an appetite."

"Me, too. Shall we grab a pizza and two-liter when you and Nolan get back?"

"Count on it, babe. It's a date."

Clarice dropped the tape's cardboard core in a pocket for a keepsake. Stuffed her useless left hand in her waistband. Grabbed the shotgun like a crutch and pushed herself to her feet, blinking away the lightheadedness and nausea that told her to lay her idiotic self back down. Staggered over to Bobby. He was still breathing, thankfully. She had no energy to help him. He needed a hospital, but she had to deal with Hector before contemplating that. She looked at the Glocks still in his hands. Dropped the shotgun and took up a pistol, thinking it would do better in the close quarters of the boat's cabin, single bullets rather than spray patterns of buckshot that could hit the kids. Not to mention the far softer recoil that was conducive to her present state.

Lightning flashed and boomed. The river continued to rise, rapids foaming near the banks, curving, leaping up in waves, spraying wildly, adding to the cacophony of the killer storm. Clarice stared at the houseboat as it bucked in the currents, tugging relentlessly at the ropes tying it to the tiny dock, which managed to stay in place by she knew not what.

She stepped off the dock, onto the deck over the boat's pontoons, her expertly trained feet the only thing keeping her from pitching into the river. She held the gun up in front of her like the Good Guys do in the movies. Finger on the trigger, a snarl warping her face as she sought her target. Sheets of rain blasted in from the side, and she couldn't determine whether the water had blinded her or whether she was about to pass out from blood loss. The water had so much pressure it knocked the earbuds loose just as Ace was trying to tell her something.

Her sight returned. She saw the cabin door, flapping open, dark inside. Turned to face it squarely. As she brought her gun down to aim into the interior another sheet of rain crashed into her, nearly throwing her from the deck. She took several steps in her boxing stance, regained equilibrium, then looked up to see Hector rush out the door at her, arm extended with something small and black in his hand, tiny bolts of blue-white electricity flashing. He jabbed her in the arm with the taser. Clarice dropped the gun.

And slugged him in the face.

"Oh, yeeaaah. That's just what momma needed," she told Hector as he crumpled to the deck, hand going to his busted lips, surprised. He looked sick, dazed, as he stuck a tentative finger in his mouth and found several teeth missing, courtesy of the brass knuckle sandwich. Clarice flashed her own abnormal grill at him. "Sucks, huh?"

He stared up at her, confounded, and she could see he wanted to ask how she was still on her feet, energized rather than unconscious. But he was hurt, confused, that metal punch having nearly knocked him out. Before she could think of a proper Shocker quip to answer his thoughts, he scrambled backwards, slipping, sliding as the boat heaved. She chased him further into the cabin, legs feeling like she could stomp holes in stone. Good arm flexing, fist twitching in anticipation of tagging him in the face again. Her head buzzed with ridiculous focus, mental acuity that seemed impossible to experience after being so exhausted only seconds ago. Her hair stood up, her tongue burned with adrenaline. She shivered as a static sensation crackled over her skin.

Hmm. I hope I don't attract lightning...

Clarice giggled at the thought, confirming her suspicion of being in shock, delusional. Hector froze, eyes wide, staring at the psychotic broad stalking him. He blinked heavily, seemed to dig deep for reserve energy and gained his feet. Turned and attempted to grab his gun belt off a shelf on a wall, knocking over a tackle box instead, lures, weights, hooks, thrown clattering across the floor, plastic box following. His clumsy, frightened hands couldn't quite grasp the gun, and he knocked the entire belt to the floor, moaning in panic.

Clarice lunged with a lead right, really extending it, cracking him in the forehead. The resounding thunk as it hit made her aware that she didn't even have to tighten her fist, the brass would do all the damage. All she had to do was throw. She instantly reset, dipped at the knees and shot another right into his lower stomach, twisting her shoulders to sink the blow deep, crying out as it hit, pain flaring from her left arm, which had automatically tried to join the party for a combination. Her rage was loud but dwarfed by the storm. He grunted explosively, collapsing, knees thudding on the wood planks. He grabbed his gut with both hands and doubled over, whimpering in pain.

His pitiful appearance had absolutely no effect on her. This man was responsible for ruining her life, her family's lives. He couldn't possibly show enough pain to elicit sympathy from her. There would be no quarter.

There would be no mercy.

He looked up at her, eyes pleading, forehead gushing blood where the metal had split him open. "Please, Miss Carter." He wheezed. "I didn't mean any harm. I'm doing this for my family."

"So am I," Clarice snarled, stepping to the right, his side, loading up her leg like a catapult, launching an overhand right missile from the hip into the side of his head, punching through it. Her step-load-punch was scary fast. The force of the blow split his cranium, the left temple caving in around the brass knuckles, a blunt machete splitting a coconut.

Crunch.

There was no cry of pain. No expulsion of breath or flailing of limbs. The devastating impact ended his life instantaneously, a light bulb popping into darkness. His body pitched over sharply, face down, a foul stench following as his bowels emptied and corrupted the clean scent of the rain.

Clarice stared down at her handiwork with satisfaction, actually grinning. She thought of how Hollywood and the media would have people believe that killing for revenge doesn't give any real gratification.

So what the hell is wrong with those people? I feel fantastic.

She walked over and kicked the crap out of him. (Literally, as it turned out). "Fuck with my family," Clarice growled.

Fan. Tas. Tic.

Movement inside the cabin smacked her back to reality, and the bloodlust pleasure faded as she recognized the sounds of a child sneaking around. A small, pale face peeked around the door that led to the main room and kitchenette, eyes panicked but determined. Spotted her and froze. Looked at Hector on the floor, dead. The boy's blue eyes brightened considerably at the sight. The door pushed open and Nolan burst into the room, ran over quickly and wrapped his little arms around her waist.

"Mom! I knew you'd come for us," he said, burying his face in her stomach.

Clarice groaned as her left arm blazed with fire, but managed to use the other one to squeeze back, smearing blood all over his Birdhouse skateboard t-shirt. She let go, stroked his hair several times, pausing when she realized what he said.

He called her Mom.

"Son…" Clarice whispered. Kissed the top of his head. She'd waited so long for him to call her that. Hearing the sincerity and passion he used with the word was vindicating in a way she couldn't quite explain. Nolan had just affirmed everything she had been fighting for. That single word from his lips had made it all worth it. The time in prison, the degrading treatment. The fights. The escape and assaults on police. All the worry about their family's future. Even her wounds. She would gladly have taken more bullets just to hear him say it again.

Nolan tugged on her arm. She looked down at him through blurry eyes, his adorable face staring up at her with intent worry. He looked just like his father. It was incredible how much he had grown in two years.

"You're hurt," he said.

"You noticed?" Clarice gave a brave smile. "I'll be fine. The important thing is that you are okay."

"Jasmine is hurt, too."

The energy that had been bestowed by the taser was transient, exhaustion overwhelming her once more. It took several seconds for her brain to register who he was talking about.

Patty's daughter, of course. "Where is she?" Clarice asked.

"In the kitchen. She's sea sick."

"I'll bet."

He tugged her arm again and Clarice followed him, staggering through the door, boat lifting side-to-side from a particularly nasty squall. Her legs wobbled, the wound in her thigh really screaming now that the adrenal ride was over. She had to grab Nolan's shoulder to keep from falling. He surprised her with his strength, guiding her into the kitchen where Jasmine lay curled on the floor.

Clarice sank down next to the girl. She was sighing, groaning. Clarice looked murmured assurances that she was safe now and would be home soon. She had no idea how she would pull off that last part, but felt sure they could figure it out now that they didn't have to worry about Jimmy and Hector.

"I told you my mommy would come for us," Nolan told Jasmine proudly. "She kicked their ass. Uh, I mean, butt." He stood in front of them, hands on waist, smiling because the circumstances allowed him to get away with cursing. He was filthy from his ordeal, but looked confident, even stronger for having survived it. Clarice was so proud of him.

And he had called her Mommy...

Clarice could get used to that.

She held up her hand for him to sit next to her. Remembered the Teacher and thought better of it, cursing. They needed to get the hell out of here. "Nolan, help me -"

Heavy footsteps pounded on the floor in the next room. The door was kicked open, crashing into the wall, thin wood splintering. Jimmy barged in with a pistol, pointed it at her. "Hello again, cunt," he said, voice gruff, in agony. Blood dripped from between his legs, spattering on the floor. He gave a sarcastic salute and said, "Goodbye, cunt."

Then he shot her.

The bullet hit her high in the chest, right collar bone going kablooie, trapezoid penetrated, lit on fire, bullet punching into the wall behind her. The pain took her to places she could never have imagined, and hoped she'd never visit again. It was so extreme that she actually wished he'd just kill her already, put her out of her misery.

She was thinking of ways to make her mouth work so she could tell the kids to run when a bolt of lightning, a freaking red one as big around as a telephone pole, vaporized a hole in the steel roof and melted Jimmy in half.

As he was aiming for a head shot, the soundless energy beam struck him in the shoulder, instantly slicing his arm and half his torso and leg off before burning a hole in the floor. The river water boiled, superheated, steaming up through the cleanly cut opening. The red lightning blinked off. Jimmy's right arm flopped to the deck, muscles contracting, dead fingers pulling the trigger of the gun still held in their grasp. The bullet went through a wall, harmlessly.

Jimmy roared, deep rage that turned shrill and pathetic as the immense pain cooked his nervous system. The smell of grilled meat filled the room, his body smoking, cauterized, the sleeve of his amputated arm on fire. He turned on his half-leg and the graphic wound made vomit come halfway up Clarice's throat. His right side reminded her of a cutaway view of an engine, sliced with a plasma cutter to show how all the parts worked together. She could see the clavicle and scapula in his shoulder, the rotator cuff muscles around it. See where his ribs were, now nubs of bone like spikes on a young buck, surrounded by fibers of interconnected muscles and loads of fat, white and bloody. As he gasped, his half-lung fluttered. The femur and quadriceps were surprisingly bloodless in his leg, and it occurred to her, from some other place, that Jimmy's corpse would be a great way to show people what happens to circulation in your legs if you become obese.

The vomit threatened again.

Nolan let out a kickass battle cry and ran at Jimmy, plowing his shoulder into the half-leg, a wet, meat-smack sound highlighting the force of his football tackle, pushing the big man toward the doorway. Jimmy's screaming increased in pitch, Jasmine matching it, and he stumbled into the next room, falling over, immense body thundering on the deck, rocking the boat.

He gasped loudly, coughed. Quieted.

Nolan stood with his arms out to his sides like a little gunslinger, balancing as the raging storm tossed the boat, panting, looking through the door to make sure the enemy was down. He nodded, turned, and ran to her, blood from Jimmy's split body covering his face, hair and shirt.

"Mom!" he cried in panic as he saw the blood thickly coating her chest. "You've been shot."

"You'd think I'd be used to it by now," Clarice grumbled. She tried moving her arms. Neither one worked. She nodded at Jasmine, who was sobbing with such heartbreaking whines that Clarice couldn't take it. "Take the iPod out of my pocket. Put it on speaker, then see if you can calm her down."

"Okay."

He carefully removed the Ziploc from her pocket. Tore it open. Grabbed the iPod and put it on speaker, sat it on her lap. Moved to comfort the girl.

"Anybody there?" Clarice gasped.

"Clarice!" Ace said excitedly, extreme relief in his voice. "Everyone okay?"

"Petunias," Clarice said, frowning, trying not to pass out. "Got a question for you."

"Shoot."

"What in geek hell was that red thingie?"

He laughed and answered smugly. "Megatron's penis."

"Awesome. Keep him around. I might want to hit that later."

He laughed again. "We'll see. The U.S. Navy might be upset about us revealing their secret space weapon. Which brings up the next issue."

"Yeah?"

"Evacuation. I could keep them out of their satellite. But using the laser will definitely bring them to the area it hit. All kinds of three-lettered agencies will be there shortly. Can you move?"

"I have one leg." Clarice brightened. "Hey. That'll be the opening line for my zombie blog."

"Ooo-kay," he replied. Then said, "Nolan!"

"Dad!" he squealed in answer, looking at the iPod on her lap.

"Help your mother. She's delusional."

"Okay. How do I fix delus, delusmal?"

"Uh. Is it still raining?"

"Uh-huh. But not as bad."

"Good. Think you can drive the boat?"

"Yeah! I'll drive it," he said happily. He frowned. "How?"

Clarice chuckled. "Honey, help me stop my chest from bleeding and I'll show you. Or tell you. I should be able to at least mumble before I pass out."

"All right!"

As he moved in front of her, a gun barked and the bullet hit Nolan in the back, knocking him on top of her. His surprised face expelled warm breath on her face before his eyes closed and he fell limp in her lap, revealing Jimmy's gruesome presence behind him. Stretched out on the floor, head and one arm sticking in the room, he pointed Hector's gun at her. He pulled the trigger. It clicked, empty.

"Cunt," he coughed, blood spraying from his lips. His eyes looked deep, completely black on his demonized, colorless face. "Ha. Damn kid. Should have done that earlier." He dropped the gun. Coughed a red spray. "Should've killed him in front of your parents. Ha."

Her mouth hung open in disbelief. This couldn't possibly be happening. They had beaten them. They were dead. Now her son lay in her lap, unmoving, bullet hole leaking from his frail body. He was happy only a second ago, ready to help his Mommy. He had called her Mommy.

Now he was... Dead.

"Nooo!" Clarice shrieked. "No, no, no..."

Clarice snarled and glared, beat the back of her head against the wall. Jasmine shrieked as well. The iPod vibrated, Ace's voice shouting, muffled under Nolan's shirt.

Jimmy laughed at her. "You ruined everything, cunt." He began dragging himself across the floor with his remaining arm, a thick, clear and pink trail of plasma marking his progress.

Her eyes moved to his destination, to the gun still held in his other hand on the other side of the room. Clarice struggled to move her arms, flailing painfully, unable to summon up her inner Hulk, her panic merely enough to throw Nolan off her lap, the iPod clattering on the floor. Black spots swamped her vision and Clarice quit before losing consciousness.

"Hahhh. You ruined my plans. Now I've ruined yours." He continued his asthmatic dragging, the sound of his burnt side sliding rubbery over the floor was sickening. "My plans, cunt. I was rich. Was gonna retire and buy a nice place in Mexico. Get a couple spic hookers, maybe take a little more of El Maestro's business."

Helpless, Clarice desperately sought a solution, eyeing the gun that was fifteen-feet from his groping hand, slowly pulling closer to it.

"I could have done it. Taken all of that greaser's business. Ha!" He paused, gasping, coughing, and Clarice thought he might be done for. He regained a little strength, and her temporary hope was dashed as he started his repulsive drag once more. He continued talking, becoming more delirious, tremors racking his entire body. "Hell. I already took part of the business. Put a bullet in that big shot greaser Jose. Pop!" He gurgled laughter, a ghastly noise, giggling like a post-apocalyptic virus carrier on *Zombieland*. "I was going to kill Hector, but you did that for me already, now, didn't you?" He stopped, looked at her earnestly and nodded. "Thank you. Hahhh!" Dragged again, his reaching arm ten feet from the gun.

Clarice began panting, eyes darting to the sides. She'd never been so terrified. Jasmine seemed to understand what was about to happen and renewed her heartbreaking wails. Clarice realized she would be killed, too. She had to do something.

Come on brain. Just one more puzzle before you throw in the towel.

The iPod vibrated again, Ace's voice too low to hear over the noise of Jimmy's effort. *I have to talk to Ace!* her blood deprived mind told her. Her arms and legs tingled as if they were asleep, completely sapped of strength or sensation. A really bad sign. She might die of blood loss before she could figure out how to tell Ace to fire the laser again. She couldn't move an inch...But Jasmine could.

She looked at the girl. "Jasmine." Her voice came out soft, weak, but was apparently at the right gentle tone for the girl to respond to. She peeked out from under her arms, and Clarice saw she had Patty's eyes. Clarice whispered to her. "I'm your mother's friend. Patty's friend." She moved her arms from around her face at the mention of her mom's name. "Patty loves you so much. She said you were strong, tough. A big girl." Clarice tried a smile, but didn't have the strength for it. Plus it hurt, dammit. "I need you to be strong, okay? I can get us help, but I need you to help me." The girl nodded, sat up, wiping her eyes. She looked at Jimmy and flinched. The horrific sight seemed to scare her into action. She looked back at her and nodded vigorously. Clarice don't know why, but she laughed. She nodded at the iPod. "Put that on my lap, okay? Hurry." Jasmine darted over to it, grabbed it and sat it on Clarice's leg. Slid over next to Nolan, hugging her legs and sobbing once more.

"...Twenty seconds! Just hang on!" Ace shouted.

"Twenty seconds until what?" Clarice said.

He paused, confused. "Did you get him?"

"Hell no. Barbecue the motherfucker."

Jimmy looked over at her and giggled.

"The laser has to re-boot. I'm sorry. I didn't think we'd need it again. I shut it down."

Clarice looked at Jimmy. He was two feet from the gun, inching toward it. They didn't have twenty seconds. He looked at her and giggled again, groping, dragging, a monster snail right out of a Stephen King story.

Fan. Tas. Tic. I'm going to be killed by an evil slug thug.

"Ace," Clarice said clearly, rivulets of tears flowing down her cheeks. "Nolan called me his Mommy." Her bravado broke and she sobbed. "That's all I ever wanted. That's all I'll ever get." She sucked in a shaky breath. "Our son's dead, Ace."

"NO!"

The stressed speaker rattled, blown by her husband's powerful cry of anguish.

"I'm so sorry," Clarice uttered between jerking sobs. "I thought, I thought…" Full-fledged distress enveloped her, emotional torture that superseded her physical wounds. Her son was dead. Her coach and mentor was dead. Her friend Bobby was likely dead by now. What did she have to live for? Without them in her life, she had no life. Fortunately, she wouldn't get to test that theory. It would be all over in a moment.

Jimmy reached the arm, growling angrily, psychotic eyes rolling grotesquely as he pulled the weapon from the dead fingers. He flopped around like a bull walrus to face her, the kitchen table and chair legs between them. He held the gun up, it wobbled, he steadied his tremors. Bared his bloody teeth and closed one eye, barrel aimed at her face, finger tightening on the trigger…

A machine gun rattled explosively to her right, incredibly loud, at least twenty bullets thudding into Jimmy, making one hell of a mess. His half-body jerked and bucked, flesh and blood shooting off in all directions, like some kind of freaky rave dance. The gun fell silent, the blast lasting just a fraction of a second. The big bastard wheezed out his last breath, dropped the gun and stared at her with sightless eyes.

Clarice's head throbbed as she turned it to watch the three men come into the room, their black tactical suits outfitted with all manner of special forces toys. The one in front, the short one who had shot Jimmy, pulled his black mask off and bowed to her.

"My apologies for the belated assistance, my lady," the Teacher said. "Company policy kept me from interfering."

"What changed your mind?" Clarice croaked.

"We had a directional microphone set up and heard him confess to murdering a friend of mine." He glared at Jimmy's body and his voice hardened. "Therefore voiding his protection under the company policy."

"Super-duper."

The other two men, masks still on, moved to the children, one of them hurriedly taking a first-aid kit from a cargo pocket. Removed a syringe and vial. Gave Nolan a shot, started CPR. It was a futile effort Clarice couldn't watch.

Jasmine was given a bottle of water, and they carried her and the boy's body outside. Came back for Clarice. She clung to the iPod, trying not to be too much of a baby as she was jarred by the man carrying her off the boat, onto the dock, then the road, as if she weighed no more than a bag of groceries. The Teacher walked next to her, Nolan in his arms, the other thug carrying Jasmine.

"We'll make sure your people are taken care of, and we'll erase any evidence of you being here," the Teacher informed her.

Clarice grunted. "I'll take care of the evidence part."

"Oh?" He looked at her with interest.

Clarice looked at the iPod gripped in her bloody, wrapped fist of death. "Ace."

"Yes, dear?"

"Get rid of the evidence."

"With pleasure."

The red lightning beamed down into the houseboat once more, unceasing, the only noise that of vaporizing steel, wood, and steaming rain. The laser began a circular motion that started in the roof's center and spiraled outward, erasing the craft, a scene straight out of Star Trek. The process took maybe two minutes, the steel cabin rendered into a molten hole of nothing that glowed where the laser had vanquished it from existence. The scraps of metal left had bright, popping edges, the wooden sections flaming despite the drenching rain, creating a funeral pyre that cremated the bodies. Steam and smoke engulfed the whole mess, a cloud with fire kindling within, a red beam jutting out of it into the dark heavens.

The laser blinked off. The remains of the cabin, stuck here and there to the two pontoons, floated off like unmanned canoes, quickly consumed by the flooded Pascagoula.

The three men stared up at the sky, silent, frozen in astonishment. The Teacher pursed his lips, looked at her. "Impressive trick," he declared.

Before blackness encompassed her with sweet, painless bliss, Clarice mumbled to him, "That was Megatron's wiener. I'm hittin' that."

Chapter XXVI

Juarez, Chihuahua
Mexico
April 18, 2012

Clarice didn't want to wake up. She fought it tooth and nail. Attacking, swinging at phantoms. Using all her skills to evade that painful, sadistic SOB known as Consciousness. She wanted no part of that sorry bastard. She wanted to stay where she was. In Dreamland. Where all her loved ones were still breathing and they went about their lives with gusto, all their teeth and body parts intact, happy and unconcerned about running from the law.

But that bright light and the screaming idiot wouldn't allow it.

"Clarice!" the heathen yelled right in her ear.

"Is she awake?" a woman said. Her English was heavily accented, her heels tapped loudly on the floor as she approached.

"Her vital signs changed, indicative of an upper-level of mental awareness."

"*El bebé?*"

"*Estable.*"

What did they say?

Spanish. Great. Clarice had taken two years of *Español* in high school, but didn't retain enough to understand much more than a Taco Bell menu. If they didn't start speaking more *Ingles*, she was going to give them a lesson in French.

Clarice groaned, opened her eyes. The room was large, with white floors and walls - white everything - and a very tall ceiling. It was a clinic, evident from the other hospital beds and patients spaced out at intervals, some behind curtains, most in the open like her, covered in white sheets, yellow-gold in places where sunlight from huge windows bathed them with its healing power. It wasn't an American hospital, that was for sure. From what Clarice could see, she was the only Caucasian there. Even the nurse and doctor that stood looking at her had boss tans and dark hair.

They continued to stare at her expectantly, smiling. "Water," Clarice rasped. "Aqua."

Her mouth was so dry it felt like she was dehydrating to make weight for a fight. Hell, it was worse than that; at least in training camp her mouth tasted like a mouth. The disgusting, haven't-brushed-my-teeth-in-a-decade thing going on in there now tasted like someone had been feeding her road kill Jell-O three times a day.

Clarice ran her tongue around, grimacing. Eyes popped open wide. Tongue backtracking, seeking the hole in her gums that was no longer there.

Her tooth...Somebody fixed her tooth!

"All right," Clarice croaked happily, smiling wide, splitting open a few scabs. "Ow, ow, ow."

"Take it easy, *señora*," the nurse said, a young, very pretty Latina with big eyes and lips, slim face with high cheekbones that glowed prominently when she smiled. "You were in a coma for nearly a week."

A week?!

Somewhere, a beeping noise began increasing in tempo. Clarice jerked her head around, seeking it. All kinds of cool medical machines were at the head of her bed, wires and hoses leading to her arms, chest and head.

The doctor, an older heavyset man with dark skin, maybe Cuban, stepped quickly to the machines, studying the monitors. "You must stay calm, *señora*," he said. He had a soft voice, one well-suited to re-assuring panicking patients. "Your excellent fitness allowed you to breeze through surgery, but you still have a way to go before you are fit for excitement."

The nurse brought her a cup of water, pushed a button on the bed to raise her head. Clarice sipped the best water she'd ever tasted, then said, "What if I wanted to stay in a coma? How come I didn't get a choice?"

Her body ached all over, especially her thigh and shoulder.

Why am I in such pain? Surely they have pain killers here?

Clarice lay her head back, staring at the ceiling, wishing she could go back to Dreamland for another week.

They shared a worried look.

"I'll go get the husband," the nurse said, heels clicking as she left.

The doctor took the cup from her hand, patted her arm. He left to check on other patients.

Ace's face appeared above hers a few minutes later, smiling. "Hi."

"Hi. Um. Who fixed my tooth?" Clarice wanted to know, sucking on the implant.

"El Maestro's guy. Cool, huh? He cleaned the others, too." He grinned widely, showing off his freshly buffed grill. "We both needed it after two years of sweat-shop toothpaste."

"Ugh. Don't get me started on Bob."

"Is she up?" a familiar voice rumbled.

Clarice turned to see Bobby walk into the room, muscles rippling under a pink World's Gym tank top. He stopped next to her bed with a bright smile. Took off his sunglasses. Clarice realized her mouth was open and closed it before anyone smelled her dragon breath.

"Surprised to see me?" he said.

"I'm surprised either of us are alive," Clarice replied, looking at his oblique. "You okay?"

"Sure. El Maestro's goons had first-aid skills. The Ocean Springs hospital handled the rest." He wiped his forehead. "Just barely avoided the colostomy bag."

Clarice shuddered.

"Had to donate to a few doctors' charities to keep the gunshot wound off the books."

"What are you doing here?"

"Well, I'm glad you're okay, too."

Clarice started to apologize, but he held up a hand, laughing.

"I'm on vacation," he said. "I've always wanted to come to Mexico."

"And Pearl allowed it?"

"Shoot, Boss. Pearl's here. Outside with the kids."

"They are riding *burros* into the desert to see the giant cacti," the Teacher said, stepping silently into the room.

He walked slowly toward her bed, hands behind his back, just out for a stroll without a care in the world. He looked nothing like the man who had burst into the houseboat wearing a ninja suit, wielding a machine gun with deadly precision. His short dark hair was combed over to the side to cover a thin spot. Smooth, unlined skin, pale for a Mexican, showed he lead a life of business indoors, and looked too young for his eyes, wizened and knowledgeable globes that missed nothing. His chin beard was neatly trimmed. His bow tie was perfectly knotted. Clarice looked at his suit, brown tweed with elbow patches. Loafers on his feet.

She shook her head and he smiled.

"Don't look at me like that," she growled. "I still owe you one." She tried to shake her fist at him, but could only wince, stiff and weak, in far too much pain for such behavior.

He nodded. "As you wish." He pointed to the cast that covered her entire left arm, shoulder to wrist. "You have a titanium rod holding your humerus together. When it heals, you may do as you will."

"Hey. I've never needed anyone's permission to knock them out."

"As you wish."

"Stop saying that!"

"Uh. Dear?" Ace interjected gently. Clarice looked at him with twisted lips. He inclined his head toward the Teacher. "He's helped more than you know."

"Yeah. He helped put us in prison."

"But -"

"I don't give a fuck how much he tries to make up for it," Clarice snarled. The pain from Nolan's and Eddy's deaths resurfaced and her arms and face flushed a deep red. The machine behind her went off like that giant wheel on The Price Is Right. Beep-beep-beep-beep...

Clarice glared at Ace. "Have you forgotten -"

"Mom! Hey, Mom's awake," Nolan announced.

"Good. Because I'm tired of sitting by her bed listening to her fart and moan in her sleep," Patty said, pushing her son's wheelchair into the room, Jasmine walking at her side.

Nolan laughed and pinched his nose. Jasmine giggled, her voice like crystal wind chimes.

Clarice choked, staring in disbelief.

BEEPBEEPBEEPBEEP...

Ace patted her arm, kissed her cheek. He murmured, "Welcome back."

"How?" Clarice managed to stutter, looking back to the Teacher.

The Mexican crime lord shrugged and waved a hand. Another day at the office. "Your son was very fortunate. My men, whom you will meet soon, were able to revive him with CPR and stop the bleeding. No organs were severely damaged. Since it's likely you would not have left an American hospital as a free woman, both of you were rushed here, to my clinic." He tilted his head slightly. "Was I wrong to take that liberty?"

Clarice scowled for an answer.

The Teacher continued. "As for your friend Patty, the governor of Mississippi kindly pardoned her after a substantial donation to his future campaign fund." He pointed at her. "A donation you paid for, I must add."

"You rich bitch," Patty said.

Jasmine gasped, looking up in shock. "You said a bad word, Mommy!"

Patty dropped her head, flipped blonde locks off her shoulder, frustrated. She sighed and looked at her daughter. "I'm trying, all right? Geez. I'm sorry."

Jasmine beamed at her.

Clarice wheezed out a pain-racked chuckle. "I'm rich, huh?"

"There was twelve million. Your cut was six," Bobby said.

"Why did I get six?"

"You know dam -" Bobby glanced at the kids. "Darn well Eddy would have wanted you to have his share."

"But -"

"Talk to the hand, Boss," he said, holding up his huge paw.

Patty jerked a thumb at Bobby. "I think I like this guy." She high-fived him, and they both folded their arms, looking at her with competing stubborn looks.

Clarice blew out a breath. Ace flinched backwards with a pooh-pooh face, then smiled. Clarice ignored him and looked at Nolan again. He was laughing with his new pal Jasmine, chatting about the potential top speed of the wheelchair and what would happen if they 'drove' it in the desert. The implications of him in front of her, alive and happy, were still sinking in. It was a lot to take in in her present condition. The relief was profound, uplifting. Knowing that she had another shot at being his mother made her want to jump up and embarrass herself with a retarded song and dance. Seeing Bobby on his feet was one hell of an antidepressant as well. Her family was okay.

Well, most of it.

Gloom battled the euphoria. Clarice turned to the Teacher and asked, "Where's Eddy?"

"He's here. His remains are in our chapel. You may visit whenever you are ready," he said.

Clarice closed her eyes, holding back tears of gratitude. When she was sure she had her emotions in check, she opened her eyes and looked at the crime boss once more. She saw him in a new light, no longer as an enemy. How could she?

"Why?" Clarice whispered.

He just smiled and shrugged. The cryptic bastard. Dizziness overcame her, followed by the sudden urge to puke up her empty stomach. Thick, salty saliva filled her mouth. Clarice waved frantically at Ace. "Bedpan!" He spun around and grabbed a plastic tub from a cart, sat it on her chest and helped hold her head up, her hair out of her face. She heaved chunks of something she didn't recognize and had no recollection of eating. It was weird. And it stank.

It stank something awful.

A collective groan of disgust from everyone reminded her to be embarrassed, the mmm-ugh-oh noises signaling the nurse and doctor to rush back over and check on their patient and the monitors.

The Teacher cleared his throat. "Doctor Mares? You may tell them now."

"Tell us what?" Ace said suspiciously. Clarice heaved again.

The doctor was the only one that didn't groan. He practically burst with pleasure, grinning. He looked at Ace, at her. "Congratulations!" he exclaimed.

"For what?" Clarice grumbled, spitting into the tub, eyes crossing from fire lancing into her shoulder, pissed off because her mouth was really funky now.

He pointed at the bedpan. "Morning sickness. You are pregnant!" He nodded excitedly, flashing his brilliant smile again. "That is why you are in pain. We couldn't give you the good stuff."

"Uh…" Ace said.

Her response wasn't much better. After Clarice got done choking on another shot of stomach acid, she gurgled, "Come again?" She looked at the vomit, expecting it to be some kind of special puke with signs she could read. Like a shaman's bones, or something. But it wasn't special, other than its extraordinary odor.

Fricken morning sickness. Oh, joy. Her head fell back, exhausted.

"Congratulations," the Teacher told them, shaking Ace's hand, patting hers with a sincere look. "The doctors said it was a miracle the baby survived. They believe your family has been blessed by Santa Maria. I wanted to wait until you were awake and together before disclosing the news."

"Thank you," Ace replied sincerely. He looked at her like he was about to explode with happiness. He looked up at the ceiling, breathing fast, smiling. He jerked around suddenly and hugged her, peppering her face with kisses, nearly spilling the bucket of puke.

When he came up for air, Clarice was laughing with her own excitement (sensory overload from pain). She told him, "Good job, stud."

"Woo-hoo! Let's fire up a -" Patty said, hands over her head to start her celebratory hump dance. Jasmine looked at her quizzically. "Bonfire," she finished lamely, moving her arms without any hip action.

Clarice croaked out a laugh with everyone else.

She couldn't believe she was pregnant. This certainly changed things, though for the better. It wasn't like she had plans to go back into boxing. With her literally shot shoulder and titanium rod, that window had surely closed. Ace and Nolan had no worries about her running off for that life again. She wouldn't do it without Eddy, anyway. This was the perfect time in her life to have a baby. They could start fresh somewhere, truly begin a new life. Ace would have to be the provider while Clarice healed, but he could handle that and would enjoy it. Nolan could help.

Yeah. This could work out beautifully.

"Hey, Bobby. Let me borrow your shades," Clarice said. He took his Oakleys from a pocket. Put them on her.

He nodded knowingly. "Future's looking bright for you, Boss."

"For all of us," Clarice responded, showing off her new tooth.

Ace put the puke pan on the cart, leaned down intending to kiss her lips. Swerved at the last instant for a quick peck on the cheek. "I love you," he said, looking at her with his *Knows Stuff* smile. He squeezed her hand then walked over to the Teacher.

As Patty and Bobby crowded her to give kudos on the bun in the oven, Clarice noticed Ace and the Teacher whispering like they were up to no good.

Clarice flapped a hand at them. "Hey, what are you two schemers up to?"

Ace smirked at her. "Scheming, of course. El Maestro is helping me with a Chester problem."

"Chester?"

"I had to help someone get out of prison to get us out. They need to be, uh, re-incarcerated. And I want to try and buy a pardon for Diamond." He grinned. "I have to put one Sister back in and get another Sister out."

"Um..."

He waved a hand. "I know that how that sounds. Later, dear. You get some rest, okay?"

Clarice looked at the Teacher. He was staring at Ace as if assessing an extremely valuable tool, considering various ways to use it.

Uh-oh.

Ace's skills with El Maestro's resources...

Beepbeepbeepbeep!

"Oh, crap," Clarice breathed.

"What? You gotta blow chunks again?" Patty said. "I could have filled up a fifty-five gallon drum when I got preggers with this little brat." She mussed Jasmine's hair.

"Hey!" Jasmine squawked, patting her hair back into place primly.

Nolan turned and messed it up again, and they began a hair-tussling match, tiny hands darting at each others' heads, giggling joyfully.

Clarice watched for several minutes, thoroughly enjoying the sight. Clarice looked around at everyone and said, "So what's next for us?"

"How about a new and improved Custom Ace and Tattoology venture in Cancun?" Bobby said, steepling his hands in front of him. "Or in Rio. Whatever you want. You're the boss."

The Teacher gave him a sharp look. Bobby stared back, raised his eyebrows.

"Whatever I want?" Clarice grinned, looked down at her stomach. She might not be able to pursue her first passion anymore, but she had another, more important, passion to focus on now. Her true purpose in life.

And six million smackaroos to help her get started. Struggling to lift her right arm, she pointed around at everyone, patted her baby's present home. "I already have what I want," Clarice said.

Dear reader,

We hope you enjoyed reading *With Her Fists*. Please take a moment to leave a review, even if it's a short one. Your opinion is important to us.

Discover more books by Henry Roi at
https://www.nextchapter.pub/authors/henry-roi

Want to know when one of our books is free or discounted? Join the newsletter at
http://eepurl.com/bqqB3H

Best regards,
Henry Roi and the Next Chapter Team

You might also like:

A Dying Wish by Henry Roi

To read the first chapter for free, please head to:
https://www.nextchapter.pub/books/a-dying-wish

About the Author

Henry Roi was born and raised on the Mississippi Gulf Coast, and still finds his inspiration in its places and people.

As a GED tutor and fitness instructor, working both face to face and online, he is an advocate of adult education in all its forms. His many campaigning and personal interests include tattoo art, prison reform and automotive mechanics.

He currently works in publishing, as an editor and publicist. He particularly focuses on promoting talented indie writers – arranging reviews, delivering media campaigns, and running blog tours.

If you're not lucky enough to catch him fishing round the Biloxi Lighthouse or teaching martial arts in your local gym, he can usually be found on Twitter or Facebook, under Henry Roi PR.